Chloe Clarke

THE AMERICAN PROFESSOR

Limited Special Edition. No. 3 of 25 Paperbacks

Chloe is a retired lab technician. She lived for many years in Oxford and now resides in Bristol with four grandchildren and two crazy dogs.

To the late Alison who encouraged me when no one else did.

Chloe Clarke

THE AMERICAN PROFESSOR

AUSTIN MACAULEY PUBLISHERS™

LONDON • CAMBRIDGE • NEW YORK • SHARJAH

A CIP catalogue record for this title is available from the British Library.

ISBN 9781528917049 (Paperback)
ISBN 9781528961776 (ePub e-book)

www.austinmacauley.com

First Published (2020)
Austin Macauley Publishers Ltd
25 Canada Square
Canary Wharf
London
E14 5LQ

Chapter 1

They came out of the pub and turned to walk up the dirty, littered street. A line of advertisement hoardings at one side hid a piece of waste ground and at the other was a row of dingy two storey terraced houses, some empty and abandoned with broken windows and gaping doorways through which piles of rubbish could be seen, others still occupied with curtains at the windows and lights on, keeping a brave toe-hold on life amid the destruction all around them.

A cold wind blew down the dark street and she shivered in her thin coat. She walked closer to him hoping to feel a little of his warmth, wishing she had something half so warm to wear on this freezing October night as the expensive looking overcoat he had on. After a few steps, she took his arm and pressed her shoulder against him, then twined her chilly fingers in his.

"Cold, sweetie?"

"Bloody freezing."

They passed under a street lamp and walked on. At the other side of the road, a small group of young people, students from the technical college, approached and passed them as they made their way home.

They came to a road junction and turned left. The advertisement hoarding suddenly stopped, and the waste ground, littered with bricks and rubbish, was now edged by only a three-foot wall.

"You want to go in there?" he asked, indicating the waste ground with his head.

"What for?"

"What do you think?"

She considered then smiled back at him.

"All right."

He climbed over the low wall then helped her over.

"This is nice. Most fellows would let me get over by myself."

The waste ground was roughly L-shaped, part of it hidden from the road by the backs of houses. It was dark where the street light glare did not reach, and they headed that way, picking their path carefully through abandoned prams, bricks and other debris. Tussocks of coarse grass caught at their feet and the wind blew their hair around their eyes, making it even more difficult to see in the half-light. Once in the dark part, she felt around with her foot, trying to find somewhere without too much litter.

"You got a torch?"

"A what?"

"Oh, you Yanks call it some funny name or other. You know, a little light with a battery that you carry in your pocket."

"A flashlight."

"That's right, what a stupid name! Have you got one?"

"Yes, here you are."

"Find me a place, no broken glass."

They searched around for a few minutes with the aid of the light till they found somewhere that would do.

"I'm not taking all my clothes off, mind you. Not in this wind."

"I know. Just your panties."

"Knickers, for pity's sake," she said, making a face at the word he used which sounded so unbearably twee to her British ears.

"All right, knickers, then. Can I put my hand down your front? It's cold."

"I'll bet it is. All right, if you warm it first."

He put his hands in his pockets and smiled as she got ready. He did like a girl who was not afraid to say what she wanted. She unbuttoned her coat, put her tights and knickers inside her shoes, and sat down on the grass.

"Hell, it's cold. Come and warm me up a bit, Yank. Wrap that smashing coat round me."

Just for a moment, he stood looking at her, anticipating the pleasure to come. Then he knelt down beside her and took her in his arms. He kissed her softly on the lips and whispered,

"You gonna be good to me?"

"Depends on what you want."

"Just the usual. Nothing fancy."

"Try me then."

He lay on her and tucked the edges of his coat round her sides. She wriggled and sighed happily,

"Oh, that's nice."

Then he kissed her, open-mouthed, pushing his tongue in as far as he could. Her breath was stale, and smelt of cigarette smoke and beer. Her skin felt greasy and her hair smelt as if it had not been washed for a month. He was instantly aroused by her griminess. He buried his face in her hair as she murmured,

"Oh, you don't half get me going, Yank. Kiss me like that again."

She opened her mouth and felt his tongue exploring inside. Like being screwed at both ends, her cousin called it. He pushed his hands inside her clothes and found her small breasts. When he did, he was rewarded with a gush of sweat mixed with cheap perfume which increased his sense of arousal. Then he felt his way between her legs.

"What's your name, Yank?" Up to now, they had addressed each other simply as Yank and Sweetie.

"Tom Bone," he answered. The first was true, the second untrue. It was a name he had devised specially for his amorous adventures. It had a slightly absurd sound, he supposed because it sounded a little like trombone and girls

9

often laughed at it. When they did, he felt as annoyed as if they had laughed at his real name. This girl did not laugh, though. She said,

"Don't you want to know what mine is?"

That was the last thing he wanted. He preferred to think of the girls he picked up as just a body, not a person, so he could forget the whole sordid business quickly.

"Yes, sweetie, tell me."

He felt he really ought to.

"Ann Bone."

No wonder she hadn't laughed! He had a momentary sense, almost of fear, as if he felt she now had some sort of gold over him.

"If a bobby finds us, I'll tell him you're my old man and we're having it off here for a bit of a change."

"Bobby?"

"Oh, cops they call them in the flicks."

"Oh, yeah. Is one likely to come by?"

"I don't think so. They've usually got enough to do, keeping an eye on the yobboes."

"Thank God for that."

"Come on, then, Tommy, aren't you going to get on with it?"

"Don't call me Tommy, I hate it."

"I can't call you Tom, that's my Dad's name." *Oh God, what next,* he thought. "Tommy sounds friendlier, anyway."

"Oh, all right, then."

He started to work on her, making her yelp with delight. As he did so, she was thinking what a good job it was her Dad couldn't see her now. Only last night, he'd smacked her round the face in a half-drunken rage when he'd found her kissing her boyfriend in the front passage. He hadn't been so drunk, though, as not to wait till the chap had gone before he did it. He knew what might have happened if he'd hit his daughter in front of a big, tough fellow who was fond of her.

She would really have to think about leaving home, because life with her father was getting intolerable. He was not too bad when sober, if you had a really thick skin and ignored half of what he said, but drunk he was a pig.

If only she could get nice and friendly with a fellow like this one. He was terrific. Not very tall, but strong and masculine. She could feel the warmth of his neck on her cheek, and when he moved, she could smell a faint, pleasant whiff of soap and the slight, musky smell of his body. Really nice. Not a bit like her boyfriend. She wondered if she would meet him again after tonight. Not much hope of that, she supposed. Better make the best of what she had and that was pretty good. He really knew how to make her enjoy it.

"Oh, this is smashing, Tommy. You can fuck me all night if you want to."

"I'll fuck you till you scream, then I'll fuck you some more till you can't sit down tomorrow. Then, if people ask you why you can't sit down, you can tell them it was because you were fucked by Tom Bone."

"Tom the Bomb they ought to call you."

"Sometimes they do, Ann Bone."

He was lingering on his own thoughts as he worked on her, none too gently, sweet and sour obsessive musings that brought tears closer to his eyes than even the cold wind could do. His colleagues at the University, wouldn't they be surprised if they could see him now? They, who only saw his public self, the veneer of the highly intelligent, smartly dressed, good-looking young man, had no notion of this overwhelming desire that seized him every little while, the desire to find some dirty, unwashed tramp of a girl, smelling of sweat and unlaundered clothing, to pick her up, fill her with beer and talk her into having sex with him in the most sordid possible situation. When the urge would come, all unbidden, over him, he would have no peace until he had slunk round the pubs and cafes in the nastier parts of the city, found a willing victim, and slaked his hated desire on her. This one was just right. He nuzzled her hair and kissed the side of her neck, wishing he was naked so he could get in really close contact with her sweaty body and make himself smell as bad as she did. What right did he have to be outwardly so clean and socially respectable, while inside he was this seething mass of filthy secret desires?

He had only been in Britain since June, but there were already several pubs he dared not go back to, because he was too well known there. With his clothes and his American accent, he stood out too much. It was easier at home – more room, more scope. This was such a miserably small country. He sometimes felt as if he was living in a cupboard.

His mind played with the thought of one of his colleagues at the Department rising at a meeting to introduce the latest American whiz kid.

"Ladies and gentlemen, may I present the newest member of our Department, Professor Thomas Di Angeli. Professor, will you tell us a little about what you've been doing lately?"

Meaning his research, of course, but suppose he was really to tell them?

Then, of course, there was Elizabeth. Elizabeth was beautiful, tall, cool and blonde, so English, so upper class, so dignified, the woman he longed above all to possess – but to possess properly, as his own lovely, gorgeous wife. What would she think? She would be utterly appalled, of course and her coolness to him would turn to repugnance.

Ann Bone was moaning and muttering softly in his ear,

"Oh, that's lovely, oh, don't stop, oh, harder, harder, oh, you're hurting me."

She suddenly arched her back and gave an ecstatic cry, clutching him with her fingers. He stopped for a moment, then started again, more gently.

"Oh, you are sweet," she said, sighing.

"Stick around," he said, anxious to do his best for her, in return for how much more she was doing for him than she knew. A few concentrated minutes later, he was pleased to obtain the same result again.

"Two," he said, burying his nose in her hair.

She shook her head wonderingly and he could hear the coarse grass crunching under it. "I never knew you could come twice in one go. Can you make me come again, Tommy?"

"I'll try," he said, but his own crisis was rushing fast upon him now. A few minutes later, he made it and lay on her limp, panting, feeling utterly drained.

All at once, she was utterly repulsive to him and everything about her which had previously been so arousing was now totally disgusting.

"Sorry, sweetie, no more tonight," he said, getting to his knees. He was conscious of the damp dirt he was kneeling on and of the mess it would be making of his trousers. He got out a handkerchief, wiped himself and made himself once more fit to appear in public, while she sat up and began to button her blouse, complaining about how cold her feet were.

This was the part of the whole thing that he hated most. If only he could now, somehow, vanish into thin air instead of having to extricate himself slowly from the entanglement! Sometimes, when it was summer and warm, the girl might fall asleep, and he could then slip quietly away, leaving a little thank-offering with her clothes, but that was not a thing that happened very often and certainly would not happen tonight. It was impossible for him just to abandon her in the middle of this waste ground. He would have to see her home, he supposed.

"Thank you, sweetie, that was great. Let me give you a little something to buy yourself a present with, from me."

"I'm not a tart," she said with sudden dignity. "You don't have to pay me."

"All the same, if you had a nice warm sweater or something like that, you wouldn't feel the cold so much."

"My Dad would want to know where I got the money from. He might wallop me. He would if he knew what I've just done."

The real Tom Bone was just as unpleasant as the pretend one, it seemed.

"Oh, I guess you can find a way round it. Here," and he tucked a small wad of notes into her coat pocket. "Don't lose it, will you?"

"Thanks, I won't." she stood up. "Oh hell, I wish I didn't drip so much after. Was that a hankie you've got there?"

"Yes."

"Can I borrow it?" He gave it to her and she scrubbed herself vigorously between the legs. "I ought to wash it for you."

"It doesn't matter."

He took it back, screwed it into a tight ball and slipped it into his overcoat pocket while she put her things back on.

"Ready?"

"Yes."

"Which way are you going? I'll take you home."

"Oh, better not do that. My Dad – you don't want to anyway, I'm sure."

He looked at her, suddenly touched by the understanding and realism.

"Are you sure you'll be all right?"

"Course I will. Lived here all my life, haven't I?"

"Well, if you're sure."

"Will I see you again?"

"Do you go to that pub often?"

"Well, quite a lot. Not every night."

"Maybe, then. I don't know when I can get away."

"The Missus keeps an eye on you, eh? I don't blame her. If you were my old man, I wouldn't let you out alone. I'll look out for you anyway. Thanks, Tommy, I've had a nice time."

"I'm glad. You're very welcome. Goodnight."

"Bye-bye."

Thus, quietly and in low key, ended one of the most important encounters of his life.

She walked away along the side road and he turned back the way they had come, past the pub, along more dirty streets till he arrived back at the town centre. At the first opportunity, he dropped the handkerchief into a litterbin, then made his way back to the car park where he had left his car. He had a long drive ahead of him, more than fifteen miles, for he always kept clear of the University town, out of self-defence.

Arriving at last back at his rented flat, he immediately turned on the shower, bundled all the clothes he had on that could be washed, into the linen basket and put the rest aside into a pile for the dry cleaners. Then he got in the shower, a lot hotter than was quite comfortable and washed every inch of himself, his hair, his ears, even inside his mouth, over and over, obsessively. He stayed in the shower for a long time till his skin was red and burning all over. Then he turned on the cold briefly and got out, gasping.

He dried and got into bed, naked between clean sheets. Even after his prolonged wash, he still felt dirty and he lay there for a long time, prey to feelings of self-disgust. Why was he plagued with this obscene need that would suddenly come over him and give him no peace till it was slaked? Then it would leave him feeling like this. How could he contemplate marriage to cool, clean Elizabeth, if she should ever become fond enough of him, with this horrible secret at the back of his mind? With his thoughts running over and over, he fell into an uneasy sleep.

Chapter 2

Mid nineteen-eighties. Less than a month after Tom's arrival in England.

The June sun reflected dazzlingly from the white painted walls of the Administration Block as he drove into the well-filled car park. He found a space, parked, picked up his jacket from the passenger seat and got out. Then, with the jacket hooked on one finger and slung over his shoulder, he strolled between green, tree-dotted lawns up the sloping path which led to his own Department. He felt utterly content. Monday, the start of another week and a new job that was shaping up nicely. He could not wait to get back to it. In addition, he had, at last, after many days' searching, found a decent flat to live in and he had spent a pleasant weekend arranging it to his satisfaction. He was really beginning to enjoy being in England. When it was like this, with the sun climbing a sky decorated with only a few puffs of white clouds, flowers blooming in the well-tended borders around the University buildings and the birds singing in the trees, he began to agree with those who said it was one of the best places in the world to be.

One of the glass-panelled doors of the building stood open and as he stepped into the sudden coolness of the entrance hall, he looked around. It was a well-proportioned, spacious area, high ceilinged, with cream-painted walls. To his right, a varnished door was propped open by a metal filing box to admit whatever cooling breeze there might be, and from within came the busy clack of typewriters and the sound of a telephone bell, quickly answered. Beyond that was the entrance to the corridor off which were the laboratories and staff offices. To the left, two other doors, both closed. Between them was a notice board sprinkled with papers, beyond that another corridor, shorter than the first, which led to the caretaker's room and some stores.

He liked this entrance hall. He admired its spacious grandeur and trim, clean lines, and he felt it would be one of the places that would remain in his mind when he left. In this, he was to be proved only too right.

Crossing from the door, he turned and walked up the corridor passing on his right two open doors, the first leading to the laboratory where he worked, the second to a small room where the glassware was washed. A few more steps brought him to his own room. Before he had even arrived and taken up residence, some mysterious Department had made a little metal plaque and affixed it to the door. It still gave him pleasure to glance at it each day, for the British had, for a wonder, managed to get his name right first time. Professor Thomas Di Angeli.

His was a medium sized room with laboratory type benching along two walls, though no laboratory work was ever done there. There were cupboards under and shelves above. The middle of the room was occupied by a table covered with books and papers, and at the far end was his desk underneath a window which gave a view of a red-brick animal house to the right and to the left an unimpeded view of the park.

After hanging up his jacket, he sat down at his desk and turned his attention to the morning mail which was waiting on a neat stack on his blotter. He had learned how to tell when Jill had brought it in herself. The secretary slung it down anyhow, but Jill piled it up with the bottom edges even leaving it pleasingly tidy. Everything she did was like that.

Not much there, a few requests for reprints and one or two circulars, nothing to keep him from one of his favourite moments of the day – the first visit to the lab. He had plenty of interesting projects he wanted to get off the ground.

Two of the three technicians were working there when he entered.

"Hi, Jill, hi, Robert. No Sally today?"

"Morning, sir. She's in, but she's washing up at the present. Mrs Simpson hasn't turned up."

Jill was the senior technician, a pleasant girl, quiet and soft-spoken, with dark brown hair and grey eyes. Within a few days of his coming to the Department, she had, he had realised, developed a great interest in his work and a considerable personal loyalty to him. She was swiftly becoming worth her weight in gold.

"Is she ill?"

"She hasn't sent a message. I think she's just taken a day off. She's inclined to be a little – um – unreliable."

"To put it mildly," said Robert.

"She's been better lately," said Jill earnestly, seeming to want to be more than fair. "I think it's the first time she's done it since you came, but she often used to have odd days off like this."

"Well, we can't have that," said Tom, "I need my technical staff in here, not wasting time washing test tubes. Will Sally have to do it all day?"

"I'll do a bit shortly when I'm free – and Robert's having a turn later."

She gave Robert a look which was easy to interpret.

"You make Robert help too?" Tom asked with a mocking smile.

"Oh yes, no discrimination here. If he tries to wriggle out of it, Sal and I administer a swift kick from either side, and send him scuttling through there like a scared rabbit."

Tom could well imagine them doing just that.

"You see what I have to put up with from these women?" said Robert, trying to appeal man-to-man.

Tom dismissed the levity with a laugh.

"You look very well on it. Now, what's happening in here?"

Jill lifted a sheaf of papers from her desk.

"Here are your results from Friday night."

"So soon?" He was genuinely astonished. "I hadn't expected these till this afternoon at the earliest."

"We aim to please," she replied, smiling at her success in having done just that.

On the basis of the results, they got down to a discussion of the rest of the days' work. He sat on a lab stool and tilted it back on two legs so he could lean against the bench, and casually stretches out his arms along the edge. As he talked, Jill stood attentively, listening, her eyes fixed on his mouth except when she occasionally made a note in a little book. He scarcely looked at her. He was used to the sight of her, flat shoes and crisp, Monday morning clean lab coat, all efficiency as always.

At the other end of the lab, Robert moved about unobtrusively, busy with his own affairs.

With everything said that had to be said for the present, the boss had a little affair of his own to see to.

"I'm gonna take five minutes, Jill. I'll leave you to organise all that, but remember what I keep saying – delegate. You can't do it all yourself, OK?"

"Yes sir, of course."

"And for God's sake, don't call me 'sir' I told you, I don't mind if you call me Tom, but if that's beyond you, make it Professor. I don't dig all this 'sir' bit."

"Yes s – Professor. I'm sorry."

"OK, don't forget it. I'll be back."

He was scarcely out of the door before he could hear Jill taking it out on Robert, but he had no time to spare for that. There was a most important phone call he wished to make.

Over the weekend, he had received an invitation from the Head of Department, Professor Ashton-Richards and his wife asking him to a dinner party a few days hence. It was, he realised, the first of a number of duty visits he would be called on to make now that he had been round long enough to be inspected and, apparently, considered fit to mingle with polite society. Now that he had a decent home of his own, he would have in due course to exert himself and do a little entertaining on his own account. He could then listen to colleagues' wives telling him what a good cook he was for a bachelor, knowing all the time that they knew every bit as well as he did that most of his dinner had come from the delicatessen in town. He smiled a little to himself at the absurdity of it all.

This invitation, however, had a distinctive spice of its own. Professor Ashton-Richards had a daughter, a beautiful girl in her early twenties – Elizabeth. He had seen her once or twice in the Department when she had come there with her father. She was tall, with pale blonde hair and blue eyes, slim and ravishingly attractive. Surprisingly, she wore no wedding or engagement ring. He had tried to get into conversation with her, but had found she was very distant with him, although friendly and even mildly flirtatious with others. He wanted to try to make an impression on this visit, and guessing that English society would be full of pitfalls for unwary Americans, he was going to phone an experienced friend and ask his advice.

"Hi, Paul, this is Tom," he said when he had finally made his torturous way through the switchboards.

"Hi, Tom, good to hear from you. What can I do for you?"

"A bit of advice. I've been asked to dinner by the Ashton-Richards –"

"Have you, you lucky devil? Good food, good wine, good company –"

"And a gorgeous daughter."

"Yeah, well, you can forget that."

"Eh?"

"I said forget it. You won't get anywhere."

"Why not?"

"Because, my dear Tom, the lady is allergic to Americans. You'll find yourself treated to the cold shoulder, the icy stare, the arms-length keep-away-boy routine. I know. I've had some."

"Any particular reason she should be like that?"

"I guess, you haven't been around long enough to have heard of Ed Parkinson, or you wouldn't ask."

"Who is Ed Parkinson?"

"Listen on. Ed was here a couple of years ago, up to last March. When he first came, Elizabeth was making out with some titled guy, younger son of someone or other, I don't rightly remember who. Anyway, I did hear that if she married him, she'd be Lady Elizabeth Whatever and I guess she'd think that was the tops. But Ed, he couldn't let anything alone. He went in, all guns blazing and before too long, she was crazy about him. She gave the other guy the push and it looked like Ed had it made. One night, he took her back to his apartment. It was meant to be the big seduction scene. He bragged in the Common Room that afternoon about how he was going to make her." A boyish, innocent indignation came into Paul Robins' voice. "I thought it was real sneaky. How mean can a guy get?"

The more sophisticated Tom smiled indulgently.

"Yeah, why brag? Everyone knows any dame can be had."

"Oh, I don't believe that!"

"If you're waiting for a real, pure maiden, you're going to have a long wait, man."

"Then I'll wait. It'll be worth it."

"What's the big deal? You a virgin or something?"

"Any reason I shouldn't be?" Paul snapped indignantly.

"None whatever. Don't get riled. Gonna finish about Ed?"

"Oh sure. Quite simple. When they got back to the apartment, there was Ed's wife, come over from the States on purpose to see what he was doing."

"Columbus!"

"Yeah. And he'd told Elizabeth he was single."

"What a louse! Some things you gotta play fair about."

"Yeah. Elizabeth's other guy didn't want to know. He'd found someone else. She hasn't spoken a civil word to an American since."

"Surely, she must be over it by now, Paul?"

"Been nearly two years and she's still bitter. Funny thing, the technicians loved Ed. Great guy for fooling around and making everyone laugh. And some of them liked him even more for what he did, because they couldn't stand her. Miss Frosty-Face they call her."

"Paul, she's gonna melt, she's gonna thaw, she's gonna learn to love blueberry pie and cookies. You watch."

"What you mean is, you're gonna burn your fingers."

"Just stick around and see."

It was great, chaffing with Paul. He was a real nice guy with a streak of innocence that it was easy to take a rise out of. Not until Tom actually picked up his fork at the dinner party did he remember that he had never gotten round to asking him for any of the advice he needed.

Chapter 3

Stunning would have been the most apposite description of the drawing room into which Tom, elegantly attired in his best suit, was conducted by Professor Hugh Ashton-Richards at eight o'clock on the following Saturday. Stunningly simple good taste, manifest yet restrained.

He had been aware of it first in the hallway of the tall Victorian house. His feet had rung on marble tiles, his gaze had been swept upward by a handsome, curving oak staircase. Nodding parlour palms in the corner had threatened with their finger-like leaves the perfection of the side-sweep of his top hair.

But here, in the drawing room! Entering in the wake of his host, he had suddenly felt like a sticky-fingered little boy let into Grandmama's best parlour and told to behave himself. The walls were white, with large wood-framed panels filled with figured red-flocked covering. The ceiling was white too, with elaborate mouldings picked out in gold. The furniture was heavy, dark and antique, gleaming with countless layers of beeswax. The antique fireplace was overflowing with a summer collection of flowering plants. The chairs were squashy and inviting – and yet, everyone was standing.

There were six guests already, grouped around the Persian carpet's central motif. One man Tom knew slightly. He occupied a room way up in the shadowy depths of the corridor of Tom's own Department. His wife was the standard-issue for the rising academician, intelligent, but not too much so, tweedily attractive, socially adept, everything in a decent moderation. No depth, Tom decided. The kind who would converse with you all evening and leave you at the end feeling as if you had been chewing gum when what you had wanted was a good dinner.

The next couple were Australian. He was an anthropologist, an enormous bull of a man, well over six feet and broad with it. His colour was startling, strawberry-blond hair and a florid complexion. His wife was large too, with a bosom that defied lechery. With spectacles pointed at the upper corners, she bore a strong resemblance to a certain antipodean comedian.

And finally, dwarfed by the Australians, hardly bigger than Tom himself, was John MacLauchlan, Scottish, dark-haired, pugnacious and a physicist to boot. His wife Nan was a pale, fair, scared-rabbit of a woman whose only response when introduced was a timid sound rather like a whimper. Tom, drinking rather too quickly a glass of excellent sherry that the Professor had handed him, felt that the Ashton-Richards, had they been trying, could hardly have assembled a group he would have found more uncongenial.

And the conversation! There is a sort of University shop which transcends disciplines and locations, and that was what they were talking. The anthropologist from Australia, the physicist from Scotland, and the biologist from England, all united in their hatred of administrators, department secretaries and purse-string holders. Well before the end of his second sherry, Tom was bored. Seduction, not small talk, was his scene, but with Elizabeth not yet having put in an appearance, there was no one to work on.

A waft of delicious odours from the kitchen. The door opened and like a stately elegant statue, grey-haired and clad from top to toe in shimmering grey, Erica Ashton-Richards appeared. She scanned the room and her eye settled immediately on the stranger.

"You must be our new American Professor," she said in a warm, pleasing voice. "It's such a pleasure to meet you – er –"

She clasped Tom's hand and turned her head slightly to the side. She knew her husband would be there and he was.

"Tom Di Angeli, my dear. Tom, this is my wife, Erica."

"How do you do, Mrs Ashton-Richards?"

"Erica, please. Let's not be formal. Hugh my dear –"

The Ashton-Richards seemed to work on telepathy. Erica flicked her eyes towards the door and Hugh went out, evidently with no need to ask what his mission was. "Now, Tom," said Erica, lowering her voice so it was masked by the renewed conversation of the others, "You were looking bored, I noticed. Come through and see my china. It's a hobby of mine. I have quite a nice little collection."

China was hardly a riveting subject either, but he had little choice. However, a surprise awaited him. Having followed her, with a certain feeling of martyrdom, through to the next room, Tom found it was in startling contrast. Everything was white and extremely modern. Carpet, walls, furniture, curtains were all white, the only splash of colour being provided by a superb flower arrangement on the mantelpiece, its effect enhanced by the white-framed mirror behind it. The china collection was displayed on glass shelves along the wall.

For the first time, his uppermost preoccupation entered the conversation.

"This is Elizabeth's room," said Erica. "We let my daughter have a free hand to decorate and furnish it as she pleased. She reluctantly allowed me to keep my collection in here, but apart from that, it's hers. The other room reflects our tastes, Hugh's and my own."

Up to that point, Tom had been thinking that the white was perhaps a little overdone, but suddenly, it seemed the most delightful room he had ever been in in his life.

"Charming," he murmured in an appreciative tone.

"Oh, here is Elizabeth now. Darling, come and meet Tom – I'm sorry, so stupid of me, I'm afraid I've forgotten your surname."

He turned sharply. There she stood, framed in the doorway.

"Di Angeli," he supplied in an absent tone.

She looked stunning. Dressed in her best, she was, if possible, even more lovely and desirable than when he had seen her at the Department. She wore a very simple white dress – white seemed to be her colour – that showed off her figure to perfection, and her gleaming hair shimmered round her shoulders and curled in wispy little tendrils along the sides of her face. He found it impossible to stop looking at her, though he realised Erica was still talking to him.

"Of course. What an unusual name. Italian, isn't it? You must tell me about its origin later. This is my daughter, Elizabeth."

"We have met," said Tom, coming to. He offered her his hand and his most winning smile.

Elizabeth looked at him frostily and extended her own hand.

"Have we?"

She allowed him just to touch the tips of her fingers and then took them away.

"Yes, at the Department."

"I expect you're right. Mother, the Bennetts have just arrived. Their baby-sitter was late."

"Oh, I must go and say good evening. You entertain Tom, darling."

"In a few minutes, Mother. I promised John MacLauchlan I'd get him another drink."

"Don't worry about me," said Tom. "I'll –"

Erica, unhearing, bustled away, followed by Elizabeth.

"– admire the china," he finished to himself. "Well, how 'bout that?" he enquired confidentially of a Dresden shepherdess. She stared back at him with marginally more interest than Elizabeth had done. The cold shoulder, the icy stare! He was beginning to see what Paul had meant!

He returned to the main drawing room. John MacLauchlan, showing no sign of having been supplied with another drink, was mooching about morosely near the fireplace, snapping irritably at his wife. Elizabeth was by the door with her mother talking to the new arrivals. Tom eyed her thoughtfully. It was not going to be plain sailing.

About ten minutes later, dinner was announced. The general conversation became chiefly dominated by MacLauchlan who began discussing politics, evidently hoping to liven things up by starting an argument. His wife watched, anxious and unhappy.

Tom was quite glad of the diversion for, just as he had been about to eat, he had suddenly found himself for no good reason acutely conscious of how British eating habits differed from his own. Finding himself with his fork in his right hand when everyone else's was in their left, it came smartly back to him that he had been so busy teasing Paul that he had not quizzed him on whether at a formal party he ought to try to conform. He glanced up. Elizabeth was looking at him. Quickly, she turned her eyes away. It did nothing to ease his predicament.

"Using unemployment as a stick to beat the Trades Unions with –" said John MacLauchlan's harsh voice as he grasped his own fork like a weapon, waving it in front of his face.

"Half of you Pommies price yourselves and each other out of jobs –" cut in the Australian on a higher pitch, tearing a piece of bread savagely.

"You don't know what it was like in the 1930's. My father –"

Mother. Tom could hear her voice, the reliable guide in all difficulties.

"Cut it first, Tom. Now your knife across the back of your plate –"

"Keep your hand under the table, boy. You conduct the band or something?"

Father. Always harsh and critical. Always mean and tight-lipped, to him, but not to Peter.

"Leave him alone, Walter. He's got to learn," and his mother would kiss the top of his head while his father muttered darkly.

Do it the way Mother said and it was always easy. He was doing it, of course. Habit had taken over. If they didn't like the way he was, too bad. All the same, he would sooner have still been with Mother in his thoughts than listening to endless arguments about rates of increased pay, money supplies, North Sea oil and OPEC. At least, no one seemed to feel the need to draw him into the discussion.

He wondered if MacLauchlan, Bennett and the Australian were even tasting any of the superb food and wine that were vanishing down their throats in such prodigious quantities. It was beautifully chosen and served, and they were gulping it down as if it was so much pizza and fast-food restaurant coffee. Erica Ashton-Richards, her bright eyes glancing from one to another as she followed the conversation, appeared unperturbed by this vandalism of many hours' work. Or maybe she did care and wished they would savour the meal with the appreciation that Tom could not help showing, even if a little too openly for absolute politeness.

It was a relief to be back in the drawing room. The women had been bludgeoned into silence by the tirade at the table but now, with the company dispersed into smaller groups, they could find an opportunity to add their milder contribution to the evening. Tom much preferred to converse with women. He hated the cut and thrust of heated male argument. Nan MacLauchlan, her cheeks a little pinker after the wine, had seated herself at one end of an inviting, cushiony settee alone, her husband being still locked in combat with Michael Bennett near the fireplace. When Tom approached, smiling disarmingly, and asked if he might sit by her, she looked positively terrified and gave merely the tiniest nod in reply.

The poor woman was probably never allowed to speak at home and it took a lot of doing to draw her out. Tom could produce nothing but monosyllabic replies till he asked about her children. She waxed quite eloquent then, and launched into talk about them, their schools, their friends, their problems and pleasures, becoming amazingly lively and vivacious.

After a little while, seeing them talking so animatedly, the Australian lady came and plumped her broad behind between them. Her intimidating appearance belied the fact that she, too, was a warm and motherly body, and Tom was soon able to excuse himself, and leaving them chatting happily and comparing notes. He had other things on his mind now. Surely, having thus done his duty as a well-mannered guest, he was entitled to be a bit selfish and see if his genial transatlantic charm could melt the frosty Elizabeth by just a degree or two?

She was talking in a group of three, with her father and the Australian. He wandered over to join them and found them conversing on the problems of travel, a subject close to his own heart. The Australian was enlarging vociferously of the deficiencies of Rome airport. Elizabeth looked bored.

"Oh, Elizabeth," said her father when the Australian paused for breath. "Why don't you take Tom out and show him the garden? It's still light enough."

"Oh, I've got to go and –"

"Elizabeth!" said her father in a remarkably sharp tone, looking at her as if she was a disobedient child.

"All right," she said sulkily and turning away, threw the words, "This way," over her shoulder to Tom. He followed her, very startled by this little exchange.

"I love your room," he said consolingly to her as they passed through it, hoping to restore her poise. Elizabeth in her normal state of mind was a tough enough proposition, but Elizabeth in a huff at being reprimanded in front of him could prove insuperable. "Your mother was telling me you chose the furnishings yourself. It's quite charming."

"Thank you," she said, thawing a little. "I wish Mother wouldn't clutter it up with her ornaments, though. It would look better without them."

"Did you do the flowers?"

"Yes. Like them?"

"Superb."

They passed through the French windows at the far end of the room and out into the garden.

It was large, with borders ablaze with colour, a spacious velvety lawn and right in the centre a bed of riotously flowering shrubs which hid part of the far end from the house. They began to walk round.

"Who does the garden?"

"Mother, mostly. It's her pride and joy."

"It certainly is magnificent." He was beginning to run out of superlatives.

"I just like to sit in it and raid it for flowers for the house. I can't bear all that boring planting and weeding."

"What *do* you like, Elizabeth?"

"Oh, the sort of thing that everyone likes. Parties, travelling – when I don't have to make all the boring arrangements – skiing, being with my friends and, of course, horses."

"Do you ride a lot?" he asked, hoping that riding might be exempt from anything that was – in what seemed to be her favourite word, boring.

It seemed he had hit on the right topic.

"Oh yes," she said with the first spark of enthusiasm that he had ever seen her show. "As much as I possibly can. I hunt every week in winter, and in the summer my friends and I hack and gymkhana at every opportunity. Do you ride?"

"No," he replied with unfeigned regret. "I never had the opportunity. Do you have your own horse?"

"Not now. I used to, but it was too inconvenient living here, and having to run backwards and forwards each day to the paddock to look after it. I tried to persuade Daddy to buy a house in the country, but he wouldn't hear of it. Oh, he is a meanie about some things! But I have a friend who owns a riding stable, so I can ride whenever I like."

Tom listened dutifully while he was eagerly told about the idle lives of the county gin-and-pearls set, stopping himself from yawning by imagining Elizabeth's trim backside in skin-tight jodhpurs. Shiny riding boots – the thought made his mouth water. A sun-dappled hideout under the trees, where he could push his hands inside her form-fitting yellow sweater, then pull her to him and kiss her while her horse wandered about cropping the grass, ignoring the humans tightly clasped together –

"Well, shall we go in?"

Back at the house already! Oh no, he was not ready to go in yet!

"Oh, let's walk round again, Elizabeth. You're real good to listen to." A lie told in a good cause didn't count, he figured. "You like dogs, too?"

"Oh yes," she said with unabated enthusiasm. "We have a beautiful Cocker Spaniel, but she's keeping to herself at the moment because she's just had a litter."

She told him all about the puppies, how extensive and superb the sire's pedigree was, and what an incomparable creature the dam was, until they were halfway round for the third time. He had spotted a varnished teak garden bench, hidden from the house by a bank of shrubs, and as they approached it, he suggested they might sit for a few minutes and admire the fading June light on the flowers. A little to his surprise, she agreed.

Casting round desperately for another subject to keep her there as long as possible, he asked her if she liked music.

"Some of it," she said, wrinkling her pretty nose. "But I don't like all that heavy stuff."

How heavy is heavy? He wondered, having been giving some thought to asking her for a date and trying to decide what would attract her.

They were silent for a few minutes, while he sat by her side. What a waste of a beautiful June evening, to be in an English garden with an English girl of such captivating loveliness and to spend the time talking about horses or dogs, or even music! Had it been an American girl in an American garden, he would long ago have tried to relate to her on quite a different level. But it was part of his received tradition that English girls were different. Cool, reserved and unapproachable. The breezy try-it-and-see method that brought him such success back home remained un-investigated as yet. He had known many girls, some almost as lovely as Elizabeth and he had never been stuck for an approach before. He had even, for differing lengths of time, owned and been owned by some of them. One girl, he remembered with particular pleasure, had moved into his apartment two hours after meeting him, and their love affair had been the most startling and amazing he could remember until, as usual, it had been terminated in a hurricane of lacerating contempt when she had uncovered his secret obsession.

But this was different. He was clean right now. There were no slums in this little town and he was full of resolve that his stay in Britain would remain uncontaminated. Barracks Street and Ann Bone lay in the untrodden future, and Elizabeth was here beside him. She was a woman, cool or not, British or not, so why not try?

"What a pretty ring," he said. "May I see it?"

"It was my grandmother's," she replied, placidly letting him take her hand in his. "She left it to me in her Will."

He stroked her fingers.

"It suits your hand. It's a beautiful hand."

She drew it away and put a little distance between them.

"Elizabeth," he said, edging after her. "I'd love it if we could be friendly."

"I am being friendly. I've been talking to you for half an hour, but it's getting cold. I think we should go in."

"There isn't any need for you to be cold," he said and boldly put his arm round her. "There, warmer now?"

"Please take your arm away, Tom," she said icily.

"Why, Elizabeth? Don't you like me?"

"Perhaps, you don't know it," she said, wriggling to get the arm off her shoulders. "But I'm practically engaged."

He did not allow the slightest flicker to betray his feelings. Instead, he carried the campaign into what he now knew was an enemy's camp.

"I like the word 'practically'", he said, bringing his face close to hers. Her perfume was ravishing.

"Please don't do that, Tom. I do dislike this sort of thing."

"Being admired?"

"Having what I think you would call a 'pass' made at me."

"I'm not just making a pass. That implies no true feelings behind it. I'm very, very attracted to you. I'd like to get to know you better."

"I've told you, I have a young man and I shall marry him one day."

"One day, maybe, but this isn't one day. This is tonight."

"I don't care to be promiscuous."

"That's rather an extreme word."

"It conveys my meaning."

"Don't you like me at all?"

"Oh, I don't say that, but Reggie – "

"– isn't here. He can't see us. Try a different flavour of a kiss. Why not?"

"Because –"

She turned her head towards him.

"It's naughty? Blueberry pie is stuffed with forbidden fruit?"

"Something like that."

Her voice was soft and low.

"Try it. With cream."

Their lips touched gently.

"Like it?"

"Not bad."

"Pecan pie's very good too."

"I thought pecans were nuts."

"They are. Try some of that, too."

He kissed her again, holding her a little closer.

"Tickety-boo," he said, with a jokey, teasing smile.

He was getting there, against all the odds, by simply being American! What a gas! Wait till he told Paul!

His triumphant mood was instantly punctured. His smile had reminded Elizabeth of Ed Parkinson and brought her smartly back to earth. Rising abruptly, she said,

"Well, I'm sure you've seen all you want of the garden," and set off towards the house, arms folded so he could not try to take her hand.

Quite a common female ploy, he thought as he followed, not trying to detain her. Giving him a little sample and then withdrawing the goods to make them more desirable. Fine. He was prepared to play any game as long as he won in the end. She would stop by the French window and turn round to be kissed again.

She did stop and turn, but instead of what he expected, she turned round and angrily hissed at him,

"Don't you ever dare to do that to me again?"

"Aw, c'mon –" he said, moving in with what he thought she wanted.

She drew herself up like an outraged duchess, intimidating even him for a moment.

"Stay away from me!"

She slammed the French window in his face.

It was fortunate he gave himself an instant to recover from his astonishment before going in, for Erica was just inside the door talking to MacLauchlan. She looked keenly at him, but by that time, he was sufficiently composed to return her a look of which she could make nothing.

Later on, he was in conversation with her and she decided to take a hand in the affair herself.

"Have you met many people outside the Department yet, Tom?"

"Very few, so far."

"Well, maybe you'd like to meet some of our younger friends. We're giving a picnic a fortnight today for Elizabeth's birthday. In Asbury Park. It's a lovely spot. Would you like to come?"

"Very much, but would Elizabeth like to have me come?"

"Of course, she would. Elizabeth! Come here!"

Elizabeth approached slowly from the other side of the room.

"Yes, Mother?"

"I'm just inviting Tom to your birthday party. He says he'd love to come."

It was a moment of delightful absurdity that Tom treasured for days afterwards. Elizabeth, fettered by social conventions, had to try to look pleased, or at least interested, when what she wanted to do was scream, or throw a tantrum, or scratch his eyes out, or possibly all three.

He, slightly less fettered, could allow his smile to be just edged with wickedness.

"Oh, good," she said without enthusiasm. "I'll look forward to seeing you there."

"Thank you," he replied with a ghost of a mocking bow.

Elizabeth was furious. She had spent a lot of time and mental effort assembling a guest list of really nice, compatible people, and now her mother had dropped this stranger into the middle of them, a man, moreover, who was showing every sign of developing a full-blown crush on her. She seemed to attract Americans the way some people with an antipathy to cats act as a magnet to the animals.

She must have been mad to let him kiss her in the garden like that! It was a serious lapse and she was going to pay for it, it seemed. Americans, damn them all! What was she going to do?

Unload him on someone else at the picnic. But who? Oh course! Sarah Myers! Her friend Sarah was going to be there and she had a definite soft spot for attractive young American males. He was attractive, no doubt about that. Bring them within range of each other, Sarah would swoop on him and her problem would be solved. A quick phone call to Sarah tomorrow, tell her all about him, and Sarah would spend the next two weeks making sure her trap was armed and baited.

She managed to keep away from the wretched fellow until the guests were leaving, when for politeness' sake, she had to take her place in the goodnight line near the door.

There was no doubt about it, he retained her hand in his for much longer than convention required.

"We're all gathering here at two o'clock, Tom," her mother said, giving him an excuse to linger even longer. "There's no point in everyone taking their own car. We block up half the park if we do. If you come here, someone will take you. If it rains, we can use a room or two in Asbury House. Lord Langton is a friend of ours. It's his house, but he's in the South of France at the moment."

"That sounds like a very sensible arrangement. But I'm sure it won't rain on your birthday, Elizabeth."

"That's kind of you to say so, but my birthdays on the Tuesday," she replied crushingly.

"I'll bring you a present," he replied, uncrushed.

She did not answer. Instead, she tried to convey with a look her thought, just make a present of yourself to Sarah Myers.

He was feeling rather pleased with himself. A little progress tonight, with the dice loaded against him and the promise of a picnic in an idyllic setting to come. Couldn't be bad!

Next day, Elizabeth got on the phone to Sarah.

"I've got a nice young man for you to meet at the picnic, darling."

"Super! What's his name?"

"Tom Di Angeli."

"What a gorgeous name! Who is he?"

"A new Professor, come to work in Daddy's Department. He's quite good looking, he's single and he's an American."

"Oh, I thought there must be some reason if you were handing out nice young men. But how exciting! I simply can't wait!"

"Well, I thought I'd let you know so you can pull out all the stops. Please do, because for some reason, Daddy and Mummy seem to be trying to push him off on me, and he was getting a bit over-familiar when he was here to dinner last night. You know how they do, Americans, think any girl's fair game."

"Well, this one is, if he's like what you say. I'll take him off your hands, don't worry, darling. Just you wait till you see me! I've got a new dress that'll knock him flat! Oh! I must telephone Angelino at the Hair Studio and make an appointment. I hope he's on good form that day. What did you say his name was?"

"Tom Di Angeli."

"I must be certain not to call him Angelino, I'm sure he wouldn't like that! Oh, how super! I can't wait! Gosh, isn't that a beautiful name, don't you think so?"

"Doesn't do anything for me." "Oh, you're so prejudiced, darling. Never mind, your loss is my gain. Mm! I wish the picnic was tomorrow! Good-looking, did you say?"

"So-so."

"Dark or fair?"

"Dark – well, darkish. Sort of dark oak."

"Eyes?"

"Didn't notice. Nice skin, though, smooth and tanned. You'll like his mouth, too. Sort of pouty and soft – looking. Nice. Mm."

There was a pregnant pause from the other end of the phone.

"Did he kiss you?"

"Well, er, as a matter of fact, yes, he did. I didn't mean to let him, but it sort of happened."

"When he was at a dinner party? In front of your parents?"

"No, in the garden, actually."

"Hey, there's an opportunist! Is he nice and tall?"

"Not particularly, for a man. About my height, five-eightish or so."

"Oh, pity. Well, I suppose you can't have everything. I'm shorter than you, so it won't matter so much."

Had Tom been able to overhear the conversation, he would not have liked this latter part of it. His lack of inches was a sore point with him.

"Well turned-out? Nice dresser?" asked Sarah, pursuing the subject relentlessly.

"Oh, very sharp."

"Sounds ideal. Lead me to him."

"I intend to. See you Saturday, then, if not before."

"I wouldn't miss it if I was to break my leg. Bye now and thanks."

"As they would say, you're welcome."

Chapter 4

Stateside, Paul and Tom had been fairly casual acquaintances, meeting and exchanging views at scientific symposia and the like, but the sight of a familiar face as Tom embarked on his new British venture had been encouraging. During the month or so since Tom had arrived, their friendship had become closer. It was Paul to whom Tom was eager to boast of his success, after the encounter on the Saturday evening.

It took all his self-restraint to prevent him from dropping, as it were casually, into Paul's flat on the Sunday, but Monday morning, early as possible, saw him on his way to Paul's Department, trying to concoct an excuse, in the form of a question, for going to see him.

Paul needed no excuse. As soon as he opened his door, he cried effusively,

"Hi, come on in! How'd you make out, then? Taking tea with his Highness the grand Professor?"

"Oh, pretty good," said Tom, perching himself on the edge of Paul's desk. "Like you said, amazing food and good wine. I have been in better company, but they sure were lively."

"But the daughter, man! The lovely daughter! Come on, quit stalling! How did you make out with the ice-maiden?"

Tom pursed his lips and surveyed his fingernails for a few moments, driving Paul to a frenzy of curiosity.

"I can't figure why you call her the ice-maiden. I found her a real warm and outgoing girl."

"Yeah?" Paul breathed in surprise.

"Yeah. I got to kiss her and she invited me to her birthday party."

Paul's astonishment at this not entirely accurate information was nectar to Tom's ego. He stared, whistled softly between his teeth and then said in hushed and reverent tones,

"Well, alleluia! How'd you do it, man? Hey!" He became lively again. "Did you act like you had a plum in your mouth, 'Oh, I say chaps, jolly good show, what?' Or did you juggle the cutlery? Tell me how you did it?"

"I just acted natural. It seemed to work OK."

"And you got to kiss her?"

"And I'm asked to her birthday party. Pretty fair evening's work, yeah?"

"How the hell did you get to kiss her at a dinner party?"

"Daddy told her to take me out and show me the garden. Gee, you should have seen her face! But I worked on her a little, got her on a garden seat under the trees and kissed her. Twice."

"Yeah, well I've heard the way *you* operate. I guess that means she moves into your apartment next week?"

Tom rocked to and fro thoughtfully, not at all displeased.

"Not her. She's the sort who'll want the long white dress, the plain gold ring, the whole till death do us part bit before *she'll* come across. You won't get her to move in till she's got you sewn up good and tight. I know the type."

"So you've crossed her off the list?"

"No," Tom stroked his chin. "Not entirely."

"Hey, what *is* this? You're not gonna fall for holy matrimony, are you? Thought it was against your religion?"

"Well, up to now, I'd have said you were right. But when you meet someone like her and something makes you wonder if there's anyone else in the whole wide world, it can make you think. And you can tell you've got to lay it on the line, but there's someone else in their pitching as well – mm. Like I say, it makes you think."

"Hey man, you got it bad!"

"Bad enough, considering the situation. Can't seem to think about anything else right now. Hey, you'll never guess what his name is!"

"Say."

"Reggie."

"Holy cow! Reggie!"

"Right."

"Like a cartoon, isn't it? Have you seen – Reggie?"

"No, but I guess he'll be at the birthday party."

"Think he'll have an eyeglass, you know, on a black silk ribbon?"

"Shouldn't be surprised. If he's a real wet, maybe I won't have too much trouble. Say, though, you've been here longer than me. What's there to do in this God-forsaken hole? I wanted to try and date her last night, but I wasn't sure what to suggest. I'm not too sure what she likes, anyway, apart from clopping around on horseback."

"Not much here. You want the big city. More scope there. Theatres, movie houses, restaurants, the lot. That's the place. Only fifteen miles. Just a gallon of gas in those things they call cars here, there and back."

"Yeah, you're right. I'll have to drive over and check it out. Haven't had time, so far."

"I'll take you there. Believe it or not, there's an American style diner there, not a bad try. Reasonably authentic. They even get entertainers from Stateside some nights. Why don't we go over, give it a whirl and maybe take in a show?"

"Sounds good. When?"

"Why not tonight? We could drive around a bit first and look at the town. We have to pass through some real sleazy bits to get there, but the town centre is fine. See you at seven, that suit?"

"Seven. OK."

Without another word or a backward glance, Tom rose and walked from the room with a faraway look in his eye. Paul stared, shrugged and went back to

31

work. Thus, in all innocence, Paul was the instrument of Tom's introduction to the Blackgate area of the city and the instigator of a chain which led directly to the meeting with Ann Bone, months of agony culminating in disaster for Tom but resounding success for himself in a totally unexpected direction.

Over the weekend, Tom had been mulling over aspects of the Ashton-Richards affair. In common with Elizabeth, he had realised that Hugh and Erica seemed to be keen on their hitting it off. They each thought they knew why and they were both partly, but not entirely, right. Elizabeth thought it was pure contrariness. They knew she had taken a strong dislike to Americans since Ed; they disapproved of this, and so her father kept finding marriageable ones and strewing her path with them. Going even to the extent of appointing one to a Departmental post was merely the latest escalation. Tom thought it was merely his personal fascination and availability.

The factor neither of them took into account was Reggie. The senior Ashton-Richards did not approve of Reggie. He was an empty-headed, idle, vain chatterer, too much – even their parental pride must admit it – too much like Elizabeth herself. True, he was rich, well connected and employed, but such brainpower as he had was mostly focused on sport. Almost anything from Real Tennis to squash with rugby, cricket and country pastimes thrown in. Dancing, good food, these received ample attention as well. Work and advancement came well down his league of importance.

The Professor and his wife wanted something better. Elizabeth, however, found Reggie entirely congenial, apart from a little reservation about the extent of his devotion to the ball and the racket. This consideration made her perverse enough to refuse his often reiterated offers of marriage. Reggie did not despair. Shallow as he was, he could see right through her and, unlike Tom, come up with the right answer.

Monday evening, as arranged, Paul and Tom set out to explore the city. Tom's eyes were everywhere as they passed through the mean streets heading for the brighter lights of the city centre. He took in the corner pubs, the dingy cafes, the people moving about and he began to feel the effect of several weeks of deprivation.

Next evening, he was back. For an hour, he wandered about seeking places where a girl and a man might go to exchange passion, and quench each other's' demanding needs, unseen and undisturbed. Then, armed with the knowledge he required, he went to buy his first half pint of beer in a British pub and embark on his search.

Three times in all he was there that week and twice the following week. There was a lot of leeway to make up and before he saw Elizabeth again, he was right back where he started, agonising over what he could not seem to stop himself doing, worrying in case she should find out with the inevitable result that that would carry in its train, and asking himself over and over why he was plagued with this wretched curse.

At work, things began to go off beam as well. It was three days before Mrs Simpson, the washer-up, deigned to put in an appearance again, and Tom became more and more annoyed by the nagging irritation. His work was inevitably held up because Jill was unavailable during the spells she had to take a turn at the sink and enquiries elicited the fact that there was no washing up staff to be borrowed from anywhere else, the Department being already short-handed.

When Mrs Simpson did come back, things proceeded smoothly for a week or two and then, when he went for his morning visit to the lab, he found Robert there alone sitting in front of several racks of test tubes, pipette in hand, hard at work.

"Hi, Robert," he said. "Where's Jill this morning?"

Robert looked up with the wary glance of one who expects an explosion.

"Washing up," he replied.

He was not disappointed in his expectation.

"What! Oh, for God's sake, this is ridiculous. I take it that woman isn't in again?"

"That's right."

"Well, I'm going to see the Domestic Supervisor and see if I can't get her fired."

"You can't do that."

"Why not?"

"Well, you can't fire people. You'll have the Union down on you like a ton of bricks."

Neither of the young women being present, Tom expressed his opinion of the Unions in a few short and forceful words. Robert, who was perhaps a little more sympathetic with the struggles of the working classes, said nothing.

"Well, what can we do? Are we stuck with her forever?"

"See if you can get her transferred."

"Would anyone else have her? Don't they all know what she's like?"

"We haven't told them," said Robert with a conspiratorial smile. "We want rid of her too."

"Good man. I'll give the Supervisor a call right away. Ask Jill to come and see me when she's through in there, will you?"

Tom found the Domestic Supervisor sympathetic, but not particularly hopeful of arranging a transfer in the near future. Having impressed on him the problems the situation was causing with his work, Tom had to rest content for the time being, but he made a note in his diary to push things along next week.

An hour or so later, Jill came back into the lab rubbing cream on her hands.

"Thank goodness that's finished for now. Oh, how I hate that job!"

Robert indicated the door with a tilt of his head.

"Chief Sitting Bull wants you to go and see him."

"Oh my goodness, what have I done now?"

"You haven't done anything. He's brooding on the sins of Mrs Simpson."

"Oh lord, that means I'm going to have to listen to his lecture again on how all this is holding up his work, can't anyone else do it, etc., etc. I had it for breakfast every day when she was off before."

"He doesn't know when he's well off. I suppose, he doesn't have to put up with that sort of thing in the United States."

"Huh! They probably have computers to do the washing up there."

"Shouldn't be surprised. I think, though, you're going to get a lecture on the British Trades Unions. He was all for getting her sacked and he was a trifle peeved, to put it mildly, when I told him it wasn't on."

"That's a fair assessment of the situation," said Tom, who had entered unobserved. He was amused to see them both jump and look embarrassed.

"I don't know what my Union would say about me doing all this washing up," said Jill, wondering how much he had heard. "Imagine, the three of us and Mrs Simpson could bring the whole Department to a standstill if we were to put our minds to it."

"Oh, you wouldn't do that to me, would you?"

Jill laughed.

"Well, no, maybe not."

"Knew I could rely on you. Now, Jill, the moment she's back, you gotta lay it on the line to her, OK? Don't mention the Unions, for God's sake and put ideas into her head. Just tell her, right? And the D.S., if you see him."

"Y-yes, I'll do my best, but, sir –"

"Do it, OK?"

Magisterially, Chief Sitting Bull stalked towards the door. Then he paused, turned and raised his hand. In a deep. Impressive voice, he intoned,

"How."

Chapter 5

It was Saturday, the day of the picnic, and even at 6am, bright and sunny.

Mornings were pretty good as a whole. After the frenzied activity of his private life over the last couple of weeks, Tom had achieved a sort of balance. The burning urge within him had abated and the terrifying visions of what happened when someone he cared for found out about it had subdued a little. No more was his mind filled with girls he had loved and lived with reacting in disgust to the truth of the man who stood before them, the man he really was. No more the remembrance of clothes being packed, of insults being hurled, of that final slamming of the door, of many doors, that echoed through the recesses and corridors of his consciousness. No more visions of himself standing in the now empty room, arms hanging dejectedly at his side, hating himself as she now hated him. All in a moment, from having it all, he had nothing. She had taken away her companionship, her body, her lips, her caring, her thighs that would part for him whenever he asked, her interest in him, her want of his concern for her, all cut off by that closing door.

He was slated for the present and he could now make those resolutions to stay clean. He would not worry, at this moment, on this morning, about what would happen if he did take the road of the plain gold ring, the whole till death do us part bit. He had never wanted to marry anyone as much as he did Elizabeth, and he had been tormenting himself with the idea of a relationship which could not be brought to an end by simply slamming a door, but which meant lawyers and finance, and bickering over shared possessions between two who had once only wanted to possess each other. But now his mind was clear of all that at any rate for today. Night time was his time for self-torture. Morning always brought hope that some time, some way, he could win.

Not that it had been easy, achieving that balance. His score for the fortnight's adventures read five tries, three girls, two failures. Failure was what he dreaded most, especially when like now he had no roommate to save him from the need to appear, defenceless, before the bar of his own self-condemnation. With the unfulfilled agony burning within him, he would make his way back to the car and drive home. Then, with the covers pulled back, he would lie on the bed, and allow himself off the hook of frustration and self-loathing with a prolonged and luxurious frig. As soon as the blessed relief of orgasm rolled its warm and engulfing forgiveness over him, he would draw the bedclothes round his chilled body and let himself be slugged into oblivion by rapidly supervening sleep.

Those were the horrors of the night, but sometimes there were good nights as well. The balance he had now achieved had been found two nights ago in company with a girl with the sort of uncomplicated attitude to sexuality that he longed for himself. There had even been a laugh, a moment of marvellous stupid childish fun.

As soon as he had established friendly relations with her, he had started to move into his familiar spiel, but she had cut him off with,

"You looking for a screw, then?"

"Something of the sort," he had admitted.

"Finish your beer then and let's get at it. Got somewhere in mind?"

"Not specially."

"We'll go to Lafford's then."

Lafford's had proved to be a ramshackle, disused factory. After scrambling over piles of rubble, they came to the place she sought. *She* did not ask his name or tell him hers. The name she coined for him was Freak. It seemed appropriate enough.

"I hope you're not one of those thirty seconds and thank you very much, Freak. You try that game on me and I'll tear your ears off."

She looked quite capable of doing it too. Made him nervous for a bit but then the funny incident had occurred and she had laughed so much it had dissolved his tension. After he had got over the initial outrage and fury, her laughter had set him off too, and they had giggled and screwed their way to an entirely satisfactory conclusion.

On the way home that night, apart from the usual intense longing for hot water and soap, he had felt pretty much at peace with himself. And the next morning when he woke, he was filled with that strong certainty that the next time temptation came, he would have no trouble putting it aside. The lapse he had just had could be pushed into the background and forgotten.

So now, after a day and two nights of emotional decompression, it was six am. And the day of Elizabeth's picnic. He was ready for it. No girl would be able to resist his revivified charm and no languid weed of an Englishman with an eyeglass on a black ribbon was going to be able to stand in his way. He felt in sparkling form and it was a day to match. Diffused rays of the bright sun were already slanting through the thin cotton curtains spreading light patches on the carpet and bed. Yawning and stretching himself, he lay there a little, enjoying pleasant feelings of anticipation. His body felt good. Strong and active. His mind felt good too. Clean. Scrubbed. Alert for any challenge. Ready to be put to the test and it was only six am!

He rose, opened the curtains just a little way, for he was naked and there were windows opposite, and looked out. What a day it was! The sky was a clear blue, with a sun so strong that it made him blink and screw up his eyes. Birds were singing, the light was glinting on the distant river and the whole world had that lovely, peaceful stillness as if waiting for something delightful to happen.

After drawing several deep breaths, he went through to the bathroom, shaved, showered and dressed in a cream open-necked fine jersey shirt, Levi's faded to just the right shade of pale blue and his old, comfortable sneakers. Then to the kitchen where he made his first pot of coffee of the day and put some eggs on to boil.

Breakfast eaten, he pottered about for a bit doing his housework. He always chose a home that needed no hired help, preferring to look after himself when he was alone and share the chores with his companion when he was not. Home was an intensely private refuge to be shared only by the chosen, not the hired. Besides, there was not much of point, for he was tidy by nature and the amount of work he made for himself was minimal. The flat had been picked out with great care too, having an eye to the streamlining of labour. It was in a newish block of custom built flats and he had rented it, via an agency, from a professional couple without family, who had gone to work abroad for a couple of years but who wanted to come back to it eventually. They had no more time or inclination for excess of housework than he had, and all the furnishings and arrangements were selected and organised with that in mind. While house hunting, he had seen several jerried-up places in dismembered Victorian houses which were described by the agent as having 'period charm'. He had soon realised what that meant in the context of a flat. Inconvenient, dingy and work making. Perhaps, the fact that he had been lucky enough to find this place was a symbol that this was to be a fortunate time for him with things going his way – things like Elizabeth, maybe?

He allowed his mind to dwell on her, the pale coloured hair, the blue eyes, the tall, erect, willowy figure – oh, she was gorgeous. To be able to put his arm round that slender waist, those kisses he had stolen in the garden – he sat down for a moment and imagined them. This story that she disliked Americans was all a fable. She had just not met one so far who attracted her enough. He could surely overcome and prejudice she might have, and as for his own feelings, only once before could he remember having been so bowled over by a girl and that was way back in his youth. There was no problem, large or small, that could not be overcome by a little determination and the incentive to succeed was there in plenty.

Meanwhile, what was he to do with the morning? He did not want to just hang around the flat and he had already bought her present, some rather splendid perfume, the scent of which had immediately brought her to mind.

In the store buying it, he had encountered another piece of good luck, in the shape of a very helpful and interested sales assistant who had willingly dabbed her wrists and forearms with at least a dozen perfumes while he had tried to explain why each one was not quite right.

Finally, she had said,

"I think I know what you want, sir. The one that's my own secret favourite. Mind you, I can't afford to buy even the tiny size on my salary, so I sneak a little squirt from the tester when I've got a special date."

And indeed, it was just right. So delighted was he with it and with her, that as well as buying a large bottle for Elizabeth, he bought a smaller one, and presented it to her. Her incredulous pleasure at this unexpected occurrence was a joy to see.

So, what *was* he going to do? The obvious answer seemed to be to go to work. None of the technicians would be in on a Saturday, of course, but there were things he could find to do to occupy himself without their aid. It would take up at least part of the morning.

Glancing at the clock, he was astonished to see it was not yet eight. He really could not go to the Department yet – it wouldn't even be unlocked at this time anyway. What could one do at this hour of the morning? Read? Yes, the newspaper. He would stroll down to the shop, get a paper, come back, read it with some more coffee and then walk to the Department instead of taking the car. It was a perfect morning for a walk, though he might perhaps regret it by the time it came to walk home, for by then, it would probably be hot if the bright days' start fulfilled its promise. Still, it would occupy a fair chunk of that yawning gap of time.

He smiled ironically at his own feelings. Not since his teens, when, with an exciting date to look forward to in the evening, the day had seemed like a century, had he had quite this excitement. And even then, there had never been anyone to match Elizabeth. Elizabeth! As he descended the stairs to the front door of the block, he had a mad desire to write her name on the wall in enormous letters. Elizabeth! To feel like this again, when the unbridled intensity of adolescent passion should be long lost, buried deep under layers of experienced and cautious maturity! Oh, happy day! Oh, lovely, incomparable specimen of womanhood! To have come halfway round the world, to find someone like her on one's own doorstep! Could life possibly hold a greater prize?

He arrived at the Department at about half past nine and went first to the general office to look through the pile of unsorted mail. Carrying two letters addressed to him, he passed the open door of the lab and was surprised to see a movement within. It was Jill.

"Hi, Jill. I didn't think you'd be in today."

"Oh, hello, Professor. There wasn't much to do at my flat this morning, so I decided to come in for an hour, and tidy up some odds and ends."

"Such devotion to duty," he said with a smile.

"Not really. My flat mate works some Saturdays and this is one of them, so, rather than kick my heels around there on my own, I decided I might as well come in here and be useful."

"Much my own feelings this morning, though I'm not sharing at present. Good for you. Anything that needs my attention?"

"Not any of this. Just minor details."

"OK. I'll go along and get to a little work myself then."

In his room, he read his letters, then sorted a pile of papers from a wire filing basket and put them in front of himself. Twirling a pen in his fingers, he looked blankly at the top page, turned to the next, rested his chin on his hand and stared out of the window. What did one wear for a formal British picnic? Jill had looked him up and down when he came in, showing surprise, perhaps even disapproval, at his appearing at work in such unaccustomed casual dress. He was not going to swelter in a collar and tie all afternoon, even to please Elizabeth. These Levi's wouldn't do, that was for sure. But the shirt was good, expensive and it enhanced his looks. Perhaps, he needn't change that. Maybe Jill could give him some guidance. Or he could try calling Paul.

No good. He made several desultory attempts to get on with it, but he was quite unable to focus, so eventually, he decided to give it up for the time being, go back to the lab and find Jill.

"It's too sunny a day for work," he observed, sitting himself on a lab stool. "Why don't you forget it for a while and talk to me?"

"In a minute," she said, busy as usual.

"Live in a flat too, do you? Where do you come from originally? Around here? Considering we've been working together, we don't know that much about each other."

"I come from Boston – Lincolnshire that is, of course. My parents and sister still live there."

"Ah, the real, the true Boston. All others are imitations. Who do you live with now? Your boyfriend?"

"Certainly not," she replied with unexpected heat in her voice. "I share a flat with another girl. I wouldn't dream of living with a man I wasn't married to."

"I'm sorry," he said, feeling abashed and to his annoyance, slightly defensive. "It's not so very unusual nowadays."

"Maybe so, but it's not what I choose to do. I know a lot of people fall in and out of bed with anyone who comes to hand, but that's not how I was brought up."

She stumped inelegantly across the lab to get something from the refrigerator, looking indignant.

"Gee, I didn't mean to make you angry. I'm just interested."

"You didn't make me angry. It's just the way people assume things. You say you're living in a flat away from your parents and they either assume that you're cohabiting, or that you've quarrelled with them. Neither is true in my case."

"Yeah, I can see why you'd get riled. What are you doing for the rest of the day then? Going out with your boyfriend this evening?"

It seemed a harmless enough enquiry, but it was still not the right one. Her face assumed the expression of one prepared to answer the same set of questions for the fiftieth time.

"I haven't got a boyfriend."

"Really? A nice young girl like you? I *am* surprised."

"I just haven't met anyone I… like enough."

He noticed the slight hesitation and wondered what it might mean. Some recent upset? Someone thrown her over?

"That's a pity. It's good to have someone special."

"Sometimes…" she started, hesitated, blushed and started again. "Sometimes things aren't that – easy. You like someone – a lot. You're just one of the crowd to them. Or like I said before, you just don't know anyone you care enough for. Besides, when you're a woman, you can't – oh, never mind."

She turned her head away, but he could see that her face was bright scarlet. He was unsure what to say. Then, after an uncomfortable pause, she appeared to gather enough composure to speak again.

"Gosh, isn't it hot? Have you got a busy day ahead?"

Feeling well and truly warned off her private ground, he replied as lightly as he could,

"Yes, I'm going to have a terribly English afternoon. I'm going on a picnic."

She leapt gladly on the opening.

"Really? How nice. You've got a good day for it." And she sat down on her stool again, partly facing him, not quite so flushed.

"Me, I guess and about twenty others. It's really a birthday party, at Asbury Park. Do you know it?"

"Oh yes, I've been there once or twice. It's lovely. Can I ask whose birthday?"

"Elizabeth Ashton-Richards," he replied, lingering lovingly over the syllables of her name. "You know, the daughter of our Professor."

She stood up abruptly, went over to the refrigerator again, opened the door, closed it without taking anything out, said,

"Oh, how nice," came back and sat down once more. After watching this performance with some surprise, he noticed that her hands were shaking.

"Are you well enough, Jill?"

"I'm fine," she replied abruptly. Then she rubbed her forehead with her hand. "I'm sorry. I don't mean to be rude. Look, if you'll excuse me, I'll go, and have some coffee and an aspirin. I've got a bit of a headache – the sun, I expect."

"Why don't you go home if you're not feeling well?"

"I'll be all right once I've had my coffee," she said, hanging up her lab coat.

He listened to her footsteps hurrying away up the corridor. What a strange girl she was! So reticent and yet, he seemed to feel an awareness of something very powerful kept suppressed in the background. She plainly did not care to be asked about her personal life and despite her sharp words to him, he hoped she would never be embarrassed by finding out how different his lifestyle and attitudes were to her own. He liked her and respected her competence, and he could not shake off a lingering wish that she had not put him down quite so sharply.

Sarah and Elizabeth were standing together on the steps of the house, watching the guests arriving.

"I say, Elizabeth, who's that beautiful man getting out of that car over there?"

"That's him."

"Oh, it's not! He's a real dish! You must be mad not to grab him with both hands."

"What about dear Reggie?"

"I'd rather have him than Reggie any time."

"Reggie," said Elizabeth with a significant look, "is English."

"Good afternoon, Elizabeth."

"Good afternoon, Tom. I'm so glad you were able to come. May I introduce my friend, Sarah Myers? Sarah, this is Tom Di Angeli."

They exchanged the usual vapid courtesies. Then Tom, with some relief, brought forward the little gift-wrapped package that he had been awkwardly dangling from his fingers.

"I'd like to wish you a happy birthday, a bit belatedly, Elizabeth."

"Oh, Tom, how very kind! You really shouldn't have!"

Feeling no longer self-conscious of his fresh blue shirt and pale-coloured slacks, after seeing the garb of some of the other male guests, Tom watched her slim fingers as she unwrapped her parcel. Watched with pleasure, for her hands, like the rest of her, were lovely, fine and delicate, the nails painted pale pink, oval and not too long, the wrists slender and graceful, a small wristwatch on one, a narrow bracelet made of flat gold links on the other.

As she pulled back the paper, Sarah cried,

"Goodness, Elizabeth, he must be psychic."

"Tom, this is my favourite perfume," she said looking at him with undisguised delight. "Such a lovely large bottle too! How did you know?"

"I had the girl demonstrate nearly every perfume in the shop to me, till I found one that seemed right for you. I'm so glad you like it."

"Like it! Goodness, what can I say?"

"You've already said more than enough. Your smile was all I wanted to see."

"Oh, I think you deserve more than that. I think you deserve –"

A kiss, he wondered hopefully. But no.

"Tom, are you free this evening? After the picnic?"

"I certainly am," he replied, wondering what was coming.

"There's a little extra laid on. A dance, back here, for special friends and people who can't make it this afternoon. Why don't you join us and I'll try to persuade Reggie to let us have one dance together. I'll wear some of your perfume, especially for your benefit."

"Well, gee thanks," said Tom, confused as to whether this remark indicated that he was in or out. "I'll be honoured to attend."

"That's settled then. Oh, sorry, I'm forgetting. We've got to get you organised to travel to Asbury, haven't we? Reggie!"

A man standing a few yards off turned round.

"Yes, darling?"

"This is Tom. He's a friend of Daddy's. He's coming with us this afternoon. Put him in a car somewhere, will you?"

She turned away and entered the front door, accompanied by Sarah, who said, "Ker-runch!" Elizabeth looked at her quizzically. "Was that quite necessary, darling?"

"Was what necessary?"

"Did you have to squash him quite so flat? Bit cruel, wasn't it? You pick him up by asking him to the dance, then drop him straight over a cliff! Fancy telling Reggie he was only a friend of Daddy's!"

"All for your benefit, Sarah darling. I'm just helping to ensure that by this evening, he's not going to want to dance with anyone other than you."

"I think you're crazy! Just because he's an American!"

"Sarah, I can't bear to be surrounded by any more walking disaster areas. You know very well that's what any American becomes as soon as he gets within fifty yards of me."

"Surely, you're not still thinking of that poor chap who stuck the fork in his ear?"

"That was just an accident and at least he was trying to please. What about the one who crashed Daddy's car?"

"True. Just as well, it was his second best car."

"And the one who smashed one of the best pieces of Mummy's china collection, an antique worth hundreds, demonstrating the latest dance to us? And there have been others. Can you believe, when that chap was at a dinner party two weeks ago, Mother actually picked up one of her favourite pieces and handed it to him? I was on tenterhooks till it was safely back on the shelf. No. Tom's very nice and very good-looking, but I'm not going to risk it. Something disastrous happens every single time I get friendly with an American. It's fate."

"Oh well," said Sarah, shrugging. "If you say so. Your loss is my gain, I hope."

"Why don't you go and see Reggie now? I gave him specific orders to put you two in the same car."

"Oh goody! Did you really? Right, I'll be off then. See you in the park."

"And make sure you get a good tight grip on him and keep him away from me."

Reggie surveyed this worm he had been presented with in a superior manner.

"How do you do, Tom?" he said in an accent that would have made the President of the United States feel inferior.

"Hi, Reggie," said Tom, faintly.

The English weed with an eyeglass had manifested as a six-footer built like a rugby fullback with, apparently, perfect vision in the level blue eyes. His head was tilted back as he inspected Tom from above. Total self-assurance looked out from the sort of face that is sometimes described as engagingly ugly. Reggie was of the breed that had built the Empire and he had but one weakness. Elizabeth. In her hands, he was putty. Anyone else had to prove merit before acceptance. Few men he regarded as his equal, even fewer as superior and a half-pint American interloper with designs on his girl came into neither category.

"You can travel with David. He's still got room. Come this way, please."

Tom obediently followed to a gleaming silver grey B.M.W. With two men in the front and the back still empty.

"Another passenger for you, David. His name's Tom. I'll find someone else to fill you up, then you can get under way."

"I can take two more if need be."

"Oh, I think we've got enough transport. Half a minute."

"This is a real fine car. Good of you to take me," Tom observed, settling into the comfortable seat.

"Oh, you're the famous American, are you? Don't shut the door, here's Sarah heading our way."

Famous for what? Tom wondered as Sarah bounced in beside him. David started the engine and the car glided smoothly out into the road.

"Isn't it a wonderful day?" Sarah said brightly. "Elizabeth is always lucky with the weather for her picnic. She's had one every year, you know, since she was little."

"Has she? Well, it sure is a different way to have your birthday party."

It was too much to hope that he would travel with Elizabeth, but he could have been a little luckier, he thought. Sarah was most definitely not his type.

"Isn't this B.M.W. of David's super?" she went on in her high-pitched, penetrating voice. "It sounds like silk and goes like a bomb. He took me to the races in it one day and we did ninety up the motorway. Got stopped by the police and it cost him a £50 fine. I think he was more annoyed by the police having a faster car than his, than he was by the fine. I hope you're not going to tank it up today, darling."

"Chance would be a nice thing on these roads. I expect you think our roads are pretty antiquated, Tom?"

"He probably carries a car like this in his boot as a spare at home – oh, that's not the right word, is it? Shouldn't I say trunk, or something like that? Americans generally giggle when we talk about bonnets and boots."

Trying to look as if he never giggled about anything, Tom merely replied, "You quickly get to understand the different terms."

"Been here long?" enquired David hastily. He decided that his mission on this car journey was to prevent Sarah putting her foot in it too far and too often.

"About two months."

"Like it?"

"Very much."

"I suppose you feel you've got to say that in case you get pitched out and left to walk all the way."

"Not at all. I was being quite genuine."

"Different from what you're used to, I suppose?"

"Stimulatingly so."

"What part d'you come from?"

The small talk continued until they came to imposing gates and slowed to take a long, narrow, bumpy roadway through tree-dotted areas with people enjoying modest picnics relaxed on the grass or strolling about, while children played. Then they came to a low gate guarded by a man in a navy uniform who let them through when David called out of the window,
"Miss Ashton-Richards party."

"You won't have the hoi-polloi gaping at you in here, Tom," said Sarah. "This part of the park's private. Lord Langton is a great friend of Elizabeth's mother and he lets her use it each year."

"Notice he always gets well out of the way first, though," David remarked. "Can't stand some of Elizabeth's friends, obviously."

He parked the car by some others and they disembarked.

Tom decided that the first thing he must do was to somehow lose this chatty, overdressed girl with the incredibly curly hairstyle. Her voice grated on all his nerve endings and she never seemed to stop talking. And that creation she chose to wear, frilly, fussy and cut low at the front. Deeply as he loved the female body, he did hate it when a girl kept pushing her cleavage under his nose and inviting him to take a look. Those alluring glimpses of the extra inch of tantalising flesh were for the quiet moments when a casual acquaintance was beginning to drift into something closer, when she leaned forward to take a glass from his hand, their fingers touched, their eyes met and the magic began to work. Not for the middle of a sunny afternoon in a car with two other people. Not only was this putting the goods in the shop window, but throwing them at his head and he simply found it off-putting. Poor Sarah! She was doing her best and managing to get it wrong ninety per cent of the time.

Erica Ashton-Richards, who was supervising the transfer of huge amount of food and drink from the boot of a Rolls-Royce to some trestle tables set up on a smooth area of lawn, informed everyone who passed her, including Tom and Sarah, that tea would be in about one and a half hours' time. Tom did not want to wander too far from the cars. He was awaiting the arrival of Elizabeth. A little stone bench beside the path caught his attention and he said hopefully,
"You go talk to your friends, Sarah. I'll rest here awhile."

"Oh, let's wander round and see the sights, Tom. Come and have a closer look at the house. The gardens are beautiful."

"I'll take in the overall view first. Don't let me stop you."

Sarah, knowing well what he was waiting for, sat by his side.

"It would be much more pleasant by the lake. Why sit in a car park? There are benches down there and you can see the house. It's very pretty by the river. Swans and ducks. Come on."

"Don't care for swans. They're nasty and vicious, and have peevish faces. This'll do me."

He clasped his hands round his knees and leaned back, trying to look comfortable.

Sarah fidgeted with the flounces of her skirt, pulling it up a little to show her knees.

"I saw that film 'Manhattan' a little while ago. I've been wondering ever since if people in New York are really like that. What did you think? Did you find it interesting?"

"Never go to the movies."

Sarah, feeling hot and uncomfortable, tugged at her beads, wondering if it was true. It was not, of course, but he was trying not to get into any unnecessary, or indeed any, conversation with Sarah.

"I don't go all that much, but I enjoyed that. Pity you didn't see it. Do you go to the races?"

"No." There was a long, uncomfortable silence. Suddenly, not too far away, Tom saw an acquaintance, one of the research assistants.

"Excuse me, I see someone I know. I'll just go and say hello."

Sarah jumped up and put her arm through his.

"I'll come and you can introduce me."

Reggie and Elizabeth arrived a few minutes later, while Tom still had Sarah clinging to his arm. Elizabeth noted this with satisfaction and hoped her friend was making a good impression.

"Let's have some games till tea," cried the enthusiastically athletic Reggie.

Part of Tom groaned inwardly at the thought of a lot of childish running about and shouting on the grass with a crowd of strangers, but the other part pointed out that in a general jostle, he could lose Sarah and perhaps, find Elizabeth.

Reggie produced three tennis balls and a sort of wild free-for-all bearing some slight resemblance to Piggy in the Middle ensued. Pleading that he must have both hands free for catching, Tom managed to get Sarah to let go of his arm. He manoeuvred close to Elizabeth, finally made a catch and tried to present the ball to her. She declined, saying it would be cheating and he had to take himself off rather sulkily to the edge of the circle.

Then someone proposed a much more promising game. It consisted of forming two teams who lined up opposite each other, then advanced step-by-step calling out nonsensical challenges and replies, until, at a given key word, the first team had to rush through the ranks of the second to a base line behind them, while the second tried to take prisoners. A little strategy saw Tom on the opposite side to Elizabeth. Twice, his team was the one to make the frantic dash, twice he got caught, once by an agile chap with a memorable line in halitosis, once by the delighted Sarah, who flung her arms round him ecstatically and nearly had him on the ground.

Then it was the other team's turn. He placed himself carefully, and Elizabeth came dodging and weaving towards him, evading out-flung hands, so intent that she did not see him. He half caught her from behind, and was about to secure her with his other hand when something hit him heavily from the side and he landed up on the turf. Reggie, who's tackling was known and feared among the local rugby clubs, smiled down at him with an air of great satisfaction.

"Sorry, Tom, I didn't see you, old man. Can I help you up?" he said in his glass-shattering accent, extending a hand.

"Thank you, I can manage," Tom replied, scrambling to his feet. The knee of his light-coloured trousers had a large green and brown stain on it now.

They eyed each other like a pair of hostile dogs. Tom regretted his misspent youth at that moment. He should have followed his elder brother's example and played American football instead of devoting himself to his books.

"Watch it, friend," he muttered. "You may be bigger than me, but I could just surprise you."

Reggie raised his eyebrows, looking pained at such an ill-bred remark.

"An accident, old man. Only an accident," he replied loftily and walked away.

It was too energetic a game to go on for long on such a hot afternoon. Everyone flopped down on the grass in chattering, laughing groups comparing captures and escapes, and Elizabeth demanded cool drinks for the assembled company. Erica decided the buffet may as well open straight away, and soon plates of chicken salad, beer, lemonade and iced champagne were being enthusiastically consumed. Reggie tossed a chicken bone at Tom, who was sitting with Sarah and Elizabeth laughed.

Sarah wanted an ice. She really wanted an ice, but she was so comfortable under the trees that she simply couldn't move. Would Tom be terribly kind and Tom would. Anything to let his eardrums rest for a few blissful seconds.

"Tom," said Erica as he approached the table. "Oh, Tom, just look at Elizabeth. She's such a naughty girl. She will *not* wear a hat in the sun and her face is getting all red. If her nose starts to peel, we'll never hear the last of it. Give her this hat and tell her I said she was to wear it. Would you?"

Ever more gladly, Tom would. But before he had taken three steps carrying the wide-brimmed straw hat, he found Reggie had come up from behind and got hold of the other side of it.

"Don't trouble, Tom. I'll take it to Elizabeth."

"It's no trouble, Reggie," Tom replied in a hard-edged voice, still keeping his hold on the hat and allowing the anger he felt to show in his face.

"I said, I will give it to her."

"Her mother gave it to me."

"*I* am escorting Elizabeth, *I* will give her the hat."

"Oh God, isn't this a little childish?" Tom snapped, relinquishing his hold and stepping away

As reply, Reggie merely allowed his eyes to flick arrogantly over Tom, reminding the latter of the mud on his trousers and thereby adding to his annoyance. Still immaculate himself, Reggie strolled back to Elizabeth. He squatted in front of her, put the hat on her head and arranged it to his liking. Then he said something, glanced at Tom and they both laughed. His face vanished behind the brim of the hat. Kissing Elizabeth was not for him a unique moment to be boasted about, but just a pleasant part of everyday life.

Tom was angry. He was sick and fed up to the back teeth of being sat on. Somehow, he decided right then, he was going to haul her out of that guy's arms and into his own. And when he did, he would show Reggie that more than one could play the sneering game

Sarah had been watching. He was walking back across the grass to her now, still staring at Elizabeth and Reggie. Maybe this was a good moment.

"Tom, you've forgotten it."

From a long, long way, he came back to her, making a perceptible effort to focus. The fact that she was still there did not seem to console him much.

"Forgotten what?" he asked impatiently.

"My ice. You went to get me an ice."

"Oh, get the goddam thing yourself!" he snarled and walked away.

46

A few minutes later, he was back, penitent, with the largest and most elaborate ice he could concoct from the goodies available.

"Sarah," he said, "Please forgive me. That was unbelievably rude. Just because others have made up their minds to spend the afternoon scoring points off me, there's no reason I should take it out on you. I'm sorry. Will you take this, with my regrets?"

"Oh, Tom, it's all right. I wasn't upset."

"Then why," he smiled, "did I see a little handkerchief work going on as I came back over here?"

She smiled too.

"Because I'm silly. Hey, I don't think I can eat all of this! It looks gorgeous, but there's so much of it! Why don't you get a spoon and we'll share it?"

"Yeah, why not? I'd like that."

It is hard to share a huge crystal dish of ice cream and whipped cream, strawberries and raspberries, nuts and slices of fresh peach with someone without looking as if you are fond of each other, and having a good time. From where Elizabeth sat, that was how Tom and Sarah looked. He pointed to something in the bow. And she got it out and spooned it into his mouth, and they both laughed as Tom lay down on the grass, legs and arms in the air, pretending to be a dead dog. He had grass stains on the seat of his light coloured trousers as well, but the deteriorating state of his garments did not seem to be concerning him. She watched them for a long time, while Reggie munched an apple and stared ruminatively into the distance.

Reggie's protective custody had been fun while Tom looked as if he was trying to break through it, but now he seemed to have lost interest, it became irksome. Elizabeth wanted to go and find out what they were talking about over there, but Reggie would be furious if she proposed that after all his careful efforts on her behalf. Unloading Tom on to someone else did not seem to be such a good idea, now he was looking like consenting to be unloaded. Well, there was always the dance – unless, of course, he had taken offence and decided not to come. Oh, but he would, certainly, he would, so he could dance with Sarah. But then, perhaps, he would take her out somewhere else. Elizabeth was pettishly conscious of a plan that, far from failing, had worked only too well.

She sighed audibly and Reggie looked at her.

"What's the matter, darling?"

"Americans! They're so infuriating!"

Reggie knew his Elizabeth and her vanity, and he was not perturbed. A little attention this evening would mollify her and she would be back to her normal cool composure. He feared no rivals, least of all Americans. Elizabeth had been his for almost two years now, far longer than she had ever cared for anyone else. Other attractions had come, stayed fleetingly and gone, and Reggie had survived them all. She had not yet accepted his oft-repeated proposal of marriage; in the end, she would.

As the afternoon grew cool, drivers began to drift back to their cars collecting groups of passengers on the way, and Erica and her helpers embarked on the work of retrieving the scattered dishes.

The dance began at seven. Those who lived near enough and were returning for it went home to change, while guests who had travelled from further away went to the house in Park Row where they relaxed in the garden with Madeira and delicious little nutty biscuits. Elizabeth made them. It was the one piece of cooking she ever consented to do and they had become rather famous among her friends. The joke was that she would only marry Reggie when he felt able to live on nothing but nutty biscuits.

Tom got, thankfully, back to his flat, threw all his sweaty and grass-stained clothing into the dirty-linen basket, and had a shower. He had been looking forward to that shower for at least an hour. The tepid water streamed through his hair and down his face, carrying away the tensions and irritations of the afternoon with the soapsuds. Then he dried, put on a short white towelling bathrobe, padded along barefoot to the kitchen and mixed himself a more than welcome drink.

Relaxed with it in his favourite armchair, he reviewed the events of the last three hours. Elizabeth had demonstrated as clearly as could be her displeasure at her mother's impromptu invitation to him and it was a pity that she had impulsively asked him to the dance. Could he duck out of it? If he did, would his absence be noticed? By Erica, not Elizabeth. Erica was the one he was concerned about offending.

He sat sipping his drink, weighing up the pros and cons. There was always the piquant thought that he could go specially for the purpose of taking a rise out of Elizabeth.

Even more, out of Reggie. For really, when he thought about it, Elizabeth had not done any of the unpleasant things that had been done to him. True, he had seen her laughing, but it was surely a bit paranoiac to assume she was laughing at him? It was Reggie who had put him in the car with Sarah, Reggie who had shoulder charged him in the prisoner game, Reggie who had thrown missiles at him at teatime, and finally, Reggie who had initiated that undignified dissent over the sun hat. Why assume Elizabeth had any hand in it? It was quite natural that Reggie would want to keep him away from her and, who could tell, perhaps she was as irked by it as he was.

He would go to the dance and test the hypothesis. One dance had been half-promised to him at any rate, and if he got it early in the evening and was ignored thereafter, he would know just where he stood. Not that he would allow it to deflect him, but at least he would know where base was.

A long, book-lined room had been cleared and music drifted from an expensive hi-fi set installed at one end. Tom, once again fresh and spruce in his best suit, his hair combed, the little curls around his ears arranged with artful carelessness to look their devastating best – there had been several girls whose favourite leisure-time activity was winding those very curls round their fingers – was as before admitted by the Professor, Elizabeth's father. He seemed to act as regular doorman in his own house.

48

The place was busy with guests, including, of course, Reggie, who, when Tom entered the library, was dancing with Sarah. They caught each other's eye and Reggie flashed him a warning look which said 'stay away from her' as plainly as words.

Tom took up a position just inside the door and watched Reggie's athletic back as he danced. He was one of those people who seem to exude health. Bodily health in repellent abundance, over-emphatic mental balance of the sort that makes the common run of mortals feel they must, in comparison, be candidates for the psychiatrist. No doubt, complete, effortless, sexual normality as well. Should any little imp of temptation find its misguided way into his thoughts, no doubt a couple of vigorous games of squash would quickly settle the matter.

Perhaps, it would have been wiser not to come, after all. He had endured Reggie making him feel inferior all afternoon and now an evening of the same was in prospect. An hour. He would give it an hour and then slip quietly away home. Plenty to do there, reading to catch up on, advance notes for lectures next term, even television if he just felt like being idle. He stifled a yawn and looked around. Lots of acquaintances there, but no one he wanted to go and talk to. Pity Paul was not one of the guests. They could have amused each other by exchanging comments on the British, not feeling they might be the butts of similar remarks themselves.

"Why don't we have that dance now, Tom?"

Gee, it was her, looking more than ever like the fairy princess! In white, as always, a long, sweeping dress, fitting closely and enticingly around her shapely breasts, high at the front, giving no glimpse of cleavage, shoestring straps over her flawless shoulders, the back plunging low almost to the waist. A diamond stud shone in each ear, a sparkling pendant on a short silver chain at her throat. For a moment, he just stared, like a schoolboy at the pantomime, completely bowled over.

"Elizabeth," he breathed, hardly able to speak. "You look fantastic."

She smiled and his knees turned to water.

"What was that funny word you said when we were sitting in the garden the last time you were here?"

"Did I say a funny word?"

His eyes were still avidly absorbing the vision before him.

"Yes, when you were talking about blueberry pie and all that sort of thing."

"I guess I said 'tickety-boo', or something stupid like that."

"That's right. Is that what you feel like now?"

"And how!"

"Let's dance, shall we?"

Magic. Pure magic. No need to grab for her, she just moved into the circle of his arm, still smiling at him and laid her hand in his. For a brief, blinding moment, his fingers touched the bare skin of her back, before he quickly laid them on the fabric of her dress. That was smooth and silky, pleasant to the senses, but compared to that fleeting caress of her warm skin, it could have been sackcloth.

49

People swirled all around them, but for him, they could have been alone in an eternity of star-filled space.

There seemed to be a touch of restrained amusement in the eyes that looked into his. She must know how he felt. Surely, it must be plain from his face that he adored her and that any little disaffection from the afternoon had been swept aside by the sight of her?

"Did you enjoy the picnic, Tom?"

"Very much. It was an extremely pleasant afternoon. The park is just as beautiful as everyone told me it would be, the food was superb and the company was fun."

"Did you get on well with Sarah?"

"She's a very sweet girl, but I can think of someone else I'd rather have spent the afternoon with."

Again, that devastating little smile.

"She liked you very much."

"Did she? That's kind of her to say so. I'm afraid I was rude to her more than once, for I was thinking of you."

The record stopped. *Well, that's it*, he thought. *That was my free ride on the carousel and from here on in, it's fight all the way.* Reggie came bustling up.

"Shall we dance, Elizabeth?"

"Not now, Reggie, I'm talking to Tom. I'll dance with you later."

Someone put on some more music and she held out her hand, tilting her head and smiling invitingly.

"Shall we go on?"

If he had not been in such a flat spin, he would probably, as a fellow student of the art of snaring the opposite sex, have admired her technique. As it was, he was just besotted beyond all reason and logic.

They danced and talked about trivia, and he wondered if she would, after all, go out with him. Just once, as a crumb thrown to a hungry bird, pecked up eagerly and swallowed, with little hope of more bounty.

"How's your dog and her puppies?"

He never heard the answer.

Unbidden, the picture leapt into his mind of himself and that girl in the disused factory. She had the dirtiest feet that even he had ever seen, and he had kissed them while she had wriggled and protested that it was ticklish. As the evening had still been warm, and they were well secluded from prying eyes, she had willingly taken off most of her clothes for him and laid them on the floor to form a bed for herself. Things had been proceeding nicely when that inquisitive and rather over-friendly dog had happened along…

"That's a very secret little smile, Tom. What are you thinking of?"

Smoothly and without a flicker, he had answered,

"I'm thinking of how lovely you are, Elizabeth, and wondering if I dare to ask you to the Bach concert next week."

Did Bach qualify as 'heavy stuff', he wondered.

That girl, she had laughed and laughed as he had leapt to his feet with a curse, and sent the dog scuttling for its life with a well-aimed missile.

"Did it lick your bum, Freak? Oh, you are funny. You didn't half jump!" and she rolled about on her improvised bed, her breasts shaking as she giggled at him.

"Bloody dogs!" he had muttered, but her laughter was so infectious that it captured him and he had knelt down beside her again with his face beginning to break into a rueful smile.

"Oh, I'm sorry, Tom, I can't. I'm going with Reggie. He's already asked me."

Damn Reggie's eyes!

"Would you have dinner with me, then, one evening?"

"Well, I don't know, Tom. I'm busy most evenings. There's such a lot of different things I do."

"You can't be busy every evening, surely? What about, say, next Wednesday?"

The music had stopped and they were walking over to the side of the room together.

"No… no, definitely not Wednesday."

"Thursday, then?"

"Well – I don't –"

"You're not doing anything on Thursday, dear, you know you're not."

It was Elizabeth's mother. Deep in conversation, they had walked right up to her, not noticing she was there.

"Yes, I am. I'm going to Caroline's."

"That's Thursday week."

"Is it?"

"Yes," said Erica, in a voice that brooked no argument.

"Oh yes, I believe you're right."

"Of course, I'm right. Dance with him again, dear, and you can make the arrangements. Roger's putting on another record now."

Tom, a little embarrassed by this deux ex machina, said, when they were out of earshot,

"You don't have to come if you don't want to. Please say, if you'd rather not."

"No… I'd like to come." said Elizabeth, looking a trifle desperate.

Tom laughed sympathetically.

"Poor Elizabeth. Are you feeling trapped? Never mind, you can always ring me next week and tell me you can't make it."

Having thus, he hoped, short-circuited that particular get-out for her, he boldly laid his cheek against hers. As he did so, he caught the eye of Reggie, who was standing watching them with a murderous expression. He gave him a fatuous smile, which clearly made him even more furious, kissed Elizabeth's hair lightly and steered her out of Reggie's sight among the crowd.

He was glad he had given her that perfume. With practised skill, she had known how to put on just the right amount, so that tantalising whiffs of it beguiled him as she moved. Sarah, in the same circumstances, would probably have used so much that it would have been impossible to approach her without breathing apparatus.

She seemed restless and anxious to get away once they had finalised their date.

"Do you mind if I go and powder my nose, Tom?" she asked coyly.

"Of course not," he replied and reluctantly let her go, wondering if he would see her again that evening.

Words with her mother were on her mind.

"Mother, I wish you wouldn't do things like that. I really didn't want to go out with him."

"But he's such a nice young man, dear. So intelligent. Much more so than Reggie, who hasn't got an idea outside sport?"

"You know what always happens when I get friendly with Americans."

"Oh, that's all coincidence. This will be different, I'm sure."

"I don't think so and I wish you'd let me make my own arrangements. I'm not a child now. I do know what I'm doing."

"All right dear, but I think you'll be pleased in the end about this."

Even Erica did not always get it right.

Meanwhile, Reggie had buttonholed Tom in the hallway outside. He was angry, jealous and slightly drunk.

"Now look here," he said with an unpleasant stare. "Just you stay away from Elizabeth. She's mine, do you understand?"

"I didn't notice her ring," Tom replied, shrugging casually and moving imperceptibly into a fine balance on his toes.

"We're not actually engaged, but we have an understanding."

"Surely, Elizabeth is capable of making up her own mind?"

Alcohol caused Reggie's tongue to lose its accustomed rigid good manners and considered sentences.

"Look, if you think you can come oiling in here and start making up to her with your fancy talk – well, frankly, I'm inclined at the moment to sock you one on the jaw."

Tom measured Reggie with the eye of one to whom subduing the jealous drunk was a not unfamiliar exercise. Girls in pubs who seemed to be alone were sometimes not so.

"I would strongly advise you not to try it," he said menacingly.

"I was the school boxing champion, I'll have you know," Reggie replied grandly, if a little unsteadily.

"Hah!"

"Don't say 'hah' to me like that, you creep!"

"Look, friend," said Tom, delicately taking Reggie's lapel between finger and thumb. "I've fought my way out of more bars than you've probably been in in your sheltered and well-bred life, and that's a whole different ball game, let me tell you. You get me riled up and the first thing I do is throw the rule book out of the window."

Reggie was impressed. Tom's manner was not inductive to taking up the challenge and besides, he was not so drunk as to seriously contemplate an exchange of blows in the Ashton-Richards' Regency hallway. Brushing Tom's hand away, he said,

"Just you watch it, that's all," and stalked off, leaving his adversary in possession of the field.

Later, Tom saw Reggie in earnest conversation with Elizabeth. They talked for a long time while she sat with her head turned to the side, staring across the room. Tom guessed that what he wanted was to announce their engagement to the assembled company, but if that was his aim, he failed. Tom made a point of kissing Elizabeth again when it was time to go.

Chapter 6

Tom went to the Bach concert because he would see Elizabeth there even though it meant seeing her in Reggie's company. He found himself placed three rows behind them and a little to the left, on the same side of Reggie as Elizabeth was sitting. To his amusement, it quickly became plain that however it was that Reggie had persuaded her to come, Bach certainly qualified in her book as 'heavy stuff'. After a quarter of an hour, she began to fidget, after half an hour to yawn surreptitiously – yawns that were carefully hidden from Reggie, but quite visible to Tom, and her relief was evident when the interval came and she was able to leave her seat and look around her. He watched them as they pushed past people to get out of their row and climbed the red-carpeted stairs. After they had vanished through the door, he got up himself and followed them out.

He found them in the bar. Elizabeth was sipping a gin and tonic, Reggie drinking a beer. Ignoring the counter which was besieged by customers, he pushed his way through the noisy crowd towards them.

"Enjoying the concert, Elizabeth?" he asked as he appeared, as it were magically, at her elbow.

Reggie scowled blackly at him and Elizabeth replied, trying to sound enthusiastic,

"Oh yes, very good, isn't it?"

"I thought the solo violinist was particularly fine, didn't you, Reggie?"

"I thought she sounded a little flat," replied Reggie, crushingly.

"Did you? I didn't notice myself, but then my sense of pitch isn't all that good. Perhaps, your ear is better than mine."

"I have an excellent ear."

"So it seems. Go to concerts often?"

"Yes," Reggie replied. "I enjoy music and besides, you meet such nice people there – as a rule."

"Yes, I must agree with you. It's a real pleasure running into you two again it's quite made my evening."

Reggie swallowed a mouthful of beer, but said nothing. Elizabeth looked around with an air of ennui.

"Last year, when I was in Barcelona –"

Elizabeth's attention was immediately caught.

"You've been to Barcelona, Tom? When?"

"Last fall."

"I don't suppose you went to a little fishing village about five miles south of there? There was a bodega –"

"The guitarist?"

"Yes!"

"Magnificent! Superb! Such technique!"

"Oh, dazzling! Whatever was his name?"

"Manuel, of course. What else?"

"Manuel, of course. I couldn't remember for a moment. Oh, Tom, I'll never forget it. I've never heard anything like it!"

"The speed with which he played! You'd never think human fingers could move so fast."

"Goodness, yes. They sold his records in the local shop and I bought one. I listen to it often. It takes me right back to the scene. I can see the whole thing, just listening."

"I'd love to hear it."

"Come round on Thursday and I'll play it for you."

"Remember the dancer?"

"Oh yes. That incredible footwork and the beautiful swirling skirt. Breathtaking."

"That's the word for it."

"What were you doing in Barcelona?"

Reggie, suddenly completely cut out, was looking from one to the other during this rapid fire dialogue, bewildered.

"I had been at the University in Madrid for a couple of months, seeing some research being done there and I saw a little of the country too, before I went home."

"Goodness! Your Spanish must be very good."

"Terrible. The Professor I went to see was American."

"Never!"

"We get everywhere. You'd be surprised."

Reggie muttered impolitely under his breath.

"Well, that must have been fascinating. I've never been to Madrid. What's it like?"

At that moment, the bell rang.

"I'll tell you on Thursday." Tom replied, patting her shoulder. Reggie looked murderous.

"Well, I'd better get back to my seat, hadn't I? See you."

"Not if I see you first," Reggie muttered to his retreating back.

"Oh, Reggie, you are nasty to him. Why?" Reggie simply snorted in reply. "Are you sure you want to stay for the second half?"

"Of course." He looked at her in surprise. "They're playing the fifth Brandenburg. You know it's one of my favourite pieces. Come on, let's get settled before the row fills up."

Elizabeth's expression was resigned as he ushered her back into the auditorium and into her seat. As she descended the stairs, she noted where Tom was sitting, and, after taking her own place, she turned round while Reggie was studying the programme and gave him a smile that was more than a little conspiratorial in quality.

Two days later, she and Tom had dinner at a smart little restaurant Paul had told him of, which was a few miles out of town. As usual, she was beautifully dressed and looked ravishing, but he quickly discovered that if they got off the subjects of horses, travelling and her various other leisure-time activities, Elizabeth really had little to say for herself that was other than shallow and jejune. She would happily express an opinion on any subject he chose to introduce, but he was staggered by the superficiality she exhibited. Deep thought was clearly and unaccustomed exercise.

But still he was enchanted. Surely, he thought, perhaps a little arrogantly, if brains were needed, he had enough for both of them? He could watch Elizabeth's face for hours. The arch of her eyebrows, the glances of her eyes, held him fascinated. The mobile pink lips and the glimpses of white teeth kept his attention focused on what was before him and away from the empty sterility of the words they formed. Memories of the conversation of past girls with IQs resembling a handy cricket score simply convinced him that they were abrasive and exacting, while she was like smooth satin, pleasing to the senses. What he was to do in twenty years' time with a wife whose only asset had been her looks, he never asked himself.

He watched and ate, and asked questions just to keep her talking. Not that that was difficult. Once well launched and with a little wine inside her, Elizabeth could keep going unassisted all evening. It was part of her training for easy mixing in good society and it had come easily to her. Even as a little girl, she had been able to entertain grown-up visitors while her parents put the final touch to their preparations, and many an elderly Professor had been intrigued by her childish, coquettish ways and artless chatter. Now grown up, she had not changed a bit.

Since seeing her reaction to the Bach concert, Tom had been giving a great deal of concentrated thought to what he could suggest as a follow-up to their dinner date. The cinema seemed a little down-market and anyway, he would prefer music. Something lighter than Bach for her, but not too unbearably popular for him. Then, he had seen that one of the theatres in the city was staging 'The Mikado' the following week and that seemed like a very good compromise. He checked the location of the building and found it was not in the sort of place where he was likely to have an embarrassing encounter, so he put the suggestion to her. To his surprise and pleasure, it was received with delight.

The evening they went to 'The Mikado' was one of the best they ever spent together. Right from the moment when he picked her up from her home, it was plain that she was eagerly and excitedly looking forward to the performance, and he found once they got there he was more often watching her, with her face lit up by the glow from the stage, than he was watching the action down there. She followed the delightful and absurd drama as it unfolded before them with rapt attention and avid enjoyment, and after each round of applause, she unfailingly reached for his hand again and entwined her warm fingers in his. She was so lovely, so beautiful and, at any rate for this evening, she was his. The girl who any of the young men in the Department would have given anything to go out with was sitting next to him, leaning on his shoulder, holding his hand. Next week, he would think of something else she would like to do, and the week after and the one after that, and before very long, she would forget Reggie and forget those prejudices of hers, and fall in love with him. It should not be too difficult. Putting aside the horses, many of the things she liked, he liked too. Those horses were an obstacle though. Being a city boy, he regarded large animals with a great deal of caution, and the thought of getting too near a beast with huge eyes, flaring nostrils and enormous yellow teeth made him shiver, let alone the idea of having the temerity to try to get on its back!

Never mind. They would have a little house in the country, not too far from the town, with paddocks and a stable, and she could have a lovely horse of her very own and a groom to come and look after it. Then she could ride, followed by her dogs, over the rolling acres, while he worked on his lectures or the book he had it in mind to write one day, glancing out now and then to see if she was coming back. Evenings, they would drive into the town to a play or concert. He would make it his pleasure to help her to the enjoyment of the music he liked and he would learn to appreciate her preferences too. And then, the nights! Oh yes, the nights! He sighed, nudged her head gently with his and smiled into her eyes when she looked at him. The nights!

The road they had to travel home climbed a long, low hill to a viewpoint which overlooked the University town in the valley below. There was an extensive layby at the highest point which was a favourite spot for picnickers and, indeed, lovers. As they approached in the car, he suggested they might stop for a few minutes and watch the twinkling lights come on in the gathering summer dusk.

She allowed herself to be persuaded. He had behaved well after their dinner date. A little peck on the lips was all she had permitted him outside her house, after which she had quickly moved away from him and he had not tried to pursue things any further. That had left her with a good impression. It was not proper that a young lady of her standing should be expected to pay for dinner by allowing undue bodily intimacies, but he was an American and so he probably thought them a matter, of course. She had been anticipating an undignified struggle, concluded by her making an indignant departure, but it had not happened and that had pleased her. So she said yes tonight, knowing she had an ace up her sleeve.

He had had the foresight to buy a car with a steering column gear change and a well-placed handbrake, so the obstacles between the two front seats were at a minimum. She let him put his arm round her and kiss her on the cheek, then put both arms round her, and kiss her on the lips, tell her how beautiful she was and how much he loved her. To the kisses, she responded, to the declarations of love, she did not reply. She liked to be kissed and he did it very nicely. Her feelings for him were now perhaps on the warm side of neutral, but no more. An occasional night out, a little mild lovemaking in the car, when she felt bored with

Reggie's company, but apart from that, Tom must be kept in his place. He must not be allowed to think he rated very highly with her, or he would start to become a nuisance.

They sat there for a long time. She had an angora shawl drawn round her shoulders and his hands strayed cautiously over its warm softness. The longing to touch her skin was intense, but he was afraid of overdoing it and being warned off. Cautiously, he caressed the nape of her neck and pushed his fingers into her hair. He was tingling all over. This restraint when in close contact with a lovely girl was not familiar to him. Those breasts of hers – they would sometimes touch his chest within the enfolding soft wool and his hand would stir on her shoulder, longing to be elsewhere. He tried to judge the depth of her response and assess his chances if he were to try. If only she would give him some little, tiny encouragement!

Finally, he could resist no longer. Slowly, slowly, he worked his way down towards his goal, pressing the soft fluffy shawl with the tips of his fingers and kissing those warm lips at the same time, hoping she might not notice, or, if she did notice, by now, she might not mind.

Elizabeth had been getting a little bored and she saw her chance to call a halt.

"That's enough, Tom," she said, drawing away from him. "I think you should take me home now. It's getting very late."

He looked at her in doleful disappointment, sitting up very straight, but reluctant to take away the arm he still had round her.

"Oh, must we go so soon? I could stay here with you forever."

"Yes, we must, really. Mother will be wondering what's become of me and besides, haven't you got to be up for work in the morning?"

"I guess, you're right," he replied with a sigh. "Let me kiss you once more, my darling. I don't ever want to stop."

As the car moved off down the hill, he asked,
"Can I see you again at the weekend?"

It was the moment for her to show him exactly where he stood.

"No, I'm sorry, Tom, I won't be able to see you for ages. We're going on holiday this weekend."

"This weekend? Where are you going?"

"To Greece. For a month."

"A month! Good heavens, won't I be able to see you again for a month?"

"No, we shan't be back till the second of September."

"Oh, Elizabeth!"

"I thought you would know. Didn't you know Father was going to be away then?"

"Well, I guess I did, but I didn't realise you were going to be away as well."

"Oh, we're a very close family, you know. We always go on holiday together."

"A month! Oh, Elizabeth!"

He felt shattered by this entirely unexpected news.

"Well, I'm sorry to spring it on you like this." Somehow, she managed to keep the smirk out of her voice. "But I really thought you knew. You must have lots of girlfriends anyway."

"Elizabeth, there isn't anyone in the world for me, apart from you. Didn't you know that?"

"Oh Tom, you mustn't talk like that. Why, we hardly know one another."

"I know you well enough."

"Now, that's just silly. I might have all sorts of bad habits you don't know about."

And so might I, he thought.

"Anyway, I can't do anything about it, can I? I'll see you when I come back and tell you all about it."

He was sunk in misery for the rest of the drive home. Just when he seemed to be getting on so well with her! Nothing could be done, of course and he would simply have to face it, but what a long time! And what were her feelings going to be when she returned? Would he have lost all the way he had gained since the picnic?

Now they were back at her house, he kissed her and said with all the sincerity he could muster,

"Well, enjoy your holiday, Elizabeth, and don't forget me, will you?"

"Oh, it's going to be bliss," she sighed happily, "The sun, the Mediterranean, the scenery – oh marvellous! I'll be so brown when I come back that you won't even recognise me."

"I'll recognise you. And you'll look more beautiful than ever."

"Silly boy," she said, patting his cheek. "Now, let me go. Mother will be waiting up for me."

"Let her wait. Give me one more kiss, one that'll last me a whole, interminable month."

Her lips touched his again, and he wondered how he could ever live without her and if there was anyone else in the world so sweet.

"Oh Elizabeth," he said with a sigh. "I can't bear to let you go."

"Tom, I'll come back. You'll hardly know I've been away."

"I shall know, every single second of the day and night. I'll think of you every minute."

His heart felt like a lead weight as he drove home, thinking of her walking away from him and letting herself in the front door. It did nothing for his misery when he suddenly wondered if Reggie might be included in the party bound for Greece. If only he had thought to ask her! Now, unless he saw the fellow, he would be wondering all the time if he was there, while he himself was here, envious and despondent.

His flat, when he let himself in, seemed very empty and lonely. He went to his calendar that hung in the kitchen and drew an enormous red square round the second of September. There was no need to write what it signified. What likelihood was there that he would forget?

He went to bed then, but it was impossible to sleep. He had been frustrated and frustration did ugly things to him. Elizabeth had aroused him, far more than he had acknowledged at the time, made him long for her and finally, left him not only empty, but in this deep pit of despair. He could not have her clean, shining body and for a whole month, he was to be denied even the lesser delight of seeing, and occasionally, touching and kissing her. And perhaps, Reggie had what he had not.

Peevishly, his mind set about punishing him for his presumption that he meant anything in the world to her, even as much as that damn dog of hers. A little house in the country with paddock and stables, indeed! Who the hell did he think he was, dreaming dreams like that and including Elizabeth in them? The sooner he reminded himself of what was really like inside this shell that he presented to the world, the better. Then he could put an end to these recurring dreams of marriage and the thought that someone might find him an object fit for their lasting love.

How wise, how much wiser than she knew, had Elizabeth been when she refused to let his unworthy contaminated hands touch her breasts, those treasures reserved for one who could match up to the privilege. In due time, Reggie would be allowed access to every treasure because he was straight and right, and every corner of his life could bear inspection. But he himself – if he wanted to satisfy those nagging lusts, he would have to go, and abase himself to one of those girls whose kind he knew so well, find her, persuade her, kiss and wallow in her, until he knew again just where his place in the world really was. He had better go soon and he had better not, as sometimes happened, fail to find one.

His mind roamed obsessively round and round like a captured beast, trampling his self-esteem, and splattering him with the mud of loathing and revulsion, while Elizabeth, who felt rather pleased at the way she had led him on and left him wanting more, slept peacefully. She was comfortable in the certainty that she had played him along just right, ensuring that he would still be around and interested when she returned. *It did dear Reggie a lot of good to have a rival,* she thought. He was so much more attentive when he thought someone else was showing a liking for her and getting a response.

Chapter 7

Jill stayed at home on the Saturday following Elizabeth's departure for Greece. She had had quite enough of work for that week. Her boss had been techy and irritable, and had given her one hell of a time. Very little problem seemed to get magnified to gigantic proportions and, to thoroughly crown a bad spell, Mrs Simpson had failed to appear on the Friday. Her professor had stamped about the lab using words that made her ears tingle and had finally stormed off to his room to shout down the phone at the Domestic Supervisor, a really nice man who was doing his best in very difficult circumstances. Jill felt this was most unfair and she was unusually relieved when he decided to sulk for an hour or two in his office.

She was looking forward to her holiday and she said so with a little emphasis to her flatmate Susan as they did their shopping.

"My word, there was a monumental row on Friday!" she said, closing her eyes at the memory. "I didn't know where to put myself when I saw Mrs S. wasn't there. I knew exactly what was going to happen and goodness, didn't it just!"

"God, he must be a bad-tempered cuss!"

"Oh, not normally. It's only when things get up his nose like this. Usually, he's –" Jill broke off and sighed. "Usually, he's ever so nice. But this Simpson business drives him mad. *He* comes in to work every day, *I* come into work every day and he doesn't see why she shouldn't as well. He's quite right, of course. I agree with him."

Susan smiled. She was quite used to Jill's indulgent attitude and she felt sure in her romantic mind that it had its significance.

"So you let him kick you around and say, kick me again, please, sir?"

"Oh, Susan, don't be silly. You don't understand. He's like a kid in a way. When something annoys him, he screams and stamps, and lets it all out, then he'll usually go off and sulk for a bit, then like a little boy, he's back all sorry, and wanting to hug and make up – metaphorically speaking, of course. I get a pat on the shoulder as a rule. It's nice. One thing, the Prof'll never have a heart attack. Everyone around him, maybe, but not him. He doesn't let the stress build up for one second. He just yells and gets it over with."

"Sounds exhausting. He needs someone like you for a wife."

Jill smiled and shook her head.

"He's got better fish to fry. Besides, he doesn't know I exist, as a woman."

"And how does that make you feel?"

"Neutral."

Susan did not believe her.

On Monday, he was not there. It took Jill some time to find out why not. On impulse, he had taken a plane and flown to L.A. Home to Mother.

Before leaving, he had called Peter, his brother and Peter was there with two of his children at the airport when he emerged from Arrivals.

"Hi, Uncle Tom!" cried the two in unison. "Brought us any British candy?"

"Hi, Katie, hi, Little Pete. Let's see what's in my pocket, now. How are things, Peter?"

"I'm not Little Pete now," said the eight year old, offended. "I'm just Pete. My Daddy's Peter. That's how you tell us apart."

"Oh gee, I'm sorry," said Tom, mock seriously, handing out chocolate bars. "I'll remember that. How's school?"

"Doesn't your voice sound funny, Uncle Tom? You've got a British accent."

"Never!"

"Yes you have, yes you have!" shouted Pete.

"Don't shout, kids," admonished their father. "Tell Uncle Tom all about school as we go back to the car."

They made an attractive group walking together and several people, women especially, looked at them with interest as they passed. Both children were dressed in jeans and T-shirts. Ten-year-old Katie had long fair hair which hung over her shoulders, straight and silky. Her face was bright and intelligent, with her mother's blue eyes and snub nose. Her brother had dark hair and eyes, the same nose sprinkled with freckles, and a stubborn set of mouth which matched his defiant and determined nature.

The family resemblance between the two men was strong. Peter had inherited a masculine version of his mother's height and build rather than his father's, and was in consequence half a head taller than Tom and broader of shoulder. Other than that, their looks were much the same, similar hair, the colour so graphically described by Elizabeth as dark oak, curling a little above the collar and around the ears, similar dark eyes, Tom's perhaps a little darker and Peter shared his brother's good looks, marred only a little by a slightly misshapen nose, the product of a youth devoted to American football, while his brother's had been devoted to his books.

Katie, skipping along beside Tom and holding his hand, said,
"I've got top grades in all my subjects at school."

"Great. Well done, Katie."

"Don't ask *him* what *he's* got. His grades are *awful*. Daddy says I shouldn't say that. Ow!"

She gave a cry as her brother ran round and punched her in the back.

"Shut up!" he said and a brief tussle ensued.

"Break it up!" Peter snapped and the protagonists resumed their former positions one on each side of Tom. After a few steps, Katie peeped out and stuck out her tongue at her brother, who replied by making a threatening gesture with his fist.

"Break it *up!*" said their father, more emphatically.

"I'm sure Lit… I'm sure Pete is doing his best at school and you can't ask more than that," said Tom, trying to restore peace.

"I'm not called Little Pete because the baby is much, much smaller than me," the boy piped up, obviously speaking on a subject near his heart.

"Oh yes, tell me all about your new brother," said Tom, seizing thankfully on a subject that seemed non-controversial. But Katie was not to be diverted.

"We had a poll in our class last month, Uncle Tom." Tom saw a disgusted expression come to the boy's face. "It was to find the most popular girl in the class and who do you think won?"

"I couldn't possibly guess."

"Katie Di Angeli!" she cried, capering about.

"Katie Di Angeli! Katie Di Angeli!" mocked Pete.

"Well, you can't deny it, I won, didn't I?"

Pete took a firmer grip of Tom's hand and pressed closer to his side as they walked. From this position of relative safety, he fired the most devastating shot in his locker.

"Katie Di Angeli sucks her thumb!"

"Oh, you little beast, did you have to tell him that?"

"Are they like this all the time?"

Peter made a face to suggest that they were usually worse.

"Come on, kids, and for heaven's sake, stop squabbling!"

"It's no wonder Maisie has been finding it difficult since the baby came. How are things with you two now?"

The Di Angeli marriage had hit a rough patch when Maisie had found herself pregnant two years ago with an unplanned third child.

"Much better, I'm pleased to say," replied Peter, starting the car. "Things were pretty bad for a long time, though. After she had adjusted to the thought of the baby coming, she made up her mind firmly that it was going to be another little girl and when she got a boy instead – oh!" he groaned at the memory.

"Yes, I remember that."

"And I guess you remember how depressed she got. All those visits to that expensive psychiatrist! Well, he was just getting her straightened out when this real laid-back, fun loving guy appeared on the scene for a while. That's what she called him. I called him something else. Why can't some guys keep their hands off other men's women?"

"Mmm," said Tom non-committedly, thinking of Reggie.

"Well, that's over now, I'm glad to say. I think, you know, in a funny sort of way it helped her, to find she could be attractive to someone other than me. Maisie knows now that she's not just Peter Di Angeli's wife, but an attractive woman in her own right. And I guess, I value her more for nearly losing her."

"That's quite something that you can look at it in that way."

"Lucky for me, things worked out. How about you, Tom? What's with your love-life? Found a brainy Brit to share your nest for a while?"

Tom brightened up. Even if he could not bring Elizabeth with him, at least he could tell.

"No, not that. I'm not interested in a temporary bedmate right now. I've got hopes of better things."

"Oh yeah? What's all this then?"

"Well, there's this girl, the daughter of a guy I work with. Gee, Peter, she's great! This is the big one, I guess, for me. Think of all the girls I've known, take the best of each and that's her. She's a real doll."

"Does she go for you?"

"On and off. There's another guy she's known for years, and you should see the way he keeps tabs on her. She likes me, though, I guess she likes me a whole lot, but she doesn't let it show. Cool, you know, reserved, just like the British are supposed to be. But she's great, Peter. One day, I'll show you."

"Well, you know, Mother would be pleased, that's for sure. She'd like to see you good and married. Hope you make it with this girl, then she can stop talking about it all the time."

They went home and there was Mother. Tall, grey-haired, beautifully dressed and groomed for the expected arrival, greeting them effusively. The children scampered into the house with a perfunctory, "Hi, Grandma." intent on television. Peter walked round to get Tom's case from the trunk, closed up the car and headed straight for the house. Not a lot of point in saying anything to those two. There would be no sense to be had out of them till they had hugged each other silly and stared into each other's faces like they were exhibits in an art gallery. Peter had seen it all before. He paused, rested the suitcase on the doorstep and looked back at them embracing at the gate like a pair of lovers. Seeing Tom in his Mother's arms after a long absence made Peter privately wonder how close it brought him to orgasm. A bit of a screwball, really, his brother. Clever, but definitely odd. Not surprising, he'd never got hitched. If this girl decided to marry him, he just hoped she'd know what she was letting herself in for. With an affectionately contemptuous shrug, Peter turned away and left them to sort it out.

"Let me look at you, Tom. Gee, it's so good to see you! Why do you stay away so long? My, aren't you thin! Don't they feed you over there?"

"Pretty well, Mother, but I miss your pies."

"Wouldn't you know I made your favourite for you today?"

"Oh, Mommy, did you?"

"Yeah. Just for you."

"Oh, you're a honey, Mommy. I do love you."

"Why d'you stay away from me so much, then? Oh, Tom, baby!"

She pulled him to her breast again, and he turned his cheek slowly to and fro against hers. This was the one love that never failed, the one he never had to suffer for. She was always there and always smiling. The answer to her question was that he went away so he could come back and even Elizabeth, had she wanted to try, would not have been able to stop him once his mind was made up.

"Better come and say hello to your Dad and Maisie – and little Steve, of course. Tell me all your news later, yeah?"

His father and Maisie were sitting in the bright, familiar living room, the former making a good pretence at reading the newspaper.

"Hi, Tom, have a good journey?" said his sister-in-law, rising and shaking his hand warmly.

"Not so bad, Maisie. You're looking good. I like that shirt. The pink suits your colouring. And that's young Steve! My, hasn't he grown in a couple of months! What d'you feed him on?"

"Bean poles," Maisie laughed. "Hey, Dad! Put that paper down and say hello. Are you asleep in back of it there?"

His Father lowered the paper by a few inches.

"Oh, it's you. Heard you were in jail," and up it went again. Maisie glanced at Tom, shrugged and spread her hands. Kate gave what she could see of her husband a look. No one was much surprised. Kate sighed and tried to redeem the situation by saying brightly,

"Well, I guess it's time to eat. You must be famished, Tom, honey. Sit down and rest, and I'll get it to the table."

"Let me help you," said Maisie, rising.

The two women went through to the kitchen. Steve made to follow them on his unsteady baby legs, and Katie dug herself from the depths of a comfortable armchair to take his little hand and help him along. Peter passed them in the doorway and plumped himself in the vacant chair. The room was quiet and brooding. The men were indolently waiting for their food, while from along the hall came the busy clatter of dishes and the sound of the women's voices.

Truth to tell, had Maisie and Katie not been around, Tom would have been in there with his mother. There was so much to talk about, but not in a crowd. He wanted to be alone with her, to sit on the floor with his back against her armchair, and feel her fingers stroking and running through his hair while he told her all about Elizabeth.

He always told her about his girls, except the secret ones. That was too shameful even for her sympathetic ears. But otherwise, he would tell her of the highs and lows, the beginnings and the endings. She would probe with questions, where he took them, what they liked to eat, what they wore, underneath as well as on top, what they gave and what they liked to take in bed. She had to know it all and he never denied her. She was too much a part of himself. Her eyes would shine, lustrous and bright, as he talked, and sometimes she sighed, happily or sadly, the precious bond strengthened with every word.

During the meal, there was family news to be caught up with and everyone wanted to know about Britain. Tom felt good, comfortable and cared-for again. He was able to repeat the pleasure of describing Elizabeth, and give his rather slanted and wishful account of their relationship.

Kate listened with interest and replied appropriately, but she doubted. There had been so many girls, nice, suitable girls, over the years, but nothing ever seemed to come of it. These days young women did not seem to know a good thing when it walked right up and kissed them on the lips. How she would have liked to see him comfortably settled, as Peter was now that silly business of the

baby and the other man had all blown over. Tom needed a sweet, pretty girl who would let his mother guide her over how to make him happy, one who would give him lots of children, and be content to stay home and look after them. That was the trouble with Maisie. She had been hankering after a job when Stevie came along. She should have tried bringing up children the way
Kate herself had had to do, with a frail husband who was often sick and every cent needing to be watched. Even now, she was plaintively whining about their behaviour.

"I find it very hard to cope with Pete when he gets the bit between his teeth. I guess maybe it's jealousy of Stevie. He won't even heed what Peter says, sometimes."

Walter, her father-in-law, had been almost silent but now he made one of his infrequent contributions to the conversation.

"Jealousy, nothing!" he snarled and turned to Peter. "You wanna use your hand, or better still your belt, on that kid's ass."

This remark fell into a thick pool of silence. Variously, everyone found it embarrassing. Maisie stirred her coffee and looked disgusted at such a deplorable suggestion. Peter looked thoughtful. Pete, the centre of the conversation, plying on the rug, heard all that was said, but took no notice. He knew his father and therefore, he knew it would never happen. Tom bit his lip, and his mother looked up and caught his eye. They knew each other's thoughts, of the same incident in the long past. Ugly, violent and damaging, it lay festering in the secret places of his mind, buried but never dead, subtly leaking its poison. He never thought of it unless directly reminded.

Kate dropped her glance to her coffee cup again and then looked up. The wrinkles round her eyes deepened into a very secret little smile that never reached her lips. Her favourite son responded in kind to this near-caress.

The silence was getting uncomfortable. Tom inhaled deeply and turned to his brother.

"Come on, Peter, let's go wash the dishes."

Peter got to his feet without the usual reluctance. He needed to get out of this atmosphere.

As they started trying to sort out the litter of debris in the kitchen, he observed,
"Dad's old-fashioned ideas don't go down very well with Maisie. Gee, did you see her face when he said that! Mind you, there have been times when I've been tempted to take up his suggestion. Young Pete's a handful, no doubt about that. I worry about him a lot."

"You wouldn't do that to him, would you?"

"Oh, I guess not, when it really got down to it. I'm a lot like Dad myself. If you remember, he was always making the most awful threats, but he never actually laid a finger on us when it came to the crunch. It was always Mother who was left to paddle our asses."

"You've known him longer than me, so I guess you should know," said Tom enigmatically. "Where's Mother hidden the dish-cloth?"

Peter was never interested in the deep currents of people's thoughts. He did not trouble to enquire what that particular remark meant.

When the time came to say goodbye, Tom's usual sadness at parting from Mother was tempered by the thought that in a very few days, his goddess would be back from her Grecian temples and he would be able to bask in the warmth of her smile.

"Do you think he's really serious about this girl?" Kate asked Peter as they stood together watching his disappearance into the Departure area.

"Hard to say. I guess he probably talked more to you about her than he did to me, but he seems to like her a lot."

"I hope things work out this time. Poor Tom, he's had so many disappointments – I can't tell why. I worry about him a lot. He's kind of – in a way – vulnerable. Do you know what I mean?"

"Oh, Mother, you don't need to worry about Tom. He's quite able to take care of himself."

"I don't entirely agree with you. There's always been a certain something about him, I hate to call it a weakness, but just something. He's not well founded and secure as you are. In the wrong hands, with the wrong woman, perhaps – oh, I don't know. I wish he could meet a nice, sensible, steady girl and hit it off with her. I guess what he really needs is a plain, homey sort of one. They're too glamorous, too full of themselves, the girls he picks. He wants a wife who'll put his dinner before her hair-do."

Peter laughed.

"Look around you, Mom. That kind of girl's out of style. Want a coffee before we drive home?"

"Yeah, let's."

The thought of Elizabeth sustained Tom during the tedious flight back and, as he drove north from Heathrow, mile after mile slipping by beneath the wheels of his hired car, his sense of excitement mounted. Three days and she would be there again. Perhaps, he would have to start over with her, or maybe she would have missed him as he had missed her. Reggie had not been on holiday with her, that much he had been able to discover, and maybe on her Greek beaches, her thoughts had been of American lips and American arms, of his voice and his affection, and maybe she would be hankering for more.

Arriving back at the flat in the early evening, he had a shower, changed and went out for a meal, though to be sure his stomach hardly knew what day it was. Sitting alone and jet-lagged in the restaurant, he looked at the women, young and old, smartly dressed for an evening out, seated at the tables all around him. Not one of them could hold a candle to his lovely darling Elizabeth. If only he could be sure she was really his!

And if only he could be sure that if she was, he would not ball the whole thing up by his own stupid irresponsible actions! He had to form the resolution again and make it stick this time. Without difficulty, he had stayed away from those girls all the time he had been away and now he was back, it should simply be a case of continuing the same. Just keep to the routine of daily living that he had established, have the quiet confidence that he would succeed and it would happen. Positive thinking. That would put aside the only obstacle to his proposing marriage to Elizabeth, and with a prize like that before him, what could he not do?

In this mood of euphoria, he did not even consider that Reggie might prove an obstacle.

Given the right circumstances, he felt sure he could brush Reggie out of his way like a fly. Perhaps, Christmas might be the right time. If he could keep himself straight till then, he would have beaten it. And if she had fallen in love with him and things seemed right, he could home in, leaving Reggie bobbing like a cork in his wash. Then time to write to his Mother the news she longed to hear. Rather a lot of ifs. Could he make it? Was anything going to stop him trying? Nothing. Only a few days till the start of his campaign.

With supreme self-restraint, he did not ring her up on the very evening that she returned from Greece, or the morning of the day after, feeling she would want to rest after her journey. Mid-afternoon, though, he got the switchboard to give him an outside line and dialled the number that had been clicking through his brain all day. Her mother answered. After a brief, polite enquiry about the holiday, he asked if he might speak to Elizabeth.

"Oh, I'm sorry, Tom, she's not here."

"Can I call her later, then?"

"Well, not for a few days, Tom. She's gone to stay with friends in the country. After Greece, she didn't feel like settling straight back to her normal routine, so she rang these people we know and more or less invited herself. They're great socialisers and the house is full of guests all the year round. She loves to go there to get away from it all."

Get away from it all! Could she possibly have meant, get away from him?

"Well, that's very pleasant for her. When will she be back?"

"I'm not sure. It depends on who's there and what they're doing. Probably about a week, I would say."

"A week. I see. Very well, I'll call her sometime after that. Thank you, Erica. Goodbye."

Erica Ashton-Richards felt very uncomfortable as she put the phone down. She stared across the hall, frowning. Elizabeth's ploy was hopelessly transparent and it was plain from Tom's voice that he had seen right through it. Really, her daughter was cruel to that young man and Erica was disappointed. Tom was just the sort that she and Hugh would like to see Elizabeth marry. They wanted a University man, one who was both intelligent and stable, firm and wise enough to keep her flightiness under control. Not that brainless Reggie. And it was obvious that Tom was in love with her. Children were so difficult! Erica sighed and went back to the drawing room, where her three friends were waiting to resume the Bridge hand which the telephone's ring had interrupted.

Tom was frowning as well. The innocent Erica was not a fair target for his anger at this deeply inconsiderate behaviour. He could only turn it on himself. If she cared anything for him, she would have known how eagerly he was counting the days and she would not have done this to him. Not out of the blue. Not without warning. Stupid, foolish besotted slob that he was, could he not see what she was trying to tell him? He was nothing. Dirt under her feet.

He got up, walked across the room to where his jacket hung on the back of the door and got his wallet from his pocket. *Have a little, Miss Unwashed of Blackgate. What would you like for reminding me of what I am, a festering ulcer under this thin skin of respectability? Tell me what you want. It's well worth it. I need to be told again that the moon is not for my grimy grasping fingers to leave smears of unspeakable filth on.* Thus, he meditated, fanning out the notes with his hand. And yet, how he loved her and how he would have struggled against his inclinations given the least bit of encouragement! But was it worth it, if she cared so little for him?

He flipped the wallet shut and put it away, sighed impatiently, and stood for a long time staring unseeingly out of the window.

Chapter 8

"But, Elizabeth, there must be *some* time you can see me."

Tom's voice, on the phone, sounded desperate even to him. Two and a half weeks. There had been times when he had been convinced he would never see her again. Jill, on holiday when he had returned from America, had come back and resumed her unobtrusive part in his life, and still there had been no Elizabeth. He had plagued the patient Erica to distraction. And now she was back and she *still* wouldn't see him.

"I'm sorry, Tom. There are so many things I have to catch up on. There are friends I must see and Annabelle's horses to be exercised and – oh, just so many things. I can't tell you how much. I haven't got a single minute to spare."

"Oh but, darling, I've thought about you so much all the time you've been away and I was so disappointed when your mother said you'd gone to friends. Couldn't you have just called me and said you'd be away longer?"

"It didn't occur to me to do that."

No, it wouldn't, he thought. *The last thing that would cross your mind, to give me a little consideration.*

"Don't you think it was rather cruel, just leaving me to find out like that? Have you forgotten already how I feel about you?"

"Tom, quite honestly, I thought it was only a passing phase with you. I was quite sure you'd have found someone else. What about Sarah?"

"Sarah means nothing to me. Yeah, sure, I've run into her a couple of times. She gave me a ride in her car one day. Nearly scared me witless – gee, what a driver! She tried to get me to go to the theatre with her but I gave her the same routine you're handing to me. I hope she didn't feel like I do right now. She's a nice kid, but not for me. I can only love one woman at a time and that one's you."

"Oh, Tom, I'm sorry, really I am. I like you a lot, ever such a lot. You're great fun and you're so nice, but I don't love you. I mustn't say I do if I don't, must I?"

"You don't need to say that you don't love me. That's perfectly plain from what you do. But if I accept that and promise to behave with the utmost decorum, wouldn't you go out with me just as a friend? You could look on it as giving your charity to the needy."

"Oh, Tom, you make me feel dreadful! Wouldn't that be harder on you than not seeing me? Try to forget this feeling you have for me, can't you?"

With emphasis and conviction he replied,

"No."

Unseen by him, Elizabeth shook her head impatiently.

"Well, look, call me again next week. I might be able to see you then. No promises, but I'll try."

"Oh, but, Elizabeth –"

"Next week, Tom."

Distractedly, he rubbed his forehead and scratched at his front hair, making it stand on end.

"All right, if that's the soonest you can manage, I must be content with that. Don't make it too long. If someone else wants to fill your time, remember who loves you. Any night. I'll break any date. OK?"

"All right, Tom. Goodbye."

Elizabeth felt a little guilty as she put the phone down. She had not a single assignment in her diary for the rest of that week. But she had returned from her trip to the country with her mind made up that she was not going to see Tom again, even though he idolised her so gratifyingly. Her father had bored her interminably on holiday about what a good catch he would be for her and that had put her right off him. Perhaps, if the Dad had let her lie on the beach, and dream about Tom's dark eyes and the kisses from his soft pouty lips, but all that tedium prospects, and the clever papers he'd published in this journal and that – well, honestly! Was all *that* what a girl wanted to know about?

She looked at herself in the gilt-framed mirror that hung above the little antique table on which the telephone stood. After smoothing her hair, she inspected her face. Her nose was getting shiny and her make-up needed renewing. Dear old Reggie! What a relief that he was not one of the interminable band of University brains with which she was constantly surrounded!

But Tom. He was a sweet boy. Even on the phone, his voice was like warm honey. Perhaps, she would drop into the Department and say hello to him. Nothing more, just hello. Show that she was still friendly even if not romantically inclined. That might cheer him up. A little generous act, committing her to nothing. Smiling, she prepared for the expedition.

Tom was not even thinking of her. When he had gone back to the lab after putting the phone down, he had found Jill looking worried.

"Oh, there you are, sir," He coughed meaningfully and she swallowed and resumed. "Professor – sorry – I was just going to come and find you. I'm afraid it looks as if we've got trouble. Those tests we set up yesterday. I read the results and they don't fit in with anything we've done before. When I gave the results to the computer, it nearly blew a fuse. It kept typing 'please check' at me. I don't blame it either. Look."

"Let me see."

"Here's the read-out chart from the recorder."

She unfolded a long sheet of paper with a series of peaks inked along its length.

"The standard readings look OK and so do the first few tests, but after that, they go haywire."

"Show me the charts from the last couple of series."

She brought them out and unfolded them, and soon, the bench was submerged in yards of paper. They slid them about and lined them up, comparing results from one to another.

"Look, what's this one here? That doesn't look right."

"Well, here it is on this chart – oh yes, it's a bit out there, only not so noticeably."

"What about the one before?"

His shoulder pressed against hers as he leaned across in front of her, avidly pursuing the rogue results from chart to chart. She looked at him out of the corner of her eye. Not often she got him all to herself like this. It was almost worth having something go wrong.

"Yes, look, here it is again."

"Been creeping up on us, hasn't it? I should have noticed sooner."

"You, Jill? They pay me a fancy salary to stamp on the bugs."

"Maybe so, but if I'd been on the ball, I'd have spotted it ages ago. Yes, look, here it is again."

"And this one's all right, so that seems to pinpoint the day we inherited the problem. When did we do that run there?"

She frowned and touched her forehead with her fingers, trying to concentrate. It was not easy with him sitting so close.

"Last – er – Wednesday. A couple of days after I came back. "

"Hmm." He chewed the cap of his ballpoint pen and stared across the lab. "But why the difference? What did we do on that day?"

"I'll get my record book."

Together, they flipped through the pages, read what she had written for the day in question and looked at each other, puzzled.

"Why should a new bottle of culture medium affect it?" "I can't imagine."

"Was it the usual brand?"

"Yes. Even the same batch as the previous one."

"Well, I'll be damned. Jill –"

"I know. I'll have to go back and repeat them all."

"Well, maybe not all. That would make a hell of a lot of labour. Let me see."

He shuffled the charts about again, lining up the peaks, scribbling hieroglyphics here and there, muttering half-formed comments, while Jill sat, hands in pockets, waiting for the verdict.

"Hell of a lot of labour. Hold us up for days. We might not need to –"

He stopped in mid-sentence and sat like a statue, listening. Jill heard it too. The tap of high heels on the vinyl flooring of the entrance hall and, faintly, Elizabeth's voice exchanging a few casual remarks with the secretaries through their ever-open door.

"Excuse me," he muttered. He dropped the charts on the bench. "Be back right away."

She saw them pass the door a few minutes later, Elizabeth bouncing along looking totally unconcerned, Tom hurrying at her side, talking to her, trying to get her attention.

Jill sighed. She did wish he would not pursue Elizabeth in quite such an undignified fashion. A little restraint would surely be more effective in the long run. It pained her, the amused comments others made about his readiness to go dancing attendance on Elizabeth whenever she came into the Department. What right had they to smirk at him? Her Professor – well, what was it to anyone else if he went at things like a bull at a gate? In anything to do with work, she had learned to control his excesses, but Elizabeth was outside her province. He was young, he was enthusiastic, naturally, his attraction to Elizabeth would make him lose his head.

With another sigh, Jill turned back to the bench where the discarded recorder charts lay where they had fallen from his hands. She would have to wait till Elizabeth was done with him before she knew what to do about them. Elizabeth had all the luck. Everything going for her. Money, good looks and half the young men in the University swooning at her feet. Even her Professor. Even him. Nothing left for anyone else. Unbidden, a tear dropped off the end of her nose on to the paper, and she hastily got her handkerchief from her pocket and wiped it off.

No point in brooding, she told herself briskly. There was plenty to do. But what? She had been left abruptly at a loose end. What was she supposed to do, go on, go back or stay where she was and await further instructions? Should she gather up the charts, or would he be back in a few minutes wanting to look at them again? Should she go off for an early lunch or was he likely to want her again soon? She decided she had better hang about and await developments.

It was a very long time before she saw him again, indeed, not till the next morning. Elizabeth was a girl who was very susceptible to masculine charm which, when he chose to exercise it, Tom had in abundance. He inveigled her into the coffee room, made her a cup and laid siege to her till she agreed to have lunch with him. It seemed a fairly harmless arrangement, she felt, curtailed as it would be by lack of time, but, in the event, he never did get back to the Department that afternoon.

Blithely ignoring the situation in the lab, the difficulties he had left Jill in and also a meeting he was supposed to be at later in the day, he spent the afternoon walking by the river with Elizabeth. It was one of those beautiful, golden September afternoons, with the leaves on the trees just beginning to turn colour. The sun was still warm, its rays glinting on the sparkling water, lighting up the depths where waterweed swayed and tiny fish darted. In the distance, a tractor moved up and down a field, ploughing, and the far-off sound, occasionally reaching them, made the silences between seem even more peaceful.

They walked along by the water in the pleasant warmth, hand in hand, Elizabeth telling of her holiday, Tom listening and wondering if she would be interested to hear about his. Mentally, he placed her in the locations he had visited, considering her tastes and wondering if she would like them. After a time, a little weary, they sat on a stone bench to rest and enjoy in silence the beauty of the day.

Before very long, emboldened by her nearness and by the pretty hand resting in his, he said,

"You've travelled a lot, Elizabeth. Have you ever been to America?"

"No and I don't want to."

"Why not?"

"Well, from what I've heard of it, it sounds a dreadful place," she replied frankly. "People being robbed and murdered all the time, and all those guns they have there! I'd be scared to put my nose out of doors. And it's so big and everything new. I like Europe with its old cities and wonderful scenery."

Surely, she could not be so naïve as to believe that the superficial stories she had read in the newspapers or seen on television represented the entire truth about a nation of several million people? He looked at her. She *did* believe it.

"There's so much more to it than that, darling. Of course, there are parts like you describe, but other parts are beautiful, and the people are just people, good and bad alike."

"I could hardly describe you as an independent judge."

"I come from a town a few miles outside L.A," he went on, undeterred by this rather rude remark. "It's not so very different from this one. I thought about you a lot and imagined you with me. I'm sure you would find the buildings interesting to look at. Then, if you travel round, you can find practically any sort of scenery in the world you have a fancy for, from deserts to huge lakes and mountains."

"Oh yes?" she replied, staring across the river and looking quite uninterested.

"I wish I could show it all to you," he said, leaning closer and trying to break through the barrier of indifference. "We could go about together and I'd show you things that would make your eyes pop. Ever seen an alligator?"

She shuddered.

"You won't see one of those in Europe, I'll bet, outside a zoo. There's swamps full of them in Florida."

"I'm not really very keen on alligators."

"Mountains. You like mountains? I'll take you to mountains like you've never seen before. We'll fly, you'll see them first from the airplane, then from below. It'll take your breath away. We could make it –"

Our honeymoon? He paused in his breathless rush. Tom Di Angeli was going to ask Elizabeth Ashton-Richards to marry him, was he? Staring avidly at her profile, he tore destructively at his thumbnail with his teeth. Two and a half weeks ago, he could have done it with a clear conscience. He could have walked straight from Mother's arms into hers. But all the time she had been in the country, he had been smashing his resolutions to pieces in a fretful orgy of self-degradation. Old girls and new, every night of the week, because she despised him. Nothing had seemed to satisfy him. There was something missing, but he could not tell what it was.

He ripped a piece off the side of his nail, making it bleed and the sharp pain jerked him back to the present. Elizabeth, who could not bear nail-biters, was looking even further away than before.

"... Make it a holiday," he resumed, squeezing his injured thumb in the other hand. "You could come as my guest. I'd look after you. You'd be perfectly safe."

She turned her head slowly and looked into the smouldering brown eyes so close to her own. A very tiny, knowing smile came to her face, wordlessly expressing her disbelief.

"Bring a friend, then, or come with your mother. She likes to travel too."

"Oh, Mother wouldn't want to do that. She doesn't really like being all that far from home. All the time we were in Greece, she was fretting, in case the house had burned down. We kept telling her someone would tell us if it had, but she wasn't really happy till she came home and found it still standing."

"Well –" he looked desperately from side to side, wishing he had the courage to say what was on his mind. "Look, Elizabeth, I know we haven't known each other for long and I'm not asking for an answer now, but I wanted you to know how I felt. If for a holiday or in any other – capacity – well, think about it now and then," he finished, all in a rush, aware that he was tying himself in knots. Capacity! What a hopeless word! It was the only one he could think of on the spur of the moment, when what he had really wanted, but feared to say was 'as my wife'. She seemed to sense what he had meant, rather than what he said.

"No, Tom, you know I couldn't possibly do that. Please don't keep asking me. You're getting far too serious and it's much too nice an afternoon for getting all solemn about things."

"But the one thing I want in the world is to get serious with you."

She pulled herself very upright and said sharply,
"If you say another word about it, I shall go home this very minute."

A little surprised at the vehemence of her response, he answered meekly,
"All right, Elizabeth, if that's how you feel. I'm sorry if I upset you. I'm sure I didn't mean to. Let's forget it then, it's not important. Shall we walk a little more?"

"No. I'm tired of walking. Remember that little restaurant we passed with the garden running down to the water and the tables under the trees? Why don't we go there and have tea? It's just about tea time."

They rose and turned back the way they had come. Tom's mind was full of dejected thoughts. How could he offer her inferior goods when she herself was such perfection? He was sure he could have broken through the barrier of reserve and indifference with his weapons in firing order, but the way things were, he loved her too much to even try. Only when everything was right – if it ever was.

Elizabeth, unaware of the underlying tormented circumstances, felt pleased to have avoided a direct proposal by the skin of her teeth. Safety, she felt, lay in unoriginal, mundane topics.

"Doesn't the river look lovely in this light? The autumn sunshine brings out the colours so beautifully. I wish we could go punting. It's the thing I like doing best on the water. I went out lots this summer before we went to Greece."

She chattered on about her various days out on the river with her girlfriends, Reggie or another faithful swain brought along to handle the wet pole, of picnics and expeditions to beauty spots, and all the idle pursuits of a young woman who did not need to work and who chose not to. He felt irritated. His impression was that she chose her subjects specially to make him feel an outsider to her charmed circle.

Ten minutes' walk brought them back to the restaurant and she never stopped talking once. A few people were sitting there, visitors, tourists, sipping tea. Nice time to be outside. Most of the flies and the wasps seemed to have died with the summer.

She chose their table, she ordered their tea. He watched her as she ran a pretty finger down the menu and glanced up fetchingly at the young man, son of the house, who was serving. As always, she was a feast for the eyes, a dessert for the intelligence. She was off talking about boating again. He and his brain seemed to be redundant, so he let it stray as it would among pleasant paths.

The alchemy of the imagination could achieve with ease the impossible. She was in his flat, in his bed. Her golden hair was spread, disordered, on his pillow. Her naked breasts, pearly pink in contrast to her tanned body, were above the turned-down sheet.

Maybe, as he lay down beside her, she would resist a little. She would put her hands against his chest and say, *no, Tom, no, please don't*. But not for long. Like he had said to Paul, she would melt, she would thaw. No problem. This was a fantasy, after all. And wouldn't he be on top form? Far out!

"Tom?"

His name, pointed and interrogative, penetrated his attention. She was looking at him expectantly. It seemed he was meant to say something.

"You haven't been listening to a word I've been saying, have you? I suppose you were thinking of Reggie punting in his best trousers and falling into the river?"

It was so ludicrous that, unthinkingly, he laughed at her. Reggie? In his best trousers?

Falling in? How far from right could she get?

Then she did it. She leaned forward and slapped him smartly on the wrist.

It was like a thunderbolt.

Never, never in all her life had she come so close to being raped as at that moment. His imaginings had left him with a passable hard-on, but that sharp little pain brought him to an acute pitch of urgency.

She eyed him nervously, as well she might.

"He's a very good punter," she said tentatively.

The boy arrived with the tray and plonked a huge, steaming teapot down on their table. It was a timely diversion. While they fussed with the cups, he had an opportunity to regain control. He could have had a rather embarrassing accident.

All the same, he thought on his way home, it was fine having fantasies about her and waking in a lather like that, but it got him no nearer his desire. As things stood, Reggie would have Elizabeth in the end and he would be left empty. They might even ask him to the wedding. He would go, of course, wish them every joy and return home again alone to his empty rented flat. Nothing would have changed. He would be a little older, his private adversary would have triumphed again, nothing different.

Letting himself in at his front door, he stood and listened to the silence. Only the faint ticking of the clock disturbed it with small ripples of sound. It seemed very lonely.

Mozart. That was what he needed. He went to the box of records that stood to hand by his favourite chair, selected something soothing and settled down to listen.

There was a niggle, an irritating worry at the back of his mind, that even Mozart could not still. What could it be? He thought. One plus in an otherwise not fully pleasing day was that he had got away from the tension created by that wretched washing up woman doing one of her disappearing stunts. Could it be that he was worrying about Jill? He'd left her in a mess, but that would be easily put right. She never carried a grudge against him. Whatever could it be? Well, it would surface in its own time. He put it aside and concentrated on the music.

Chapter 9

It surfaced next morning almost as soon as he was through the door. Before stopping to read his mail, he went to the lab to straighten things out with Jill, to find she was waiting to give him warning of the wrath to come. The recorder charts were piled up, folded, on the end of her bench, work which would have been dealt with if he had been there.

"Professor Ashton-Richards was really awfully annoyed," she said anxiously after he had mumbled a routine apology to her.

"You mean he came checking up on me?"

"Yes, well, you see, the visitors —"

There was no way he could conceal the horrified recollection. He clapped his hand to his face and swore fluently.

"Forgot all about the bastards!" he concluded. She went a little pinker. Generally, he moderated his language in front of her, for he knew she was sensitive to invective. "Was the Chief real mad at me?"

"I'm afraid he was. He kept on coming in, and asking where you were and I didn't know what to say."

The Chief *would* be mad. A group of visiting senior academics from a German University had stopped of specially. They were touring the important Universities, the ones with clout and the only thing that would bring them to this tin-pot seat of learning was to question Di Angeli on the work he had been involved with in the United States. Maybe even to ask him why he had abandoned it to come here of all places. They only had an hour or two to spare. That was why his technician had been having a torrid time trying her best to save his bacon while Di Angeli, that love-struck idiot, had been walking by the river worrying about not feeling able to propose to Elizabeth.

"Well, I guess he knows where I was now and I don't suppose it's helped me any."

"Why? Where were you?"

"Out with Elizabeth. Trying to convince her I'm a really nice guy. I think I failed. What I didn't know was that I was failing with Daddy as well."

"Oh!" said Jill, for the lack of any other reply.

"I guess I'll go see him now and get it over. Maybe it'll score with him if I put my head on the block before he asks."

The telephone rang. Jill picked it up, listened, said, "I'll tell him," and put down the receiver.

"Professor Ashton-Richards' secretary. Will you go and see him right away?"

He made a wry face.

"Not my day, is it?"

Naturally, Professor Ashton-Richards was the soul of politeness to a near-equal colleague, but he still made his displeasure abundantly clear. Elizabeth seemed not to have mentioned the afternoon with him, so Tom had the feeling of no ground under his feet. It was a pretty gruelling interview.

Returning to base, Tom was looking for a cat to kick. It could have been the patient Jill who endured his wrath, but fate presented him with a better victim before he got to the lab. At the far end of the washing-up room, he caught a glimpse of Mrs Simpson's broad back and behind.

Discretion made him pause before roaring in. He had asked Jill to tackle her and probably she had done so. Better check.

"I asked you to speak to that woman about her absences, Jill. Did you?"

She blushed slightly and looked uncomfortable.

"No, I didn't actually, I –"

"You surprise me. Scared of her?"

"N-no, it's just that – I felt these things –" he had the feeling she was dragging every word out with extreme unwillingness. "Are better done – by a man," she concluded hastily. By now, she was beetroot red.

"All right," he said, shaking his head. "If that's how you feel. I'd planned to anyway."

After he had gone, Robert turned to her. She was gazing at the door.

"What on earth made you say that? You'd tell God Almighty off if you thought he had it coming."

Instead of answering him, Jill said softly,

"He'll think I can't do my job, now."

"If you're trying to melt his heart by being feminine and fluttery, you haven't a hope. It's just not you, Jill, love."

Jill's strange behaviour put the capstone on Tom's mood. Steaming with resentment at the world in general, he marched aggressively into Mrs Simpson's room and demanded to know why she had not been at work. Mrs Simpson looked surprised. She had hitherto been used in this Department to people who seemed to regard her comings and goings as part of the natural order of life.

"Had to look after my daughter's kiddies, didn't I? She's got the cold and we can't let the nippers get it. One of them's got a weak chest, gets bronchitis very easy."

A good, human story, calling for sympathy and understanding, normally easy enough to extract, she had always found, from your average academic.

Tom was in no mood to be sympathetic and in any case, he did not believe a word of it.

"I'm not putting up with any more of this. While you're working for me, your daughter will have to find someone else."

"There ain't no one else."

"Well, she'll have to try. You're paid for working here, not for looking after her children. Besides, surely, it's a very strange cold that gets better in one day? Are you sure you didn't take a day off to do some shopping?"

Mrs Simpson looked as indignant as anyone who has just told a thumping lie and had it disbelieved.

"Are you calling me a liar?"

"Yes."

She snorted and tore off her rubber gloves so savagely that she ripped the cuff off one of them.

"I'm not stopping here to be insulted by no bleeding foreigners. I'm going to see my supervisor. I'm not standing for this!"

"Go on, then. I'd like to have a word with him as well."

"You will. Don't worry."

She stormed off and he went to his room to await the inevitable phone call. About half an hour later, it came.

"Mrs Simpson tells me you insulted her, Professor."

"I probably did."

"She tells me that unless you apologise, she will not only resign, but go this very minute."

Tom yawned audibly.

"Fancy!"

"Have you anything to say to her?"

He had, and said it, adding,

"You can pass that on to her, suitably amended, of course."

The Domestic Supervisor became serious.

"Look, I must be honest with you. It won't be easy to replace her. This is a rich little town, you see. People sneer at the sort of wages we can pay. And they're not worth travelling from the city for."

"I think we can take it. At least, we'll know where we are from one day to the next, not like now."

"Well, as you like. I'll get an advertisement in for a replacement right away, but I can't hold out much hope for a speedy outcome."

"I'm putting a burden on the technicians, but I think they'll think it's worth it to be shot of her."

Now he had to face the lab with the news.

"Folks, I think I've blown it. Mrs Simpson is leaving us this very minute as I understand. She's not inclined to work any longer for such a boorish foreigner. It's going to make things tough in here for a while, I guess. The D.S. is going to put in an ad right away, but he's not hopeful of quick results. I'm sorry, Jill. I'll try to lighten your load as much as I can."

"Oh, I expect we'll cope. I can always come in Saturdays."

"Gee, I don't want you to give up your free time because I can't keep my temper."

"It doesn't matter. If I haven't got anything special to do, I'll come in. OK?"

He always liked the way Jill took the ups and downs of life in her stride. The only time he had seen her off balance was when he'd questioned her about her boyfriends. Otherwise, nothing seemed to fluster her. Surely, things would be better now without the tiresome Mrs Simpson.

Jill's mind was fixed on what awaited her that evening, burdening her more and more as the day went on. Her classes at the Technical College were starting up again for the winter, and she was certain to meet Richard.

She really felt badly about Richard. She felt guilty about throwing him over so abruptly but when she had suddenly felt there was no meaning to their relationship any more, it had seemed the kindest thing to do. For several weeks, he had phoned her at work, every day at first, until, meeting with consistent firm refusals, he had finally given up. She hoped that by now, he had found someone else.

He had not. When she was in the cafeteria in the break between classes, he came over, drew up a chair and sat beside her.

"Hello, Jill," he said, pitching his voice low so it was covered by the continuing conversation of the group of friends she was with. "Nice to see you. How are you?"

"Very well, thanks. What have you been doing all summer?"

"Thinking of you."

She turned her head away.

"Oh, Richard, I was hoping you'd forgotten all about that."

"Jill, I'm still nuts about you. I've been looking forward to seeing you and hoping you might feel different. Look, come over to the table by the window. I must talk to you alone."

"There's nothing to say, Richard."

"Let's just talk. Come on, Jill, please."

She excused herself and they took their coffee to the other table.

"Jill, do you realise this is the first time we've met face to face since that night you announced out of the blue that you didn't want to see me anymore? I've never had such a shock in my life! Can't you tell me why you did it? I've thought and thought to try to remember if I said or did anything, but I'm stumped. Tell me why, Jill, before I go bonkers."

"Oh, Richard, if only you could understand. You didn't say or do anything. My feelings changed and there seemed to be no meaning in what was between us. It's purely an emotional thing on my side. I realise it may seem trivial to you, but to me it's overwhelmingly strong. I'm truly sorry for all the distress I've given you, but there it is."

He looked penetratingly into her face.

"You're right. I do find it hard to understand and, yes, a bit trivial as well. Look, why don't we try to suss this thing out, Jill. See if we can't get it together again. Let's go out a few times, to the flicks or the disco. You've been brooding all summer on something that maybe doesn't matter. Forget emotion. Try a bit of solid fact. Come out with me and see how you feel when we're together again."

"No, Richard," She tugged at her front hair. "We've made the break now –"

"You've made the break." She was silent. There was nothing she could say to explain. "Is there someone else?" he asked. "If there is, just say so and that'll be it. That I can understand."

"I never go out with anyone else."

"That's not quite an answer."

"It's the only one I can give you. Find someone else, Richard."

"There's only you for me, Jill. Do you think I'd still be waiting around if that wasn't the case?"

"Oh, you do make me feel such a heel."

"Look, let me walk you to the bus stop tonight. Hell of a miserable walk down Barracks Street. We could talk then."

"I'm going with Sue and the girls. Try to see, Richard, I'm trying to spare you pain."

The bell rang.

"Hell! Well, I'll see you tonight, whether you want me to or not. Back to good old Business Studies for now, though. You'll be sorry when I've got a seat on the board and a six-figure salary, see if you're not."

Every aspect of life looked black for Jill and her boss. Their private lives were mocked by tantalising visions of what they could not have. Each wanted a loving partner, each had only a will--the-wisp that danced forever out of reach, which was their private lives. The problem that had arisen at work the day Tom had gone walking by the river, resisted all Jill's best efforts to solve it. Tom prowled the lab like a caged lion, endlessly seeking that fine adjustment that he was convinced was all that was needed. Hampering him was the chaos the place was in after two weeks without a glassware washer. Only a spark was needed to light the fuse of the explosion that was to blow them all sky-high.

"These results are absolutely hopeless, Jill," he said, tossing the latest recorder charts disgustedly on the bench. "Why in heaven's name can't we find out what's wrong?"

"Well, I'm at my wit's end," she replied, looking worried. "I've been through the method step by step, I've made up all the solutions again, I've checked everything I can think of, I just don't know what else to do."

"I'll be glad when they come to check the instruments. When did you say they would come? You rang them last week, didn't you?"

Jill opened her eyes wide, then closed them, hand to her cheek, horror on her face.

"I forgot to do it," she gasped in a scarcely audible voice.

"Oh, for God's sake!" he cried, slapping his thigh. "How the hell are we supposed to make any progress if I can't rely on you to remember anything?"

"I'm sorry, there was so much to think of, it went clear out of my mind."

"How long do they usually take to come?"

"About a week. I'll get on to them right away and tell them it's urgent."

"A week?" he uttered some expletive under his breath and then banged the bench with his hand. "I'd get on a damn sight better here, if they hadn't landed me with a totally incompetent technician! You get in there and get them right away, if it's not straining your resources too much!"

With that, he turned and marched angrily out of the lab.

"That's a bit unjust!" said Robert indignantly. "Incompetent my backside! Everyone knows you're one of the best technicians in the Department!"

"Oh, it's all right. He's just in one of his moods. It doesn't bother me."

"So I see," he said, looking at her distressed face. Then he muttered, "Bastard!" under his breath.

"Don't say that, Robert. I was wrong, wasn't I? I should have phoned them and I forgot. Anyone would get annoyed."

"Anyone wouldn't have blown you up in public like that."

"Well, he's been a bit touchy because of all these problems. I can understand that."

"A bit touchy! He's been like a bear with a sore head all week. I could have thumped him a few times, the things he's said to you."

"Oh, he'll be all right again, once we get this sorted out. I'd better go along to the office and call them. If it hadn't been for the washing up, I could probably got it straight by now."

The Domestic Supervisor had been quite right in his prognostications. It was now a fortnight since Mrs Simpson had left and they seemed no nearer getting a replacement than they had on the day she went. Advertisements had brought no result whatsoever and the local job centre had been unable to interest anyone in the vacancy either. It made a lot of extra work for Jill, reducing the amount of attention she could give to her proper tasks. She tried, she really tried, for she would do anything in her power to please her Professor, but when things were not going well and he was in one of his awkward moods, it was very difficult to keep him happy.

While she was walking along to the office to make her call and try to cajole the engineers to come sooner than they normally would, he was in the scientific staff common room, soothing his ruffled feelings with a cup of coffee.

He sat in an armchair with his feet up on a low table as no one else was in the room and reflected on how nothing seemed to be going right. These problems at work were infuriating and he could not put them away even at night, as he spent most evenings alone. Elizabeth was unapproachable at the moment. Her shell of resistance to him seemed to have hardened and nothing he could do would persuade her to see him at all. He was in despair. She came into the Department fairly frequently, if anything, more often than before, and whenever he heard her voice when he was in his room or the lab, he would drop everything to go and try to speak to her. He felt sure he was making a public spectacle of himself and his feelings, but he cared little for that. Anytime she was around, he felt irresistibly drawn to be near her, even if she would do little more than say hello.

Something else was drawing him irresistibly into its net as well and that was the chief cause of his irritability. Elizabeth's continued rejection of him had lent force to his opposing desires and he had been fighting them hard for the last week. Each evening as he sat alone at home, he longed to get out the car and drive to Blackgate; and each evening he had managed to resist the wish, but he knew it was not going to take much to tip him over the edge of the precipice whose brink he continually trod. If Elizabeth only knew what she was doing to him! Perhaps, if she did, she wouldn't look so smugly pleased when she said,

"Sorry, Tom, not this week. Next week, maybe."

What would she do if she knew she was killing him by inches? Sweet damn all, most likely. Just look more pleased than ever.

He sighed and finished his coffee. No more time for self-pity, duty called. Then he thought of Jill. Poor girl! He had been beastly to her of late, shouting at her over the last thing. Imagine saying that she, of all people, was totally incompetent! *How unjust could you get?* He felt angry that he had so far forgotten himself as to take out all his frustrations on her and decided that things must be put right straight away.

Robert was alone in the lab when he returned. He glanced up from his work with a look that spoke volumes.

"I'm going to apologise to her," said Tom.

Robert did not reply – it was scarcely his place to do so, but he sniffed and that spoke volumes as well.

Tom wandered aimlessly about the lab, picking things up and putting them down at random, until Jill re-appeared. As soon as she saw him, her expression became tense and defensive.

"They're going to come on Monday," she said quickly, "or Tuesday at the latest. That's about when they would have come if I had phoned them when I was meant to."

"Thank you, Jill, well done. Look, I'm sorry about what I said to you earlier. I was quite unjust, as I'm sure you know every bit as well as I do. It's a difficult spell right now and I know you're doing your best. I said I was going to make things easier for you and instead I'm making them harder."

"That's all right," she said, smiling with relief. "It was silly of me to forget, but if they come when they say, we won't have lost any time."

"Look, I've had my first good idea in weeks. Until they come, there really isn't any more we can usefully do on this. Why don't we call it a day for now and stop picking at it, eh? Instead of beating our heads against a wall, why don't we concentrate on something else for a bit?"

"Yes, I'd be very glad to do that. There are several other things we haven't touched all week."

Amity was fully restored at once. Later, as the afternoon wore on, he remarked conversationally to her,

"Going out tonight?"

"Yes, evening classes again," she smiled, ruefully.

"Looks as if it's going to be a cold night for it."

"You going out?"

"Yes, I think I'd better." He came to a sudden decision. Damn Elizabeth! Jill did his chores and brought his coffee, soothed his ire, and acted as his hands and feet. She deserved to have him in a good mood, not jumpy as a frustrated stallion. Not an orgy, just one night, to take the pressure off. She would be pleased with the results, even if she would have strongly disapproved of the means. Good thing she didn't know, with her high-minded ideals! It would shatter her image of the dedicated researcher living only for his work.

"A meeting?"

"Sort of… yes, a meeting, that's right."

"Well, I hope you enjoy it. I wish I could stay in and toast my knees at the electric fire."

"What's it tonight?"

"Physics. We're studying sound and light. I could study it better at the disco, I'm sure."

"Fond of discos?"

"Well, so-so. I occasionally go to one with Susan."

"Not my scene at all. I prefer concerts," and he whistled an air from Bach.

"Nice. I like that. My Dad's very fond of Mozart." He looked at her with one eyebrow raised. "Something tells me I said the wrong thing."

"Never mind. At least, you try, which is more than can be said for Elizabeth." She turned her head away.

"Doesn't she like music?"

"Evidently not, apart from flamenco guitar."

"You should – try to educate her, then."

He smiled.

"I've got a deputy doing that but not, I think, doing very well."

"Oh!"

Later that evening, two men and a girl were sitting in a pub in Barracks Street. They sat round a small, circular table which had pools of beer all over it and an overflowing ashtray in the middle. Each had a beer and the girl was smoking a cigarette. The pub was full, the air loud with the sound of voices, the clink of glasses and the thump of darts from a group in one corner. A brief noisy dispute broke out about the correctness of someone's subtraction of the score, numbers were rubbed off the board with an oily sleeve and scrawled up more accurately in chalk before the game resumed amid the grumbles of the player whose arithmetic had been doubted.

"Noisy lot," said Darren, one of the two young men. He swallowed the last of his beer, wiped his mouth with the back of his hand and added, "Well, I'd better be going. Got to be up at six for this new job. It's a clocking-in caper, so you better be there."

"Wish I could get a new job," said the girl, stubbing out her cigarette and spilling several butts on the table as she did so. "I'm brassed off with that bleeding factory. Same thing every bloody day and that bitch of a supervisor – the day I leave, I'm going to tell her just what I think of her, the old bag."

"Or the day you tell her will be the day you get chucked out," laughed the other man.

"Either way would suit me. I'd leave tomorrow if I could find something else – or a rich sugar-daddy."

"You won't find one of those round here anyway."

"Mmm. Some hopes. Mind you, my cousin, the one who's always picking up funny boyfriends, she met a chap of about 60 at the Locarno dance hall who said he'd set her up for life if she'd go with him."

"And did she?"

"Not her. She likes them a bit funny, but she said grandfathers aren't in her line. If he'd been really loaded, I could have just put up with it, mind you. I'd put up with quite a lot from a chap with plenty of cash."

"You'll have to go to the Locarno, then and see if you can spot him."

"I might just do that."

"Hey, how about this geezer who's just walked in? He doesn't look as if he's short of a bob or two."

"God, no! Look at that coat! That must have set him back a few quid!"

She watched him push his way to the bar and buy half a pint of beer. He was of medium height, with well-cut and neatly combed dark hair. A nice looking fellow. Clean and respectable. Stood out in this scruffy pub. He leaned on the bar, took a mouthful of beer and looked around. She stared at him with undisguised interest and a moment later, he caught her eye. His look lingered on hers and then passed on. Beginning to feel the warmth of the crowded bar, he unbuttoned his coat, and she could see that the suit and shirt underneath looked equally smart and expensive.

"Never seen him round here before," Darren observed.

"I saw him – oh – about a month ago in that pub round the corner. He's a Yank, or maybe he just pretends to be so he can pull the birds better. He was making time with that girl who works the pumps at the White Star Garage. Don't know what he saw in her, she fancies herself as a mechanic and she never bothers to wash the oil off. I'm not that fussy, but she's a bit yukky even for me."

"Well, no accounting for tastes," said Darren, yawning. "I'd better get along."

"I'm going too. Got to be up in the morning as well. Coming, Ann?"

"No, I'll stay for a bit and finish my beer," Ann Bone replied.

"She's hoping to pick up the Yank," Darren said, nudging his companion.

"Well, you never know your luck."

"Go for it, Ann. See you."

"Bye," said Ann absently, still staring at the stranger as the two men left. She took a crushed cigarette packet from her bag, shook one out and lit it with a match.

The man at the bar watched her companions leave then glanced back at her. She returned his gaze steadily. He looked her over from head to foot, picked up his beer and came across the room to her.

"Mind if I sit here?"

"Help yourself," she replied with a slight shrug.

"Can I get you another beer?"

"I wouldn't say no."

"What are you drinking?"

"Bitter."

"Pint?"

"Yes, please."

If he wasn't an American, he was making a damn good imitation, she thought. While he returned to the bar, Ann got out a grubby comb and tidied the front of her hair watching, as she did so, every move he made.

At coffee break at the Technical College, Richard came and sat by Jill. The first time he had ventured to do so since their previous conversation some weeks before.

"Jill, it's such a cold, dark night. Please let my walk with you to the bus stop, just this once."

"Richard, I don't think it's wise. I don't want you to think –"

"I won't think anything. I'd just like to walk with you."

"You know I generally walk with my two friends."

"Let me come too."

"It means you're having to spend more time in the cold."

"I'd have to do it anyway, waiting for my bus. Can't I go with you instead of just hanging about?"

"All right, Richard, but don't read anything into it."

"I won't," he promised, but his face lit up. "I'll wait for you at the main door, OK?"

The group of four set off for the bus stop, the two girls in front, Richard and Jill behind.

"What a night. It's going to be a long, hard winter if it keeps on like this," said Jill.

"Biting wind," Richard agreed, taking this as a cue to put his arm round her waist.

"Now, Richard," she said, trying to move away.

"Oh, just for old times' sake, Jill."

Lacking the heart to say no, she made no further demur and they walked on in silence till they were about half way down Barracks Street.

Her eye was caught by a movement. It was a couple coming out of a pub ahead of them on the other side of the road. She glanced at them, looked away and then suddenly looked back, his attention so riveted that she almost came to a stop. A man of medium height walking with a short, slight girl.

They were in a pool of darkness between two streetlights so it was impossible to see their faces but as they approached and passed, then receded into the distance, she watched, turning her head to look over her shoulder after they had gone by. Surely, there was something familiar about the walk and general appearance of the man? It was hard to distinguish much as he was wearing a heavy overcoat and they were a good way off, but surely it couldn't be…

Richard looked to see what she was staring at so intently, just in time to see the girl take the man's arm.

"Someone you know?"

"Well, I don't think so. For a moment, I thought it was – but no, it couldn't possibly be. Just for a moment, I thought it was my boss. But he'd never be in a pub in Barracks street, surely?"

"Does he live here? It's a terrible dive, that pub. I went in one night with another chap who wanted to get some cigarettes. It's really rough."

"As far as I know, he lives close to the University. I just thought for a moment that man looked a bit like him, you know, his walk and carriage looked familiar, but it couldn't possibly be. Stupid of me to even think it. He'd never be in a place like this."

"Well, there's no accounting for tastes, but it does seem a long way to find a particularly scruffy pub."

"Oh no, it couldn't possibly be him."

They waited five minutes or so at the bus stop while Jill's feet got colder and colder, and she wished she was snuggled up in bed with a hot water bottle. When the bus finally came, the three girls went upstairs where they hoped it would be warmer and sat side by side on the long bench seat. Jill took off her shoes, and tucked her legs up under her and put her hands in her sleeves, seeking what warmth she could. They were all tired so there was little conversation. As they sat, Jill thought of the man she had seen, and wondered in consequence what her Professor Di Angeli might really be doing and where he was right at that very minute. A girl called Ann Bone could have answered her questions with great precision.

Quite a long time later, he was driving home, enjoying the warmth of the car heater, but wishing passionately he was in the shower, washing the lingering dirt of the nights' proceedings from his body, watching it go down the drain and away. He kept brushing the knees of his trousers with his hand, thinking of the damp grass he had been kneeling on in that vacant lot behind the hoardings. He sniffed his hand and made a face. It smelt unmistakeably of the intimate parts of a very unwashed girl. Taking his remaining handkerchief from his pocket, he wiped the steering wheel, and kept the handkerchief between his fingers and the wheel. Strange how reckless he was before the event, seeking out dirt and nastiness so eagerly, and so obsessively fastidious afterwards!

Strange, too, the jolt it had given him to find that girl tonight had the same name as is fictitious one! He ran his tongue round his teeth, longing for a toothbrush, not liking to think of the enthusiastic way he had kissed her. She probably hardly knew what a toothbrush was for.

Perhaps, he ought to choose a new name. He liked Tom Bone, though, he had an affection for it and he could hardly tell them his real, rather outstanding name. Apart from the risk of discovery, they probably wouldn't believe it anyway. Oh, to be home! He pressed his foot down and watched the speedometer needle creep up. The road was quiet and familiar, and he could drive with only half his mind. The recollection of Ann Bone was refusing to be pushed away so easily. He could feel the small, firm breast cupped within the cold fingers of his hand and the slight body, little bigger than that of a well-grown child, beneath him. When he thought of her pleased response to his lovemaking, he sighed. Why couldn't Elizabeth be like that? A girl who, he devoutly hoped, he would never see again in the whole of his life, had said,

"Thanks, Tommy, I've had a nice time," when all she would say was, "No, I'm sorry, Tom, I can't go out with you tomorrow evening, or the next one, or the one after that."

He would even forgive Elizabeth for calling him Tommy.

After parting from him, Ann walked half the length of the street before she unfolded the wad of notes he had put in her pocket. Twenty-five quid! Now there was a thing! Twenty-five quid for a five-minute screw she'd have given him for nothing!

She tucked the notes inside her bra. Dad mustn't see these or he'd have them off her and drink them in nothing flat. Twenty-five quid on top of the weeks' pay due in a couple of days could be a nice little springboard to better things. A girl used to making a lot out of not very much could bring some changes to a life that badly needed them.

Mum had washed the kitchen floor while she had been out and spread old newspapers on it. Ancient history now, she supposed, but just for fun, she got down on her knees on the gritty surface and started to read the situations vacant page. Half way through she stopped, looked again and tore a little slip out of the paper. The fuse was spluttering into life.

Chapter 10

The engineers came. For a day, the lab was littered with their tools and the inward parts of scientific equipment. Disembowelled cabinets stood like reproachful ghosts, dragged from their familiar corners and dumped disrespectfully wherever a space could be found. Undisturbed dust and long-dead spiders were swept away by the ruthless duster of Sally, who tutted and made faces as she worked. She hated spiders. From being a laboratory, the place had briefly become a workshop smelling of oil and overalls.

Finally, the last screw was tightened and they left. When they sent in their report and their bill, the verdict was that apart from the odd bit of fluff in the corners, nothing was wrong. Being told that would cost a sizeable chunk of the Department's annual budget.

Nevertheless, by one of those quirks familiar to lab workers the world over, things from that moment started to go right again. They began to get results that made sense and were repeatable. It cheered them up like nothing else could have done.

Then, on the Monday of the following week, Jill greeted him with the happiest smile he had seen for a long time.

"Good news, Professor. New washer-up starts today."

"Well, thank goodness for that. I hope she'll be more reliable than the last one."

"I hope so too. She's quite a young girl, I understand, so maybe she won't want to stick it for long."

"Well, she's here now. That is just great. That is the tops. Have you seen her?"

"No, she's with the janitor and the head cleaner. After they've shown her the ropes and explained things, she's coming along."

"Jill, I feel we've turned a corner. I've got good vibrations about all this. And listen, I gotta thank you for what you've put up from me lately. Believe me, I don't know why some days you didn't poison my coffee. Most technicians would, after my bad temper tantrums."

"What bad temper?" she smiled.

He laughed, patted her shoulder and stood up.

"Let's get Friday's results listed and go tell that damn computer what we think of it."

"Here they are."

She handed him a sheet of paper.

"Do you ever actually go home? When on earth did you do these?"

"Oh, I floated in for an hour on Saturday morning."

"You make me feel like a slouch."

"Keenness is my middle name."

The computer drew them some pretty graphs and gave them pages of predictions to mull over. It was coffee time before they finished. Tom ripped off the last sheet of paper with satisfaction.

"Great! You go have your break and we'll get our heads down over these when we come back."

He decided after coffee to take a moment to look in and see if their new glassware washer had arrived. Nothing like establishing friendly relations with all the staff, however humble. He was a great believer in it.

She was there, standing with her back to the door, a slight girl with dark haircut short, shiny and clean. They had found her a lab coat that was a reasonable fit and over it, she was wearing a waterproof apron tied at the waist. Her black low-heeled shoes were scuffed and worn, and a thin ladder meandered up the back of one stocking and out of sight. She was not working yet, just looking from side to side to see where everything was.

"Hi, Miss, I don't think we've met."

She turned round and he experienced a jolt of surprise. Her face was vaguely familiar, but he could not quite place it. She had no such problem.

"Bloody hell, if it's not Tommy Bone!"

"Ann!" Stunned, he stepped into the little room and closed the door behind him. "What the hell are you doing here?"

"Use your eyes. I'm working, enn' I?"

Trying to control the rising tide of panic, he said, wishing his heart would not race so fast, "So you're the new washer-up?"

"Domestic assistant, please. Well, fancy meeting you here! Isn't that nice now. I thought you weren't going to recognise me for a minute. Got a short memory, haven't you?"

"I got such a surprise, seeing you here."

"I bet you did. And I bet you're going to be nice to me, en't you, Tommy?"

"I'm nice to everyone," he said, trying to collect his brains.

"You'll be extra nice to me, won't you, though, Tommy Bone?"

Irritably, he shook his head.

"Not Tommy Bone. Professor Di Angeli, get it?"

"Gawdstrewth! You're my bloody boss! That's who they said I'd be working for!"

"Yes. And I'd be grateful if you keep your mouth shut about what happened between us."

She picked up a pair of bright new orange rubber gloves. Slowly, deliberately, she drew them on, smoothing them down finger by finger.

"I bet you would, too," she said at last.

"It was just a – you know."

"Yeah. I know. Twenty-five quid's worth of how's your father. That's a lot of money to be able to throw about."

"It was meant to be a present. A thank you."

"Want to know what I used it for? To get away from my Dad and find a new job. So you're the reason I'm here, see? What d'you think of that, Professor Di Angeli? What a bloody posh name. I knew you'd be too posh to have a common name like my Dad." She minced up to him, saying mockingly, "Good morning, Professor Di Angeli, yes, right away, Professor Di Angeli, whatever you say, Professor Di Angeli," then, when she was right up against him, her expression turned to a sneer, "Professor Di Angeli, picker up of common little tarts like me!"

"Keep your voice down! Anyway, I thought you said you weren't a tart?"

"Oh, you do remember something about it after all? Well, I did think about it for a bit, it was nice to find a wad of cash in my pocket, but then I saw the ad for this job and I thought it would be safer. Didn't expect a bonus like this. Are you thinking about how you're going to get me to keep quiet, Tommy Bone?"

"Who do you think is going to believe you?"

"Where've you been? I don't know what it's like where you come from, but here folks love to believe things like that. No smoke without fire, that's what they say. So you're going to be extra nice to me, aren't you, Tommy?"

"I guess so," he muttered, reluctantly.

"That's better. Now, on your bike and I'll let you know. Don't want them to think we're necking in here with the door shut, do you?"

"God, you cow!"

"Out, sunshine. I'll let you know."

Agitatedly, he strode along the corridor to his room and sat down at the desk. He picked up a pencil, chewed the end of it, then snapped it in two and threw the pieces into the waste paper basket. Getting up, he walked round the room two or three times, thought,

Oh, this is ridiculous, sat down and tried to think rationally about the conversation he had just had.

Were people going to believe her if she started to spread gossip about him? Undoubtedly, as she had said, some would. Did it really matter? The details he would rather not have become public property were unknown to her, after all and surely, people went off the rails occasionally? She only knew of one isolated incident and that was not so very terrible, was it? He tried to imagine some of his colleagues putting it into words and talking about it to each other. The idea did not appeal at all. Who else might hear about it? Jill? He realised he cared quite a lot about what Jill would think. Elizabeth? It would surely kill stone dead any chances he might have with her.

What did she mean about 'being extra nice to her'? Money, he supposed. Well, he could cope with that, at least for a little, but sooner or later, he was going to have to get his head out of the noose. Even if the worst came to the worst, it would be very difficult for him to simply cut and run, for, personal considerations aside, to walk out on his research at this stage without some very good reason would not recommend him to anyone else with a vacancy to fill and the fact that a girl had got her claws into him, would hardly be regarded as a good reason.

He felt himself gripped by a rising tide of panic. Turn this way and that, there seemed to be no escape from this sudden, dramatic change in his fortunes. To think that only this morning he had been in that euphoric mood, thinking that all his troubles were over! It seemed like a lifetime away. If only he had let Mrs Simpson go on in her own sweet way. If only he had not gone out that particular night, or to that particular pub. If only – if only –

Chapter 11

Jill sighed. Her boss had been taxing her patience to the limit all week and it was still only Thursday. Nice to be back home in the cosy flat with the undemanding and companionable Susan in the other armchair, washing up done, and a free evening ahead.

On Monday morning, when the new glassware washer had started, he had been so chirpy and cheerful, but then after coffee, he had disappeared for ages and come back so preoccupied she could hardly get a word out of him. Then it had been back to the same old story. Jumping down her throat for the least little thing. Grumbling at her about everything. It was all very unsettling.

"Things still rough?" Susan asked, observing how Jill sat staring at the wallpaper, the book lying in her lap unread.

"Awful," Jill replied frankly. "I feel as if I'm walking in a minefield all the time. I'll bet it's that stupid dumb blonde he's in love with. She gives him the run-around all the time, and he comes back and takes it out on me. I wish he'd forget her."

"And find someone else?"

"Maybe, as long as it's not someone who treats him like dirt the way she does. She despises him, you can tell, but he can't get enough of her."

"I bet he's one of those people who like to suffer. A masochist."

"Oh, come on! That's bosh! He's as straight as a die. Not the least bit peculiar. Just – touchy."

"Oh yes? And how do you know? Been to bed with him lately?"

"Susan, do you mind? Of course, I haven't been to bed with him! The very idea!"

"Well, how can you tell what his proclivities are, then? You should try it and see what he asks you to do."

"Oh, Susan, what an idea! As if I would do that!"

"Hey, it would be exciting, wouldn't it? Suppose he took off his trousers, and asked you to beat him till he screamed and then drag him by his hair into bed –"

"Susan, will you shut up?"

Jill's pulses were throbbing wildly and her face was bright red. A tight band seemed to squeeze itself round her chest and her lungs could not suck in enough air. She gasped and clutched at the arms of the chair.

"You could take it out on him for all the things he's done to you."

"Shut up, shut up and shut up!" Jill cried, looking frantic.

"Listen, I bet he really fancies you but he daren't say anything because he knows you'd be shocked out of your wits. You ought to try giving him a bit of encouragement. If you were to ease up, you could probably see that blonde piece out of the door. I think you're in there with a good chance."

"Susan, he doesn't know I'm alive and that's the simple fact. Gosh, you've made me feel really queer! I'm going to make a cup of tea."

Tom was seated in a relatively clean cafe in Blackgate Street watching two girls together at a table sipping milk shakes and talking quietly. Oddly, it was the last thing he wanted to be doing.

After Ann had thrown him so unceremoniously out of her room on Monday, he had walked away and hidden himself in the library. It was some time before he could gather courage to go back to the lab. Suppose she came in, and started saying indiscreet things in front of Robert, Jill and Sally! But Ann had said absolutely nothing. Not one single word then, or all week. Not so much as a good morning. His nerves were in shreds.

But the tension had a curious and interesting effect. Whereas since the first time he had seen her, his dreams had been of no one but Elizabeth, he now found they had marginally but distinctly changed. Once he had thought Elizabeth was perfect, but now he dreamed of a perfected version of her. And instead of sitting on a hard chair in a cold, almost empty cafe in Blackgate, what he really longed for was to be in his comfortable, centrally heated flat making love in bed to a girl who cared for him. The cold November night could do its worst outside the closed curtains, for he had made their little nest so warm that they could lie naked with no covers and not a single shiver would spoil the magic. She would be blonde, of course, beautiful, what else? And she would love him. There lay the difference. A fresh, new affair, untried and untarnished. It was so long since he had had that.

The undefined girl in his dreams would be warm, generous and forthcoming. She would lie on her back, and spread herself, uninhibited, her legs, arms, breasts and lips forming a cup into which he could pour himself, welcome, eager. Her loins would move in harmony with his, she working just as hard as he for the final consummation. After her orgasm, he would take his own pleasure and then that most blissful rest in all the world, his head pillowed on a cushiony breast or a white thigh.

But instead here he was looking for a substitute for Ann. The looks she gave him chilled him to the bone and filled his mind with foreboding. Her silence was almost worse than anything she might say. He dared not try to have it out with her, for he shrank from waking the sleeping dog. Yet, the dim delineation of the body he had so lately enjoyed, concealed and revealed in turn by the easy fitting lab coat she always wore, perversely tantalised him and turned him on at the most inconvenient moments, such was the power of the memory of that night.

Only one of the two girls he was watching seemed aware of him and his scrutiny, but she was very aware and very interested. She kept glancing in his direction, her gaze lingering on his a little longer than was strictly necessary. She would raise one eyebrow and smile very slightly, then look back at her friend. In her mind as well as his, was the thought of how she was to ditch her companion and get him on her own.

Her fingers, the nails painted with chipped bluish-red varnish, were curled round the short, thick-stemmed base of her milk-shake glass. Looking at them, he thought of the hands of his imaginary lover. Just like Elizabeth's, dainty, pink and clean.

The girl at the table was looking at him speculatively. He made a tiny movement of his head towards the door and she inclined hers with the ghost of a nod. Her eyes were brown, as was her hair. Her face had a tough, hard-bitten appearance, far removed from the more conventionally feminine looks of the girl in his imagination. Yet, he knew that if that girl existed, she would have her own brand of inner toughness. Strong women always appealed to him, from his Mother right down to Elizabeth. Elizabeth might be fickle and flighty, but the ruthless way she could play on his feelings and keep him dangling, showed that she too had what he craved, and that kept him enslaved to her as much as her beauty did.

He drained the last of the coffee from his cup and headed to the counter to get another, making a slight detour so he could brush against the back of brown-eyes hair as he passed.

"Another coffee, Yank?" enquired the Greek who owned the cafe. His name was Constantine, and he was a cheerful, fat man with wavy black hair, a drooping black moustache and a thick-lipped mouth which broke easily into a smile, a smile enhanced by a gold-tipped tooth right in the front. He took a happy and inquisitive interest in his customers, which Tom found a little embarrassing. Having been in the cafe three times before he was treated as a regular, which meant being kept abreast of the latest doings of Constantine's extensive family.

"Yes, fill her up," Tom replied, leaning his back against the counter and surveying the sparse sprinkling of customers, including, of course, the brown eyed girl who was watching him surreptitiously.

Constantine pulled the handle and with a whish, coffee began to run into the cup.

"Andreas, my third boy, he's in trouble at school again. Always fighting, that boy! Everyone got it in for him. Always got to be a fall guy, wherever you go."

"Yeah, tough," said Tom briefly, his back to the Greek, watching the girl.

"Up in front of the head again. Got six."

"Didn't know they did that, these days."

"He does. Private school. Greek Orthodox. My girl Sophie, she adores her brother. She cried. Thought more of it than he did. He said it was nothing."

"That's boys for you."

"My Sophie, she'd make a lovely wife. Soft hearted as a baby, helps her mother, looks after little Nicolai. Sorry to lose her one day."

"Yeah."

Tom picked up his cup and dropped the money into Constantine's plump hairy paw.

"She's a great girl. Not many girls here tonight. You got a wife?"

"No."

Constantine stroked his moustache.

"My Sophie's a bit young for you. Pity. She'd like to go to the USA."

Not with me, Tom thought, conveying polite regret with a restrained American version of the proprietor's expressive Hellenic shrug.

Just as he was sitting down, a flood of young people came in. Constantine, who obviously knew them well, bustled over to take their orders.

"Hey, look, Marion, there's Bobby and Jack, and their crowd. Let's go over and have a laugh, shall we?"

"You go. I'll come in a minute. I'll just finish this, then I want to go to the bog. I'll come after."

Marion got a packet of cigarettes from her bag. Turning to Tom, she said, "Have you got a light?"

Tom had long ago learned that one of the most massively useful pieces of equipment he could carry with him was a box of matches. He had lost count of the number of times he had managed to get into conversation with a girl by offering, or being asked for, a light. Moving to the chair her companion had vacated, he lit her cigarette for her and she blew out a stream of smoke.

"Haven't seen you around here before."

"No. I'm pretty much a stranger in these parts."

"You an American?" she asked with a coy smile.

"S'right, Marion."

"Hey, how do you know my name?"

"I'm psychic."

"Oh, I know, I expect you heard Jo say it and you're just trying to be a clever-clogs. What's yours, then?"

"Guess."

"Oh, don't play silly buggers. How can I guess what your name is? Is it one of those nutty American things, Elmer or Herman, or one of those?"

"No, it's quite an ordinary name."

"Well, come on then, tell me."

"Tom Bone."

She giggled

"What a funny little name."

"What's funny about it?" he asked huffily.

"Oh, I don't know. It's so short. Short and sweet I suppose you'd say. What do you like to be called, Tom, or Tommy, or what?"

"Just Tom."

"I know a chap by that name who likes to be called Toss."

"That's a weird idea."

There was a brief lull in the conversation. The subject of names seemed to be exhausted.

"Have another milk-shake?"

"Oh, no thanks." She stretched her arms and smothered a yawn. "I should be getting home."

"It's too early for that, surely?"

"Well…"

"Stay a little. I thought you said you were going to the bog, anyway," he said innocently.

"God, you can't say anything in private around here, can you?"

"Is it far from here?"

"What?"

"The bog?"

"Are you serious? Don't you really know what it means?"

"Quite serious. What is it?"

She laughed.

"The toilet, you nitwit, the bathroom." She put on a bogus American accent for the last word.

"Oh well, if you mean the john, why don't you say so?"

"The john!" she cried in mock disgust.

"The bog? That's a new one on me."

"Oh, you have to keep your ear to the ground in this here little ol' country if you want to learn anything."

"Well, I used to, but dang my hide, if people didn't keep treading on my nose."

She burst into a merry peal of laughter and he knew he was well on his way. He moved his chair closer to her. Yes, she was interesting. His nostrils twitched gently. Easily two weeks since she had been in close contact with soap and water.

"Feel like a walk?"

"What, at this time of night? It's dark and freezing cold. Where could we walk to, anyway?"

"Barracks Street?"

"That dump? What would we want to go there for?"

"I know a nice quiet place, if you felt like a cuddle," and he nudged her shoulder with his.

"Hey, you're a bit fast, aren't you? Are they all like you, over there?"

"I'm well known as the fastest gun in the west."

"I should think you are," she replied, giggling. "Where's this quiet place of yours, anyway?"

"Behind the hoardings."

"What! I'm not going in that dump! You could break your neck there, in the dark."

"Not if you know it well."

"How come you know it so well? I thought you said you were a stranger in these parts? I think you're a damn great liar."

"What do you want to do, then?"

"I didn't say I wanted to do anything."

"Don't you?" He put his hand on her knee, under the table.

"Gerroff!" she said, pushing him off, not very convincingly.

"Sorry," he said, not very convincingly either.

"You're much too fast to be allowed out alone. Tom Bone, the fastest gun in the west – no, it doesn't fit, somehow."

"Oh well, if you're going to be rude, I'll leave, right now."

"Oh, don't do that. It was only a joke. Stay and talk to me. You're nice. I like you."

"Do you?" He took her hand and this time met with no rejection. "What do you want to talk about?"

"Dunno. The weather's the usual thing, isn't it?"

"Damn cold. Too cold for cuddling."

"You've got cuddling on the brain."

"I was agreeing with you. You said you didn't want to."

"I didn't say that. I just said I didn't want to go to that dump behind Barracks Street."

"Where, then?"

"You are keen, aren't you?"

"Who wouldn't be with you around?"

"Idiot!" she cried, thumping him on the shoulder.

"Where's your favourite place?"

"Who says I've got a favourite place? What do you take me for?"

"A girl who knows what it's for."

"What a damn cheek! I'm going home this very minute!"

"You might meet some real nasty man on the way."

"I've met one now."

"I'd protect you."

"From yourself?"

"Sure. Go away, you creep. There, he's gone. All right?"

God, what a game it was, he thought. Would any man, in love with a girl like Elizabeth, be sitting here making a fool of himself with an unsavoury girl like this, if he wasn't a candidate for emergency admission to the funny farm?

"You are absolutely stone bonkers," said Marion contemptuously.

"Gee, I wish you'd talk English in this neck of the woods. 'Bog', 'Stone bonkers', what are you talking about?"

"Oh, get lost," she laughed, but in a friendly tone once more. "Can you understand that?"

He put his arm round her again. Tonight, the game must be played out. Tomorrow, he would get back on track, Ann or no Ann.

"Come on, then. Just for the information. Where's this place of yours?"

"Well, in my opinion, the best place around here is the shelter at the kids' playground in the park. Mind you, I have known there to be a queue."

"Far away?"

"No."

"Come on, then, let's go."

"I didn't say I was going with you. I just said it was the best place."

"Didn't your mummy tell you it's naughty to tease?"

They continued to skirmish around the position for a little longer before they finally stood up, he helped her on with her coat and they left the cafe together. As they passed, he heard her erstwhile companion say,

"Well, alleluia, look at that! She doesn't waste much time, does she?"

He smiled to himself and put his arm round her waist, then turned his head and caught the other girl's eye. Flustered at being overheard, she looked away, blushing uneasily.

As they walked along the length of Barracks Street, Marion called out to various acquaintances as they passed, leading her prize like a captured bull on a string. Past the defensive line of iron railings, by the impressive entrance gates, securely locked, till they came to a place where the metal strip which ran along the ground holding the posts together, had been broken in two places. This allowed three or four of the uprights to move back and forth in the upper sockets, and, with time and use, they had become loose enough to make a gap that could be slipped through. She pushed him through it, omitting to mention that it was on top of a steep bank. He slithered down the slippery grass with more speed than grace, and landed on his hands and knees at the bottom. He was up in time to catch her as she followed him down, laughing inordinately, kissed her and slipped his hands inside her sweater.

"What a nice little boob."

"Yes, and guess what, she's got a sister."

"Oh yeah? Where is she?"

"Naughty boy."

He kissed her again. Oh yes, she would do very nicely.

"Onions."

"What?"

"You've been eating onions."

"Gosh yes, at tea time. Can you still smell them? Sorry."

"Don't care. I like onions."

He kissed the side of her neck and her ear so he could bury his face in her hair. That really turned him on, that and the smell of sweat. Not enough of that around. He pushed his hands inside her jumper again.

"Let's just stay here."

"Keen, aren't you?"

"Desperate."

Marion laughed. There was nothing she liked better than this, to be in the arms of a man who was full of desire for her, holding her so tightly that it hurt. At these exciting moments, they kissed her like at no other time. Her lovely American was doing that to her now, grunting urgently as his fingers explored her moist and warm secret parts. A moment later, he had her on the ground and was tugging at her skirt.

"Come on, Marion, give a guy a chance."

"You don't need a chance, you just take it. Come on, darling, wind me up a bit first."

"I can wind you up fifteen different ways. Which would you like?"

"Anything, anything," she whispered rapturously, engulfing him once again in a cloud of oniony breath.

It was as well for Marion that she did not realise how abruptly his desire changed to revulsion the moment their climax had passed. She was surprised at the way he suddenly pulled himself out of her arms, rolled away from her and knelt on the grass a little distance off. He was actually struggling with a wave of nausea, caused by those very same onions. He took several breaths of the clean cold air and the feeling began to subside.

"Tom?" her voice came to him, faint and puzzled.

"Yes, sweetie?"

"Come back to me. I'm cold."

With an almost superhuman effort, he crawled to her and took her in his arms again, his head turned to one side.

"Kiss me again, darling." He gave her a tiny peck on the lips. "Not like that. The way you did before."

He took another deep breath.

"In a minute, sweetie. Hadn't you better cover yourself up? You'll get cold."

She took his hand and put it on her breast. He stroked it mechanically and tucked it back inside her bra.

"Come on, sweetie, get dressed again, you'll freeze."

"What's wrong with you all of a sudden?"

"Nothing. I just came over a bit funny. I'll be all right in a minute."

She put her clothes straight, looking curiously at his face. He longed to ask her not to stare.

"Feeling better yet?" she asked solicitously after a few minutes, standing looking at him as he sat on the ground.

"Yes, thanks," he said, getting himself up. "I'm sorry about that. I don't know what came over me."

She firmly refused to take any money from him, in fact, she stared in astonishment when he offered it. She did, however, allow him to walk her home. She lived on the first floor of one of the tenement buildings in Blackgate Street, one with a close open at both ends, leading from the pavement to the back area, with two doors opening off it to ground floor flats and with the stairway about half way along. This was a wide concrete flight of steps with treads worn to a dip in the middle and a metal banister worn smooth from innumerable hands.

The cold wind funnelled through the open close but there was a little alcove at the foot of the staircase, concealed from everywhere but the stairs themselves, just made for lovers. Here, they stopped and leaned against the shiny tiles of the wall. Marion put her arms round his neck and they kissed. He was a good kisser and she never knew what an effort it cost him.

"See you again?" she asked as they nearly all did. He gave a version of his usual answer.

"Maybe. I'll be around now and then."

"Won't you take me to the flicks some time?"

"Can't, sweetie. I'm a married man."

"What, you old devil! I thought you seemed to have had plenty of practice. All right, look out for me next time you're on the town."

"I will. So long, sweetie."

"Bye, gorgeous."

They parted after another brief kiss, and she climbed the stairs and entered the short narrow hallway of her family's flat.

"That you, Marion?"

"Yes."

"Want some tea?"

"No thanks, Mum. I think I'll go straight to bed. I've been to the cafe, so I don't want anything."

"All right. Night-night."

She walked into the small bedroom which she now had all to herself, her sister having got married a few months ago and having taken all her clutter with her. Sitting down on the edge of the bed which was covered with a cheap Indian cotton bedspread, she put her hands in her coat pockets and thought of him. What a smashing man! She could go for him in a big way, given the chance. Pity he was married, but then, it didn't always take, did it? And everyone knew Americans were apt to get divorced at the drop of a hat. Perhaps, if she was to meet him a few more times and he got keen on her... She pushed her hands further into her pockets and rocked to and fro, dreaming. Suddenly, the fingers of her left hand encountered something unfamiliar. It felt like a folded wad of paper. She pulled it out and inspected it by the dim light of the bedside lamp.

It was a five-pound note folded into quarters.

"What the..." she muttered and opened it out. It was five five-pound notes folded together. "Oh, you sod!" she said quietly and rising, she crumpled the notes into a ball, and threw them on the dressing table. "I'll tell you a thing or two when I next meet you!"

She hung up her coat, feeling annoyed. It seemed to take the edge off things, somehow, that he had given her money after all. It made her feel insulted and cheapened. If her mother hadn't been up, she might have gone and thrown the money into the fire. She felt more than angry and insulted, though. Tough and experienced as she was, there was something about it that made her heart feel heavy and her eyes sting. He had stabbed her in the back somehow and she couldn't quite figure out why.

Then it came to her. Of course. This was a final goodbye, when she had thought things were vaguely open-ended. Despite what he had said, he never wanted to see her again. Lies, all of it! She, who ought to have seen through him like a pane of glass, had been used, duped, taken for a ride as easily as a sixteen-year-old kid. And yet, and yet, it had been lovely, hadn't it? If only he hadn't given her that damned money! She picked it up, screwed it up savagely in her hands and threw it in a corner. Then she started to get ready for bed.

Suddenly, when she was only in her bra and pants, she sat down on the edge of the bed and cried.

"You sod, you filthy screw! I'll kill you, I will, I'll kill you!"

But it was too cold for such histrionics to last for long. Soon, shivering, she put on her nightdress and got into her chilly bed. She lay there thinking and gradually began to see the bright side. She was disappointed and angry, but realistic nonetheless, and there were several different things she could do with an unexpected windfall of twenty-five pounds. Want it or not, she had it, so why throw it away?

She switched on the lamp, climbed out of bed, and groped in the dim and dusty corner till she found it. Then she got back into bed, put out the light and lay in the darkness, lovingly smoothing the much-abused banknotes between her fingers, considering various interesting alternatives.

Chapter 12

Marion had done him a lot of good, in spite of her onions. Cleared away the gremlins.

When he woke the next morning, he felt free and fit for anything. For a while, he lay in bed with his hands behind his head and enjoyed feeling like an untroubled member of the human race again. She would be pleased to find the present he had slipped into her pocket, he guessed. Nice to have a bit of mad money to spend on oneself and she had earned every penny. Chatting her up had been great. Just what he liked, to find an easy-going, willing girl like that who would put up just enough resistance to make it fun, while still letting him know all the time that he was going to get there in the end.

He rose, opened the curtains and looked out. A grey day, with rain threatening. Well, so what? Life was all right. He felt good. Maybe he would call Elizabeth today and see if she would go out with him. Better to call her when he was like this, with enough resistance not to be dashed if she said no and plenty of bounce if she said yes.

Jill was pleased to see him come zooming into the lab throwing off coloured sparks like a Catherine wheel. He greeted her effusively and hugged her round the shoulders with one arm as he asked about progress.

"You're very cheerful this morning, Professor."

"Well, why not, why be glum? Enjoy life when you're feeling up and make it hell for everyone else when you're feeling down. That's my style. You must have noticed."

"Oh, er… Well, that's difficult to answer, without putting my foot in it."

"Then don't answer. Make the most of it while it lasts."

"Good morning, Professor."

It was so startling to hear Ann actually speak to him that it brought him to a momentary halt.

All the same, he smiled, even at her, so good did he feel.

"Good morning, Ann. And how are you today?"

She looked at him long enough for it to be disturbing, before,

"Well enough. I want to talk to you."

Jill turned her head and looked round at her. A bit rude, that. Not even 'please'?

"All right. You want I should come and see you?"

"Yes."

Jill stared even more. There was an uncomfortable pause.

"OK. I'll come along later."

104

"Soon."

With that, she walked out.

Jill glanced to see how he was reacting. He was aware of it. Ann must be made to show at least a veneer of civility, whatever her private attitude might be. Irritated by the curtness of the exchange, he left it as long as he dared, before slipping out unobtrusively, as he hoped, to her room. Jill was aware of his going and wondered.

"Well?" he demanded of Ann's back as he arrived at her room. She did not trouble to turn round.

"Shut the door."

He kicked away the retort stand that acted as a doorstop and pushed it closed.

"Very chatty all of a sudden, aren't you?"

"Got something to say now."

"Like what?"

She had a fine grasp of timing. Meticulously, she went on scrubbing the handful of test tubes she held for a full half minute before dropping them back into the water and swinging round to face him.

"Like, I've got you by the short and curlies now. You've made a bloody great booboo, you damn clot." He disdained to answer. "You *are* a naughty boy, aren't you? Saw you last night, didn't I?"

"Can't have been me. I was at home."

"Balls! It was you all right. You were as close to me as you are now, but I ducked down behind a fellow so you wouldn't see me. There was about six of us. In Constantine's. She stopped to squeal at us so we'd see what she'd got. Remember, someone said she ought to put you in her pocket."

He remembered. If it had been a man who said it instead of a girl, there might have been heads punched.

"You was with that Marion Kaplinsky. I know her. She's the fastest lay on the Blackgate."

His foolish crack about being the fastest gun in the west came back and hit him with almost physical force.

"Oh yeah, Marion," How many times had he had to say those words? The name might vary, the girl accusing him might change, but it was always the same desperate story, accompanied by the same often vain hope that it would be believed. "Oh yeah, Marion. She's a friend of mine from way back. We ran into each other, we had a coffee and a few laughs. Then I walked her home. Why should I have to tell you my business?"

"Don't you tell some whoppers! I've never known Marion let anything in trousers get away from her since she was about fourteen. She was expelled from school for having it off in the boys' bog, you know. And you expect me to believe a story like that! I know what you were doing all right."

"What an imagination you've got."

"Well, aren't you the little goer! I expect you want me to keep my mouth shut about that as well."

"There's nothing for you to keep your mouth shut about. Just don't start spreading any lies about me, that's all."

"I don't need to. You can tell enough lies for the both of us. The truth'll do. Our clever little Professor spends his evenings sloping around Blackgate looking for easy bit of skirt to lay. Wouldn't your brainy friends like to hear that? Wake them up. Wouldn't it?"

"Look," he sighed wearily. "OK, so I picked up a girl. So you saw me. So I took her to the park and screwed her. It was just a bit of a gas, for both of us. She enjoyed it, you ask her. Nobody lost out. What's so terrible about it?"

"I dunno. You tell me. You're the one who denied it."

"Well… it's just one of those things I like to keep under wraps. It's my private life. What's it to anyone else? I don't want it talked about. Suppose I started talking about you? You're not such an angel yourself, now, are you?"

"Listen, who's going to be interested in what I get up to? It's different for you, though, isn't it? You've got a position to maintain, God help us. Us at the bottom of the heap, we can do what we like, but you up there, you've got to be whiter than white. Think of what happens when a bishop or a politician gets caught out. They shoot them down with their arses on fire. Do the same to you if they knew, wouldn't they?"

Of course, they would. Wasn't that just what he had always dreaded? What she knew was nothing to what there was to know, but he didn't care to have it spread about that he was a regular chaser of girls. Apart from the gossip it would engender at work, it would surely sink him with Elizabeth.

"Look, can't you just keep quiet?"

"I might, if you could make me want to."

"What's that supposed to mean?"

"Got something to sell, haven't I? What are you going to pay?"

He looked at her for a long time, chewing the tip of his thumbnail, considering. It was a nasty situation. If mud started to be thrown about, there was no knowing what someone might dig up. There were plenty of past indiscretions that could come to light. The United States was not a universe away and people had acquaintances all over. Painfully aware of what he was doing, he took his first tentative step into her net.

"Well, what do you want? I'm making no promises, mind you and I'm not prepared to go very far to hush this up."

"Come and see me tonight, at my bed-sitter."

It came out pat, obviously prepared.

"What for?"

"The dame as you gave Marion, of course."

Was that all! That was a let-off! Pity, she was so squeaky clean though. She held not the slightest attraction for him now. He shrugged and said indifferently, "If that's all you want. What time?"

"Don't look so enthusiastic, will you? Don't you want to?"

"Does that matter? This is something of a business deal, isn't it? As long as you're satisfied and you're prepared to keep your mouth shut, there's no reason why I should have to enjoy it."

"Well, what's wrong with me all of a sudden? There must have been half dozen girls in the pub that night but you picked me out. I suppose I must have taken your fancy then, so why do you feel so different now?"

"It doesn't matter. What time?"

"But look, I don't like this. I don't get it either. Have I changed?"

"Yes – no – oh God, will you stop asking questions? Look, it's nothing. Forget it. You've got make-up on and I don't like girls in make-up. But I'll come. What time?"

She snorted contemptuously.

"You can't have had a very good look at our friend Marion, then. That's not the reason, you just made that up. Come on. Out with it!"

He shook his head like a bull troubled by a cloud of flies. How on earth had he got into this? Even more, how was he to get out of it? What could he say to shut her up?

"Persistent, aren't you?"

"Tell me!"

"Look, this conversation is crazy. There's absolutely nothing to tell. I just like to choose my own girls, that's all. I don't like having my arm twisted, all right? Is that so hard to understand?" He realised his voice was rising to a hysterical shout, so he paused, pulled himself together and added patiently, "If you want me to come and see you, please just tell me where you live and what time. I've got work to do, believe it or not. I can't spend all day in here jawing with you."

"Are you kinky?" she suddenly asked.

"Course I'm not bloody kinky."

"I think you are. I don't think you'd get so uptight about just picking up a few girls. It's not because you don't want your missus to find out. You're not married. I know that. I asked around. Well, if you're that fond of girls, why aren't you married?"

"What the hell is that to you?"

"I'm just interested. If all a guy wants is a screw whenever he feels like it, he gets married or moves someone in. If he goes to all the bother to get in the car, and go and find it every time, he's looking for something else again. Like I said, he's kinky."

"Shit!"

"Deary me, such language! What on earth can it be? It's not the way you do it. That seemed quite straight and normal to me. Must be the girls, then. Marion? She's not kinky as far as I know. She just likes it fast, hard and often. And me, I did before but I won't do now, so you reckon I've changed, eh?"

"I never said that! You said it! I don't know where you got the idea from, but I wish you'd forget it!"

"Oh, wait a minute! I get it! You're one of those blokes who never likes to have it with the same girl twice, aren't you?"

"That's right. You've got it. It bores me."

"Well, if you want me to keep quiet, you're going to have to put up with me again."

"I've already said I will."

She looked at him, frowningly. He very much wished she wouldn't.

"I've got a feeling there's more to it than that. You wouldn't be so uptight about people knowing that."

"Maybe you wouldn't, but I would."

"It's a hell of a long way to Blackgate. Why go as far as that? There's girls everywhere. Plenty of variety right at your own door."

"Well, I don't want anyone here to see me, do I?"

"Yeah, but why Blackgate? Who'd go to Blackgate if they didn't have to? It's bad enough living in a dump like that, but to go there for a bit of fun – you've got to be kinky."

"How do you know I don't go to other places? I have a high turnover rate. I've just worked my way round to Blackgate lately. Next week, it'll be somewhere else."

She stared at him, still thinking about it. He had perched himself on the edge of a table which held glassware waiting to be washed, and now he rocked to and fro, staring unseeingly at a basket of dirty test tubes.

"I'm different. How am I different? Oh, I know, you fancy yourself as the last of the big spenders, don't you? You like to pick up girls who look as if they haven't got a bean, and stuff fivers into their pockets so they'll feel grateful to you and think what a great guy you are."

"That's right. It gives me a kick to think about it."

Anything, however unpleasant, would do, as long as she failed to drop on the truth.

"Well, I'd still be grateful for a fiver or two. They don't pay me much for doing this job, and I've got my rent and food to pay for now, so I'm worse off than before, really. I haven't changed a bit, that way."

"All right, so I'm quite happy to come and see you."

"Shut up and stop confusing me! There's something I'm trying to remember – something about Blackgate. What was it now?"

He sat inspecting his thumbnail, passionately wishing she would leave the subject alone.

"The White Star Garage!" she cried with sudden inspiration. "You've been going to Blackgate for ages, haven't you? The girl from the White Star Garage, who fancies herself as a mechanic!"

"How the hell do you –" it burst from him before he could think what he was saying. "– know about her?" he finished lamely.

"Oh, you'd be surprised what I know about you and your little goings-on, Professor. Now, what was it that David said?"

"Who the hell is David?" He was beginning to shout again and he had a dull, sick sensation in the pit of his stomach.

"He's a friend of mine. He knows about you too. You're quite a local celebrity. Now, what did David say about her? She never washes the oil off. She goes about in her dirty dungarees all the time. She smells, too. I've been stood beside her in the pub sometimes and she stinks. Oh, I know, he said he wasn't that fussy, but she was a bit yukky, even for him. Is that what you like? Do you like them yukky?"

"I haven't the slightest idea what you mean by 'yukky'," he replied, knowing only too well.

"Oh, you know sort of –" she waved her hands expressively. "Dorty. Messy. Doesn't wash very much." She thumped the bench with her hand. "That's it, isn't it? You like girls who don't wash very much, and that's why you go to Barracks and Blackgate. Of course, it's obvious, isn't it? Why didn't I guess it right away?"

"This is just stupid. I don't know what you're talking about."

"Yes, of course, I get it now. The whole thing. Marion, yes, that figures, she's still living in Blackgate, but I can have a bath easily now at my bed-sitter. That's why I'm different. Well, it's obvious, isn't it? Honestly, who'd have thought it, looking at you? I mean, you're so clean yourself, it's, like, one of the first things that hits anyone looking at you, how clean you are. All sort of pink and shiny. And you like girls like that! You've been prowling round Blackgate for months. It was weeks ago that you met me and David said it was ages before that that he saw you with that other girl. Don't you tell some fibs?"

"It wasn't that long ago I started going there," he said desperately, trying to stem the tide.

"Oh, get out! And if you're going there, it's because you like slummies. I mean, who'd go there if they hadn't a reason?"

"I'll tell you the reason, the real one. It's because I don't have to work too hard. You and your friends are a crowd of cheap tramps and hookers. All you have to do is say, how about it and they can't wait. None of them. It's too easy."

If he thought he was going to get anywhere by being insulting, he was wrong.

"Listen, haven't you heard what University students are like? It's in the papers every day. Besides, if all you want is an easy lay, why did you turn me down?"

"I didn't turn you down. I said yes, didn't I?"

"Yeah, just about and only because I twisted your arm. Besides, if there's that much choice, why go for the garage girl?" She looked him up and down. He was wearing a gleaming white shirt, plain dark tie and neatly pressed navy trousers. "I mean, look at you! You always look like a tailor's dummy, and you smell like you're just out of the bath, soapy and nice. What were you like after you'd been with her? I bet you had oil all over your shirt, for a start."

He had had to throw the shirt away, because it had been impossible to get the stains out. Suddenly, he didn't care anymore. All his life, he had felt miserable and guilty about his obsession, and always he had had at the back of his mind that he ought to be made to suffer for it one day. Each time he had looked like getting caught out, he had either lied his way out of it or run away, but now he was tired of running. There was something about the sharp witted and tenacious Ann Bone. She seemed to be able to make rings round him while he stood bemused and helpless in the middle. It felt like fate, the final reckoning. He was almost glad it had come. Perhaps, somehow, in this way lay the acceptance of himself and the peace of mind that he could never seem to have. A reckless disregard for the consequences filled him and he answered her,

"Yeah. All over it."

"Did you take her to the same place as you took me?"

"No. I know lots of places."

"Tell me some."

"Oh, all over, back of the old laundry, some of those empty houses, all over."

"Geesh!" she whispered. Then she wrinkled her nose. "Didn't she make you smell? I mean, going home after, couldn't you smell her on you?"

"Yeah."

"Is that one of the things you like?"

"Yeah."

She moved closer, with a sort of horrified fascination on her face.

"Did you give her a French kiss, like you did me?"

"Yeah. Both ends."

She stared, her previous look augmented by puzzlement.

"You mean you kissed her arse?"

"Yeah. A French kiss. You know what that means."

This was getting too much for him. He shifted about uncomfortably on the edge of the table, then stood up. Ann Bone wrinkled her nose again.

"Let's see your tongue." He stuck it out briefly for her inspection. "You mean – you actually shoved it in her?"

"Yeah."

"But her – didn't you get diarrhoea?"

"No."

"Well, you were damn lucky. Why'd you do it?"

"I like it. Not every girl'll let you do it, but when she will, it's great."

"Why didn't you ask me?"

"Too cold that night. I didn't want you to freeze."

"Would you do it at my bed-sitter?"

"If you want."

"Gee! I don't know if I *would* want. I'll have to think. Hey, I'll tell you what, though. Would you fancy me again if I *did* smell?"

"I might."

"What do you like best?"

"Hair, when it's not been washed it gets a smell – gee!"

"What else?"

"Sweat."

"No deodorant?"

"Right."

"What else?"

"What only a girl has. You don't wash that bit that makes you a girl, then just give me a tiny sniff of it and – kapow!"

"God, what a nut!" she whispered. "All right, I'll do it. I won't wash, not even my face. Will that turn you on again?"

"I'd want your body, but no more than that."

"That's not very nice, is it?"

"Do you want the truth, or a load of crap?"

"I'd rather you said you liked me."

"What does it matter? I'll give you what you want and the only price I ask is your silence. Role-reversal, that's the name of the game, honey. You're the client and I'm the cheapest hooker on the block. You leave the soap alone and I'll make it worth your while. You won't even notice that I hate your guts."

Her eyes flashed angrily.

"You're a bastard!"

He shrugged.

"When's our date, then?"

For a long moment, she stared at his impassive face.

"I really have got you by the short and curlies now, haven't I? You've told me a load of stuff I bet you don't want anyone else to know. Why'd you do it?"

"You guessed most of it."

"Yeah, but you could have just kept saying no. Now I know it's true."

"Yeah."

He thought, why had he done it? After all his years of careful circumspection, he had recklessly flung himself into the hands of a girl he scarcely knew, because of that sudden impulse that she was his destiny, for God's sake! The price she would want to extort for her silence could be mind-boggling. No getting out of it now. He would have to go through with it and what the end might be lay beyond the reach of his imagination. He felt both frightened and angry. Angry with himself for his foolishness and angry with her for having wheedled him into this position. Might there even be, at this late stage, some means by which he might bluff his way out of it?

"Swallowed that little lot like a dream, didn't you?"

"What little lot?"

"All that stuff I've been feeding you. Believed it all, didn't you? You must be crazy, to believe garbage like that!"

It was her turn to stare and consider, and chew the tip of her thumb. Then she shook her head decisively.

"You meant every word of it, I could tell."

"Not a word. I made it all up."

"You never did. That business with the White Star girl proves it. Besides, you said you'd fancy me if I got sweaty again."

"Aw, listen, no one would choose that type of girl. It was a story."

"I've got a cousin. She's got a sort of kink, you'd never believe. She just likes oddballs, any brand at all. She collects 'em. Rubber fanciers, black leather guys, the queerer the better. She's got a cupboard full of weird gear to keep them happy. Some of the stories she tells! Mind you, she'd love to meet you. Might introduce you one day. No. There's all sorts and you're one. All those other things I thought of you tried to tell me that was it, but you couldn't carry it off. This was the truth. You're kinky for slummies. You'll never make me believe different."

He was dished and he knew it. Even if it had not happened to be the truth, he would never have convinced her. The anger and rebellion faded again, to be replaced by a sort of stubborn, childish compliance.

"Have it your own way, then. Do what you like, I don't give a damn, long as you keep quiet. Dress up in a mermaid costume with a flower behind your ear, if you should happen to decide that's what turns me on, next time you think about it. It's all the same to me. I don't care. I'm sick of all this. For God's sake, tell me when you want me to come and screw you, then let me go away. I hate the sight of your stupid face."

His shoulders drooped and he looked at her with a hangdog expression.

"Golly, gee, a real charmer! OK, next Friday. Week tomorrow."

"Yeah, All right."

"And you be a good little boy, stay home nights and don't go visiting Marion or any more of her friends. You'd better be pretty hot stuff when you do come or I'll stamp all over you with my high-heeled boots and see how you like that!"

"Oh, drop dead!"

Turning on his heel, he walked out of the room, to go and brood unhappily in his office.

The week passed. Ann Bone formed plans in her sharp and cunning mind. She kept a show of politeness to him in public, for the outward normality of their work relationship was important to her now in her long-term ideas. It must seem that they were simply the boss and one of his more lowly assistants, but he must be made very conscious that it was no more than that, just an appearance, and, moreover, it was as fragile as eggshells.

Meanwhile, everyone could see how her hair became lank and greasy, and her neglected skin sallowed and sprouted a fine crop of pimples round the chin. She wore the same clothes every day and her blouse collar was soon begrimed with dirt.

Covertly, he watched all this. It was a new experience, to have a girl set out to make herself the way he really wanted and to have it happening before his very eyes. Many times, he had stood in the bedroom of an elegant apartment to watch his latest attractive blonde room-mate arrange her hair, and put on her stylish clothes and makeup – in his public life, he never had truck with any but the lovely, well-dressed blondes, and with his own good looks he had no problem finding eager takers – and as he looked at them, he would think of how little they knew of the desires of his real self. To walk into smart restaurants and theatres, or to go to a party accompanied by shiny hair, expensive clothes and seductive perfume was to display the Tom Di Angeli that was concocted for the world's eyes. To watch Ann Bone degenerate again into her previous self was a very private excitement.

She scarcely spoke to him that week, beyond the barest courtesies of normal communication, but when their eyes met, there was no need for words. The secret, mocking knowingness of her look would revive in him that oddly exhilarating self-disgust which he felt when he submitted himself to his longings, and the promise of fulfilment she embodied kept his motors running day and night in subdued but mounting expectation.

When she knew Jill was watching them, which was most of the time, she would casually brush against his back or touch his shoulder, watch for her reaction and never fail to get it. For what was hidden from Tom, because he was so close up against it, was quite plain to Ann and she stowed away the knowledge in her treasury of things which might be useful.

On the Friday morning, when he was in the lab, he heard the technicians talking together.

"I can't think why that girl took a job as a washer-up," said Robert. "I don't get the impression she's that fond of water, had you noticed?"

"I know what you mean," said Jill.

"I'll say," Sally remarked. "This morning, she leaned across in front of me to pick up a basket of tubes for washing and phew! The smell nearly knocked me over!"

"Perhaps, someone ought to tell her about B.O." said Robert in an exaggerated whisper behind his hand.

There was a moment's silence and then Jill spoke.

"Well, I'm not going to for one. That's a tough little piece of goods in there. Say one word out of line and she'll probably knock your block off!"

"Yes, you're right. Professor Di Angeli must think we're an awfully catty lot, talking about people behind their backs like this."

"She's a good washer-up, Sally, what more can we ask? Her private life's her own affair, I guess."

"That's very true. You hardly ever have to send anything back because it's not clean."

"And she comes in every day."

"So far."

Later in the morning, Ann called to Tom as he was passing her room.

"Well, will I do? Come closer. Come right up to me. Will I do?"

"You'll do." He dared not get too close.

"No one else will come near me. I don't even like coming near myself. I've heard of some kinky ideas but yours takes the gold-plated biscuit."

"Well, I didn't wish it on myself, I promise you."

"Just make sure you're there at nine on the dot, and you do whatever I say and no messing. All right?"

"All right."

As he turned to go, she said mockingly,

"See you later, Professor Di Angeli!"

Chapter 13

A little before nine, he turned his car into the street where she lived, decided he did not like the look of it and parked, instead, in a different street, a short distance away, under a streetlight. The road he sought was lined on either side by narrow-terraced dwellings, three stories high. Most had had the front walls of their tiny gardens demolished and been paved to accommodate a car, or contained piles of rubble or a scatter of children's toys. Most of the peeling front doors had two or three doorbells. It was dark and cold in the ill-lit street and the wind tugged at the lapels of his coat as he searched for the address he wanted, using his pocket torch now and then to read the grimy, paint-splattered numbers.

Two motorbikes, on a patch of rough grass, stood in front of the house he sought. He walked up the cracked concrete path, pushed open the front door and entered. His nose wrinkled. The place smelled of boiled cabbage, chip pans and not very clean lavatories. The sound of a broadcast voice came from somewhere, but otherwise, all was silent. He climbed to the first floor as instructed, taking his hand quickly off the handrail when a touch showed that it was in imminent danger of collapse. On the landing, a few steps brought him to a door with a small square of cardboard pinned to it reading 'Miss Ann Bone'. He knocked.

She opened the door, still wearing the same dirty clothes, her jaws working rhythmically on a wad of chewing gum. Indicating with a tilt of her head that he should come in, she turned her back on him, walked around the room and sat down on the arm of one of the two easy chairs that stood by a gas-fire hissing on the wall. He pushed the door shut behind him and stood looking around.

The room was about ten feet square with the gas fire on the wall to its right and a coffee table in front of it. A single bed stood with its head to the wall on the right and behind the door, was a large, old-fashioned wardrobe. Against the wall facing him was a drop-leaf table, its leaves folded down, holding on its remaining surface an electric kettle and jars of coffee and tea. Above this, on the wall itself, was a glass-fronted kitchen cabinet with cups and saucers, biscuits and other odds and ends. There was a door beside the gas fire, *perhaps a cupboard*, he thought. The floor was covered with a thin, threadbare carpet which had once been red with a floral pattern.

"Not very luxurious, is it? Not what you're used to, I should think."

He said nothing but simply stood there, looking and waiting. The cheapest hooker on the block, ready to cope with the client's fancies.

Eventually, after they had watched each other in antagonistic silence for some moments, she said, "Well, what are you standing there for? I think you ought to kneel, don't you? You want me to do something for you, so kneel down and ask for it."

He still said nothing, but leaned his shoulders against the door and gave her a look. The latch clicked into place behind his back. She rose and walked over to him.

"Go on, kneel."

"Get lost."

"You're going to do what I say, and no messing, remember? You're not the boss here, I am. Kneel."

He sighed impatiently.

"Well, if you find it so very amusing," he replied and bumped down on his knees on the thin carpet.

She knelt down in front of him and smiled contemptuously, right in his face.

"That's a good little Professor."

He eyed her warily. It was going to be a tough evening.

"You're going to give me a bad time, aren't you?"

"Clever boy."

"You've been planning all week what you're going to do. You've got me right where you want me, and you're gonna make the best of it, yeah?"

"Ten out of ten."

"What are you going to do with me?"

"Make you crawl. Show you you're not such a big shot as you think you are. Not with me. I know you're just a dirty old man and I'll tell everyone else unless you're a good boy."

"What do you want me to do?"

She shot out her hand, grabbed his tie and gave it a sudden jerk, so that, taken by surprise, he found himself on all fours.

"I want to play puppy dogs."

"Well, I don't."

"Have it your own way. You don't play with me, I shan't play with you, and you know what that'll mean, don't you? Besides, you want to go to bed with me, eh? Take a sniff at me, lover-boy. Don't I smell nice? Like a bloody dustbin. Going to play puppy-dogs?"

"I might."

"You've got to."

"Woof woof."

He spent some time crawling around on the floor performing all sorts of silly antics at her behest while she encouraged him with slaps, kicks and insults, shrieking with laughter.

"Oh, I do wish the people at the Department could see you now!"

"I'm sure they'd find it hilarious," he said, wincing from a particularly vicious kick. "I don't know why I'm letting you do this to me."

She knelt on the floor beside him.

"Don't you really, Towser?" she cooed, patting his hair. "Don't turn your head away like that, or you won't get any dog biscuits."

"Oh, for God's sake!"

"That cousin of mine – told you about her, didn't I? She knew a fellow once, exactly like you."

"Oh, my goodness, did she have some fun with him before she got fed up and chucked him. He was a real nut. The worse she treated him, the more he liked it. The stories she'd tell us! She had us all in fits. I was never quite sure if she was shooting a line at the time, but I can believe it now. You're just the same, but in a different way."

"No, I'm not," he said, indignantly.

"Yes, you are. You just can't face up to it, that's all. You wouldn't be here tonight if you didn't have a secret yearn to be kicked up the backside. You knew I'd make it hot for you. That's why you came. You've been winding up for it all week. I could tell."

He got into a sitting dog position, partly to save that part of his anatomy from further assault.

"I'm here," he said sharply, "because I had no choice. You made it clear that if I didn't come, you were going to make my life pretty miserable for me. It's not easy to fight blackmail. If you spill the beans, I'd surely have to resign from my job and it means a hell of a lot to me, this post. Believe me, I wouldn't have come a hundred miles of you tonight, if I could have thought of a way out."

"Yes, you would. You love to suffer. You're loving all this."

"Let me up," he said, trying to disengage his tie from her grasp. "I'm going home and damn the consequences."

"No, you're not. You're going walkies again."

"Let go, for God's sake. I'm sick of this game. It's damn hard on the knees."

Perceiving that she had gone too far, she let go.

"All right, why don't you go to the bathroom?"

"Don't want to."

"Well, I want you to. There are a few bits of things I've got to do, so you can have your little treat."

"I doubt if it'll be worth it," he said sulkily.

Without a word, she put her arms round his neck, looked into his resentful eyes and kissed him. Little by little, she shuffled forward on her knees till she was touching him all the way, up and down, pushing against him with her body, making him embrace her, limply and reluctantly at first, but gradually with more fire. Every move she made, offered him a little sample of the fulfilment she could give to his obsessive needs, right from the moment when she raised her arms and put them round him. Face to face, they knelt, holding and hating each other— she, almost sorry for the poor mutt and what the rest of the evening was going to cost him; he, wishing he could keep a grasp on reality with his head in a tantalising cloud of sweat.

She turned her head to the side and brushed his mouth with her hair. Pushing his fingers among the greasy locks, he caught and held her there, his chest swelling as he inhaled slowly. No good. He was hooked. The future was nothing. Even if it meant knocking down everything he had built for himself, at that

116

moment he cared little about it. He must have her, whatever happened. Burying his face in her hair, he nuzzled her ear with his lips, kissed it, nuzzled it, kissed it again. Then he worked his way round to her mouth, leaned her back in his arms, laid her on the floor. The buttons popped easily on the front of her blouse, it was so old and worn, and her cheap, washed-out bra sagged loosely around her small breasts, giving ample scope for his exploring fingers.

"What do you think?"

"I'll take it." They rocked to and fro on the carpet, clutching each other. "God, Christ, I can't resist you. I'll be sorry, I know, but I guess I gotta have you."

"Let's get on, then. Go to the bathroom, let me get ready for you. Then we can have our bit of fun."

"I don't want to go to the bathroom. I want to take you right now. What have I got to go to the bathroom for?"

"What do you usually go for? Come on, you're getting what turns you on, so let me have what turns *me* on. Fair, isn't it?"

"Oh…I guess so."

"OK. Well, go to the bathroom, count slowly to a hundred and take your clothes off. Do it the other way round if you want to admire yourself. I'll call you when you can come back."

It was a risk, letting him cool down like that, but one that she had to take. The bathroom was behind the door near the gas-fire and even though she called out, "Count slowly, now," as he closed it behind him, she was still in a fever to get everything accomplished that had to be done. After what seemed an infinity of minutes and suspicious noises, it was ready. She lay in the bed and looked around her. It seemed all right. Then she walked round the room surveying it from every angle, but even after that, her stomach was still twitching anxiously as she lay down again.

"Can I come back?" he called.

"Yes, all right."

She tried to sound careless and casual. But she had the feeling it had not entirely come off.

He had stripped to a pair of dark-blue Y-fronts, which she noticed looked satisfyingly bulgy. His clothes were hooked on one elbow and he draped them over the nearest armchair.

"Well?"

She looked. It was well, worth looking, at. His skin was pale-gold in colour, slightly, but not emphatically, tanned and the effect against the dark-blue was riveting. Although he was short and not especially broad, the muscles of his limbs, chest and abdomen were, like his tan, enough to make her catch her breath, but not so much as to be overdone. From the neck down, he looked solid, compact, condensed power. From the neck up, he looked so tentative and uncertain that the contrast was almost comical. He was unused to not being in command and it showed.

"Come over here. Unless you're one of those long-distance lovers, that is."

"What is going on?" he asked, glancing around at the strange sight that the room now presented.

She had pulled all the covers off the bed and dumped them in an untidy heap on the floor. The coffee table had been moved to a position between the bed and the wardrobe, and lined up on it, were three table lamps which had previously been dotted around the room. They were all lit, as was the ceiling lamp, so the bed was flooded with light, almost like a stage.

A story had come to her mind. Not a very good one, but with no time to consider, it would have to do.

"I like to kid I'm in one of those sex shows, you know, in the clubs where they have it off on the platform with the audience cheering them on all the time. I just like it that way," she added sulkily, as if she thought he was going to argue.

"Anything you say, Ann, dear."

Her eyes flashed and she looked at him as if she thought he might be teasing her, but seeing he looked quite serious, she lay down again and said,

"Come and take my clothes off."

"That must be the noisiest bed in the country."

"Awful, isn't it?" she agreed, moving about and making the springs creak, like a small orchestra tuning up. "I spoke to the landlord about it, but he's just not interested. Says to think I'm lucky to have a bed at all."

He came and sat by her feet, producing another protesting groan from the bed and took off her shoes and tights. Then he worked his way upwards, dropping discarded clothing in a heap on the floor.

"You're sure, you want to go through with this?"

"'Course I do. What's wrong?"

"You're uptight as hell. You feel like you're made of wood."

"Just get on with it, for goodness' sake."

"What do you want?"

"Straight."

"Nothing else?"

"Just do what I say."

He shrugged. His blue Y-fronts landed on top of the heap of clothes and he started to try to get her going a bit, but she would have none of it.

"Don't bother with all that. Just screw me. Come on, do it now, but slow."

He got to work slowly, like she said, resting after each stroke, wondering what was wrong with her. Her fingers were cold on his back and she shivered delicately each time he moved.

After a few minutes, she suddenly said,

"Put out all the lights. Go on, all of them. The fire, too."

He got up, did the rounds and groped his way back to the bed in the darkness. When he got there, he found she was holding out her arms to him. As soon as he touched her, she seized hold of him and pulled him down to her.

"Start again," she whispered in his ear. "Do what you were going to do a minute ago before I stopped you. Kiss me, like you did that night behind Barracks Street."

"Sweetie, I don't know where I am with you. Why do you keep changing?"

"Ssh. Talk quietly."

"Why, all of a sudden?"

"These walls are like tissue-paper. You don't want everyone to hear us, do you?"

"The way this bed creaks will give them a fair idea of what's going on."

"Well, talk quietly anyway."

He said no more, but kissed her the way she liked it. She gasped softly as he exchanged the fresh minty taste of his mouth for the stale nicotine of hers. She had discarded her chewing gum at some point and any cleansing effect it had had was gone. Her tongue was like a warm, soft, pink cushion, lying inert, as he probed and explored with his, exciting her by running it round the inside of her cheeks.

"Like it?"

"Oh, yes!"

"Want I should try what we talked about last week?"

"Ssh! Not yet. In a minute, maybe."

He kissed her breasts and sucked gently.

"Put your arms up so I can smell the sweat."

"You're the queerest guy I ever met. Don't you like some funny things?"

He made no reply. With his head pillowed on one breast, he was breathing as if he was in a rose garden. Working her over with his hands, he wound her up and himself too, until the aches of desire in his limbs and loins were keyed to breaking point.

"Let me try it now, sweetie. You'll like it."

"Oh. No, no!"

"Yes, come on. Ease up. Let me get in there."

He slid down and pushed his face between her legs. The tangle of pubic hair got in his way. He ran a finger up the crease and found his target. Despite her pleads for silence, she squealed as she felt his tongue touch her.

"Oh, stop! It's disgusting! Come up this end. This is the end you're supposed to kiss."

"I'm not just kissing you," he said, indistinctly.

"I know you're not! Oh, stop it, stop it! Not when I haven't washed! You'll get germs!"

"Who cares?"

"Come on, do it proper. If you do that with your mouth, what'll you do with your other end, I'd like to know?"

"I could show you a few things."

"Well, don't. Just do it proper."

"I'm sorry, Sweetie. I thought you'd like it. If you'd only try."

"It's filthy," she said sulkily.

"Give you a kiss to make up."

She pushed him away as soon as he got near.

"Oh, you smell disgusting. Wipe your face with your hankie, or you'll make me puke."

"Where would I have one stashed, right now?"

"Oh, use the sheet then, but do it, for goodness' sake."

He pulled out the corner of the sheet and rubbed hard round his nose and mouth.

"There, that better?"

"A bit. Now, no more fancy stuff."

"What about you and your high-heeled boots?"

"Oh, I never really meant that. I haven't even got a pair. Come on, look, I'm ready for you. Are you going to take all night?"

"If I can."

"Oh, you're a shocker!"

He pleased her in the end and she was feeling benevolent.

"This is better than that mucky old waste ground, isn't it, sweetheart? You don't have to put your pants on and go straight home. You can have a kip first. Won't that be nice?"

She pillowed his head on her shoulder and in a few minutes, he was fast asleep.

His sleep was brief but profound. When he woke up, he could not orientate for a moment. The stuffy, shabby room with its cracked ceiling and dingy walls affected him with the oppressiveness of a prison cell. There was a movement and a little puff of steam. He raised his head from the lumpy pillow. The gas-fire was warming the room again and she had thrown a blanket over him. She was wearing a short, thin, cotton nightdress through which her body could dimly be discerned and she had combed her hair.

"I was just going to wake you, Tom. There's some coffee for you. I thought you might want it."

He had never heard her speak in such a soft, gentle voice and she looked at him tenderly, almost lovingly. She seemed to have forgotten why she had dragged him there. Or perhaps she hoped he had forgotten. Her tough, hostile nature was cloaked and she looked as if she wanted nothing better than to climb back into his arms and love him again.

It was obvious what her little plan was. She was going to seduce him into showing even more weakness than he had already, perhaps even try to make him love her, then batten on to that advantage to have her way more than ever. Well, it wasn't going to work!

Calling him Tom, that was a nice touch. Normally, she would call him absolutely anything else. In private, Tommy, because she knew how he hated it, at work by his title, because he had ordered her to, but in a way that made it seem like a slap in the face. Never 'Tom', until now, when she thought it might help her to get around him a little more.

He tasted the coffee. It was weak and very sweet, but he was thirsty and it was reasonably refreshing. He swallowed it quickly, in three or four scalding gulps, then said, "Well, do you want me for anything else or can I go home now?"

"Oh, stay the night. Don't you like to be with me? We can have another cuddle. That'll be nice."

"No, as a matter of fact, I don't like being with you much, since you asked. I can't remember signing up for spending half the evening nose-down to a very dirty carpet, for example."

She looked a little ashamed.

"I don't really know why I did that. Yeah, I suppose I wanted to take the mickey a bit, because we all have to do what you say at work. It was only meant in fun."

"That wasn't the impression you gave at the time. You kicked me and called me every name you could lay your tongue to. If that's your idea of fun, it sure as hell isn't mine. You humiliated me because you knew I had to take it. OK, you made me want you, I'll give you the credit for that, but I don't know if the result was worth the price I had to pay. I don't much care being made a fool of."

"Oh, but Tom, you did like it, when we were in bed together. I know you did. Can't you forget all that silly stuff we did first? Half an hour ago, you were loving it."

He noted that he was still 'Tom', but not for much longer, he suspected. Leaning on his elbow, he looked at her.

"That little quirk of mine that you talk about so much. That was what I was enjoying it in bed, back then. I was just kinda hanging about, cheering it on."

She wrinkled her brow and shook her head. This concept was evidently too complicated for her to grasp.

"But Tom, for a whole week I've been letting myself get dirty and niffy to please you. You don't think I like being like this, do you?"

"And it did please me. I appreciated it very much. But remember what I said last week. I wanted your body, nothing more. Can I go now, please?"

"That's OK then, if it pleased you. Aren't you going to say what a nice girl I am for doing it?"

"No."

"Why not?"

"Because you're not a nice girl. You're a particularly nasty, vicious girl. You're about the most unpleasant girl I've ever met."

That did it!

"Go on, get out!" she screamed, her face furious. He leapt to his feet and started to get dressed as fast as possible, pushing his tie, pants and socks into his pocket for speed. "You'll regret this! You'll be sorry you spoke to me like that. You've done yourself a bad turn, you'll find out." He laughed, quickly buttoning his shirt. "You can laugh now, but you won't be laughing on Monday, wait and see."

"What's the matter, can't you think of anything else to call me? Run out of names earlier on?" She glared at him, fists clenched at her sides. "Go on, try. You're disappointing me. I'm sure you can think of something to fill the bill."

She made wordless noises of impotent fury, so, as he opened the door, he said, in a fair imitation of her sarcastic voice,

121

"Goodnight, Professor Di Angeli!" and slammed the door behind him. He heard some missile hit the door and smash on the floor – he guessed it was the coffee cup – and he laughed quietly to himself as he went downstairs. Thinking of her furious face, he felt that, taking things as a whole, he had come off best in the end.

Next day, at about lunch-time, there was a knock at the door of Ann's bedsitter. When she opened it, a young man was standing there.

"Have you got them?" she asked eagerly.

"Have a look."

He stepped in and handed her a small package.

"Oh-ho-ho-ho!" she laughed, delightedly. "Just wait till he sees these! His eyes'll pop out on stalks! Barry, you are a total star!"

"Annie," said the young man, putting his arm round her shoulders and giving her a hug. "I think we've got it made, you and I. He'll give you the moon now, if you ask for it. He's yours, every day of the week."

"I'll say."

"I didn't like you being with him like that, though. You won't do it again, will you?"

"Do you think I'd two-time you?"

"First chance you get."

"Oh, get out of here!"

"You'd better not," he said, playfully showing his fist.

"Oh, like that, is it?"

"Got to take care of you, haven't I? You're my little pot of gold."

"And don't you forget it," she said, pushing his fist aside. "Sit down and have a coffee. One of us'll have to use a cup though. Smashed my mug last night. Threw it at him."

"Hit him?"

"Nope. That's what it would have done to his head if I had," she said, putting her finger on the dent in the door.

"Never mind. He can buy you a gold-plated one now."

"What d'you mean, plated? Solid gold, more like."

"That's my girl. Sure you can handle him?"

"Him? He's a pushover. I can't wait to see his face on Monday. It'll be like a wet weekend."

Chapter 14

Euphoria can evaporate surprisingly quickly and Monday morning found a very worried Tom driving to work, wondering what he was going to be faced with. All weekend, he had been kicking himself for his stupidity in throwing away anything he had possibly gained by letting Ann make a thorough ass of him, by indulging in those few stupid ill-considered remarks just before they parted. She was not likely to forgive them easily. Even though he had kept his part of the bargain, she might well use them as an excuse not to keep hers, and the thought of her sitting with the rest of the domestic staff, giggling over how she had got that American Professor to come to her room and sleep with her, and telling them all she knew of his sexual preferences, made him curl up and die with agony inside. Over and over, he had tried to tell himself that there was not one single thing that she could prove, and if he just kept his head and denied it all, there was no reason why anyone should believe her, but he was not convinced. People would devour the dirt as eagerly as pigs at a through. No smoke without fire, they would say and his protestations of innocence would fall on deaf ears.

But there was more to it even than that. The grip she had on him was subtly strengthened. The simple need to keep her quiet was now only half of it – maybe even the weak half. Even while he was driving to work, the remembrance of the luscious and languorous delights he had found in every corner of her foetid body lingered in his mind, arousing guilty feelings of remembered pleasure, making him long for her again, reckless of all danger, regardless of his dislike for her, despite any vestige of common sense. That evening had marked the apotheosis of his passion. The rapture of the two naked bodies, his and hers, on that stripped, narrow, creaking bed in the run-down room had not, as it usually was for him, been followed by feelings of disgust and remorse. Anxiety the next day, yes, but that was different. How light his spirits had been as he had gone home that night. If only he could recapture that feeling now and lose this nagging worry that some catastrophe was about to happen.

His mail was piled up on his desk, waiting for him, and after taking off his jacket, he warmed his hands briefly on the radiator and went to look through it. The room was chilly, so he picked the bundle up and went back to lean his behind against the comforting warmth, while he flicked through the letters for anything of special interest.

Right in the middle, he was surprised to find a cheap-looking white envelope with nothing written on the outside. That was odd. It was thick and curiously stiff and rigid. With a puzzled frown, he put the rest aside and tore that one open. Hastily, he pulled out the contents, took one look and groaned aloud,

"Oh, my God!"

His sense of foreboding was amply fulfilled. In his hand was a bundle of photographs, clear, sharply and expertly printed, and the one on top was a panoramic view of himself from behind as he lay beside Ann trying to arouse her. One after another he turned them over. There were quite a lot of them, showing the whole process, even him getting up to turn the lights off. Not much in the way of identifiable faces, but several excellent views of the mole on his left hip. Well, who would be able to recognise him from that? No one here, at any rate.

However, the photographer was not done with him yet. After the victim had fallen asleep, he had got his flashgun into action and there was no question then of who the two people involved were. Ann was looking very pleased with herself – and no wonder! Compromising would be a mild description of the product of her evening's work.

The last picture was a real gem. Ann had gone and was no doubt standing at the shoulder of the camera artist, urging him not to miss the final scene, the image of her now destroyed Professor, sprawled out on her bed, legs apart, blissfully asleep, totally naked and utterly abandoned. Not a shred of dignity or concealment left to him. Just the poor duped fool lying there, sated with his little adventure, sleeping it off while the tart he had despised and her unknown assistant were completing the preparations for leading him a dance all-round the houses for who knew how long.

Suppose Elizabeth was ever to see these – or anyone else, for that matter! He was sweating now and not with the heat from the radiator either. Stuffing the photographs back into their envelope, he buried them under the papers in the top drawer of the desk and turned the key in the lock.

So now he knew why Ann had seemed to let him down so lightly. Her words came back to him,

"You won't be laughing on Monday," and, by heaven, she was right. She, on the other hand, in an infinitely strengthened position, could now laugh all she wanted. He cursed himself for a naïve fool for not having realised what he was being set up for. If he had not been so besotted, the odd arrangement with the lights should have given the whole thing away. So much for his brains! If he had thought with them instead of with his guts, he would not have been in the mess he was in now.

Wiping his forehead, he thought over the fated evening and, with hindsight, the whole thing was sticking out a mile. Not only those lights – and had she not said they made the bed like a stage – but her wild variation of mood and response. Her inhibition at first when she knew they were being watched and her anxious desire for quiet when the lights were off. Then, after the third party had gone, the relief must have produced that sudden rush of friendliness, almost affection, which he had been foolish enough to reject so summarily. Those few minutes of triumph were going to cost him dear.

It was not long before he heard the expected knock on the door. In answer to his summons, Ann came in, smiling confidently. Someone was walking past in the corridor and for their benefit, she said in a voice which sounded respectful but was in fact full of irony,

"Someone said you wanted to see me, Professor."

"Yes, come in, close the door."

"Well, what did you think of my little present?"

She sat on the edge of the table facing him, lit a cigarette and blew a stream of smoke at the ceiling.

"What am I supposed to think? What would anyone think? I've never seen anything so disgusting and obscene in all my like. How did you work it? You might as well tell me, now you've got me over a barrel."

"I've got other boyfriends besides you, you know."

"You mean you've got boyfriends. Count me out."

"Well, my guy works for a photographer. He took them."

"But how?"

She laughed.

"Oh, it was the oldest trick in the book. Such an awful old trick that I really didn't think it was going to work. He was in the wardrobe."

"All the time?" he asked anxiously, thinking of himself crawling about on the floor.

"No, I let him in when you went to the bathroom. That's why I made you go. He borrowed a smashing modern camera you can hardly hear, but even at that we probably couldn't have done it without that good old bed. The way it creaks, he could most likely have dropped the thing without your hearing. Then he left while you were asleep. My goodness and don't you just sleep! I thought he was taking an awful chance using the flash, 'cos I thought you'd wake up straightaway, but he insisted because he wasn't sure if we'd had enough light. He kept the door half open so he could get out quick, but you were sleeping like a baby and we got a nice lot. Isn't that one of you on your own a smasher? That's my favourite, that one."

"And now I suppose you want me to pay you some exorbitant amount for the negatives?"

She laughed unpleasantly.

"You should be so lucky! I wouldn't sell them to you for any amount. Think of the fun I can have, just having them!"

For a few minutes, she sat smoking her cigarette, looking thoughtful, flicking ash all over the floor.

"Now," she went on at last. "You've seen my bed-sitter. Not very nice, is it? Pretty awful area for a girl to live in, all alone. Don't you think I should have something better?"

"I'm not paying your rent for you, if that's what you're after."

"Oh, no?"

"No. You can rot in that damned room of yours till kingdom come. Find another idiot, if you want someone to keep you."

He owed himself a little whistling in the dark before the final, inevitable capitulation.

"Oh, come on. You know damn well you've got to. You wouldn't like people to see pictures of your little dingle-dangle, now, would you?"

"You're in 'em as well."

"Yes, but I don't care. You do, that's the difference. Besides, isn't there one of you all alone?"

He looked at her thoughtfully with pursed lips.

"If I was ever to pay someone's rent for them – and I'm not saying I ever would – I should revert to type, and become very old-fashioned and Victorian. I'd expect, in fact, I should demand, the usual conditions. An affectionate, submissive, obedient mistress who'd jump to my command and do exactly what I say, not one who thinks I should do what she says. One who'd know her place, and realise she's got to give me everything I ask for and believe me, I'd ask for a lot. One who's always at my beck and call. Would you do that? You'd have to promise to, before I'd agree."

She looked astonished.

"I've got to hand it to you, you've got a nerve! Do you think I'd do that, when I've got those pictures? Not bloody likely. Besides, there's my boyfriend. He wouldn't like it. Wouldn't like it a bit. He's very jealous, you know. What d'you reckon he thinks of what you've done to me already?
He's not happy. And he's big, you know, bigger than you. He could smash you into the ground, easy."

"Let him pay your rent, then, if that's how he feels."

"Haven't got no rude pics of him, have I?"

"If I gave you fifty pounds, would that keep you quiet?"

She laughed mockingly and flicked her cigarette end into a little sink let into the bench against the wall, where it expired with a tiny hiss.

"Fifty pounds? I thought you Americans were supposed to think big! Fifty pounds! You must be kidding!"

"Well, I'm not giving you anymore. That's more than those pictures are worth, anyway."

"Fifty pounds? I wouldn't sell one of them for that."

"Well, take it or leave it."

She leaned back and ran her hand through her hair, smiling at him with the confidence of one who knew, struggle as he would, the fish would be hers in the end.

"Suppose I just popped a couple of them in an envelope and sent them to your lady-love?"

He inhaled sharply.

"What do you know about her?"

"Elizabeth Ashton-Richards. That's her name, isn't it? I know where she lives. Found her in the phonebook." She put on a lovelorn expression. "I've seen you mooning about after her, gazing at her like a pet spaniel. I could do it, easy. Shall I?"

He glowered at her. The fish was flapping helplessly on the bank.

"Find an apartment," he snarled. "A reasonable one, mind, not some fancy place and I'll think about it…"

"Now you're being sensible. You can give me that fifty pounds you were talking about a minute ago too, just for starters. I'm behind with the rent of my bed-sitter."

"You're not getting fifty pounds and your rent paid! For God's sake!"

"Come on, you've got to give it to me. I need it, or forty anyway."

With a muttered exclamation, he threw five ten pound notes on the desk.

"There. Now get out. I hate the sight of you."

"I'll bet you do. I'll just bet you do, Professor Di Angeli. You'll hate me more, too, before

I'm done with you."

She picked up the money and flounced out, banging the door behind her.

It did not take her very long. Three days later, she was back.

"I've found a flat," she announced, coming into his room right behind him as he was going in himself.

"How much?" he asked resignedly, hanging up his jacket.

She named a figure which was by no means exorbitant, considerably less than he had expected, in fact, in view of the rent of his own flat.

"My boyfriend wanted me to find somewhere posher, but no, I liked this place. I hope it's not too much," she added, with a surprising touch of anxiety. Evidently, she was not yet fully into the role of ruthless extortioner.

"Anything is too much. What do you want me to do, send a cheque to your landlord each month?"

"Oh, no, give it to me, I think," she replied, looking flustered.

"What's wrong? Don't you want him to know you're a thief?"

"I'm not a thief," she replied indignantly.

"A blackmailer, then, which is the same thing, only worse. Why don't you really grind my face? Tell me I've got to take it round to him and say, here's the money for Ann Bone's rent. I've got to pay it for her or she's going to wreck my life for me. Would you like me to do that? I guess you would, because you must feel very proud of yourself. You'd be better off as a hooker. At least, an honest way of earning a living."

"You're a real swine!"

"What did you expect of me? Gratitude?"

"Yeah, why not? Most girls in my position would have just blabbed it all out. At least, I'm giving you the chance of keeping it quiet."

"Well, thank you and goodnight! You're too good to me!"

There was a moment's hostile silence.

"Well, come on, then, are you going to give me the money?"

"Have I a choice? How much do you want right now?"

"Well, look, it's a bit complicated. He wants just the rent for the rest of the month – that's only a week – but I have to pay a deposit, in case I give a wild party and wreck the place, I suppose – " she giggled nervously " – and then pay the next month's rent on the first – and my electricity, of course."

She was trying to look tough and uncompromising again but not succeeding notably.

"Electricity? I've got to pay that as well?"

"Well, you don't get your electricity thrown in with your rent, do you?"

"I pay my own rent," he said, glowering at her. "Well, come on, then. Is it possible to find out how much?"

"I've got it all written down here,"

He looked at the slip of paper she handed him from her lab coat pocket, then in his wallet.

"I haven't got enough here. I'll have to go to the bank at lunchtime. Come back this afternoon."

In fact, he had more than enough to cover the amount, but he thought he might as well give himself the satisfaction of making things as uncomfortable as he could for her. The more she had to sweat for her money, the less she might be inclined to ask for.

"Oh," she said anxiously. "I'd promised to bring it to him at lunch time. If someone else comes along wanting the flat and they've got the cash –"

"Well, you'll just have to take a late lunch and worry about it till then. What time is he going to hold it for you?"

"Two o'clock. No later, he said."

"All right. I'll see you get it on time."

If he didn't, he thought, she might find somewhere else more expensive.

"And make sure you do pay the rent. I'm not paying it twice if you spend the first lot on clothes. I'm going to get a notebook and write down what I've given you, and you're going to countersign it so you can't say you didn't get it. "

"All right."

He could see that this move towards putting things on a more business-like footing bothered her and he was glad he had thought of it. Sitting down at his desk, he began to open his morning mail. Irresolute, she stood there, obviously wanting to say something else. He ignored her.

"Wouldn't you like to come and see the flat, maybe one day next week?" she asked timidly.

"No, thank you."

"I'd like you to."

"Oh, I expect your photographic friend has passed it as suitable. No doubt he's carefully inspected the wardrobe, to make sure it's big enough for him."

"Oh, you are a beast!"

He looked at her out of the corner of his eye and gave a little bitter laugh.

"I'd like you to see it, though," she paused, then went on, a little more boldly. "Why don't you come and warm the bed with me?"

He pushed his chair round sideways from the desk and looked incredulously at her.

"Are you crazy? Are you absolutely, totally insane? I've had sex with you twice and look what it's got me into! I'd sooner cut my hand off."

"Look, there won't be any more of that sort of thing, I promise. My boyfriend – well, I wish we hadn't done it, in a way –"

"You can have my vote on that."

"I mean – oh gosh – I wish things were different with you and me. I wouldn't ever do anything like that to you again, truly, truly."

"Get out!" he snapped.

"I'd like you to see the flat. I like you ever such a lot, I really do. Go on, say you will."

"Well, thank goodness I'm not one of your enemies, if that's the way you treat your friends. Get out!"

Suddenly, without warning, she sat down on his knee and put her arms round his neck.

"Please, please, I really want you to. Shall I let myself get dirty again for you?"

"Get out!" he hissed furiously, right in her face.

"Oh, why won't you be nice to me?" she cried desperately, on the verge of tears.

"Isn't it obvious?"

"Please, Tommy!"

He swore and stood up so fast that she had to clutch at the edge of the desk to avoid falling on the floor.

"If you ever call me that again, I'll break your thieving little neck for you! I've told you already, when you're here you call me Professor Di Angeli, and you don't say it as if you were spitting and when you're anywhere else, you don't call me anything because I shan't be there!"

"Oh – look – I'll tell you what. If you'll come I'll let you do anything you like to me. I shan't stop you."

"I wouldn't dirty my hands even touching you!"

"Oh, but I love you, God help me, I love you!"

She threw her arms round his neck and kissed him on the lips.

Staggered by this unforeseen happening, he put his hands on either side of her waist to push her away from him and at that precise moment, with the accurate timing of a well-rehearsed farce, there was a brisk knock at the door and Jill stepped in.

She always came in like that. It was what he had told her to do.

"Don't wait for me to answer, Jill," he had said, "Just knock and come in."

And why not? There was normally no reason why she shouldn't.

Startled by this sudden intrusion, Ann jumped away from him. Blushing furiously, Jill said,

"Oh, I'm sorry, I didn't – I'll come back later." And she quickly shut the door again.

He turned on Ann in an almost uncontrollable fury.

"You're nothing but trouble to me, you little slut! See what you've done now? Are you satisfied or do you want to do me any more damage? Get out before I throw you out and bounce you three times off your ass up the corridor!"

White-faced with terror at this sudden onslaught, she turned and fled from the room, while he sat down at his desk with his head in his hands, fluently cursing the entire race of women.

Quite some time later, he heard a timid knock and after a hesitation, Jill came in looking embarrassed, carrying a sheaf of papers.

"I'm very sorry. I just wanted to give you these."

She turned to go but he called her back.

"Jill, about what was happening just then –"

He stopped. The prospect of trying to explain seemed impossible. What was he to say? That she had made a pass at him? Did that sound likely?

Jill looked at him with those straightforward, level eyes of hers.

"I'm not a gossip, Professor. And especially not about you and your affairs."

He smiled.

"Perhaps 'affairs' wasn't the best word you could have chosen. That was more in the nature of a momentary lapse. But I appreciate what you've said. Very much. Thank you."

She was a serious girl and didn't often venture to have a joke with him, but she did now.

"If you have momentary lapses like that a lot, perhaps, I should come in here more often! I didn't see a thing. Don't worry about it."

After she had gone, he found he felt better than he had since he had opened that packet of photographs. Dear Jill! Now there was the one woman in his life who never gave him a moment's hassle. When he was out at lunchtime, he decided, he was going to buy her a box of chocolates. Was that likely to be misinterpreted? Oh, what the hell. He was going to do it anyway. She had dispersed the unpleasant feeling left by Ann's visit and that in itself was worth a token of appreciation.

Chapter 15

He was still working hard on his other problem. Elizabeth seemed totally recalcitrant. He telephoned her endless times and spoke to her, or tried to, each time she came into the Department, but to no avail. She never seemed to have any time free for him and whenever he asked her to go out with him, he simply met with one excuse or another, or just a blank refusal.

However, one lunchtime, a few days after that encounter with Ann, as he was passing through the entrance hall on his way out for his lunch, he saw a notice on the notice board advertising a performance of Die Fledermaus, to be given by the University Operatic Society. Now there was an inspiration. If she liked Gilbert and Sullivan, perhaps she liked Strauss as well. Lunch forgotten, he turned back to his room to ring her immediately.

To his surprise, she answered the phone herself straight away and to his even greater surprise, she agreed to his suggestion with delight.

"Oh yes, Tom, that would be wonderful. I'd just love to see it."

Hastily collecting his wits, as he had been prepared for nothing more than a 'no' of one sort or another, he asked,

"Which evening would suit you best? They're performing Thursday, Friday and Saturday."

"Oh, I think the Friday."

"That's the first of December. Good. I'll see about tickets right away, then. Oh, Elizabeth, I'm so glad you can come. It'll be wonderful to see you again."

"I'll look forward to it, Tom. Goodbye."

As she put the phone down – it was an extension which stood on her white dressing table, and happened to be connected because she had been speaking to Sarah just before Tom had called her – she looked at herself in the mirror and smiled with satisfaction. How humbly grateful his voice had sounded when she had said she would come and how hard, but unsuccessfully, he had tried to hide his incredulous surprise! There was nothing like keeping men guessing, she thought, to have them attentively dancing on her string. Now, Reggie was getting much too complaisant. Only last week, he had refused to take her to a dance because he was playing in a badminton tournament, of all things. She was not going to stand for that sort of thing at all. He thought he had safely seen Tom off, but he was going to find out he was wrong. No doubt, he would want to take her to this Strauss thing – it was just the sort of boring rubbish he was always dragging her off to – 'improving her mind, giving her an appreciation of good music' and all that sort of twaddle. Well, Reggie was about to find he wasn't the only pebble on the beach and, if it did not bring him quickly to heel, he might find he was the one swept away by the tide.

In any case, Tom was nice, if one could overlook the tiresome fact that he was an American. He had affectionate gentle eyes and such a soft pleasant polite way of speaking, if you could forget that awful accent. At least, he refrained from using any of the more appalling Americanisms and when he was with her, he was always so attentive, unlike Reggie who was getting very off-hand lately and treating her as if he was quite sure of her feelings. Well, he would find he had better think again. Elizabeth did not like being taken for granted – not by any means.

The telephone's sharp ring broke in on her thoughts, making her jump. It was Reggie.

"Hello, Elizabeth. How are you?"

"Well enough," she replied coolly. "And you? Still stiff from your badminton?"

"Stiff? Me? I never get stiff. I'm make sure I stay too fit for that. Have you seen that the U.O.S. are doing Die Fledermaus?"

"I had heard."

"Lovely music. You'll like it. We'll go on Friday. I've got a couple of tickets."

Oh, have you, indeed, she thought. *Taking me for granted again. Well, look out!*

"Sorry, Reggie, I'm booked to go with someone else."

"Not that wretched American again?"

"What particular wretched American did you have in mind?"

"Oh, you know the one – what's his name – Di Angeli or something fanciful like that."

"Yes, I am going with Tom, if it's any concern of yours."

"Any concern of mine? Elizabeth, what are you trying to do to me? I thought we had an understanding? I thought we were going to get married sooner or later? Don't you feel anything for me, Elizabeth, that you happily go out with anyone who happens to ask you?"

"Don't be so insulting, Reggie! Of course, I don't go out with anyone who happens to ask me. I just like Tom. Can't I have other friends besides you? Anyway, I've never said I was going to marry you."

"I think he's more than a friend. He kissed you at your birthday party, deliberately right in front of me. Twice."

"Oh, Reggie, don't be such a prig. Lots of people kissed me at my birthday party. People often do, when they give you a present. David, for instance, and Jack and –"

"Not the way he did it, though. He flaunted it, right under my nose and then he grinned at me in that go-to-hell way that he does. I could have thumped him – I would have if it hadn't been at your Mother's house."

That would have been fun, she thought.

"Oh, Reggie, don't be such a fool. You're so insanely jealous, you make me tired."

"Of course, I'm jealous. Don't you know how much I love you? I'm absolutely nuts about you. I'm jealous of anyone who comes near you. Please don't treat me like this."

"Look, Reggie, calm down, will you? You're getting hysterical over nothing. I'll go with you to something else, but please stop going on."

"Going on? Getting hysterical?" he shouted. "Elizabeth, don't you understand…"

"Oh, I'm not going to talk to you when you're in this silly mood. Phone me when you're feeling more civilised. Goodbye." And she put the receiver down, shutting off his protests.

She smiled at herself again in the mirror. If that did not bring Reggie round to dance attendance on her again, she was mistaken in her man. She looked at her watch. Lunch would be just about ready. Time to go downstairs. Smoothing her hair down with her hands, she rose and left the room.

Meanwhile, Tom had returned to the notice board to find out where he could get tickets and was just heading for the department where the Operatic Society secretary worked, when he suddenly had a thought. Ever since he had agreed with Elizabeth to make it the first of December, he had had a nagging in the back of his mind. He felt that date rang a bell and he suddenly remembered – Ann's rent, of course! With Ann's rent to pay as well as his own, he was going to have to be more careful than he had been accustomed to being for some time. Elizabeth had expensive tastes and it would be too humiliating to find he could not take her out because he could not afford to. He would have to make some fresh calculations, but the treasury should run to the tickets and a little supper afterwards without too many problems. He wondered, not for the first time, how it would all end.

He decided when the day came, that, as he had a lot to do at work, to take his best suit, a clean shirt and his electric shaver with him, and change after work instead of going home first. He told the caretaker he would be in the building until about half past six and, at half past five, the caretaker knocked at his door, told him everyone else had gone and that he was about to go too, and would he pull the outer door closed behind him and make sure that it locked. Tom agreed and went on with his writing.

About ten minutes later, he was surprised to hear quiet footsteps in the corridor followed by a knock at his door. It was Ann.

"What are you doing here at this time of night? I thought you'd gone long ago."

"Well, I haven't. I heard you say you was working late so I stayed in the bog till everyone had gone. I wanted to see you."

"Well, you're seeing me. What do you want?"

"You," she replied simply.

"Me?"

"Yes, you. I made up my mind I was going to have you again and, if you won't come to my flat, it'll have to be here. We won't be interrupted. Everyone's gone home, including Madam Jill."

"Didn't I make it abundantly, crystal clear to you the last time you were in here, that if there was one thing I was never, never going to do again, it was that, with you? I thought I'd got my point across, pretty forcibly."

She smiled. Having been brought up for all her twenty-two years with a father who was violent when drunk, and boorish and argumentative when sober, she knew just when male anger was to be avoided at all costs and when it could be shrugged off as 'him going on again'. She had been alarmed by Tom's fury before but she had the measure of him now and she had come to understand that despite the show of aggressiveness and sophistication that he liked to assume with her, he was in reality as harmless as a pussy-cat, and as susceptible as a teenager. It was this latter attribute that she meant to work on now.

"Oh, that's what you say, but I don't pay no attention to that. You do talk ever such a lot, don't you, Professor? But I've seen the way you look at me when I'm in the lab. If I was to say, 'come on, boy, let's go then', you'd have your trousers off before I could cough."

He put his hand over his mouth and looked at the ceiling.

"You are coarse, aren't you?"

It was true what she said, though. Impossible to deny it. Ever since the initial heat of anger over the photographs and her use of them had abated, he had found himself watching her covertly as she moved about the place, and thinking with a foolish and perverse longing of their encounters. Now, as she let go of the door handle and moved across the room towards him, he felt his breath coming a little quicker and a pulse in his temple made itself noticeable. She was, despite the fact that it was a cold early winter day outside, wearing a thin cotton dress and apparently no bra.

"I say what I think. I'm getting to know you, anyway. You're getting the urge again, aren't you? You'd like to go on another of your little pub crawls, wouldn't you?"

"Well, what's it to you if I am?" He was worried. Was it really that obvious? It was true, though. His thoughts about Ann, combined with what had been up to now a firm intention to have nothing further to do with her in that way, had sent his mind off seeking alternatives again.

She pushed her hands into the pockets of her dress, making it abundantly clear that she was wearing no bra.

"If you were to have it off with me, here and now, it would save you a fortune in beer, wouldn't it?"

"This sudden concern for my finances is rather out of character. I don't want to, as you say, have it off with you, here, now, or ever. Is that clear?"

"Why don't you try me?" she said, sitting on his knee and putting her arms round his neck. "I don't think you'll tip me off this time."

He closed his eyes, seized with overwhelming longing.

"How long since you last had a bath?"

"Not since you came to my bedsitter that time. You might have noticed before, if you hadn't been so busy shouting and making a scene. Keeps my electricity bill down too. Come on, say yes. I like it with you."

"Doesn't that boyfriend of yours have something to say about that?"

"Him?" she said with contempt. "He's just a great ape. Doesn't have any idea of what girls like. But you – well, it's different with you. You're nice." She tugged at his tie, took it off and unfastened his collar button. "Come on, gorgeous, loosen up a little."

"I'm not stopping here with you," he said, but his eyes were still closed and those guts of his were again acting as traitors to his brain. "I've got to go out."

"Ah yes, the lovely Elizabeth. Well, you won't be handicapped, will you? You don't have it off with her, do you?"

"Certainly not," he snapped. "My relationship with Elizabeth is rather different to the one I have with you – such as it is. I may not be handicapped, but I may be late."

"Would she tear you off a strip? Would she shout at you? Would she slap your face?"

"Certainly not. She's much too well bred. A lady, unlike you."

She said a rude word and set to work on his shirt buttons.

"Will you leave me alone? I've got to go out."

"Not yet. You're not going anywhere until I say so."

She put her arms round his neck and kissed him again. He shook his head, but he was responding to her, despite himself. Putting his arms round her, he said, "Leave me alone, you bitch, can't you? Do you want everything I've got?"

"Every single thing."

She hunched her shoulders and looked in his face, prodding him in the chest with her finger till he opened his eyes, and looked back at her.

"You hate me, don't you, but you still want me. You want me so much it hurts. Hurts down here, doesn't it?" She put her hand on him. "Oh yes, I can feel that it hurts. I'll bet you hate yourself too, for wanting me so much."

"Leave me alone, you bitch."

"You're getting a bit boring. Can't you think of anything else to call me? I can think of lots of things I'd like to call you."

"What have I ever done to you?"

"Not a thing, sweetheart, but you can't get away from me and, for all your brains, there's not a damn thing you can do about it. Why don't you take my dress off? You want to, don't you?" She pressed herself against his bare chest. He put his hand up, found the zip at the back of her dress and pulled it down. Then he slipped it off her shoulders and found that not only had she on no bra, but she was entirely naked underneath it.

"Surprised you, didn't it?"

Standing up, she let the dress fall to the floor, sat down at his feet, took his hands and pulled him down on the floor with her. Without any resistance, he came. Then she lay on him, kissing him and squirming about until she had him in a frenzy of desire.

"Will you let me get at you," he gasped.

"Not till I'm ready." She got hold of a handful of his hair and pulled. "Not till I'm ready, understand?"

"Ouch! Let go! You little slut, what are you trying to do?"

"To remind you of where your place is, lover-boy. You do what I say and when I say, and you make it good."

"I shan't be able to make it good if you won't let me do it soon."

"Go on then, get going. I'm staying on top, though."

"No you're not. There's limits to what I'm going to take from you."

A brief struggle then –

"Oh, oh, what have you got there, a cucumber?"

"Serves you right for making me wait so long."

They squirmed about on the floor, fighting as much as making love, till they ended up halfway under the table with honours even on both sides.

"Well," he said, when peace was finally restored. "Did you get what you came for?"

"What about my rent?"

"You'll be found dead in a ditch one day, you bitch."

"Well, they'll all know who done it, anyway."

"Rent! I don't know how you've got the nerve!"

"If you offset the beer and petrol you've saved, it'll hardly come to anything."

"I don't have that much trouble finding girls."

"I should think half of them could hardly believe their luck."

"Thanks for the compliment. Can I get up now?"

"God, yes. I'm being flattened."

"Choose someone your own size next time, then."

He extricated himself from under the table, banging his head on the edge as he did so and started to straighten himself up a little. She watched, still sitting naked on the floor.

"How I'd like to tell the lovely Elizabeth what you get up to in your spare time. Having it off on the floor with the girl who washes the test tubes! It'd shock the pants off her!"

"Don't be so vulgar! And you stay away from her or I really will break your neck."

"You're never going to get anywhere with her, you know. She doesn't really like you."

"You're an expert, I take it?"

"Of course, I am. You don't like me, she doesn't like you and it's a bloody stupid triangle. All it needs is for her and me to set up home together, and the whole thing would be completely nuts."

"Will you put your clothes on and push off?"

"If you like. Don't forget my rent, though."

"I'll give it to you tomorrow."

"Putting it off again? Oh, I get it. You're expecting her to take you to the cleaners, I suppose."

"Not at all. I just like to know I'm covered."

She giggled.

"Which is more than you were a few minutes ago. Zip me up. Will you?"

"Oh, get out, for goodness' sake and leave me alone."

He couldn't help laughing himself as he said it.

"All right, sweetheart. I'll go. I wonder what she calls you."

"She calls me Tom, what else?"

"She might call you a few other things if… all right, I'm going, I'm going."

As he advanced on her, she fled from the room, laughing like a child. He found himself smiling after her and reflected that, if he was not very careful, he might actually get to like her. Then he thought of that envelope of photographs, carefully hidden in a drawer in his desk and of what she might do with them. The feeling quickly evaporated. He looked at his watch. Quarter past six! Good heavens, and here he was, unshaven, unchanged and no doubt looking extremely disreputable too!

A frantic twenty minutes or so later, he was starting his car, looking much more like his usual trim and elegant self. Ann seemed to have disappeared but as he stopped at the gates of the campus before turning into the main road, there she was, waving to him from the pavement, with that all-too-familiar mocking smile on her face. Suppressing a desire to make a rude gesture at her, he merely lifted his hand briefly in reply and swept off to meet Elizabeth.

Elizabeth, despite her expectations, found him not entirely satisfactory company that evening. He seemed a little vague and distracted as if he had something on his mind. This puzzled her as, usually when he was with her, his attention was completely centred on her. Could it be that she had played him along too much, she wondered? Perhaps, she had better be more accessible, at least for a time. The thought of having an admirer, even one who was well down the list, slip through her net, was not agreeable to her.

Chapter 16

"Mind you, Christmas parties aren't what they once were," said Robert, "I don't know if people worry about getting drunk in front of the boss, or about being breathalysed on the way home, but things just don't go with the swing they once did."

"It was fun last year, though," said John, one of Professor Ashton-Richard's technicians. "When that chap Ed Parkinson was here. Do you remember him doing his Red Indian rain dance for us?"

"Yes, he was a lot of fun. I miss him. It worked too, didn't it? Wettest winter for twenty years, or something like that," said Sally.

"And didn't a few people bless him when it was still raining when he left in March?"

"What we want," said Robert sagely, "is to get the scientific staff stoned to the eyeballs, while the technicians stay… well, not exactly sober, but fit enough to watch the fun. Get some of these old fogies of Professors dancing the cha-cha with the washers-up. In particular, I want to get Chief Sitting Bull sloshed, so he'll kiss Jill under the mistletoe."

"Quiet!" said Jill with anxious emphasis. "Remember, walls have ears in this place."

"Oh yes," said Robert, laughing. "We were talking in the lab one day when he came pussy-footing in and made us all jump out of our skins. I often wonder just how much he heard."

"I'll tell you how much he heard, the lot."

"How do you know?"

"Because, the next time I went to his room, he produced a feather from somewhere, stuck it in his hair and said, 'welcome to my teepee, number one squaw'. I didn't know where to put my face!"

"Doesn't like being sent up, does our Jill," said Robert, giving her a friendly hug.

"It's not that so much, but I spent the rest of the day trying to remember what I'd said. I'm sure I wasn't being very polite."

"Well, it can't have been too awful. After all, he's still speaking to you. Serves him right for sneaking in in his creepers, or creeping in in his sneakers, or whatever it is he calls them."

"Anyway, he's not going to kiss me under the mistletoe. He's got better fish to fry."

"Ah yes, the boss's daughter. I suppose she's going to be there."

"You bet. Never misses a chance to show herself off to the chaps," said one of the girls tartly.

"Well, he's welcome to that dame. I'd just as soon go out with a marble statue," said John.

"Yes, all show and no substance," said his crony Roger.

Jill sat with the tips of three fingers touching her slightly parted lips, dreaming of being kissed by the man she would have best loved to do it. He was not much taller than she, so he would not have to bend his dark head down very far to reach her. She thought of his face coming close to hers, of his soft, slightly full lips touching hers. She imagined his skin a little bristly, his arm round her shoulders, holding her gently, but so firmly that she would feel quite melted and weak. She touched the tip of her middle finger with her tongue and the salty taste brought her back to reality. A nice fool she was, sitting here daydreaming about things that would never happen! An even nicer fool, to have broken with a pleasant, easy-going boy like Richard, to whom she might now have been engaged. She had thought the world of him, before the other man had come along. People often said she was sensible, but surely, the sensible thing would be to make up with Richard, who would have her back any time, and try and forget this stupid infatuation? She spread out her hands on her lap. Square, capable hands, the nails cut short, the skin rough and stained with laboratory work. Useful hands, workmanlike hands, not the kind a man would dream about or want to kiss. She was Jill and functional, rather than glamorous, was the word to describe her. What hope? None at all.

Robert was saying, as she came back to earth,

"Anyway, this isn't getting us anywhere. What *are* we going to give this lot to drink?"

"If you want to get the scientific staff stoned to the eyeballs without their knowing it, I know just the thing," said John. "I was at a party last month and the chap who was giving it made some stuff he called 'dynamite punch'. It tasted like fruit juice but it had a kick like the proverbial mule. He let some of his special friends into the secret, and we spent the evening watching everyone else getting higher and higher. The party ended with the floor littered with bodies, but everyone had a great time before they passed out."

"Sounds just the thing. Have you got the recipe?"

"Too right I have. I wasn't going to let a thing like that pass me by."

"Well, tell me what's needed and I'll see about it. I don't suppose anyone's got a punch bowl?"

"You're joking, of course."

"We've got two of those big yellow mixing bowls in our flat," said Jill. "I don't know why they've given us two, they must think we're terribly domesticated. We never do any baking anyway. They're not very pretty but they hold a lot, and I suppose we could cover them with some foil and decorate them with a few bits of holly. I could go home and get them at lunchtime."

"Just the job. Have you got a ladle as well?"

"Yes, I'll bring that too."

"Good. Well, the vital thing is to make sure that the technical staff know what's what. Is everyone here?"

"No. There are two or three who must be still in the labs."

"Well, we'll let them know and everyone must be sworn to secrecy. Anyone who spills the beans to any of the Profs will be sent to Coventry till next Christmas."

Jill and Sally set about their appointed tasks. As they went, they discussed who best to tell. Some of the domestic staff who they thought could be trusted to keep the secret they put in the know. As they approached their own lab, the question arose as to whether to tell Ann. Jill refused to give any opinion. She had come to heartily loath Ann. She had seen, when they had not realised she was around, the insolent and disrespectful manner with which she treated Tom, and had noted the inexplicable way in which he seemed to defer to her instead of putting her firmly in her place. She treated him with due respect in public and private, and she certainly failed to see why Ann, of all people, should not do the same. She would have been inclined to say nothing about the punch, simply because she never wanted to say anything to Ann about anything at all, so she withdrew from the whole affair and left Sally to decide. Sally felt, on the whole, that Ann slightly drunk was a better proposition than Ann very drunk, so she warned her that the punch was going to be very strong, but told her no more of the story, hoping for the best that she would not discuss it with anyone.

Someone else, too, was worried about the prospect of a slightly drunk Ann. Tom knew that Elizabeth was coming to the party and he was rather dreading an encounter between the two women, as he never knew what Ann was likely to do. He had no reason to suppose for a moment that she was particularly reliable and the thought that he could pay her rent and do her bidding from now to kingdom come, without the slightest assurance that one day if she felt like a little gossip, or got a little drunk, his secrets would not become public knowledge without a second thought on her part, meant he was never entirely easy in his mind. And where was a more ideal setting for a girl to get gossipy or drunk, than at a Christmas party? He had a very strong inclination not to go, but he realised that it would be better if he did, so that, if any trouble looked like blowing up, he could at least be there to try to nip it in the bud.

Despite what he had resolved about making her sweat for her money, he had given her, her end-of-December rent early and he had not demanded a signature for it either. In addition, hating himself for doing it, he had given her a Christmas present, hoping to keep her sweet. Her knowing smile as she took it had done absolutely nothing to soothe his feelings. He felt he was permanently on his hands and knees when she was around, and he hated the feeling and hated her too for making him feel like that. None of this, though, made it possible for him to ignore the powerful sexual attraction that she held for him – a situation which she understood only too well and intended to exploit to the full.

At lunchtime, all work was suspended and everyone gathered in the library, a handsome room, long and lofty, which a benefactor had refurnished about ten years ago with solid oak furniture, tables with chairs for readers, all of which had now been moved to against the walls where, covered with white sheets, they acted as bars and buffets. The two mixing bowls, artistically decorated by Sally, stood ready, filled with Robert and John's devil's brew, destined, they hoped, to be the downfall of many. Paper garlands were pinned along, hanging down in colourful swags before the serried ranks of solemn books which lined the walls. Glasses and bottles, corkscrews and openers were put at the ready, and, at the other table, plates of food, salad, cold meat, cheese dips, crisps, sausage rolls and all the other necessaries for a proper Christmas celebration. Robert took personal charge of hanging a huge bunch of mistletoe from a lamp just inside the door, and proceeded himself to kiss Jill, Sally and any other girl he could get hold of under it.

Robert poured a glass of sherry for each of the helpers and with a toast of, "Happy Christmas and here's to the downfall of the ruling classes," everything was set for the party to begin.

Within about half an hour, various members of the Department began to drift in, in ones and twos, remarking appropriately on the technicians' efforts. It took Robert a little time to persuade anyone to try his punch, but once he had succeeded with one brave soul, others had a taste and soon the level in the first bowl was falling rapidly, to a point where John was getting ready to bear it off to some secret place where he had the necessary ready for replenishing it.

As tends to happen at parties of working colleagues, there was a certain dichotomy at first, with the technicians in a knot at one end of the bar, the scientific staff in two or three groups dotted around the room and trying, in general unsuccessfully, not to talk shop, but as the party spirit, or maybe the punch, began to take hold, people began to wander about and speak to each other.

Professor Ashton-Richards came up to Jill who was still anxiously watching for the arrival of her Professor.

"Marvellous party, Jill. You technicians have really surpassed yourselves. You've done magnificently."

Professor Ashton-Richards prided himself on knowing everyone in his Department by name.

"Thank you, sir. It's always fun, doing it."

"Tell me, how are you getting on with your new Professor? Of course, he's hardly new now, been here since summer. I expect you're well used to each other's ways by now."

"Oh yes, we get on very well."

"Glad to hear it. He's a very gifted young man, highly intelligent and sometimes one finds that such men can be a little difficult to get on with socially, perhaps too demanding, or even lacking in common sense," he finished with a smile.

"Oh, I don't find that at all," Jill replied enthusiastically, "He's very easy to work with. Very pleasant indeed."

"Good. I know the Chief thinks highly of him. One of the brighter ornaments of the Department."

Jill responded with a pleased smile and glanced towards the door again. Professor Ashton-Richards leaned towards her and said confidentially,

"I know Professor Di Angeli thinks highly of you, Jill. He told me you're one of the best technicians he's ever had, including the ones he had in the United States."

"Well, that's very flattering, but really, I only do what I'm told."

"There are ways and ways of doing that, my dear. A good technician can be like an extra right hand."

Jill smiled again and mentally ascribed his flattering words mainly to the large glass of punch he was holding.

A few minutes later, Tom appeared. He paused in the doorway and looked around, then headed for the buffet to get himself something to eat before approaching the bar.

Sensible man, Jill thought approvingly. *Lacking in common sense, indeed!*

She watched anxiously as Robert ladled him out a large glass of punch – she felt sure it was considerably bigger than he had given anyone else. He tasted it, made what was obviously an approving remark and vanished from her sight among the crowd. It seemed no time at all before he returned for a second shot and Jill decided that, at whatever risk of disapproval from her colleagues, she must try to warn him. She did not mind anyone else being caught out, but she did not want to see her boss acting in an undignified manner. So she went in search of him and encountered him a few minutes later, well down the second glass.

"Hello, Jill, aren't you having any of the punch? It's very good."

"You want to be careful of that stuff," she said quietly, glancing round to make sure she was not being overheard. "It's stronger than it seems. I don't know what Robert's put in it."

"Oh, I think it's pretty innocuous," he said in an ominously cheerful voice, "You really should try some."

"Well, I think you should stick to what you can be sure of."

Someone dug an elbow into the middle of her back and, as she looked round, she saw Robert carrying a tray of glasses. He gave her a warning look. Tom leaned his head down towards her and said quietly,

"I'll take your advice in the lab, Jill dear, but not here." He tapped her gently on the nose with the tip of his finger, smiled at her and turned away.

Jill shook her head despairingly at his retreating back and went to find Robert.

"I'll murder you, Robert. What on earth did you put in that stuff?"

"What's wrong, your precious boss getting squiffed? I think you've got a crush on him, you know."

"No I haven't. I just don't think it's fair – on any of them."

"You didn't say anything this morning."

"No I didn't and I wish I had, now."

"Oh, I say, look who's here. Golden girl herself."

Jill turned round. Framed in the door stood Elizabeth, looking, as always, breathtakingly beautiful. She wore a close-fitting gold coloured dress and brown high-heeled sandals. Round her shoulders was a short jacket of white very fluffy fur, almost like swansdown, and her hair, smoothly brushed and curled in at the ends, gleamed under the lights like silk. Jill saw Tom go over to greet her, inches ahead of the field and conduct her to the improvised bar. She declined the punch, and had a gin and tonic instead.

They stood together talking for a few minutes, Tom's gaze riveted to her face, while her eyes wandered round the room, looking to see who else was there. Then she excused herself and went to talk to someone else. He watched her as she went, absently refilling his glass from the punch bowl, letting quite a lot of it dribble over the edge. She moved on to talk to someone else, while he watched, licking his fingers. Then, unable to stand it any longer, he swallowed a large mouthful of punch and set off in pursuit.

"Time for some music, I think," said Robert to John. "Have you got your cassette player?"

"Right here. Where's the nearest socket?"

He plugged in and put on some lively dance music. Soon, a small group was dancing while the others moved closer to the walls leaving the centre of the room clear. Tom had lost track of Elizabeth, but after a few moments, saw her dancing with one of the young research assistants, a lad of about twenty, who gave the impression that he felt several inches off the ground.

Tom, who was beginning to wonder why he felt quite so high, and was trying to remember how many drinks he had had, took up a station near the buffet and watched them.

Suddenly, he heard himself hailed by an American voice. He had been in Britain now so long that to unexpectedly hear an American accent was as startling to him as it would be to the average Briton.

"Hi, Tom! Say, what goes on here? This is the liveliest party I've seen for months! The joint is really jumping!"

"Oh, hi, Paul, good to see you. What brings you here?"

"Came in to see one of your profs and what do I find? Everyone having a whale of a time. What on earth is everyone drinking? What have you got in there?"

"Oh, it's some punch. Have you tried some? It's very good, but I'm beginning to think it's pretty strong. The technicians made it."

Paul looked horrified.

"You never risked drinking something the technicians had made? If they're anything like our lot, it's probably got marijuana in it."

"I'm beginning to think you're right," said Tom, looking ruefully into his glass.

"You should have stuck to Scotch. Are any of them drinking it?"

Tom looked round the room, then shook his head.

"That's what I thought. Look at your chief! He'll have a heart attack if he goes on like that."

"I think I'll have a few crisp words with a certain young man in the morning."

"I doubt if you'll be capable of it." Paul took Tom's glass and sniffed the contents. "My God! It smells lethal! There are going to be a few headaches around here tomorrow." Tom glowered at Robert, but that young man was too occupied to catch his eye. "Anyhow, now I see you, how are you making out with Miss Ashton-Richards, if you're capable of remembering, that is. You told me you'd got as far as taking her out a few times, several weeks ago, but I haven't seen you since."

"Oh, pretty well," said Tom, looking around for her. She was no longer dancing, but he could not see where she was. "It comes and goes, you know. Sometimes she's friendly, sometimes not."

"Hmm. Well. You seem to be getting on better than most."

"Oh, she's a lovely girl," said Tom, with an expansive gesture that missed Paul's glass by a hairsbreadth. "You've noticed, of course. That face, that figure, that hair – absolutely marvellous. What more could one ask, you may say. Well, between you and me, Paul, there is one thing. Don't nudge me like that, you'll spill my drink. Brains, Paul. What the lady has in looks, she lacks in brains. *Will* you stop nudging me? The original dumb blonde, is what you might call her. The brainless wonder."

"Shut up!" Paul hissed emphatically in his ear.

Then, from the other side, he heard a quiet voice say,

"Well, now I know what you really think of me, don't I? The truth can be very interesting, when you get it plain and unvarnished."

Elizabeth, her cheeks very pink, her eyes bright and looking close to tears, tossed her head, and walked purposefully from the room, leaving Tom blinking and trying to collect his wits.

"Boy, I think you just blew it," said Paul, not unsympathetically, but Tom heard not a word of it. He was already halfway to the door. He had put in a lot of work on Elizabeth and he was not going to let it be wasted for a momentary indiscretion if he could possibly help it. As he went, he shook his head, trying to clear it.

When he got out of the crowded library, she was already several yards down the corridor, he heels tapping briskly on the shiny dark brown vinyl flooring. The hem of her skirt flicked from side to side as she walked and the little fur jacket, bouncing on her shoulders, expressed her feelings as plainly as words.

"Elizabeth!" he called, but to no response

He caught up a little, but she ignored him and walked on.

"Elizabeth!"

"Leave me alone!"

As they reached the door of his room, he drew level with her, caught her firmly by the arm and drew her in. Letting go of her, he put his back against the door. His head was clear now.

"Let me out! Come away from that door and let me out! I'm not staying here with you!"

He shook his head slowly, saying nothing. She stared at him incredulously. "Let me out at once or I'll –"

"Scream?"

"If necessary."

"And just how far do you think that will take you, my sweet? That crowd in there are making such a noise that they wouldn't notice if you dropped a bomb and most of them are so drunk that they wouldn't care either."

"You're drunk too."

"I was, I admit, when I said what I said, but I'm not, now."

"Well, let me out, then."

"Not till *you've* said what *you* want to say."

"I don't want to say anything to you ever again."

"Oh, I think you do. I think you could go on for at least ten minutes without stopping. Come on, let's have it, all of it. Don't spare me. We may as well have it all at once, then we can talk and see if we can't put things right."

She turned her head away and looked out of the window her lips pressed tightly together.

"Come on, say it," he urged.

"All right, I will, then," she said, turning back to face him, her eyes bright with anger. "I think you're the rudest, most ill-mannered man I've ever met, standing there discussing me with your friend as if I was some two penny-halfpenny pick-up! And as for what you said, I found it very insulting and hurtful. I may not be very clever, I don't pretend to be, but there's more to life than brains, you know." She stopped for a moment and turned her head away, to let her voice steady and to blink back the tears from her eyes.

"Any more?"

"Quite a lot. You're presumptuous. You think you just have to wave your hand and any female within a hundred yards will fall at your feet. Look at the way you went on, kissing me and taking all sorts of liberties, that first evening you were at our house at Park Row, as if you only had to ask and you would be given. As if I had been waiting all my life for you to come along and carry me off. You're like that all the time, too pushy and – and –"

"Brash?"

"Brash," she echoed and continued relentlessly. "You just have no idea whatsoever how to behave in polite society. Just like every American I've ever met, in fact."

"Ah," he said with satisfaction. "Now we're really getting down to it, aren't we?"

"Perhaps, we are. You all ought to be made to stay in your horrible country until you know how to behave in decent company."

"And just how are we supposed to learn that, if we're never allowed any? Are you going to send missionaries to the poor benighted natives?"

"What a good idea, as long as I don't have to go."

He said nothing. There was a long pause.

"Finished? Run out of ideas?"

She disdained to reply.

"Well, I expect you'd like to have your prejudices reinforced. Nothing in this world like being proved right, is there? Let me see now, what can I do for you? Well, I don't just happen to have my gun with me right now, but how about this, for starters?"

He took three packets of chewing gum from his jacket pocket and, without leaving his vantage point at the door, tossed them on to the table beside her. Actually, he had bought them for Ann at her request and forgotten to give them to her, but no matter. The effect was what he wanted and he achieved it. Elizabeth looked at them disdainfully and turned her head to the window again.

"Of course, there's a couple of rival gangs both on the lookout for me too, I wouldn't feel at home without that. One lot are drug-pushers and the other feel I've muscled in on their protection racket. Well, the result of all this is that the Home Office are about to start proceedings to deport me as an undesirable alien, which will be a little embarrassing, as the FBI are gunning for me as well."

She was having a shade of difficulty controlling the corners of her mouth.

"Then I must have told you, I simply must have, about the three times I've been divorced? Oh, did I forget? Well, I've got so used to it that it often slips my mind. That's the reason for all the crime, of course, to keep up with the alimony. If you only knew what it was like, my dear! I had the brother of wife No. 2 in here yesterday, demanding –"

"Oh Tom, stop it, you are a fool!" she cried, shaking with laughter.

"That's more like it," he said, stepping away from the door and taking her arm in his. "Come over here and sit down."

Since Ann had taken to sitting on his knee, he had acquired another chair hoping that, if there was something else to sit on, she might not sit on him. He rather regretted it now as, had it not been there, he might have been able to persuade Elizabeth to sit on his knee which would have been much nicer. Somehow, though, it was not something he felt she might do spontaneously.

She perched on the chair and he drew the other close to it.

"Now, Elizabeth, will you listen if I apologise?"

"Oh, Tom, there's nothing to apologise for. I can't even remember what you said."

He leaned forward and kissed her cheek.

"Say you forgive me anyway."

"Of course, I forgive you, darling."

"Good. I'm glad. I couldn't bear to think of such a foolish remark coming between us."

"Please don't think any more about it, Tom."

He was about to kiss her again when she suddenly half rose and, to his astonishment and delight, his lovely delectable Elizabeth was sitting right there on his lap.

She was a good deal heavier than Ann, he guessed perhaps approaching a hundred and thirty pounds compared to Ann's rather slight hundred or so. She was several inches taller than Ann too, in fact, standing up, he and she were almost eye-to-eye, so she did not fit him so neatly as Ann. He had to stretch up quite a long way to kiss her, but how infinitely worth it when he got there!

"Am I too heavy for you, darling?"

"Of course not. I could sit here and hold you all day, and it would be no strain at all. This is so delightful. Perhaps, we could find somewhere more private later. Meanwhile, will you do something very sweet for me?"

"What's that, Tom darling?"

"Will you come back to the library with me so people can see you've forgiven me? Quite frankly, I want to make all those young men jealous."

Just before they re-entered the library, he put his arm round her waist with a proprietorial air and made a point of steering her over to talk to Paul, whose expression when he saw them was quite priceless.

Over by the bar, Robert said,

"Are you all right, Jill? You've gone very pale suddenly."

"Yes, I'm all right," she said with a catch in her voice. "Give me a whisky, please, Robert."

"I thought you didn't drink spirits?"

"I do just now."

She turned her back to the room and stood with her head to the side, her face only partly visible to him. Something had clearly upset her. He poured her a stiffest whisky, added a splash of water and handed it to her. Then he looked to see what she had been looking at a moment ago. The group was still there at the other side of the room, the two men, one dark, one fair, in their dark suits conversing with the tall attractive woman in her bright clothes. When he looked back questioningly at Jill, she had already swallowed half the contents of the glass.

"Hey, steady on, that stuff's strong, you know."

"Let me sit on the chair behind you, Robert. Just stay where you are."

She sat down and he stood shielding her from the room. When he looked over his shoulder at her a moment later, she was wiping her eyes with her handkerchief. He liked Jill despite her decisive, downright manner and he felt concerned.

"Cheer up, old girl. It's not that bad. As they say, it might never happen."

"It has happened, probably several weeks ago," she said indistinctly, burying her face in the handkerchief. "Oh Robert, Robert, what am I going to do?"

Chapter 17

There was a light shower of snow falling, the flakes drifting gently down through the still air from a heavy, grey sky. The lawn outside the window of Tom's room was gradually acquiring a thin carpet of white as were the trees in the park beyond. The roof of the red-brick animal house too was turning white, the whole scene taking on that fairy-tale loveliness that only snow can give. A few people were walking about in the park, leaving trails of black footprints behind them on the paths. Later, no doubt, when the schools emptied for the lunchtime break, there would be groups of children playing, shouting to each other, sliding and throwing snowballs, but, at the moment, all was quiet and calm.

Tom sat at his desk, leaning on his elbows, dreaming of walking in the snow with Elizabeth. He thought of little else but Elizabeth these days. Since their tiff and their reconciliation at the Christmas party three weeks ago, things had been quite idyllic between them. Since then, she had been his. All of a sudden, his. He doubted if she saw Reggie at all. She went out with him whenever he asked and all her iciness seemed to have melted. She was warm, friendly and quite adorable all the time. He knew from past experience she was inclined to be fickle and that there was no telling how long this mood would last, but he was not going to worry about that now. In fact, he was strongly inclined to throw caution to the winds and ask her to marry him, letting any problems that might arise in the future take care of themselves.

Now he sat, chin on hand, imagining Elizabeth with flakes of snow settling on her blonde hair turning to sparkling drops of water. Snowflakes settling on her shoulders and on her pretty nose, her cheeks pink with cold, her eyes shining. As they walked along, she might ask him to hold her hands to warm them. The thought made him smile as he sat there alone.

Then, perhaps, she would go back to his flat with him, and they would have coffee and buttered toast. What a pity he did not have a log fire for her to thaw her chilly face, feet and hands by! An electric fire did not fit in with his romantic dreams. He gazed out of the window for a little longer, lost to the world.

Suppose, then, they were in his living room, cosily sharing one of the big, black leather armchairs. Suppose her head was resting on his shoulder and his cheek was against her blonde hair. Her delectable body softly pressed to his, the rhythmical movement as her breath came and went stirring within his arms. Suppose. Would he have the courage to say, "Elizabeth, I adore you. Let's get married."

And would she say, "Oh yes, Tom. I've wanted so long to hear you say that!"

If she said yes, it would have to be soon. He could never wait for anything, least of all that. He would take her away to Europe, to some tiny place where they could be quite alone to enjoy each other, then to America to meet his folks. His mother would think she was just right for her favourite son and even his father would have to admit that he had done pretty well, this time. Then bring her back here, to watch everyone being jealous.

And Ann would be waiting for him. Waiting with all her weapons at the ready, to destroy his newfound happiness. Every few days, she was in asking for money over and above her rent, and she was not going to relax her grip easily, especially if she knew he had so much more to lose. Possession of those photographs meant she held all the trumps.

Even so, the situation was not entirely hopeless. She did not act as toughly and ruthlessly as she liked to think she did, and with practice, he had found he could wheedle her and often send her off with less than she had come for. She could never entirely be extinguished as a threat to his peace of mind as long as she was around, but if he played his cards right, he felt he might be able to keep her within bounds that he could compass.

Ann was well aware of all this and she was not happy about it. To be presented with such a golden opportunity for milking an easy touch surpassed her wildest hopes and she knew acutely that she was not making the most of it. Time to tighten the screw a little.

To have his money at her beck and call was very pleasant, but she wanted more than that. Very much more. To have a man like him, who represented all she most hated, the rich, easy living boss class, the oppressor, the exploiter, the sort who at a whim could throw he father of a family on the dole, or walk away leaving a girl with a child she neither wanted nor could support, or refuse a young man a job because of his clothes or his hair-style, to have such a man, for that was how she saw him, in her power, filled her with a deep and savage destructive joy. She wanted to dominate him, to humiliate him in every possible way, to make him dance to her tune and do her bidding, whether he wanted to or not. Coming from a neighbourhood where most people were always a nod or a wink from destitution, she knew well the power of the men she ranked him with. She had seen people, her own father and his friends, having to knuckle under to such men in order to keep their families afloat, and she was going to have it out on him for what she had seen.

Her plans were made and in connection with them, she had scanned the advertisements in some masculine orientated magazines her boyfriend liked to read, to find the things she needed. The postal order she had sent off had been bought with some money she had got out of Tom and it added a special spice to think she was making him pay, all unaware, for his own discomfiture.

He had finally stopped daydreaming and settled down to some serious work when he heard her knock at the door. When he saw who it was, his first thought was that his other chair was not in its best place, but was right up at the other end of the room, where he had been using it to get some books down from a high shelf. To put himself, therefore, in a better position to avoid undue intimacies, he stood up and leaned against one of the side benches. She closed the door behind her and advanced into the room.

"When are you going to come and see me again?"

"Never."

"Oh yes, you are. You do what I tell you, remember?" And she sat down in his chair, put her elbows on his desk, her chin on her hand, and looked up at him.

"Nuts."

It was irritating, the way she could make him feel like a visitor in his own room. Bringing her cigarette packet from her pocket, she lit one and dropped the match on the floor.

"You're going to come round to my flat and you're going to give me a nice evening. You'll put on your best suit, the one you wear when you're taking her ladyship out and a clean shirt, not the one you've had on all day, and you'll come and be very polite to me, and ask me nicely to go bed with you. I want that and I'm not doing it here no more. The floor's too hard for one thing and you need a lock on that door. I can't enjoy it if someone might come walking in any minute, like *she* did that day. Besides, I've got a little treat for you, something you're really going to like and here wouldn't be the place for it."

"What treat?"

"You wait and see."

"Huh! I doubt if it'd be worth it. I'm not coming to your flat, for definite."

"Why not?"

"I'm just not going to, that's all."

"Give me a good reason, come on. It's quite a nice flat in not a bad district, much better than that bed-sitter. Don't you want to see what you're paying for?"

"Not if it's got you in it. If you want a reason, it's because you disgust me. Look at you now! You walk in here and you take over the place. You make it stink with your smoke and when you're gone, I'm left with all that mess on the floor. There is an ashtray, you know."

"Fussy, aren't you? You're not so particular when you're around Barracks Street," she said challengingly, adding some more ash to that which was already on the floor.

"Damn Barracks Street! I wish I'd never seen the goddam place!"

"I'll bet. All right, your flat then, if mine's not good enough for your lordship."

"No!" At all cost, he was not going to have her in his flat. It was his refuge and the thought of Ann's' contaminating it was not to be borne.

"What's wrong, do you think I'll make it dirty?" she asked with her usual acute perception. "I should think it's dirty enough with the likes of you living in it. You've got more kinks than a scenic railway. I bet you're gay as well. Do you take your boyfriends there?"

"Shut up and get out! I've never met anyone with such a filthy mind!"

"I have, oh yes, I have and I could point to the place he's standing on. What makes you think you've got the right to say things like that to me, you bloody hypocrite! I think you'd better apologise."

"Go to hell!"

"I probably shall, but not yet awhile and I'll be in good company when I do. I'm not going to stand here and be insulted by the likes of you. Come on, apologise."

"Get out!"

"All right, have it your own way. Looking forward to coffee time? You can think of me showing my photographs to my friends in our room, while you're having it."

"Oh, God, no!"

"Apologise, then."

"I'm sorry."

"That won't do, you know damn well that won't do. Apologise properly, you creep. Come on, properly."

It took a great deal of abject crawling on his part before she was finally satisfied.

"All right, then," she said at last. "I'll tell you what we'll do. You can book us a hotel room for the night, a decent hotel, mind you, I'm not going to any flea pit." She leaned back in her chair with a thoughtful look. "Try to get a room that's really private. No point in going to all that effort if we're worrying about giving the folks in the next room a free show. Then we'll have a nice dinner and a few drinks to put us in the mood, before we go up and have a bit of fun. Let me see, now, we don't want everyone to know we're being naughty, so you'd better book us in as Mr and Mrs Di Angeli."

"No!" he cried, appalled at the prospect.

She jumped to here feet, swung her arm back and slapped him viciously across the face.

"You'll do as you're bloody well told!" she screamed.

"For God's sake, don't shout like that! Everyone will hear!" he implored, swaying on his feet at the shock of this sudden assault.

"I don't care if they do!" she cried, hardly any more quietly. "Let them all hear, I don't care!"

He collapsed into the chair she had just vacated, holding his hand to his stinging cheek.

"Look," he said after a moment to recover. "We can't use my name. Suppose someone who knows me was to see it on the register – it's not impossible. They'd know it was me – there's no one else around here with that name, I'm sure. If my reputation, to use your charming British phrase, was to go for a Burton, where does that leave you, eh? Takes the edge off that knife you're so fond of sticking in me, doesn't it?"

She considered this for a moment.

"All right, make it Bone, then. A stupid fancy name like yours is a bit noticeable. We'll be Mr and Mrs Bone."

"All right, yes, all right," he said desperately.

"Good. You make the arrangements then and I'll see you tonight at eight o'clock."

His heart sank at the thought of another tussle with her, but there was no avoiding it.

"Not tonight. Tonight's impossible. Quite impossible."

"Why can you never do anything that I want? You've always got some excuse or other. I want to make it tonight, so there. You'll just have to tell your bit of fluff you'll see her another time."

"It's not that. It's a meeting. I'm the principal speaker. I can't possibly get out of it."

"Tell them you've got flu."

"Professor Ashton-Richards will know that's not true. Ann, I can't possibly get out of it."

"You could do it if *she* wanted you to."

"I couldn't do it for Elizabeth, or for the Queen of England for that matter. As long as I'm on my feet and capable of speaking, I've got to be there. There are a lot of important people going. I must be there, or there'll be all hell to pay."

"All right, tomorrow then. He-he! You can think about it while you're boring the pants off them tonight. What's little Ann going to do to me tomorrow? Still, you'll have to do something to make it up to me. I know. Buy me a nice, frilly, lacy nightdress. And do it yourself, don't send your little slave in the lab out to do it for you. Size eight, remember, lacy, frilly and expensive. Something really nice."

He looked at her, his shoulders drooping.

"How do you think them up?"

"Easy. I just have to look at you and all sorts of clever notions come into my head. I say, you do look pretty with one red cheek. You'll have to miss your coffee unless you want everyone to see it."

"Thanks. Anything else you want to inflict on me this morning?"

"No, I don't think so. I'd better go and do some work, then. You don't want me to get the sack, do you? Keeping me in here like this, alone in your room with you – you ought to be ashamed of yourself."

"Ask Jill to come in here when you go, will you?"

"Please?"

"All right, please."

"I'll tell her to keep one eye shut if she doesn't want to get a shock."

"Don't be smart. Just ask her to come."

"All right, she'll love that. There's nothing she likes better that coming to see her precious boss. Goodbye, sweetheart, see you tomorrow."

She kissed him on the back of the neck and bounced out of the room.

Jill came in a few minutes later.

"You wanted to see me, Professor?"

"Yes, Jill," he replied with his head well tucked down. "Can you get me a cup of coffee, please? I haven't got time to go along there this morning."

"Yes, of course. Are you all right?"

"Perfectly. No sugar, please and make it strong."

"Anything I can do to help?"

"Just the coffee, please, Jill, quickly," he answered, trying to keep the testiness out of his voice.

"No sugar, you said."

"That's right and strong."

She came back a few minutes later with the cup of coffee and put it on his desk. While she was away, he had moved his chair right over to one side so it was impossible for her to approach from the side where she might see his left cheek.

"Sure I can't do anything?" she asked solicitously. "Shall I take these letters to the office for you?" and she leaned across in front of him to pick them up.

"No! Leave them alone!"

She jumped back as though she had been stung.

"I'm sorry," she gasped. "I'm just trying to help."

"Well, don't. If I want your help, I'll ask for it. Just leave me alone."

"All right. I'm sorry."

She left looking upset and he sat chewing his lip. Why did one always take things out on the one who least deserved it? Jill, who would do anything in her power for him, who put up with his moods and smoothed his path with unobtrusive thoughtful efficiency, was always the one who got the rough edge of his tongue when things were not going well. There was no earthly reason why he should snarl at her because Ann had chosen to twist his arm. He would really have to make an effort to be pleasant to her this afternoon, when he had dealt with the ordeal he was faced with at lunchtime.

First of all, there was finding a suitable hotel room. Taking to heart Ann's dictum of 'somewhere that was really private', he inspected the available rooms in three different hotels without finding anything that seemed to fit the bill. He got some very strange looks from desk clerks as he tried to explain what he wanted and the whole thing became highly embarrassing.

Entering the fourth hotel, he suddenly had the inspiration to say that he was a very light sleeper and he needed to be as quiet as possible. This was immediately accepted by the young man at the desk, who said,

"Yes sir, I think we can find something suitable." And conducted him upstairs. He wondered why he had not thought of it before. The clerk showed him to a room on its own, right at the end of a corridor, with a private bathroom next to that of the adjoining room.

"And the room next door is not booked at present, sir. Of course, I can't guarantee it will remain so, but that's the position right now."

This seemed ideal. He booked it for the following night, enquired about the availability and timing of dinner, and left, wishing that his other task was finished as well.

He decided that the least painful way would be to buy from a department store rather than a more specialised shop, so he went to the best one in town, ascended to the ladies' clothing floor and tentatively approached the what seemed to be the right counter which was staffed by two young girls. With much blushing, he explained what he wanted whereupon they exchanged significant glances and swooped on the shelves. Within minutes, the counter was covered with a bewildering froth of white nightdresses, both girls chuckling gaily and vying with each other to hold each creation up in front of her, so he could see what it was like.

"Getting married, sir?"

"No, it's for my sister's birthday."

"Lucky sis."

Finally, having made his selection, he left the shop with his parcel, sighing with relief. Passing Ann's room on his way in, he tossed it through the door on to the table where she put her clean glassware before returning it to the lab.

"Here you are."

She said nothing at the time, but a little later, she put her head round the door of his room without the formality of a knock, said,

"Absolutely smashing. What a clever boy you are. I knew you could do it if you tried."

He deduced that she was pleased.

Chapter 18

When he met her the next night, at a neutral point in the centre of town, near neither her flat nor his, she was carrying a large plastic shopping bag, which, he supposed, contained the nightdress together perhaps with a change of clothing.

"I hope you're not planning on carrying that about with you all evening. It doesn't do anything for you at all. Apart from that, you're looking very nice."

This was not true. Her best was not markedly less shabby than her workaday clothes, but she obviously had made an effort to look smarter than usual and he appreciated it. It seemed she did not want to let him down too badly, in public at any rate.

"Well, what am I going to do with it? I'll want to have it with me later. I'll need it then."

"Put it in the room, if you like. It'll give you a chance to see it and say if it's what you wanted. Your instructions were rather vague."

"Sounds all right."

"Where do you want to have dinner? We can eat at the hotel, unless you had anywhere else in mind. We shouldn't see anyone we know."

"Why not? Save us a lot of effort. I suppose we can have a drink there, can't we?"

"Of course."

"Good. We'll do that, then."

"The car's parked just up the road – that was the nearest I could find. Come on."

"I say, what a smashing car," she said, bouncing up and down on the seat like a child, and making it rock on its springs. "You do yourself well, don't you?"

"Oh, it's not so bad," he replied casually. "But you should have seen the one I had last year, in the States. I could have strangled you, put your body in the trunk, and it could have been bought and sold three times before anyone found you."

"Oh, don't say horrible things like that! You make me go all creepy!"

"Don't you think I'd like to do it? It's a dangerous game, blackmail. Don't ever forget that. You could very easily wind up dead, if you push too hard."

"Shut up!" she said and he could see she was perturbed. One up to him, he thought.

They drove the few streets to the hotel, parked and, after checking in, went through to the bar where she asked for a Babycham and he had a Scotch. In fact, she had two Babycham and he felt she was trying to put out of her mind what he had said.

The hotel's menu was not extensive, but she was quite dazzled by it. She dined on tomato soup, roast chicken and a disgusting concoction called 'trifle' while he had grapefruit, an appallingly overcooked steak and cheese. He also let her drink most of their bottle of wine, hoping it might make her sleepy. Then they drifted through to the almost empty bar for an hour where they made desultory conversation to a background of music, until ultimately, she said, "Shall we go?"

"Any time you like."

"Come on then."

They climbed the stairs slowly, Ann looking as if she was almost asleep on her feet. She put her arm round his waist and leaned her head on his shoulder as they walked along the corridor. Smiling at this rather touchingly childish gesture, he remarked,

"Hey, this won't do. Remember, we're supposed to be married."

"Don't care. I'm nearly out on my feet. Are all these rooms full?"

"The desk clerk said the one next door wasn't booked. That was yesterday, of course. Might be taken by now. Does it matter?"

She did not reply. She had seen the room before, of course, in token of which, her carrier bag stood on one of the beds. Nonetheless, she still looked around in wonder.

"Got everything, hasn't it?"

She gazed at the shiny Formica topped dressing table with its immensely wide mirror, the wardrobe with another mirror, full length, at the broad bed with its silky green spread and the cunning headboard with little strip lights let in.

"You could watch yourself, whatever you were getting up to, in 'ere. You stay in places like this a lot?"

"I've been in better than this," he said, swishing the curtains closed over windows black and shiny with the night.

"All right for some, enn' it? You should see the bedroom my sister and I had to share at home. Yeah and then we 'ad to fit 'er baby into it. I was glad when I got out."

Still looking drowsy, she headed for the bathroom and he heard the sound of water splashing. When she returned, spiky bits of damp hair were clinging to her forehead and she looked much more alert.

He sat on the edge of the bed. Having agreed, for the usual price, to give her, her idea of a 'nice evening', he decided he had better start delivering the goods. Invitingly, he held out his hands to her.

"Come here."

She stood still, looking at him, thinking. Whatever she had in mind, she was wavering. It seemed a good idea to encourage this.

"Come here, Ann. Let's get it together."

She was wavering all right, between the warm flesh and blood of the man before her, and the idea she had chosen to equate him with in her mind. It would be sweet to lie in his arms and yet – would he ever have been here without her forcing him to? He despised her, his skivvy, his wash-up girl. It was not his choice that they were here.

The plastic carrier bag, innocent looking, lay on the bed.

"I expect you're wondering what I've got in here."

He was, anxiously. It was tightly packed and knobbly but it was impossible to guess the contents. From the top, she took out the nightdress, shook out the folds and laid it on a chair.

"Shan't need that just yet."

Then she emptied out the other things from the bag and spread them out for him to see. It contained a black Basque corset, a pair of black thigh boots and a whip.

"There now, what do you think of that?"

Panic seized him like a tiger's claws in the chest.

"No, Ann, no please."

"Turns you on, doesn't it?"

"No, Ann, you've got me all wrong, you really have."

But had she got him all wrong? Why these strange sensations?

"Don't give me that! It's you that's got yourself all wrong! Come on, Professor, get your clothes off. We're going to have a bit of fun, you and me."

She was tossing her own clothes on to a chair with gay abandon as she said it.

The blood was hammering in his ears and his face felt suffused. Mentally, he seemed to be whirled back to his eight-year-old self-watching in terror adult fingers fumbling with the buckle of a heavy belt. A strong irresistible adult, an adult with authority –

But he was grown now, and this was a girl years his junior, thin and light, and shorter than himself.

"No!"

He took her by the wrist with his fingers.

His father had grasped his arm so fiercely that there had been bruises on the pale pink skin over the skinny biceps for days afterwards. But not this time. He was going to take the lash of that whip, and wind it round and round her soft, defenceless throat –

"What will you do with the body, Professor?"

"How d'you know what I'm thinking?"

"Written all over your face, enn' it?"

"Then why aren't you scared?"

She tugged.

"Let go my wrist." He released her and she sat down. "Been livin' with my Dad, enn' I? He doesn't say nuthin'. He just gives you a mouthful of knuckles. But you, you're all talk and no do. You're softer'n a girl. You're a pussy cat."

"Thanks."

"Don't mention it. I'm gonna put on the gear, and in a minute, you're gonna lie down and let me do you over. First, because it turns you on, second, because you know you damn well deserve it."

"What makes you think that?"

"Which?"

"Both."

"You deserve it because of all the girls you've made cry. Do you know you can make people cry? I cried for you that night."

"You? You never cried for anyone, least of all me."

"I did. Think of all those other girls. What must they have thought? You're a looker, I suppose I've got to give you that and you're American. They must have thought it was like being screwed by their favourite film star. Then you walk away and they never see you again. Of course, they'd cry."

He did not like that thought one bit.

"Well, what about the other?"

"I know it turns you on because of what you were like that night at my bed-sit. Seemed there wasn't nothing bad enough I could do to you. I'd have tried it then if it hadn't been for him in the wardrobe. You've been wanting someone to fix you up for a long time ever since – what? Who done it to you then? Your Ma?"

Slowly, he shook his head, wondering if it was made of glass, she seemed to read his thoughts so easily.

"Not Mommy. I was her favourite, I guess."

"Dad. I should'a known. All the same, bloody Dads. Did you have it coming that time?"

"Yeah. You could say that." He sat down on the bed beside her with a feeling close to relief. "Put your kinky gear on."

"Why?"

The look of a victim resigned to his fate was in his eyes as he glanced at her.

"Because I guess it'll turn me on. Y'want me to tell you about last time?"

"Yeah."

"Why?"

The confident smile of one with four aces in her hand answered him.

"Because it'll turn *me* on."

"Yeah? All right, then." He lay down on the bed as if it was a psychiatrist's couch while she put the whip aside and continued to take her clothes off. With astonishing ease, the tale which he had always considered untellable began to be told.

"I'll never forget it. I've had three real bad days in my life and that was the first. I was eight, maybe nine years old and I wanted a toy gun. Just a plastic space gun with a flashing light and a buzzer, because all the kids had them that year. But my Daddy wouldn't buy me one. We were too poor."

She had been pulling her slip over her head, but at his words she suddenly stopped. She stared at him from under the tattered lace edging, astonished.

"Too poor?"

"Oh yes. We were a poor family."

"I thought all Americans were stinking rich."

"Well, you thought wrong, sweetie."

"Hey!" She dropped the slip on a chair, and stood in her bra and panties looking at him with new eyes. "How d'you get to be a Professor then?"

"By being such a smart-assed whiz-kid that the College practically paid for the privilege of teaching me. It can be done."

"Pity you changed. If you'd still been hard up, I'd have liked you better. Go on about your Pa."

"If I had been, you'd never have met me. Well, like many poor people, he was real uptight about money and meeting his bills on time. He had little boxes where he used to save for all the regular payments. That's where I took the money from. I thought he'd never notice – some hope! He always knew what was in there to the last cent. But, in fact, it was the gun he saw first. I thought he was out and I came swaggering in with it stuck in my belt like a real little cowboy. Naturally, he wanted to know where I got it. Bad luck on me, Mommy was out. He'd never have got to do what he did if she'd been there."

"He belted you, eh?"

"And then some. After he'd shaken the whole story out of me, he made me throw the gun in the garbage. Then he got to me. I've never had my wagon fixed like it before or since."

"Don't you have some funny expressions?"

The whole thing was flooding back in clear, sharp detail. How he had heard through his screams and the sound of the merciless leather on his flesh the crash of the front door, and his Mother's feet flying up the hallway. At the sound, his father swore and let him go, but blocked him in a corner by the big faded couch to stop him running to his mother the moment she came in. He could see them as he saw them that day from where he stood, sobbing and almost naked, peering over the high arm of the old-fashioned Chesterfield, standing among his scattered clothes yelling at each other.

His father:

"All I ever hear from you. Oh my good little Tom, oh my clever little Tom, oh my precious little angel, on and on till I'm sick to my stomach. Well, your darling kid's a thief and a liar. He stole money from the rent box and the rent's due in three days. I can't make it up, can you? We're going to have to owe it. I've never owed the rent in the whole of my life. That's what your darling kid's done to us. I sure hope you're proud of him."

His mother:

"That's not true. How dare you say that of him? He'd never touch your boxes."

Himself:

"Oh, Mommy!" Longing for her arms but dreading what would happen when she found out that the accusation was true.

"I don't believe a word of it! He'd never do that!"

His father looked so angry that he had trembled for the safety of his precious mother.

"Are you calling me a liar? That just goes to show, you think more of that thieving little brat than you do of me!"

"Don't you talk of him like that! How do you know he did it?"

"He did it all right. He admitted it to me, after telling me a pack of lies first."

"With you yelling at him like that, he probably didn't know what he was saying."

His father grabbed the gun from the wastebasket and thrust it under his mother's nose.

"All right, where's the money then, and where did he get this from?"

She had thought about it and then turned her eyes on him.

"Oh, Tom!" was all she had said, but the tone of her voice, and the sorrow and dismay of her look had hurt him more than all his father's anger and violence. Frightened him more, too, for if he had lost his mother as an ally, what would happen to him now? But that ultimate disaster had not occurred. She rallied to the attack again.

"Well, all right, it was very bad of him, but to beat a child of that age like that – it's brutal! There's no need for it! You could have got it across to him without all that. When I heard him screaming, I wondered what on earth had happened."

"So now I'm brutal, am I? I suppose you want your darling kid to grow up to rob banks and mug old ladies?"

"Oh, for heaven's sake, don't be so stupid! All because of one childish indiscretion!"

"Indiscretion, you call it!"

His father had been going angrily on, but his mother had come over and, despite his relatively advanced age, had picked him up in her arms. She could do it quite easily, for he had been small for his years even then and carried him away to his bedroom – away from the terror of his father's fury. He had wound his arms round her neck and cried into her hair. It was the last time he could remember crying and he recalled having been glad that his school friends couldn't see him.

As she carried him upstairs, he had whispered to her between his sobs, "I'm sorry, Mommy, I'm really sorry."

"Never mind, darling, just try and forget it."

"You still love me best, don't you?"

She had hesitated a long time. She carried him into his room, sat him on the bed, and busied herself getting out fresh shorts and socks for him. Then, at last, she had said, a little shyly,

"Yes, I do, darling, but don't tell the others, will you?"

He had thrown his arms round her neck, and kissed her adored face over and over. Of all the embraces he had ever had in his life, that had been the sweetest.

Ann was ready.

"What do you think of it?"

The corset was of black shiny boned satin with lace over the breasts and it fitted her like a second skin. Below it was the dark triangle of crisp hair. A few inches of white thigh tapered to the glossy black boots with their sharply pointed toes and high heels. As he stared at her, she pushed a lock of hair from her eyes and picked up her whip.

"Well, come on, speak up," she said, grinning at him impudently.

He rolled off the bed and stood in front of her.

"My dark angel."

"Do I turn you on?"

"Not yet."

"Wait a bit. We'll see about that. Get your jacket off."

He hung it on a chair and she started to undress him, slowly, caressingly, leaning against him, and letting him feel the stiff fabric and scratchy lace in which her warm flesh was constrained.

"You're going to do it all for yourself in a minute. You're going to take the covers off that bed, 'cos we don't want to mess them up, do we? Then you'll lie right down on your front, and keep still and take what's coming to you. Because I know you're a naughty little boy who knows he deserves to be whipped, aren't you? Right across here," she added, stretching her arm across his shoulders. "Oh, it will hurt and won't you love it!" She pushed him in front of the wardrobe mirror and got his arms behind him. "Look for yourself. Are you trying to tell me you're not turned on?"

"OK, I'll admit it. When do we start?"

"Now."

Knowing what she wanted, he stripped the bed to the bottom sheet. His hands were trembling, in fact he was trembling all over. It took more guts to lie down than it did to square with an angry guy whose girl he had been propositioning. Ann stood watching him, her arms folded, the lash of her whip snaking down at her side. She gave no hint of what she was thinking.

He pressed his forehead to the pillow, gripped the sides of it and said, "OK, I'm ready."

She needed just a little help to get going.

"You can still get off with it, you know. Just ask me round to Sunday tea at your flat."

"Go climb a tree!"

"What about Elizabeth?"

"Now you're talking. I'd ask her any time. Uhh!"

She had smacked the whip diagonally across his back from hip to shoulder. It hurt about twenty times more than he had expected.

"Hey, Ann, take it easy. That hurts."

"Meant to, enn' it? Keep still."

Ten more crosswise strokes working down from shoulders to waist while he grunted and writhed under the assault. His back was burning and smarting with pain when she decided to stop, and tossed the whip aside.

"Turn on your back."

He groaned pathetically.

"Doubt if I can. Christ, I hurt! What a bitch you are!"

"Come on, you great baby! Don't men make a fuss about nothing! I didn't feel a thing."

"Yeah. Very funny."

"You're bleeding a bit. Good thing we took the spreads off. Give the chambermaid something to think about in the morning."

"Bleeding! What the hell –"

"Get over. You won't die."

"Bleeding! Look, Ann, quit fooling. This is serious!"

"Stupid! It's only a little bit. Get over."

Despite his protests, she rolled him over on his back where he lay groaning as if he were about to die. After what she had put him through, his erection needed some freshening up, so she got to work on that. Soon, she had it good as new. Then she climbed on the bed and got astride him on her knees.

"Hey, what the hell d'you think you're doing?"

"Going to screw you, aren't I?"

"Not like this, you're not."

"You just lie still and behave yourself. Remember who the boss around here is."

"But I don't – I like to be on top. I think it's right."

"Not tonight, it's not. Lie still."

She got hold of him and plugged him in with a practised hand. She started to rock her bony pelvis on his and put her hands on his shoulders, pressing him down on his painful back. He made no protest, shut his eyes and let her work on him. He was hooked. Every other Tom Di Angeli seemed to have melted away before this one. The well-tried stud, collecting girls the way some people collect stamps, the clever and admired scientist collecting honours, and adulation in much the same way. The smart socialising young man who had eaten at the Aston-Richards' table and waltzed with Elizabeth in their library. Every alter ego except the one he was in now.

A little before eight, he could be seen, having unstuck himself from the bedclothes, walking rather stiffly down the stairs with Ann. Just as they were about to enter the dining room from which came an appetising smell of breakfast, he was accosted by the hotel manager, who had been hanging about in the corridor near the foot of the stairs.

"Could I have a word with you, sir?"

"Of course. You go on, Ann. I'll join you in a few minutes."

The hotel manager conducted him into his office.

"Sit down, sir."

"Thanks, I'll stand," he said, eyeing the rather hard chair he was offered and realising he might have some little difficulty getting up again.

"Now, sir, we normally do everything in our power to respect the privacy of our guests here, but when one of our night staff was making his routine rounds last night, he said he heard very strange sounds coming from your room." He looked at Tom, who was staring at a corner of the desk. So much for no-one knowing! "I'm told you particularly asked for a room that was very private."

"I'm sorry if we caused a disturbance."

"You must understand, sir, that it's very easy for a hotel to lose its reputation and we try to run a respectable establishment here. I must ask you not to use my hotel for such purposes again."

"Of course. I'm sorry. You don't mind if we have our breakfast, I take it?"

"Please do, but I must ask you to leave as soon as possible afterwards."

"I intended to."

"I hope you understand my point of view."

"Perfectly, perfectly. Is that all?"

"It is, sir. Good morning."

He sat down carefully at the table which Ann already occupied and sighed.

"Life with you, Ann, is full of new experiences. I've been thrown out of many places before but this is the first time I've ever been thrown out of a hotel."

"Threw you out! What for!" she cried indignantly.

He leaned towards her across the table.

"Because, my dear Ann, they don't like people indulging their little fancies in their bedrooms, especially if they're the sort of fancies that make a lot of noise. Lowers the tone of the place, you know. Let in one sort of undesirables and before you know where you are, you have every queer and lesbian and God knows what pouring in from miles around, and your hotel has become a byword for permissiveness."

"What a cheek! I'm going to tell him where to go!" And she half rose from her chair.

"You stay right where you are! I've had enough embarrassment for one morning. You and your kinky gear! The things you get me into! Never, never again!"

"Oh, I think you will, don't you?"

Chapter 19

She was quite right, of course. In fact, this incident very nearly marked his total, unconditional surrender to her. Before many days were out, he found himself aching for her skinny body with the small, firm breasts, with a longing that grew on him all the time. He thought constantly of her in her corset and boots, dominating him, making him do what she wanted, reducing him with such ease to a writhing, whimpering mass, pleading with her and ready to promise her anything if only she would stop, or not stop, or let him make love to her, or beat him some more, or he hardly knew what. His need for her became greater as days went by and he knew that she was not going to have to come to him this time, it was going to be him seeking her.

For nearly a fortnight, he stuck it out, trying not to brood over what they had done together, but his thoughts and his dreams were haunted by it, day and night. Wanting to repeat the experience and yet dreading it. Wanting to somehow salvage some of his self-respect, yet not knowing how to. Resisting the strong and insistent call as long as he could. Gradually, an idea came into his mind how he could exploit the fact that he was a man and she a woman, to show her that she only seemed to be in total control because he let her be. He did not like it very much at first because it went right against all the principles he tried to hold to in relating to women – all women, even those like her. It was sneaky. It was unfair. He always tried, if nothing else, to be open and above board. Perhaps, not always with success, but he tried.

Besides, it was going to make her angry and resentful, and that meant inviting a much more violent beating than he had got from her before. It was a thoroughly nasty, underhand little plan and bit by bit, he came to love it. It seemed to give him some sort of excuse for pandering to these unbearable longings. Ultimately, he knew, its only effect would be to leave him even more securely in her grip, but what the hell. He would do

So he went along to see her and by that time he was so eager that she achieved the grip-tightening bit long before he meant it. She glanced up from her work as he entered the washing-up room and shut the door behind him.

"Hi," she said casually and carried on with what she was doing, taking no further notice. She picked up a handful of test tubes from the water with a gloved hand, scrubbed each one with a brush, rinsed them under the tap, then from the distilled water bottle and stacked them in a partly filled wire basket at her elbow.

"Want something?" she asked, after a few minutes.

"Yes," he replied, then stopped, at a loss for how to express himself. Her room was tiny, just about the width of the double sink with a draining board which stood at the far end under the window. She had let down the venetian blind and tilted the slats to reduce the glare from the low winter sun shining straight in.

"Would you like – will you – I want –" he began and then stopped again. So hard to put in words what filled his mind!

She tutted.

"Well, come on, if you've got something to say, spit it out!"

Her voice was impatient, but she felt a tingle of excitement, for she knew very well what was in his mind.

"Shall I book another hotel room for us?"

"What for?" she asked, pretending to be casual.

"Same as last time."

"All of it?"

"Yes."

"Mm."

"Well?"

"Oh, I don't know. I'll think about it."

"Oh, come on, Ann. Do you want to or not?"

"I don't know. Maybe."

"Ann!"

"I'll think about it."

"Oh, come on, Ann. Say yes or no. You must know."

"Stop bugging me! I said I'll think about it."

"Look, if I book a room for tonight, will you come?"

"Oh, I don't know what I'm doing tonight. Come back later and I'll tell you."

"How much later?"

"Oh, I don't know. About four o'clock."

"Look, you must know what you're doing tonight. If you decide now and you'll come, I can find a room at lunchtime."

"Oh, go away! I said I'd let you know."

She picked up another basket of dirty test tubes and started transferring them by handfuls to the washing up water.

"Ann," he said desperately. He walked the two or three steps across the room towards her and took her by one rubber gloved wrist. "Leave that for a minute and make up your mind."

"Oh, leave me alone," she cried trying to pull her hand away.

He drew her across the room, leaned his back against the door and kissed her.

"God, not here! Are you nuts?"

He walked quickly to the window, and closed the blind fully, then came back to her, took her in his arms and kissed her again. This time, her back was against the door.

"Come on, Ann, for heaven's sake. Make up your mind and say yes. I don't know what the matter with me is. I hate to think of what we did and yet I can't get it out of my mind. Once more,

Ann, just once more, then we'll forget the whole thing. It's so sordid and yet I can't leave it alone." He looked at her for a long moment and then closed his eyes. In a scarcely audible voice, he said, "I want you, Ann."

His breath was coming fast and hard. He wanted her, now.

"Don't rush me," she said, trying to control her own feelings and keep command of the situation. Then she looked at him, smiled her mocking smile and said, "You are keen, aren't you?"

She leaned against him, against his heaving chest and he was flooded with uncontrollable desire.

"Has this door got a lock?"

"No."

"Lean against it hard, then."

"What are you doing? Stop it!"

He was pulling up her skirt with one hand.

"Ann, please..."

"Stop it! Stop it! Oh, Tommy, Tommy!"

She was breathing hard as well, now.

"Ann..."

"Oh, stop it! If someone was to come in!"

"You're a bit too small to make this very easy. I'll have to lift you up..."

"Oh, Tommy, oh, Tommy, oh Professor!"

He had found his mark now.

"Oh, you are a naughty boy! Oh, Professor!"

"You like it, don't you?"

"Oh, yes!"

Nothing to be heard for a few minutes but their breathing in unison.

"Ann..."

"You ought to be whipped, really hard, for doing this to me."

"Do it tonight, sweetie."

"I will, I will, I'll do it, all right."

A few minutes later, he was leaning limply against her.

"Oh, Ann, sweetie, the things you make me do!"

"Do you still want to see me tonight?"

"Sure. Plenty more where that came from."

"Do up your zip, for heaven's sake. If anyone was to see you like that –"

"I only came in to speak to you about not getting on with your work fast enough and here you are, idling about again!"

"Oh, you! I'll get you for that, I will!"

"You little vixen! I was never like this before I met you!"

"If I remember right, you were much, much worse. At least, I'm keeping you off the streets."

"H'm, yes. Well, shall I book a room?"

"I think you'd better. You want teaching a lesson."

"Hey, I'd better go. I've got a roomful of students waiting to be taught a lesson, right now. Shall tell them why I'm late?"

"Yes, do that, then they'll all be along here at lunchtime, queuing up for their turn."

"Naughty! See you later, sweetie."

"You will, don't worry."

No prolonged negotiations this time. His part was just to strip and lie down for her right away, to co-operate with her every move, and let her think he was completely submissive till the moment came. So, as soon as they were in the room, with the door firmly closed and locked against the prying eyes of the world, he took her bag from her and they sat on the bed together as he emptied it. He was taken aback to find that she had put in with the other things two pieces of thin rope. That was a shaker. If she tied him, he would have no chance at all.

"You won't need those. I'll be still for you."

"I just thought I might work off a few variations. We'll see."

"You going to get changed?"

"All right, junkie. Can't you wait?"

Quickly, he folded and put aside the top covers of the bed, had his own clothes off, and was ready and waiting with his arms tucked under his chest, while she was still wrestling with the tightly fitting corset. "Come and love me a little first, sweetie," he said in his best wheedling voice.

She sat on the edge, put her arms round his waist and began to kiss his bare shoulders.

"I'm going to whip you really hard, you know that?"

"I know."

"And you know why, don't you?"

"Mmm-hm."

"Why?"

"Because I got you against the door of your room this morning and I screwed you."

"Yes. And you didn't ask me if you could, either. You don't screw me without getting my permission first."

"You liked it though, didn't you? Was it a nice fuck? Did you have a lovely come?"

"Smashing!" she sighed happily. "But that doesn't alter the fact that you were very, very naughty. If I was to let you go on like that, next thing you'd be telling me, I'd got to come to work with no knickers on."

"What a good idea! And you'd have to do it, wouldn't you, because at work, I'm the boss and you have to do what I say."

"I suppose I would."

"Well, what would happen then? Let's have a little fantasy. Let's see. I'm in the lab, say and you come in with some clean tubes to put away. I say to you, did you do what I told you, Ann? Have you got any knickers on? And what do you say?"

"Are the technicians there?"

"Yes, of course. They're always there. All of them."

167

"Oh! Well, I suppose I'd just ignore them and say, yes, I did what you said, Professor. I haven't got any on. And what do you say?"

"Well, I'd look stern and say, you don't always tell the truth, do you, Ann? I guess you'd better come right over here and let me check."

"Oh, Tommy, you're turning me on."

"Me too." She lay half on his back and started kissing his hair, with one hand on either side of his head. "Then you come slowly over to me, pulling up your skirt, but I say, just you leave it alone and let me do it. So I lift it up and sure enough, you haven't got any panties on."

"Then what do you say?"

"I say, oh yes, that's nice. What a pretty little thing. Shame to keep it covered all the time. Hey, how does it feel right now? Is it excited? Like, is it wet? And I'd put my hand to find out. Is it wet?"

"Yes."

"What a sexy baby you are! Well, then I'd say, all right, Ann, since you're such a good girl, I've got something real nice for you. Look here. Come on, look down here. Then I'd bring it out and let you see it. What would you say?"

"Oh, Tommy! Oh, you can't half get me going!" She wriggled about, pressing her breasts against his shoulders. Covered with the fabric of the corset, they had a delectable kind of firm squishiness. "Well, I'd say, gosh, isn't it big! Is it all you?"

"And I'd say, yes and it's all for you for being such a good girl. Do you want it now?"

"What are the technicians doing all this time?"

"Staring in amazement, I guess."

"I'd say yes, come on then, let me have it."

"Right up?"

"All the way. Every inch. Oh!" She was getting quite carried away by the picture. "What an imagination you've got!"

He was ready.

"I can do more than imagine, sweetie." he said, turning over and getting his arms round her.

"Now just you cool down. It's my turn first."

"You haven't a hope. Keep still."

"Not till I've had my turn," she gasped, struggling with him. "Let go, come on, it's my turn first!"

"No. Lie still, if you don't want to get hurt."

"Look, you know damn well – oh, stop that! You've got to do as you're told!"

"Try and make me!"

He grunted as he tried to get her under control. Fighting like a cat, she tried to scratch him, but he trapped her arms to her sides.

"Come on, come on!" he muttered.

Never before had he done it to a woman like that, but no woman had ever done to him what Ann had done. Thoroughly aroused now, he overcame her by sheer physical strength, and took her unwillingly, hard, fast and with no regard for her feelings. It only took a couple of minutes, and as soon as his grip on her relaxed, she struggled out from under him and scrambled out of bed. She was wild. She was furious. With the adrenalin beating through her veins, she stood there, eyes blazing, her breast heaving with anger at the outrage.

"You raped me, you sod!" she cried.

He nodded, smirking with self-satisfaction. He knew he was going to have to suffer for it in a minute, so he was going to make the best of his triumph for now, while it lasted.

"You raped me, you bastard! I'll kill you! I'll cut you to ribbons!"

"Yes." He was still smiling in an infuriating way. "I raped you and you couldn't do a thing about it. With all your whips, and your photographs and your dirty little secrets, you couldn't stop me. I raped you and you couldn't stop me."

He could hear the breath whistling in her nostrils as he lay on his front, his head turned towards her. She moved quickly out of his sight and he knew it was coming. He clenched his fists in anticipation, digging his nails into the palms of his hands. While he could still speak, though, he continued to say, "I raped you, Ann Bone and you couldn't do anything about it. I – uh – raped you – uh – and you – uh – couldn't stop me." He could hear her grunt each time she brought the whip down, exerting every ounce of her strength. He clenched his teeth. He was not going to give her the satisfaction of hearing him cry out, or of having him ask her to stop. All that she wanted to give, he would take.

Blood was trickling down his shoulder and dripping on the clean hotel sheet, but he didn't care. He had shown her she could not have her own way in everything and for that, he would gladly take what was coming.

His ordeal was shorter than he expected. After half a dozen vicious strokes, she gave a little cry and threw the whip across the room where it fell with a clatter at the foot of the wardrobe. Then she pulled off her corset and flung herself on his back.

"Oh, Tommy, what am I doing to you?"

He pushed and held her away from him. Her breasts and arms were smeared with his blood.

He was pale and trembling but he managed a ghost of a smile.

"You couldn't make me yell," he said, quietly.

"Oh, Tommy!" she said again, starting to cry.

"Crocodile tears," he said contemptuously, wiping one away, none too gently, with his hand.

"Oh, Tommy, what can I do – tell me – anything?"

"Stop calling me Tommy for a start, and get the handkerchief out of my pants pocket and wash the blood off my back."

She found the handkerchief, wetted and soaped it at the washbasin, washed his back, and dabbed it dry with the hotel towel, leaving bloody smudges on that as well. She was incredibly gentle. Little whimpers escaped her as she worked, kneeling on the bed beside him. The soap and water made the whip cuts sting, but the satisfaction of having got the better of Ann for once made anything worthwhile.

169

When she had finished, she said in a quiet remorseful voice, "I lost my temper. I'm sorry. Is it better now?"

"A little."

She rinsed the handkerchief, wrung the water out of it and draped it over the edge of the washbasin. Then she lit a cigarette, got the ashtray off the dressing table and put it on a chair by the bed. She sat on the edge, put the cigarette to her lips with a shaking hand, took a draw and blew out the smoke.

"I wish I didn't love you so much," she sighed.

"You've got a very funny way of showing it."

"I don't know what I feel. Sometimes I love you, sometimes I hate you so much, there isn't anything bad enough I can do to you. Oh, sometimes I wish I'd never met you."

Tears were running down her cheeks again.

"I agree with you on the last part."

"Don't you love me, even the tiniest bit?"

"Not the tiniest bit. Why should I? What have you ever done to make me want to? I said once you were the most unpleasant girl I've ever met and I stick by that."

She stood up and walked away from the bed. He twisted his head round, and watched her as she went over to the dressing table and leaned her hands on the edge. The smoke of the cigarette between the fingers of her right hand rose in a thin straight stream and dispersed in a cloud by her hanging head. He could see that she was still crying.

He looked at her for a few moments and sighed. She was going to get him again, he was going to give in to her and let her get the upper hand once more, but there was nothing he could do about it. He couldn't lie still and watch her cry. Reluctantly, he eased himself off the bed, went over and stood behind her.

"Don't cry, Ann," he said softly.

"Why shouldn't I? I'm so miserable. You hate me, everyone thinks I'm rubbish, they think I'm stupid because I'm just the washer-up. I want you to like me and sometimes I think you do, then we do something like this and you make me mad, and – oh, God!" She shook her hanging head despairingly.

"Let's pretend I love you just for now, even if I don't."

"Oh, you're hateful. Do you think that would make me happy?"

"Ann," He took the cigarette from between her fingers and threw it into the washbasin. Then he took her by one shoulder and turned her round. Her face was streaked with tears and she was still smeared with is blood. He put his arms round her.

"Ann," he said again.

"You don't care about me. You hate me."

"When you're like this, I could almost – change my mind." He pressed her quickly to him, before he said anything too unwise. As he did so, he felt a thin trickle of blood start to run down his back again.

"Oh, Tom, Tom," she sighed.

"Come on, let's clean you up a bit and go to bed. Let's forget about minds and just enjoy each other's bodies. It's so much easier that way."

They got the handkerchief again, washed each other, kissed and stroked until they were ready to make love. As they got back into the blood stained bed, he observed,

"We'd better not come back here either. They'll never let us in again when they see this mess."

"We're going to run out of hotels at this rate."

"No we're not. This'll be the last time – and I mean it."

"I'd quite miss it if you stopped saying that."

Her mocking smile was back again. The old familiar Ann was beginning to re-assert herself and he felt glad. In the mild and penitent mood, she had been in earlier, he could all too easily have come to love her, and of the complications that would have brought in its train, he could not even begin to think.

She slipped into his arms.

"That was fun, earlier on, when we made up that silly story, I liked that, but you really scared me when you had me like that after. I didn't know you were so strong and you looked as if you were – oh – going to do something awful to me. I was really scared."

"No you weren't. You know your stupid great Tom, you know just what he's like. He's just a sort of brainless punch bag. You can do what you like to him and he never hits back. You weren't frightened. You knew it was just a game."

"Yes," she said wonderingly, then, shaking her head, "I never met anyone like you in my life before."

Thus, carelessly and without a thought, he tossed back to her the advantage he had bought and paid for. He had never really felt comfortable with it anyway. It seemed that to disclaim it, put things the right way round with them again.

Ann now had him inextricably entangled in her net. Before anything in his life in which he would look important or impressive – a scientific meeting at which he was to feature, or a particularly glamorous date with Elizabeth for instance – he seemed to need her to pull him down and put him in his place. She got to know this, and she would tease him about what he would think when Elizabeth put her hand on her bruised and swollen place on his shoulder that she made a point of leaving there when they were going to a dance, or how he would feel when sitting on a hard chair on the platform, waiting to rise and give his talk.

Everything he was and everything he had was in the power of this girl. There was no way he could stop her, if she felt so inclined, from telling people about the secret self that she knew only too well and every time he was with her he gave her more ammunition to use, but, all the same, as soon as she put her whip down, he would be on his feet, catching her in his arms, pulling her corset off her, kneeling at her feet to take off her boots, often getting kicked as he did so, then carrying her to bed to seek the final dissolution in the bittersweet delight of ecstatically mingled pain and pleasure.

Then, at these moments, he would please his sweet tormentor to the best of his ability for the relief she brought to his troubled mind at the expense of his cowering body, given to her, willing and defenceless, for her amusement. What did it matter that tomorrow he would be gritting his teeth and pulling his hair to try to distract his mind from the thoughts of what he had let her do to him? That was tomorrow, but this was tonight, and tonight the pain only added to and enhanced the pleasure as he dug himself into her, covering her face with kisses, and whispering her name over and over. Tomorrow, he would be Elizabeth's polite and elegantly dressed escort, but tonight he was

Ann's victim, naked, and in pain and happy, punished for and relieved of those uncountable sins and misdeeds that hung so heavy on his conscience.

The endless cycles of highs and lows seemed beyond his power to break. He longed for some way to tear himself from the grasp of these appalling desires, but he seemed to have been sucked into an endless whirlpool from which he lacked the ability, or

indeed, the will, to escape.

Chapter 20

Jenny was standing on a street corner when he saw her, just outside the heavily barred and padlocked door of the Bricklayer's Arms. It was late afternoon, hot for so early in the summer and Tom was feeling exhausted. After an afternoon spent shopping in the town centre, he was prowling about the Blackgate Street area, wondering if it was worth the effort, or if he should just go home.

For one thing, very few people of any sort seemed to be about. Perhaps, everyone was at home getting their evening meal and the girls, the sort he liked, were busy in the kitchen with their mothers, or maybe they were watching tennis on television. At any rate, they certainly were not in evidence walking about the pavements of Blackgate Street.

It was so hot. Although he wore only a short-sleeved shirt and a pair of lightweight slacks, he felt uncomfortable, his shirt sticking to his back and his feet throbbing with the heat from the dusty pavements. He was thirsty and beginning to get hungry too.

And then there was Jenny. Alone on the grimy street looking very small and frail as if the hard, unrelenting surroundings might swallow her up at any moment and snatch her from his sight. Her face was shiny in the heat, and her naturally pale city skin was flushed red over the nose and cheekbones. Her brown hair straggled untidily down the side of her face and a long, badly cut fringe hung almost into her eyes. She wore a stained and limp cotton dress, no stockings and canvas open-toed sandals, the kind that are piled in baskets outside the doors of the cheap shoe shops. Her feet were dusty. But she was pretty and he liked what he saw.

Nevertheless, he glanced around nervously as he approached. Ann's family lived nearby and what would be more natural than that a girl should go to see her family on a Saturday afternoon? If she saw him, she would know at once why he was here and she would be jealous. He knew that and he also knew only too well what would happen to him if he made Ann jealous.

He had found, in spite of everything that he still craved the sweaty bodies and the dirty hair, and Ann would not give him that any more. She said her boyfriend didn't like it. But when he had said recently that he would like to go and find such a girl again, she had flown at once into a rage, and it had taken him a great deal of time and effort to calm her down again. Oddly enough, she never seemed to care how often he went out with Elizabeth. She apparently came into a different category.

Watching Jenny from the corner of his eye, he saw that she kept glancing in one direction up the road, sighing occasionally and looking annoyed, with the air of waiting for someone who was well past their time. He decided to try his luck.

His accent was, as always, useful. He could assume the air of a weary and bewildered traveller. He went up to her and said,

"Pardon me, Miss, do you know where Exton Street is?"

She turned her eyes to him, and three little lines came between her brows as she tried to focus on him and his question. Then her brow cleared and she gave him accurate, concise directions.

"Sounds a long way."

"I'd say fifteen minutes' walk."

"Whew!" He shifted the jacket he was carrying to the other arm and glanced at the pub doors. "When do they open?"

There was a turret clock on the opposite corner and she looked at it.

"Just over half an hour."

"Gee! Well, I may last till then. You waiting for opening time?"

She looked indignant, as well she might.

"Indeed I'm not. I'm waiting for my boyfriend. At least –" she added in a sudden bitter tone, "I thought he was my boyfriend."

"Late, is he?"

"Nearly an hour."

"I'm sorry. I wouldn't leave a girl like you standing around on the street alone."

She smiled wanly with the eternal patience of the female and looked up the street again. Then, as if it burst involuntarily from her, she said,
"He often makes me wait like this. It's to show whose boss."

"Pretty dumb attitude. If someone gets good to you, he'd lose you."

"If someone got good to me, he'd smash his face and mine too," she sighed. "Look, if all you want is a drink, not beer, you could get a lemonade at the cafe. At least, it's wet."

She pointed to one over the road and smiled in a more friendly way.

"Why don't you come and have one with me? I need someone to talk to and you could watch for your boyfriend from there. If he comes, you just go. Come on, why not? I'll take a chance if you will. At least, you'd be sitting instead of standing."

She considered the proposition and then said impulsively,
"All right, I will."

They crossed together, and he bought some lemonade and chocolate, and they sat down to console themselves and each other.

"What's your name?"

"Tom. What's yours?"

"Jenny."

Interesting, that. He had felt no need to say 'Bone' and hide behind his other self. And he wanted, really wanted, to know who she was. Strange? Ominous? Maybe.

They talked. He told her of his imaginary tour of Britain, and she told him of her extensive family and of the boyfriend who thought so much less of her than she did of him.

"I don't think he's going to come, do you?" he said at last.

"No, it doesn't look like it. I suppose I might as well go home for my tea. Not that I want any now, after all that chocolate. Thanks!"

"You're welcome. But look, they're opening up the pub. Wouldn't you just as soon have a beer with me? You're real nice to talk to."

"Yeah, why not? Mum'll think I've gone to the flicks with Jason. Sure, you've got the time?"

"All the time in the world, sweetie."

She looked at him with one eyebrow cocked disapprovingly and he wondered what he had done to displease her. Then he realised he had introduced the word 'sweetie' rather early in the conversation. Perhaps, Elizabeth was right and he was too pushy. Better slow down a bit.

They crossed the road and entered the dim coolness of the Bricklayer's Arms. Several thirsty customers were already lining the bar. He bought them a beer each which proved to be just a fraction cooler than the lemonade and they sat at a small table drinking it in silence while he considered his next move.

He was just about to ask her where she lived when he heard the sound of the street door behind him opening. Jenny glanced up and stiffened suddenly.

"Lord, it's him," she whispered. Fear stood on her face. Someone came up behind him and stopped by his chair, bumping arrogantly into his shoulder and making beer slop over his fingers. He put his glass down and got out a handkerchief.

"What're you doing in here, Jen? Told you to wait outside, d'in I? Where did you pick up this poofter? Can't you keep your hands off the men for five minutes?"

Tom looked up from his beer wiping. Jason was a tall, brawny young man with greasy black hair and a pimply face. Despite the heat, he wore a black zippered leather jacket adorned with studs and emblems, and a pair of faded, ragged jeans.

"You were supposed to be here at half past four," she said indignantly.

"Couldn't make it then. Come on, let's go."

"I'm not going anywhere with you. I'm fed up having to wait every time you feel like being late. You were supposed to be here at half past four."

"I said, come on."

"Didn't you hear her? She doesn't want to go with you."

"Well, I'll be doggone! If it isn't John Wayne!" said Jason in what was presumably meant to be an American accent. Then in a menacing British snarl, "Stay out of this, Grandad, or I'll knock your block off."

Out of the corner of his eye, Tom saw the barman call his companion over. They stood together, alert, watching.

"Leave me alone, Jase. I don't want to come with you," she implored.

"Come on, unless you want your face smashed," he said, taking her roughly by the arm and dragging her to her feet. She looked desperately at Tom.

"Take your hands off her," he said, standing up. His eyes were about on a level with Jason's ill-shaven chin.

"Who's going to make me? You, old man? I could take you with one hand tied behind my back."

"Leave her alone, or you're going to have to."

"Don't you talk big, for a little fellow? I might spoil that pretty face for you."

"And I might improve yours."

"I'd put you through that window right now, but I don't usually mix it with old age pensioners."

"Take your choice. It's me or them," he said, indicating the two barmen who were making a move in their direction.

"Outside, then."

"Lead on."

Jason pushed his ugly face to within an inch of Tom's and grinned.

"I'm going to take you to pieces, you know that? It'll take them a week to find all the bits."

"Save your breath. Let's go."

Under the watchful eyes of the two barmen, the procession left the pub, Jason first, swinging his shoulders as he walked, the lights glinting on the studs of his jacket, Tom following, his shirt feeling damp and clammy against him, surveying the other's broad back as he walked, wondering how many pounds in weight he was giving away besides the six or seven years of age, Jenny behind him looking anxious and unhappy.

"There's an alley round the side."

"Suits me."

It was a typical back-of-the-pub alley, a wide door for deliveries, not as smartly painted as the front, another door leading to the gents' toilets, stacks of crates filled with empties by the wall, empty beer kegs awaiting collection and, at the far end, a washing line with three or four tea towels hanging limply in the heat. The ground was littered with crown caps and discarded beer mats, especially round three very smelly dustbins near the washing line.

The moment they were out if sight of the pavement, Jason swung round, his fist already at chest level. Fast, but not quite fast enough. He didn't actually see Tom's fist move, but he felt the impact and then he felt his back crash against the wall. He slid into a sitting position and stared at him, amazed and temporarily stunned.

"Bloody hell!" he exclaimed and scrambled to his feet, only to find himself a moment later sitting on exactly the same spot.

He got up again. This time he was ready. So he thought.

His fist connected with Tom's head just above the ear but it was a glancing blow compared with what he got in exchange. He tripped over a crate and staggered, trying to regain his balance. Tom's fist crashed hammer-like on the back of his shoulder and three more swift punches felled him with a noisy clang among the beer kegs. He felt no inclination to face this tornado again unarmed.

His fingers scrabbled for a weapon. Seeing this, Tom grabbed his jacket from the ground with one hand and Jenny's arm with the other.

"Let's get the hell out of here. I'll take you home. "

They fled.

"Where do you live?"

"Barracks Street. I'll show you."

"I know it."

He had forgotten that he was meant to be a tourist, but there was no time or breath for questions.

Meanwhile, the discomfited Jason had extricated himself from the beer kegs. He stood for a moment, scowling after them, with his fingers tenderly exploring his jaw, then he walked away briskly from the alley towards Constantine's cafe. He pushed open the glass-panelled door and walked up to a table where five other young men were sitting, of similar age and appearance to himself.

"Hi, Jase. Want to sit down?"

"You guys doing anything?"

"Nope. What's up? You look a bit miserable."

Jason glowered at the wall.

"Some bloody Yank's gone off with Jen. He socked me, the blighter, behind the Bricklayer's Arms and he's gone off with her."

"God Almighty! Who was he, the Incredible Hulk?"

"Some little short-arse, but he's so bloody quick I couldn't get near him."

"Blimey!"

"He's taking her home. If we nip round to Lemon Street –"

"Yeah. Come on. We don't want no wise guys on our patch. He can't be quick enough for all of us."

They rose in a body and headed for the door.

Jenny and Tom were about half way down the street, which was hemmed in by the usual high brick houses, rising straight up from the pavement, with no vestige of garden or front area before them, when a group of half a dozen young men appeared at the other end. There was an indefinable air of menace about them, like that of a pack of wolf's intent on its prey. Tom eyed them uneasily as they approached and the feeling was confirmed when they suddenly fanned out across the road, blocking it completely as they continued to advance on them. Jenny, who had been watching the situation too, suddenly said,

"It's Jason and his pals." And her eyes widened with fear.

Tom stopped, completely at a loss.

"I can't handle that lot."

There seemed no-where to go. Even precipitate and ignominious flight, which he would have indulged in if he had been alone, seemed impossible with Jenny in tow and he could not leave her to their tender mercies. He had been about to tell her to run for it and prepare to do his best as they continued to bear down on them, when she suddenly said,

"Come on!"

She dived up a close off Lemon Street. He followed but when he got to the back of the houses she had vanished into a maze of low walls, coalhouses and outside lavatories. He looked around, bewildered.

"Where the devil has she gone? Jenny! Jenny!"

No one answered. In the distance, a dog barked. Passing traffic made a subdued hum. High, crumbling tenement buildings loomed all around, half empty. Dirty rags of curtains still flapped pathetically behind broken windows, like hands waving vainly for help.

Reaction hit him with a numbing wave of exhaustion. Darkness coming on, a crowd of enemies nearby, frightened, and alone in this weird and unknown landscape, he could have dropped where he stood.

"Jenny!" he called again.

Like magic, she appeared right in front of him from round an angle of wall.

"Where d'you get to?" she demanded, pushing her fringe out of her eyes with dirty fingers. "I was miles on. I thought you was right behind me."

The relief at seeing her dispersed his exhaustion at once.

"Well, you just, like, vanished."

"Come on."

She took him by the hand and dragged him stumbling after her. He followed her as she picked a swift and tortuous way through a maze which was clearly as familiar to her as his own flat was to him. They scrambled over walls, dived through narrow spaces between buildings, skirted piles of rubbish and even once found themselves walking on the roofs of two adjoining brick sheds. Finally, panting, they arrived at the open back door of a derelict house.

"Come on in."

The ground floor was awful, stacked with rubbish, but she led him up some still solid stone steps to the first floor. The flat door stood open and she stepped boldly in. There were no tramps, but they had been here not too long ago. The place stank and an empty wine bottle lay on its side in the dust.

"Where are we?"

"Barracks Street."

He glanced briefly through the remains of a dusty window.

"Oh yeah. Just on the downtown side of the hoardings."

Now she had the leisure to look suspicious.

"Thought you said you were here on holiday?"

"Did I also tell you I'm the world's biggest liar?"

"No, but I believe it." She moved closer to him. "I don't care very much about that, though. It's what you did that counts. You saved me."

"Oh that. It wasn't so much. It's easy to hit someone who's not ready for it. I've always been quick. It's saved my ass more often than I care to think. Anyway, you saved me as well. I hope I haven't got you into trouble. Will he come and take it out on you?"

"I've got two brothers. They'll look out for me."

"I hope you're right."

"I shan't have nothing more to do with him anyway. A chap who keeps you waiting for two hours and then can't even fight for you without all is friends to help."

"That doesn't signify. If I'd given him a chance, it would have been a very different story, I can tell you. He wouldn't have needed any friends at all."

"I still think you were great."

"Thanks. Would you have picked me up if it was me left lying among the beer kegs?"

"But it didn't happen, did it?"

"It might just as easily. I guess I'll go look out of the front window and see if anyone's in sight. If they're not, we'll go."

He turned from the window and found Jenny was right behind him. She pressed up against him and it was plain what she wanted. It accorded with some deep primitive instinct, to complete his victory with the woman of his vanquished foe and she clearly liked the idea as much as he did. But that troublesome feeling of honour which stopped his mouth when he wanted to propose to Elizabeth picked this moment to chip in is two cents' worth.

"Jenny, you don't owe me that. Anyone would have done what I did."

"That they wouldn't. They'd have faded into the crowd. Why get landed in someone else's fight? You were great. I've got to pay you."

"Not like that. I couldn't take it as payment. But if you say, because you like me. Or maybe, because we're friends –"

"Because we're friends."

"Here?"

"Good as anywhere."

With her back against the doorframe, he kissed her, leaning his whole body on her and enjoying the pleasant sensations of arousal. Blows and kisses. How strange that the primitive instincts should still be so close to the surface! It was a very long time since he had shown such aggressive behaviour and the memory of what he had done that evening made its opposite seem all the sweeter.

He could not forget, though, that Jenny had neatly and resourcefully rescued him from a very ugly and dangerous situation, for he had no doubt that those half a dozen pugnacious youths would have worked him over pretty thoroughly for what he had done to their leader. For that, he thought, he owed her rather more than a little transitory physical pleasure.

He looked at her as she stood there against the doorway, eyes closed and arms tight across his back, her lips seeking his again. What could he do for her? He kissed her again and suddenly had an idea.

"Come over here," he said.

They sat on the dusty floorboards in a corner out of sight of the window, leaning against the damp, peeling wall. He put his arm round her and, with the other hand, started to slowly unbutton the front of her dress.

"Jenny," he said, "I'm going to say something to you that you might think it's not my place to say, none of my business, in fact. You can slap my face if you want to, but I think you should hear me out."

"Go on then, and I'll let you know."

"Look, you're a pretty girl, nice face, nice figure, nice legs –"

"Keep talking, I like it."

"Nice hair, too, if it was washed and cut properly. If it were to have it done, and keep yourself clean – told you I was going to be rude to you, didn't I? – and get a pretty dress, you could have someone much better than that lout Jason," – or me either, he added mentally – "You could have the pick of the young men of the town. Why don't you? It's not much of an effort."

"It is, though. You don't know what it's like around here. These houses are all condemned and the Council won't do nothing to them. There's nine of us in the family and we've got no bathroom. My Mam has to bath us in a tin bath in front of the fire. I help 'er, 'cause I'm the oldest girl, you see, and by the time we've boiled kettles and bathed all the little ones, well, I've just had enough. I can't often be bothered bathing myself."

He stared at her unbelievingly. Did people really live like that nowadays?

"It's quite true and there's lots more like us."

"Are all the houses round here like that?" he asked, suddenly enlightened.

"Oh yes, most of them. All the ones in Barracks Street."

"Oh? What about Blackgate Street?"

"They're even worse. There's more of them since they're tenements. They've got a toilet on each landing that all the families on that floor share, a kitchen sink with no hot water and that's your lot. They're all due to be knocked down, you see and the Council says it's not worth their while modernising them, 'cos we'll all be rehoused in a year or two. A year or two, maybe. I'm not holding my breath."

So that was it. A perfectly simple explanation of why the district had proved such a fruitful source to him, and of why the names of Barracks and Blackgate had been enough to allow Ann to ravel out his secret, and make his life hell for the past six months. Nothing more mysterious than a penny – pinching local council!

"Incredible!" he whispered, then, aloud, to Jenny, "Why don't you move out then? Find yourself a flat?"

"I'd like to, but I can't afford it. I don't earn much as a typist. Besides, I don't want to live alone."

"Share a flat then, with some other girls. Then you'd share the rent and the expenses, so it needn't be too much."

"I don't know how to find one."

"Look in the paper. There are columns of people every night advertising for people to share their flats. Then all you need are some pennies for the phone and, if you put your mind to it, you could be in a flat next week."

"Easy as that?"

"Easy as that."

She mused.

"My sister's old enough to help my Mam, she's still at school, but she can do all the things that I do for her. My Mam would have one less to cook for, too. Jason couldn't find me either, could he?"

"Probably not."

Her eyes lit up.

"I'll do it. Do you know, I think you've changed my life."

"Good. Great."

She looked at him with soft and loving eyes.

"You've changed my life, Tom, you really have. How can I ever thank you?"

"There's no need at all. It's I who should be thanking you. Didn't you save mine?"

"What are you talking about?"

"From our friend Jason and his cronies."

"Oh, Jason wouldn't have gone that far."

"I'm glad to hear it."

"No, finishing you off would have been too kind in his book. He'd rather have let you suffer."

"What a delightful young man."

"Still," she added, stroking his cheek, "I'm very glad he didn't get hold of you. You wouldn't have been so good-looking by now if he had."

"Gee, yes. I don't know about good-looking, but I sure would have looked different. I shan't forget what you did for me, Jenny. I'm very grateful."

He gathered her in his arms and she slid down a little.

"Come on, show me how you do it."

"Haven't you done it before, Jenny?" he asked anxiously. The prospect of initiating a virgin under such circumstances would have given him furiously to think. To his mingled relief and amusement, she said,

"Course I have, but never with a gentleman."

He shook his head emphatically.

"Don't fool yourself, Jenny. You're not doing it with a gentleman now."

"If you knew some of the fellows I know – gosh, I wish I could share a flat with you."

"I don't live here. Besides, you wouldn't like it after a bit. I'm not really nice to know. What does this dress of yours do now? I've unfastened all the buttons and it hasn't got me very far. Has it got a secret combination lock somewhere?"

"Silly! It's got a zip at the side, look. I like you anyway, whatever you say."

"Would I be sitting here doing this to you if I was nice to know?"

She laughed.

"You wouldn't have been doing it at all if Jason had got his boot in. He'd have stamped on that hand good and hard, and he wouldn't have missed the other bit either, know what I mean?"

"I know. Well, here's to Jason's downfall. I hope he never gets within range of me again."

"Socked his jaw and had his girl. He'd break every bone in your body, you'd better go back to America while you're still in one piece."

181

"Not yet. Up to now, I've only socked his jaw."

"Come on then, what are you waiting for?" She put her arms up so he could pull off her dress. "Mind you, my slip's nothing to write home about. I didn't expect anyone to see it."

"Doesn't matter. It's what's inside that counts." She was painfully thin. He could feel her backbone like a series of knobs. "You don't seem to eat very much."

"Well, when my Mam can't afford much for dinner, I let the boys and the little ones have mine. I just say I'm not hungry."

He loved the way she said 'little ones' without pronouncing the 't's'.

"Poor Jenny. You'd be much better off looking after yourself."

She shrugged.

"I don't really mind, if it helps Mam. You're not thin, anyway. Let's have a look at you, come on. Fair's fair, after all. I want to see the famous arm that socked Jason."

"Go ahead, then. My shirt buttons are at your disposal."

She pushed the shirt off his shoulders and said,

"Oh my word, wow!" She stroked his chest and his shoulders, then peered down his back. "I say, do you know you've got red lines all over your back?"

He hunched his shoulders with embarrassment.

"I guess it's from where I've been leaning against the wall. I mark very easily."

"Doesn't look like that," she said, trying to see again.

"Never mind my back. Let's concentrate on your front. That's much more interesting. What would Jason say if he saw me now?"

"Are you asking me to use language like that? Sod Jason, I don't care what he'd say, the ugly bastard. I'm finished with the likes of him. I'll find a chap who'll look after me properly but Tom – I'll never forget you."

"I'm not worth remembering."

"I'll remember. Always."

Jenny was sitting on the floor of the damp, abandoned bedroom rolling her head ecstatically against the peeling wallpaper. Tom had eased one soft little pink breast out of its hiding place and he was kissing it. No one had ever kissed her breasts before and it was lovely.

Observing her reaction, Tom deduced correctly that Jason was a species of Vlad the Impaler intent only on gratifying his own need. It was sad to think of this sweet and affectionate kid linked to a lot like him. It occurred to him that he might have even made things worse for her by his hasty well-intentioned action.

"Jenny, that guy, is he likely to come round and take it out on you?"

She shook her head.

"My brothers'll look after me. They've been telling me to get away from Jason for ages. I don't want 'im no more. Not since I saw you put 'im on the floor."

His heart felt so full of tenderness for this sweet and affectionate girl that he hardly knew how to contain it. They began to make love and after a few minutes she said,

"Oh Tom, you're so – gentle."

"Aren't you used to people being gentle with you?"

"No I'm not. Jason just likes to show how tough he is. He hurts me."

"Jenny, Jenny, don't ever let him hurt you again. Oh Jenny, I can't bear to think of him hurting you."

She stirred and he got an arousing puff of her body smell. This was the apotheosis of his passion. Because Ann punished him so adequately, there was no need for him to regard Jenny as a punishment. He did not have to wallow and degrade himself. He could kiss her breasts instead of her feet. He reached up to stroke her hair but she turned her head and kissed the palm of his hand.

This unexpected touching gesture affected him like the flicking on of a light. He raised his head and looked at her ecstatic face, seeing in it the faces of countless girls, here and at home, that he had turned into symbols, catalysts in his ingrown reaction on himself, used and discarded. He curved his fingers round her cheek and felt its softness. He needed something to feel good to him then because a shattering avalanche of sharp-edged realisation had swept unanticipated over his mind. He could see with painful clarity what he was doing for what it really was. Wallow? Degrade himself? Regard her as a punishment? What was he thinking? She was Jenny, a girl with needs and problems that shrank his own into insignificance. She was a daughter, a sister, third child and oldest girl in a family of nine, a friend to her cronies, above all a human, human being. Not something for him to use in his self-centred search for mental easement. He could see, he was behaving worse than Jason! She was not just a body. None of them had been just bodies. Even Ann, the tough, streetwise Ann.

"I won't let him hurt me ever again. Oh Tom –" And suddenly, she began to cry.

"What's the matter, Jenny? Oh, don't cry. Do you want me to stop?"

"No, I don't, but you will stop, and then you'll go away and I'll never see you again."

She burst into a storm of tears, and he rolled over, sat up and held her in his arms, her head on his chest. He held her gently, stroking her hair and trying to sooth her while she cried uncontrollably, clinging to him desperately as if she was drowning, her little, underfed body trembling against him, racked with sobs. Still overwhelmed himself by his sudden self-realisation, he had a lump in his throat the size of a football and he felt as near to tears as he had been since he learned that 'big boys don't cry'.

Jenny began to recover a little. She wiped her eyes with her fingers, leaving dirty smears on her face from the dust on the floor. He found his handkerchief, not the one that smelled of beer, gently dried her eyes and wiped the dirt away.

"I'm sorry, Tom, I don't know what came over me. It was all too much, all of a sudden."

"Oh, Jenny, it's all right –" he said and then choked. Bound hand and foot by the convention that said that tears were unmanly, he closed his eyes, clamped his jaw and leaned back against the wall, longing for some relief from the force of self-knowledge that was tearing him to pieces within. Jenny looked at his distressed face and, in a deeply compassionate voice she said,

"Why don't you cry, Tom? You look as if you want to."

"I can't," he gasped.

"Yes you can. You'll feel better if you do."

"I can't, I can't, oh, Jenny –" He buried his face in his hands, fighting a last desperate battle not to lose control.

"Yes you can. Look, no one will know except me and you can be sure I won't tell anyone.

"You can cry in front of me, after all, you won't ever see me again –"

Her voice broke and when it did, the shell of years of customary restraint and self-control fell away, and tears streamed down his cheeks.

It was her turn now to comfort him as he sobbed in her arms, his face hidden in her bony shoulder, crying, not like a child, but with the hard, racking sobs of one weeping in spite of himself. It was several minutes before he was able to collect himself and lift his head with a long, shuddering breath. He felt dizzy and his head ached, but the dreadful tension was gone, and he felt able to face up to things again.

"Aren't we a pair of great babies, sitting here howling over each other like this?" he said with a lop-sided smile. "Where's that handkerchief of mine?"

"No, we're not," she replied, handing it to him. "If more people did this sort of thing, they wouldn't end up in the nut house."

"Let it all hang out, man, and how! Seriously, though, Jenny, you don't know how much you've done for me today. I think you've done more for me than anyone has done before. When I came up and spoke to you this afternoon, I just wanted a girl, any girl, didn't matter who, for my own fun. Who you were meant no more to me than, say, what chair I chose to sit on. But, Jenny, when I saw how that lout Jason treated you, I was so angry, not only that he would treat any girl like that, but that he would treat you in particular like that, I had already got to like you, you see, though I was still, I'm sorry to say, thinking of nothing more than how I could persuade you to let me lay you. But there was something about you that made me – really forced me – to take the risk of swapping punches with him. I was really scared, Jenny, make no mistake about that. He's a big fellow and I knew that one slip on my part would have let him take me to pieces, just like he said. Well, thankfully, I got away with that, and, since then, I've come to like and admire you so very much. When you told me how you let the others in the family have your food when there wasn't enough, I thought, what a girl, what a marvellous girl. But when you cried because you wouldn't see me again, it broke me up like nothing ever has before. Jenny, if you knew what I'm like, if you knew –"

"Tom, you're all right."

"You don't know the half of it, Jenny. You just don't know. If you did, you wouldn't be able to see the back of me quickly enough."

"You're all right, Tom. If you weren't, it wouldn't worry you whatever it is."

"I wish I could think that."

"You think it. It'll work out. You've got to be a nice fellow, Tom, whatever you say. Look what you did for me this afternoon. You could have just walked away when Jase started throwing his weight about. I'm sure most chaps would have done that. Wouldn't have wanted to get involved. None of their business. But you didn't. Then, even after you'd hit him, you could still have left me to go home alone. You might have known he'd be the sort to get his pals and come looking for you."

"I guess I should have expected that, but, to be honest, the thought never crossed my mind."

"Tom, I wish I could help you."

"You have helped me, Jenny, more than you could ever know."

"Do you want to make love again?"

"Jenny, I'd love to, but I honestly don't think I can now. Do you mind?"

"I can understand. Well, then, we'd better get down to some thinking, hadn't we? You're not out of the woods yet. He must have heard you say you were going to take me home, so they'll probably be hanging about the house. Where have you got to get to?"

"I've got to get back to the town centre. My car's in the multi-storey car park. It'll cost me a fortune to get it out after all this time."

"Well, you can't walk there alone, you'd never make it without running into one or other of them. And you couldn't wait at the bus stop either. Tell you what, if we get back to our house, I'll get my brothers to go with you."

"Will they want to?"

"If I tell them what Jason was doing to me and that you socked him, you'll be their best friend. They can't stand him. They were always on at me to get away from him. We needn't tell them any of our secrets."

"That sounds great."

"I'd better put my dress back on, hadn't I? If you stay here, I'll have a quick recce and see what's what. I can keep out of sight on my own."

After a few minutes, she slipped out of the front door, looked around and worked her way from shadow to shadow in the gathering dusk. Then as he watched from the window, carefully keeping out of sight, he suddenly saw her disappear into another house. He waited for several minutes, tense and alert to every sound in the quiet street, the occasional car humming past, distant shouts, creaks and clicks from the old house he stood in, every sound, however tiny.

It was quite dark inside the house now and he felt the hair beginning to prickle on the back of his neck. A small sound came from the direction of the door – was it her? He listened, listened and then started violently as something brushed against his legs. A loud mew. Nothing but a stray cat. Restraining himself from kicking it across the room, he listened again, hardly breathing. Then he jumped again as, with shocking suddenness, the streetlights flashed on and flooding part of the room with dazzling light. He moved back into the shadows and waited.

Another movement and a whisper.

"Tom!"

"Jenny! Is it you?"

"Where are you?"

"Over here, out of the light."

She came into the room, glimmering in the half-light. He was never so glad to see anyone in his life.

"Well?"

"Jason's a little way down the road on this side, the way you have to go. Two of them are on the other side near our house. We'd have to pass them to get there. One's further up the road the other way and I don't know where the other two are. Tom, we're in dead trouble."

Chapter 21

"What can we do, then?"

It was borne in upon him anew how deadly serious all this was. Alone with this young girl in this derelict shambles with a horde of louts outside intent on grievous bodily harm with him as the target. The bottom seemed to drop out of his stomach and he felt sick and faint with fear. He stared at Jenny, trying to fight off the fit of panic. On unknown territory, handicapped by her –

"Right. No more messing. Out the back, we'll work our way down the street that way – you don't mind a bit of climbing? Well, you'd better not. Then we'll cut through Lemon Street and you go off on your own. Can you find your way from there?"

"Sure. What about you?"

"Oh, I can sneak back. I'll get into the house the back way."

No good. No good at all. If they were covering the front of the house, they'd be watching the back as well.

"I'm taking you home, Jenny," he said, trying not to think what his words could be leading him into.

"Don't be stupid. They're looking for you, not me. What're they going to do to me?"

"Ever heard of a gang-bang?"

The short, brutal words brought her up short. Her eyes looked deeply into his. Then he heard her breath sigh out.

"Um."

"Um is right. I'm not going to let you take that risk. I'm staying with you until you're in your house and safely in the care of your brothers, whatever happens to me. I'm not letting you face them alone. You mean far too much to me for that."

"Do I really, Tom? OK. We'll go down this side a bit, cross the road where they won't see us, work our way back, and we'll just have to try and dodge them behind the houses."

"Yes. Right." He hoped he sounded more resolute than he felt. "If they see us, I'll hold 'em as long as I can and you run for it. Scream for your brothers. Don't worry about me. Get inside out of it. Let's go now."

But she did not go at once. He could see little more of her than her eyes by then, but they had never left his. Suddenly, she flung her arms around him.

"Tom, oh, Tom, I got you into this."

"Don't give it a thought. We'll see it through together." He put his fingers under her chin and tipped her face towards his. "Together."

They kissed. A sweet, magic kiss in the face of mutual danger. When their lips parted, he was smiling and the adrenalin was beginning to flow. His fear had left him and he felt ready for anything.

They crept downstairs hand in hand. It was almost pitch dark by now and the vile back courts were lighted only by fitful gleams that found their way from the street lamps through the empty buildings. Still holding hands for the fear of getting separated, they stumbled for what seemed like miles over broken ground littered with bricks, bottles and all kinds of traps for unwary feet, and climbed over dividing walls until she picked a close and peered out cautiously into the street.

"Can't see any of them."

All the same, venturing into the open road under streetlights that felt like searchlights was a nervous business. As they crossed, walking as coolly as they could to avoid attracting attention, his skin was tingling every moment in expectation of a shout, running feet, a blow from behind, Jenny screaming, blood, pain. And that hazard negotiated only marked the beginning of the most dangerous part of their journey.

Quietly, breathlessly, with eyes and ears alert, they slipped back up Barracks Street behind the opposite houses. More of these were occupied but the windows were curtained so the light exposed their whereabouts without giving any idea if their attackers were near. It was a ghastly journey. Before long, Tom had quite lost his bearings. They stopped behind a bin-shelter.

"There it is," she whispered, pointing to a kitchen window.

It was as well she whispered it right in his ear, for suddenly, almost at their elbows, a voice said softly,

"Got a fag, Ken?"

"Yep."

They were just on the other side of the shelter. Tom and Jenny, stopped, frozen in their tracks. A cigarette was given and lit, and then the first voice said, "I'm getting fed up with this. What say we nip over to the pub for ten minutes? I don't think they'll come this way."

"Yeah. Come on. If Jase can't keep tabs on his own bird, I don't see why I should spend my Saturday night doing it for him."

They moved off noisily. Tom and Jenny breathed again.

"I hope that's all," he murmured.

They stopped by the wall, just beside the kitchen window, hidden in the shadow. They waited, but there was no movement and no one challenged them.

"Seems all right."

"Wait, Jenny, before we go in. I might not get another chance to say this. You've done more for me tonight than you could possibly know. I gotta thank you."

"I never knew no one that wittered on the way you do. What you on about now?"

"Never mind. If we don't see each other again –"

With a little half sob she was in his arms and seeking his lips with hers. In the dark of that summer night, in that urban wilderness, he kissed the girl who had set him free as if he would kiss her forever.

"I'll never forget you, Tom. I'll find a new guy, but I'll never forget you. "

She tried the handle of the back door. Lights were on in the house but the door was locked.

"Who's that?" said a suspicious voice.

"It's me, Mam, Jenny."

"I heard some boys outside so I've locked and bolted the door. Come in the window, it'll be quicker than unlocking it again."

The sash was opened and they scrambled in over the chipped stoneware sink, into the stuffy kitchen smelling of past meals and present ironing, Jenny and her biology professor who was mentally comparing her courage and resourcefulness with the attributes of a certain rich young lady of his acquaintance. Favourably.

"Hi, Mam. Are the boys in? This is Tom. He needs a bit of help."

"How do you do, er, ma'am," said Tom, realising suddenly that he had no idea of Jenny's surname. Jenny's Mum simply looked him up and down, and nodded, in response to both his greeting and Jenny's question. She was a little, scrawny, used-up rag of a woman, but there was an indomitability in her eye which her daughter had inherited.

"Yes, they're through the room."

Entering the living room behind Jenny, Tom saw that it gave the same impression as the kitchen, shabby and well worn, but clean. The walls were covered with brightly coloured floral paper, badly in need of renewal and a cheerful fire burned in the grate of an old-fashioned fireplace. An American detective story was showing on the large colour television, easily the most handsome object in the room and the sound of gunfire echoed from the walls. Two large young men sat in sagging armchairs and the settee was filled with an assortment of small children who stared at the stranger with large curious eyes. One of the young men glanced up.

"Home early, Jen."

"Ben, Mike, this is Tom, a friend of mine. He's in trouble. Needs a bit of help."

Ben, the elder, half rose and turned down the sound to a chorus of protest from the younger viewers.

"Shut up, you lot," he said curtly and silence fell for a few seconds.

Jenny began to tell the tale of Jason's bullying and then about the fight which she described with hero-worship in her voice. Tom was enormously amused to see the two young men staring in ever-increasing astonishment at his relatively diminutive figure as Jenny told how he had repeatedly floored the terror of Blackgate without taking a single solid punch in reply.

"I wish you'd tell me your secret, man," said Ben enviously.

"I'm fast. Because I'm not so big, I have to be fast. Get them before they get you, that's my motto. It's saved my ass more times than I like to think."

Ben laughed.

"Where did you pick up a Yank, Jen?"

"I told you. We was in the pub –"

"Well, I gotta thank you for what you done for my brainless sister, but what help do you need? Sounds as if you can take care of yourself damn well."

"Against eight of them?" Jenny snapped.

The boys were furious when she told them how the house was staked out. Ben peered through a crack in the curtains and estimated six. Then he went to a corner of the room, got a pole like a long broomstick and gave a series of complicated knocks on the ceiling.

"We'll get Jack and Tom down. Fellows who live upstairs. We've got a code, and they'll know there's trouble and to watch it as they come. Go and open the door for them, Mike."

A few minutes later, a flood of young men came in, all great husky brutes. The boys upstairs had been playing cards and having a few drinks with friends. Tom began to feel a lot better. They heard the story, and were as impressed by him as Ben and Mike had been.

Ben said,

"I might have stepped into something like that for my own sister, but I wouldn't have done it for someone else's. Jason put a guy in hospital last month."

"I'm sure glad I didn't know that."

His namesake from upstairs who was about seventeen and half a head taller than him, shook Tom's hand enthusiastically and proclaimed himself proud to share his name. Tom concluded Jason was not universally loved.

"Well, what's the plan?" said young Tom eagerly.

"We take 'em out," said Ben. "Get out there and keep them busy while the Lone Ranger here makes a run for it."

"Run for it be damned. I've done all the running I plan to do for tonight."

"You with us, then?"

"Yeah."

"Great. I'd say we've got about ten minutes. Someone'll phone for the rozzers when they hear the racket and it'll take them around that long to get here."

"Enough time to crack a few heads."

They sallied out into the close in a tight bunch. The cool evening breeze and acute nervousness made Tom shiver but still, he had no wish to use the invitation to run. Kev Aston was the first antagonist they saw.

"Aston, get yourself and your pals off of our patch."

"Free country, ennit?" came a growl from the street.

"Not for you lot. Clear off if you know what's good for you. You've got till I count ten."

He began to count to a chorus of defiance from outside. Mike turned to Tom.

"When you see a jam butty, scarper. It's everyone for hisself then."

The count finished and they were exploding from the close entrance, leaving Tom not a second to ponder on the meaning of this strange message.

Jason had been looking forward to a pleasant, easy revenge but because of the card game and defections in his own forces, he found himself outnumbered, outgunned and outmanoeuvred. He and his friends were quickly ringed round, and were taking a terrific beating. Kev's knife and a cosh someone produced both went flying across the street, and out of reach almost as soon as they appeared. Boots, fists and heads were indiscriminately in use. It was a good average Blackgate scrap with one side getting pounded. Jason was not used to it being his side and he was almost relieved to hear the wail of a police siren.

"Get the hell out or they'll bang you up for the night!" Ben yelled to Tom as the 'jam butty' swept round the corner.

"Thanks for the party, guys," Tom shouted and ran. A constabulary voice ordered him to stop and a whistle blew. He ran faster. There was an angry cry and a terrific crash. He glanced over his shoulder. Young Tom had tripped the policeman and been collared by another. He hesitated but the lad waved him on. Remembering Mike's words 'it's everyone for hisself', he started to run again. The sacrifice would be useless if he stuck around. He would find out what happened to young Tom and do what he could to help.

He put a lot of distance between himself and the dying remains of the fight before he stopped, and took stock. Under a streetlamp in a quiet area, he paused panting and looked himself over. There was quite a lot of blood on his clothes and some of it must be his because he could feel it trickling from a cut over his jawbone. One ear was singing and when he felt it, it was swollen. Various parts of his body felt bruised. All the same, he had been in dirtier fights and come out in worse shape. It had been quite an experience but the toughest bit was yet to come. He had to face Ann, and tell her he was done forever with Blackgate and with her and her whippings. Compared with that, Jason and his friends had been easy meat.

Chapter 22

He spent most of the day following this adventurous Saturday in bed, nursing his injuries and considering his position.

After shower and a very gingerly shave, he exposed his battered torso to infrared heat from the health lamp he usually used on ultra violet to keep his Californian skin to its normal tan even in the depths of a British winter. He put a fresh dressing on the bruised and ragged cut on his jaw, and ice packed his swollen ear and another swelling on his temple. His hands were in bad shape, stiff and tender, but he hoped those they had been in contact with felt worse.

With his bodily hurts soothed, and the big electric coffee pot full and steaming on the bedside table, he lay back and reviewed the social implications of his incident-packed evening with Jenny.

Almost a year he had been in Britain and a pretty comprehensive mess he had managed to make of things. He always fell in love with girls like Elizabeth and he always furtively offered himself to girls like Ann, but never before had he encountered one who had accepted the offer so whole-heartedly. Those regular floggings she had made him submit to had pushed him to the depth of self-disgust, but in driving him to the point where there was no way but up, they had also prepared the way for Jenny.

And Elizabeth. Her predecessors had each responded to his blandishments, and shared his life for a while, filling one set of bodily and spiritual needs, while the Anns had filled another. Elizabeth was currently in Dorset for the weekend. She had resisted him and he had thought he wanted to marry her, but now he was not so sure. All at once this morning, her flaws seemed all too clear. Just as his had done to the first of those beautiful girls in his life, whose name, oddly enough, had been not dissimilar. She had been called Elise.

He had met Elise while they were both at college, innocent, optimistic kids full of big plans for the years ahead. He had told her how his folks were poor and she had said it didn't matter, but in the end, it had mattered too much. Her experience of life had been too limited for her to cope. One vacation, she had taken him to meet her family, and, dazzled by their possessions and a life-style beyond his wildest dreams, he had gone home at the end of an amazing week with a head full of plans of what he would do for her when he was through with his studies.

Then he had invited her to his home. He had had to budget carefully to see he had enough for a cab when he picked her up at the airport and he could remember the way her face changed as they left the prosperous parts for the poorer streets. When the cab had stopped at the house, for a moment, he had feared she actually was not going to get out.

She had, but then she had made him put her suitcase just in the hall. Then she had met his folks, and taken a swift and disdainful look at the way they lived. To his surprise, she had then asked him to show her the back yard. Once outside, she had rounded on him, and called him a fraud and a jerk, and every other name she could think of and told him she wasn't staying in this run-down slum another minute. Then she had taken her suitcase from the hall and walked out. He had run after her to find her in a call box getting herself a cab. He had pleaded with her till the cab had come and whirled her away leaving him on the pavement utterly humiliated.

In his shock, he had wandered off down town, a prey to bitter thoughts, till he had found himself in a really tough, poor ghetto. Then he had decided that if that was rich girls, he was through with them and he was going to find the poorest girl he could to take Elise's place. He had gone out that afternoon a virgin but an hour later, he was one no longer. He was on a vacant lot with a half-caste girl to whom a pure white college boy was an unattainable dream and an innocent one the seventh heaven of bliss. She made all the mileage she could out of is initiation and he was a willing pupil. But when it was over, that awful revulsion had hit him for the first time. He had just upped and run for it. Years and maturity had taught him a degree of subtlety, but basically nothing had changed – till Ann. That day of his rejection by Elise had been the second of those three bad days in his life and in its turn, it had led directly to the third.

His desire for girls like the one who had taken his virginity kept returning with increasing frequency, followed inevitably by the revulsion and the desire to shower in agonisingly hot water till his skin was on the verge of peeling. He became frantic, unable to cope with the lack of control of his own mind, falling behind with his studies, without even the support of Mother, for he felt unable to expose this shameful sore even to her loving eyes. Eventually, he dropped out.

For many long weeks, he hid up in L.A., living in a rundown two room apartment, doing jobs building, labouring, anything to bring home a few dollars and endlessly chasing girls. He met a guy who appealed to him and they prowled the bars in tandem. Then, one night, in a sleazy dive downtown, they got caught in the crossfire of someone else's shootout. His friend was shot and badly injured, and he himself was pulled in by cops used to dealing with the tougher elements of society. Working in kid gloves was not their scene and to them, he was just another punk. They worked him over pretty efficiently before they let him go.

Somehow, he had got back to his miserable lodgings, fallen into bed and slept for many hours. When he woke, he knew it was time to look at himself and ask what the hell he thought he was doing.

Going home was the worst part. Half a dozen times, he had walked past the gate before getting up the courage to go up to the house. But when he did, the look on his Mother's face was worth it all. She had hugged him and cried over him, given him milk and cookies, and hugged him some more, exclaimed over his untidy and slightly battered appearance, and hugged him yet again.

When his Father had come home, he had simply looked at him disdainfully.

"Humph. I knew it wouldn't last. Thought you was finally becoming a man. I even began to feel proud of you."

His Mother had stared at him in astonishment.

"What do you mean, you felt proud of him? Did you know where he was?"

"Course I did. Jim Preston saw him in a bar and kept an eye on him. He told me what he was up to. The guys respected him and the girls couldn't get enough of him."

His Mother's fury was plain.

"You knew how I was worried out of my mind about him and you knew where he was all the time, and you never thought to tell me?"

"Course I didn't tell you. I knew what it would be like if I did. You'd just go get him back. I wanted my son to be a real man."

"I could murder you, Walter Di Angeli, truly I could. When I think of the sleepless nights I had and you knew all the time –

The argument went on for many minutes while he just sat there with his head down and surreptitiously gorged himself on homemade cookies.

Next was college. They were not keen on re-instating dropouts lest it should encourage others to try it. But they did take him back, reluctantly, because of the hitherto outstanding record. And then it was all over.

Except for the obsession. There was no escape from that. So he pragmatically built it into his life and constructed the flimsy cover of his alter ego, Tom Bone. In all honesty, few covers can have been blown with such monotonous regularity. But here, today, now, it really was over. All of it. Every bit. Tom Bone was dead and buried, laid to rest by a frail little kid called Jenny. And now he had to tell Ann. She was going to be wild. Power, money, influence over his life, all swept away in one hectic evening and she hadn't even been there. Oh yes, she was going to be wild.

He called her to his room on Monday afternoon, knowing she would think he was going to ask for an evening of her ministrations. He was ready for the storm. It was the first time he had let her get a close look at him that day and she stared, as everyone else had done. He had told the lab staff the old story that he had walked into a door and in the face of their patent incredulousness had simply refused to elaborate.

"Must have been a wrap-round door," he had heard Robert mutter to the girls.

"God, what the hell happened to you?" Ann cried in her shrill, confident voice. "Get in an argument with a double-decker bus?"

"Not quite," he said quietly. He had resolved to stay cool and unruffled whatever she literally or metaphorically threw at him. "I had something happen to me that you'd better know about. It affects you materially."

"Is this a one fag or a two fag story?"

"A two drink story, more like. But if you must destroy your lungs, go ahead." Pointedly he opened the window and pushed the ashtray towards him as she sat down, uninvited as usual. "And you're not going to like it, not one bit."

"Oh, give us the works, then. Don't pussyfoot."

"All right, short and crisp. It's over, you and I, finished."

"Over! Finished! Hah! Yes. Well, now we've had the funnies, tell me what you really wanted to see me about."

"Just that. Saturday night, I had a number of experiences and the marks you see are the results of the least of them. I learned a lot in a very short time. Now, I've got to thank you for one thing. You and your whip put me in a state of mind so I was ready to learn. And now I don't want to go chasing girls like the ones from Black gate anymore. I'm not a naughty boy, like you love to call me, so I don't have to let myself be beaten. I hope we can be civilised and agree to regard that part of our lives as closed. I'll be happy to pay for the things you bought, the boots and such."

Her finger tap-tap-tapped on the white paper of her cigarette and a fine shower of ash fell, some of it even into the ashtray. She watched it as it fell, a tight little smile on her face. Then she looked up.

"It's not so easy, sunshine. I can't pay the rent of that flat myself."

"I'll pay another two months to let you find another."

"Don't want another. I'm gonna stay there."

"Then you'll have to find the means to pay, Ann. No one owes you a living. I owe you a lot, but not that much."

She inhaled deeply, her chest expanding inside the lab coat, slightly damp from her glassware washing. Sadly, regretfully, she smiled at him. Pityingly.

"No go, darlin'. You try and rat, you know what I can do. I can tell 'em all about your funny little habits."

"Tell 'em then. Enjoy yourself. Let me know how it goes."

She rose to her feet looking utterly incredulous. With a flick of her thumb, she shot her cigarette end out of the window where it lay smouldering among the close-cropped grass, a thin, unwavering stream of smoke rising in the still, warm air.

"Have you gone raving mad?"

"On the contrary, I guess I've just come to my senses after about twelve years of being out of 'em."

She jerked out a desk drawer, turned the contents upside down on the blotter and thrust the envelope which had been buried in them into his hand.

"Take a look at them pictures, sunshine. Refresh your memory."

With a thud, the whole lot landed in the green metal waste bin. He did not take his eye off her. The crisis was fast approaching.

"It's over, Ann. Finished. I don't need you anymore."

He expected her to fly into a rage. Instead, her lips trembled, and her eyes looked hot and bright.

"Finished? Is that all you can say?"

"Yes. Let's be civilised about it, shall we?"

"But I – but I – Tommy, didn't you know I love you?"

That shook him. It was not the answer he expected. She had declared love for him long ago, but he had dismissed it as a passing emotional quirk and forgotten it. Till now, she had never mentioned it again.

"I'm sorry, Ann. I'm truly sorry if that's the case, though I think if you do love me, you hate me at the same time even more. I've always made it perfectly clear that I didn't love you and I never will. I can't tell you how bad it makes me feel if you feel more for me than I ever could for you. I realised I've used you in my search for peace of mind, but I think, not unfairly. Admit it, you were having a hell of a good time watching me squirm. Well, you were entitled to it, but now it's finished. Let's make it a clean break."

A tear trickled down her cheek as she made her last throw. She stepped forward and took his hand.

"Tom."

Gently but firmly, he pulled it away.

"It breaks my heart to see you cry, Ann, but you won't change my mind."

She dashed the tears away with the back of her hand.

"Right!" she gasped, barely able to speak. "Right, you bloody hypocrite. You think you can treat me like dirt, chuck me out when you're tired of me. Well, they're all going to see whose dirt now."

"I can understand how you feel, but what good is it going to do you to wreck my life for me?"

"A hell of a lot of good, that's what. I'm going to laugh like a drain to watch you drop into it. Oh yes, oh yes. A hell of a lot of good."

And she was gone. He stared at the door for a long time. Then he did something he had never done before. He went up the driveway to the Students' Union shop, bought half a bottle of whisky, say down in his room and drank the lot. It had not the slightest effect on him.

He was changing his shirt that evening for what was probably going to be his last ever date with Elizabeth, when he heard the rattle as the newsboy pushed the local evening paper through his door. Cramming the shirttail into the waistband of his trousers, he went to get it. There it was, half way down the front page. 'Affray in Barracks Street' He read:

"Three youths were arrested on Saturday after a scuffle in Barracks Street and appeared before magistrates this morning. Following the incident, another youth was taken to hospital and detained with suspected concussion."

Only three! Their legs must have been in good order to escape from the eruption of cops he had seen in his backwards look. Unless Jason had a Tom in his gang, it looked as if Jenny's pugilistic neighbour had not escaped. The other two arrested seemed to have come from the other side. And reading between the lines, he guessed it was none other than Jason himself who had come off worst. The defendants had been given a severe ticking off and fined £25 each. He could find the house again. That money was not going to come out of the family finances of his young ally.

While putting on his tie, he dwelt with amusement on what the paper might have done with the story that had got away. 'University Professor in Punch-up?' 'Don slugs local villains?' Gee, if only they knew what they had missed!

The telephone rang. He tutted and looked at his watch. Quarter to seven. He hoped it was not someone too garrulous, for he had to leave within the next ten minutes. Two pink theatre tickets for Guys and Dolls were tucked in his wallet, and the curtain rose at 7.30.

"Hi, Tom Di Angeli," he said cheerfully to the receiver.

The voice at the other end was recognisably Erica Ashton-Richards' but he had never before heard her speak in such tones of pure, super-cooled ice. She addressed him as 'Professor', which gave him a nasty jolt and then she said, "I'm afraid Elizabeth cannot see you. We have had a very unpleasant occurrence."

He asked what it might be.

"About ten minutes ago, we found a letter on the mat, delivered by hand and addressed to her. It contained – goodness, I hardly know how to say this – it contained, well, some photographs of you, Professor, in what I can only describe as a highly compromising situation. They were accompanied by a filthy and obscene anonymous letter. Elizabeth is deeply shocked. I would not, I think, be exaggerating if I say she seems in danger of a nervous breakdown."

For a moment, he was quite unable to answer.

"Mrs Ashton-Richards," he said at last, taking his form of address from hers. "I can't tell you how appalled I am. Please believe me when I say, I wouldn't have had this happen for the world. It sounds melodramatic to say it, but I have an enemy who has chosen to revenge herself on me in this particularly dreadful manner. I can't apologise enough. If I had had any idea this would happen, I would have done all in my power to prevent it."

"Well, Professor, I'm sorry for your troubles, but my first concern must be for my daughter. I think it would be better if you didn't see her again."

"If you think that best, then of course it must be so. If Elizabeth would speak to me just for a moment, I should like to apologise to her personally for what has happened."

"I don't think she will, but I will ask her."

There was a murmur of voices and then he heard Elizabeth shout hysterically, "No! I won't! Get him off the phone! I told you what would happen if I mixed with any more damn Americans! I won't!"

"I'm sorry, Professor. I expect you could hear how things are. She is terribly over-wrought. I must go to her now. Goodbye."

He put the phone down with the finality of that 'Goodbye' ringing in his ears. What a tragic waste! His innocent romance, killed by the malice spawned by his own failings. Only a year ago, in this very flat, he had had that mad desire to write her name on the wall in enormous letters. That carefree day seemed an infinity of time and space away. Sadly, he got the tickets from his wallet, scrunched them up and threw them in the kitchen pedal bin.

He made some coffee, carried it through to the living room, put it on a small table by his favourite armchair, sat down and looked around. It was an agreeable room, the walls painted pale primrose with a few pictures here and there. A unit of shelves lined one wall holding some things belonging to the people from whom he rented the flat, and some books and records of his. There were the usual dining table and chairs, and the two handsome leather covered armchairs with soft squashy buttoned cushions. A pleasant room, clean, modern, anonymous, empty, utterly lonely. He felt as if someone had just taken him and put him down there to get him out of the way.

Here he was, thirty years old, miles and oceans away from anything he could call home, with his life in ruins around him, and no one he could turn to. He sipped his coffee and his mind was full of girls crying. Jenny crying. Ann crying. Elizabeth's voice full of bitterness and tears. For so many things, his change of heart had come too late. So many heartbreaks, given and taken. Who had the power to free him from the burdens of the past?

Some calm, competent, level-headed girl to whom he would be able to fearlessly tell everything and who could take his problems in her stride. A girl with common sense and just a little toughness. Where was such a one to be found, though? Not a vengeful Ann, or one of the intolerant beauties like Elizabeth to whom he was so fatally drawn, but a girl with some of his Mother's precious virtues. She would be lost to him now, surely. In her longing to redeem the sinner, she would have made the mistake of marrying a lout who got drunk every week, came home and bruised her pretty face with his fists. The patient forgiveness she would have expended on him was given and taken already. She must exist somewhere. If only he had been the one to find her first! Perhaps she had once been right there beside him, loving him, but too timid to say so!

He sat for hours, brooding. On tonight and what might have been. On tomorrow and what an enraged Professor Ashton-Richards would say to him. On what he was going to do after his resignation had been offered and accepted. On how fortunate it was that he did not know where Ann's flat was. On what he might have done if he did. On how with one neat stroke she had shattered his increasingly shaky academic career and wrecked his hopes of personal happiness.

On the utterly imponderable result of meeting her face to face tomorrow.

On someone who would stretch out her hand –

And do what?

Chapter 23

Next day was Tuesday. Tuesday was often quite a relaxed day; experiments and investigations started at the beginning of the week would be maturing, and there would be time to get together with Jill and talk over results already achieved.

Tom decided to walk to work even though he had slept very badly. It was not far, indeed, he often felt guilty about taking the car, but consoled himself with the thought that it was there to hand on the rare occasions that he needed it. Now and then he had considered acquiring a bicycle, but it being a student area, he knew that bikes were endlessly being stolen. If he had got one, he would have to hump it up the stairs and store it in the hallway of the flat. A bike in the hall was really too studentish to contemplate. He felt he had moved beyond all that.

He really knew in his heart of hearts why he was walking, to put off the moment when he arrived at the Department, where he would be constantly trying to assess if he was getting strange looks, wondering what Ann had been saying and to whom since she had stormed out of his room the previous day. Sooner or later, he must meet her face to face in the corridor. How to react? Simply say good morning as if it was a common day with nothing at all unusual in the air? Walk past her in silence? That, he felt, was to invite mockery for sure.

He could have been a man going to his execution as he walked up to the double glass and oak doors, only a little later than his usual time. So, in a way he was. The boss's daughter outraged, the boss himself no doubt acquainted with the fatal photographs, the whole place about to be abuzz with rumour and speculation. Approaching the door, he was surprised to see a little knot of people standing in the entrance hall. Someone near the door looked out and caught his eye, then turned partly round and said something, following which several of the people walked furtively away.

It was hardly necessary to be furtive, for he would have noticed nothing less dramatic than the ground opening under his feet. High up on the wall, just below the lofty ceiling, were affixed four enormously enlarged photographs, the pick of Ann's collection, so hugely blown up that every detail could be clearly seen. No one who had come through that door could fail now to recognise him from the mole on his left hip. Beside them was a sort of poster made from wallpaper, mentioning, should it have been necessary, who it was in the pictures, followed by a list of strange practices which he was supposed to have made her do with him.

As he stood transfixed with horror, he heard a soft voice at his ear,
"Oh, Professor!"

It was the one who was always at his side, Jill, of course, looking as stricken as if they were photographs of herself up there.

"Why doesn't someone get them down?" he gasped at her.

"We haven't got a long enough ladder. Caretaker's gone to get one."

"Well, hell, why doesn't he hurry?"

"He is, I promise you, he is," said Jill with a look which made it quite clear who had told him to hurry. If he had taken any notice of that look, he would be running all the way.

"How the hell did she get them up there, then?"

"They must have brought their own ladder. I say 'they' because one couldn't have done it alone. Must have broken in last night, after the caretaker had gone. Through a side window so the alarm didn't go off. Must have had a van or something. There's tracks outside."

He could stand it no longer. Without another word, he walked quickly to his room and shut the door.

A few minutes later, Jill knocked at the door and came in.

"Caretaker's got them down now. He said, should he put them in the incinerator. I said yes. Was that right?"

"God, yes."

"I'll make sure they get properly burned. There's no point in asking you what you want done today. I'll come back later."

She left and went along to the lab where she wandered about, doing meaningless little jobs to keep herself occupied and answering Robert's questions in a vague and distracted way. She felt as if it was her own world that was falling about her ears.

She wanted desperately to go and talk to him, to try and comfort him, but what on earth could one say? How to console someone whose most intimate secrets had just been revealed to a startled world? Why had she gone away and left him on his own, when she might be at least trying to help? How to get back in there with him? Oh, of course, that was no problem. A regular, routine little task. His mail.

The talk in the office fell silent as she entered, shoulders squared, chin jutting defiantly, very conscious of showing the flag before the chief source of departmental gossip.

"Any mail for Professor Di Angeli?" she asked in a firm voice. Normally, she would just say, 'Anything for the Prof this morning?' but today, she felt she must make a gesture of some sort, however slight.

One of the secretaries handed her a bundle of letters, eyeing her uneasily.

They're treating me as they would treat him, she thought and she felt pleased about it.

She carried them to his room, knocked and went in as usual. He was sitting at the desk, chin on hand, pale, looking shattered. He even still had his jacket on. He must have been sitting there not moving ever since he had come in. She was deeply, sincerely moved for him in his terrible plight. Her heart ached for the still figure who had not so much as raised his head when she entered. And yet, and yet, somewhere deep inside her, a mischievous little imp danced with optimistic delight. Her golden, unapproachable idol, knocked off his pedestal and sitting in the mud, and only she was there to put out her hand and help him up. An excitement stirred within her and inextinguishable hope turned its flame minimally higher.

All the same, she knew she had no subtlety. Without doubt, she would kill any chance she might have by ineptitude. Trying to think resignation into the uppermost place, she put his letters in front of him.

"Here's your mail," she said, looking intently at him, trying to read his thoughts.

"Thanks," he said absently.

"I'll carry on with what I was doing yesterday. You'll feel better in a little while. Then we can discuss what else you want doing."

He sighed wearily.

"There's only one job for you today. I'm sitting here mentally drafting my letter of resignation. When I've roughed it out, you can take it to the office to be typed and start wondering who your new boss will be."

"You don't need to resign, surely? All this will be a nine days' wonder. Next week, someone else's head will be on the block and they'll have forgotten all about you."

"I wish I could believe that."

"It's true. You know it is. That's the way things always happen."

"Well, even if it is, I think the boss will gratefully accept my resignation."

"What! I'm sure he thinks more of you than he does of that little – of Ann Bone."

"Where is she, by the way?"

"Not in. I doubt if she'll dare to show her face again. Heaven help her if she does."

"Well, that's some consolation. I must have finally got her off my back at last. But at what a cost, phew!" He realised this must be all Greek to Jill. "She's been riding me pretty hard over the last few months. I don't suppose you could have noticed, but she'd managed to get her teeth into me over one or two things and she was making the best of it."

"I had realised there was something strange going on," said Jill reflectively. "Her attitude to you seemed – unusual, but of course, I didn't know the ins and outs of it. Still, she certainly won't come back after publishing such a pack of lies to the world."

"Why should you assume they're lies? I doubt if many people will. No smoke without fire, that's what Ann said. You can tell people anything and they'll say, no smoke without fire, and believe it. And indeed, there is a certain amount of fire. Most of it was lies, but the photographs were true. I did sleep with her, several times."

She chewed her lip at that, but said stoutly,

"Well, so what? I doubt if there were too many people in the hall this morning who could afford to cast stones. Gosh, if you knew how hard I tried to get them

201

to go away, so I could wait by myself for you to come in, but they wouldn't move. They wanted to be in at the kill."

"I appreciate your efforts, but there was little point once even one person had seen those pictures. You can bet your sweet life there isn't a single department where it's not being talked about right now – and you can imagine what people are saying. No, the simple fact is that Ann has won. She's won, totally and completely."

"But you don't have to let her win."

"What am I supposed to do?"

"Fight it!"

"How can I possibly do that? Don't you realise what she's done to me? She's taken everything from me. I've been publicly humiliated. I'm most likely going to lose my job, maybe my whole career, you'd be surprised at how these things can follow you about. My personal life is in tatters. She's left me nothing, nothing at all. She's won, Jill, there's no way of getting round that."

"But these things will pass. Don't give in!"

"What the hell am I supposed to do, then?"

"Get out of here. Write your letter to the Chief first, if you feel you must, but then get back in the lab, do your work, act like you always do and defy anyone to say anything. It's the only way to salvage anything out of the situation."

"No. I'm just going to get shot of this place as soon as ever I can."

"No, you're not. You're going to stay, unless you're fired and that's not going to happen. You're not going anywhere. You're staying."

"Says who?"

"Me, of course."

"Why should what I choose to do or not to do be of such particular interest to you?"

"Because I love you, you stupid blind idiot! Don't you know that? I love you and I've loved you since the minute you walked in here. I don't want you to go, I want you to stay because I love you, you great blundering fool, will you get that into your thick head? Now go on, tell me I'm fired. We might as well make a clean sweep of the Department while we're about it."

She thrust her clenched fists into the pockets of her lab coat and looked defiantly at him. He stared back, open-mouthed.

"You love me, even after all that's happened?"

"Especially after that. I always had you on a pedestal before but I think I like you better like this, sitting on the ground with your trousers in the mud. Aren't you going to tell me I'm fired for insubordination?"

"I can hardly – Jill –"

"It's all right, I know you don't love me. I know Elizabeth's first in line. I just wanted to let you know there's someone batting on your team, that's all. I'll go now, before I insult you again. See you in the dole queue."

"Just you stay right where you are."

She stood still, looking worried.

"Now, here's something for you to get into your thick head and it must be thicker than I thought if you mean what you've just said. Thanks some more to Ann, I am now a back number as far as Elizabeth is concerned. She has firmly given me the push, without the slightest likelihood that she will ever change her mind."

"Oh, I'm sorry."

"You're not the least bit sorry. You're delighted. I know you never approved of my interest in Elizabeth."

"It was hardly for me to approve or disapprove."

"You did disapprove, though. It was quite clear from your demeanour."

"I'm sorry it was so obvious. May I ask what happened?"

"You may. Ann sent her those photographs last night, that's what happened and you can imagine what *she* thought of them, particularly, I fancy, that incredible one of me looking like a floored heavyweight boxer in a nudist colony."

"Poor Elizabeth."

Jill put her fingers over her mouth, feeling the laughter beginning to bubble up in her. The corners of Tom's mouth began to twitch.

"A floored heavyweight boxer in a nudist colony – oh!"

"Poor Elizabeth, can you picture her face. Oh, it really isn't funny, you know."

In a moment, they were both giggling hysterically, helpless with spasms of laughter, infinitely relieving to the feelings after the tensions of the morning.

"Oh, I think that's the funniest thing I've ever heard. A floored heavyweight boxer –"

"It really isn't the least bit funny, you know."

"If anyone comes past and hears us laughing like this, they'll certainly think we've flipped our lids."

"They'll probably be right. Jill, why have I never really noticed you before?"

"Always around. Just part of the furniture, that's me."

"Never again. Not ever again, to me. But listen, that list on the wall. Surely, if I got up to all that, you would find it shocking? I didn't, as it happens, not all of it anyway."

"I knew that. What a lot of nonsense! I don't believe any of it and I don't think anyone else will either. Saying she whipped you and you liked it so much you begged for more. I mean, I ask you!"

"Amazing! You have managed to pick the only one that happens to be true and I can prove it. Look!"

Before her astonished gaze, he pulled off his jacket and threw it on the desk, scattering papers everywhere. She checked an automatic move to pick them up, feeling there were weightier matters on hand. He was pulled open his shirt buttons and let it slide off his shoulders. Then he turned round and showed her his back. She stared, dumbfounded. A whole series of red lines, some faint and old, others fresh and new, marked the skin.

"Look!" he cried, "Take a good look, go on! What do you think of that? That's where she whipped me. She did it at least half a dozen times and she was quite right, I did like it."

He pulled his shirt on his shoulders but did not button it and started to pace up and down.

"She didn't even have to tell me to take my clothes off, after the first time. Shall I tell you what we did? I got a hotel room for us, and when we were there, I just took my clothes off and lay down on the bed for her to whip me. Can you picture it? Pleasant thought, eh? Look at me. I'm supposed to be intelligent. There were people, up to this morning, who even thought I was a pretty nice guy to know. Not anymore! I could have stopped her any time. I could have just got up and taken the whip away from her, you know how small she is. No sweat. But I didn't. I just lay there like a great booby, and told her to keep doing it and harder. I kept my arms under my chest, like this, see? So I wouldn't get marks on them, because if I did, people might see it. But, after a time or two, that wasn't enough for her. She wasn't humiliating me enough. One night, she brought a piece of rope and told me to put my arms behind my back. I was scared stiff. She hurt me enough when I was free and we both knew I could have stopped her, so what was she going to do to me when I was tied up and helpless?

"'Put your arms behind your back, Professor', she said, gloating, just like that. She knew I'd have to do it in the end. 'Do I always have to tell you things half a dozen times?' Well, I did it, very slowly. Do it, go on, do it yourself and see what it feels lie. God awful, that's what it feels like. So I put my arms behind me but no, that still wasn't enough. She got one arm, twisted it up like this, so my hand was under my shoulder, then the other one the same and tied them together like that. Do you know what it's like? No, of course, you don't. In a few minutes, your arms and shoulders are aching so much you'll do anything to get them free. I pleaded with her, I begged her, yes, I went on my knees to Ann Bone to get her to untie me because it hurt so much. She did it in the end, when she was good and ready, just to give her a clear field so she could whip me again – with a whip she had bought with my money, how about that? And I still liked it. I still begged her to do it harder and not to stop. What do you think of that, eh? I'll bet you've never been so disgusted. I walk about here, acting like I'm a minor deity and all the time I'm a nut, a screwball, a pervert. What do you –"

"Will you please bloody shut up for one minute!" shouted Jill, exasperated beyond measure with this recital.

They stared at each other in disbelief. She could hardly believe she had spoken to him like that, using a word she had never used before, except in its literal sense. *Well*, she thought, *I've done it now, might as well be hanged for a sheep as a lamb.*

"There's only one thing you are and that is a socking great fool," she said, staggered by her own temerity. "Not because of what you did, I know perfectly well that people enjoy some strange things and, if there's no harm in it, why not? But because you're skulking in here wallowing in self-pity about it. What do you imagine people will think if you come and hide in your room like this, holding your poor head and telling yourself how badly you've been treated? Of course, they'll think it's all true."

"I am astonished. I am appalled. Never in my whole professional life have I been spoken to by a technician like that. You are in very serious trouble, young lady. Come over here. No, over here."

He moved over and put his back against the door. As she looked at him, puzzled, a tiny frown line between his brows faded into a smile.

"What?"

"Come here. I'm going to kiss you and I don't want any nosy technicians walking in, OK?"

OK? Of course, it was OK. She practically threw herself at him, flung her arms round him and hugged him tightly.

"Ouch! What the hell's that? Look, you've scratched my chest with that great long sharp pencil in your top pocket. Take your lab coat off, for goodness' sake."

With her lips against his and her arms round his neck, Tom felt as if he had known her and loved her all his life. Why on earth had he chased after the moon and raked in the gutter, with this treasure right under his nose? So sweet, so adorable, so understanding – understanding! The word brought him back to earth with a jolt. There was so much more for her to understand! Here was a girl, very like the kind he had been thinking of last night, moreover, one who already at work took his problems in her stride, who had said she loved him, and plainly did and who already understood so much. How would she react to the whole of the truth? Did he have the right to burden her with it? And yet, if anything was to come of this magic moment, she must know. There must be truth between them. For good or ill, he had to take the chance.

"Jill, dear."

"Yes, Tom – oh, is it all right if I call you that?"

"Of course. We must talk, though. There are things I've got to tell you."

"Later."

"No, now. It must be now."

"I can't bear to let you go."

He sighed to think how differently she might feel in a few minutes.

"Now, Jill. It's important."

He put her gently away from him.

"Come over to the desk and sit down."

"What is it, Tom? You look very serious."

"I am. Deadly serious. There is more, Jill, and you might change your mind about me if you knew everything there is to know."

"I wouldn't."

"You might and if you did, I'd be very sorry, but I must tell you. I've been living a lie for years and, although I think it's over now, you've got to know about it and judge me on the whole of the truth. Can you bear it? I've got to warn you, it gets pretty disgusting and sordid in parts."

"I'd like you to tell me. If you think it's so important."

"It is to me. There must be truth between us. There has to be someone with whom I don't have to pretend I am what I'm not. Stop me anytime if you find it too unpleasant."

He went right back to Elise and told her everything, about his obsession, about his meeting with Ann and how she had wormed out his secret, and, as a result, gradually come to dominate him more and more. He told her about Jenny and even, with no little difficulty, how he had wept with remorse in her arms in that derelict house a night or two ago. He told her every detail he could remember, bad or good, to his credit or against it, until with her there was absolutely nothing left to hide. Most of the time he was speaking, his eyes were lowered to where his hands lay clasped in his lap, but when he did occasionally glance up, her face seemed to register nothing but sympathy and interest. She sat absolutely silent until he had finished, when he said,
"Well, there you are, that's my story, every bit of it. How do you feel about me now?"

Once again, he lifted his gaze, almost shyly, to her face, wondering what he would see there now. Her eyes were lowered, and she looked solemn and sad. With a gesture he had come to know well, she tugged a lock of her front hair and pressed her forehead with the tips of her fingers as she tried to marshal her thoughts. She was silent for what seemed an interminable time.

He longed to put his arms round her again, to feel her sweet lips against his as he had before, but he knew that he must not. She alone must decide whether to accept or reject him and, if her decision was to have any meaning at all, it must be uninfluenced by him.

He wished that she would speak, say anything at all, to put him out of his suspense. He tried to brace himself for the rejection which he felt sure was coming, but he shrank, wincing, from the prospect. It would be kindly and gently worded, he felt sure, but for all that, he knew it would hurt and wound him unbearably.

At last, with her eyes still down, she said,
"Tom. You know what you felt like this morning when you came in and saw all that stuff on the wall. Imagine, then, just for a minute, what I felt like when I saw it. I had got used to the thought of Elizabeth, she seemed like the sort of girl I would expect you to go for and, although it made me sad to see you with her, still I could understand. But to see you like that with Ann – well, I was just simply floored by it. But, Tom, although I felt like that, my love for you didn't waver for a single minute. I couldn't understand, but I still loved you. Then, all that stuff written on the poster – gosh, I didn't even know what some of it meant, but even if it was all true and I knew you had done it all fifty times over, it still wouldn't have made any difference. And the same applies to what you've just told me. I don't think, Tom, there's any way you could stop me loving you."

"But, Jill, I know how you feel about these things – about moral behaviour, let's call it. How can you say that?"

"I can say it because it's true. Of course, I wish you hadn't done these things – didn't do them – but I never thought you were a knight in shining armour,

Tom." She lifted her eyes and smiled suddenly. "Wouldn't want one anyway. How could you get near him for all that sheet metal? I just wanted a human, natural man, the one who happened to be you. I'll say it again, I don't think there's any way you can stop me loving you. Got any more ghastly secrets?"

"Not a one. You know all my faults from personal experience – how short my temper is, how I take it out, usually unjustly, on the nearest person, who generally happened to be you, lots of other things like that, you must know them all."

"Vividly," she said, smiling again, "and I expect you know a few about me as well. Do you suppose there aren't things about me that I'd rather not have published on the wall of the entrance hall? I've got my little quirk too, but no one's ever photographed it."

"Never! You?"

"Me. I'll tell you about it one day and you'll be surprised, I can say that with certainty. But, Tom, you won't ever let her do that to you again, will you?"

"God, no. The very thought – well, all I can say is, I must have been nuts."

"Remember the day I walked in here and found you kissing her – or rather her kissing you?"

"I've told you what really happened that day and what I said was true."

"All right, I believe you. No need to get defensive. Shall I tell you what I did after that?"

"Go on."

"Well, first of all, I went to the lab and shouted my head off at Robert about something that wasn't even his fault, then I went to the ladies' room, and cried and cried."

"Jill, did you? I couldn't tell. You didn't look as if you'd been crying when you came back."

"I made very sure I didn't. I didn't want you to know. You made me cry another time, too."

"What a louse I've been! When was that?"

"At the Christmas party. You went out with Elizabeth and when you came back, you looked so pleased with yourself, I felt sure you had got engaged."

"We'd just had a little spat and made it up. Jill, if only I'd known. I guess Ann knew how you felt. I recall some things she said which should have given me the hint, if I'd only taken notice. Let me kiss you again to make up. Bother this room! I'll have to lean against the door again. I'm going to have a bolt fitted so I can carry on my love life in a decent privacy."

To feel her weight, her whole body pressed against his, Jill the inhibited, uninhibited, Jill the straight-laced, unbound, magic like no other, no easy conquest, no knowing experienced cookie, but Jill, pure, clear, loyal, unselfish, understanding, forgiving. She knew it all and if Ann came back, she would be his bulwark. If she shared his life, she would never turn away from him and slam the door in his face. This was the real, the true, the one he had always waited for. Her lips against his were so very, very right. He felt as if he had known and wanted her all his life. The irrepressible Di Angeli ego was climbing out of that mud patch and getting to its feet. Never in his wide-ranging career had he fallen in love so hard and so fast.

"Jill."

"Mm?"

"I love you."

She stepped away from him at once.

"Don't be silly," she said crisply.

"I mean it. I won't try to insult your intelligence by telling you I've loved you all along and never known it, but I do know I love you now."

"Oh, look, come on. You're emotionally bouncing round like a rubber ball. You only think you love me because I came along with my little brush and dustpan to pick up the pieces. It's too quick."

"How long is it supposed to take? Look, you said you've loved me since I came here. Here's a scenario. I've just walked into the lab for the first time. How long did it take?"

She pursed her lips as if calculating.

"About ten seconds."

"It's taken me all of five minutes. How can you say it's too quick?"

"All right, granted."

She stepped back to him, pushed her hands inside his shirt, which was still loose and unbuttoned, and slid them over his back. When they encountered a fresh welt, one from Ann's last assault on him, she pressed it with her fingers till she saw his mouth twitch. Then she smiled in his face.

"What was that all about?"

"Just a little game, Tom."

"Oh! Well, here's another scenario for you to consider. Suppose the boss accepts my resignation. What will your biology professor be then? Just an ordinary guy, not a big shot, not the boss, jobless and perhaps needing support myself. Unemployable in the academic world? Maybe. Gossip gets about, you know and no one wants a pariah in their department. Present damnable, future could be worse. I could end as a used car salesman or something of the sort. What do you say? Would you take me on those terms?"

A little line of puzzlement came between her brows.

"I don't quite – I can't – that sounded a bit like a proposal."

"That was a proposal."

"But Tom –"

"'But Tom' isn't an answer. Yes or no. Don't talk about time again, because we've had plenty. For a year, we've known each other in good times and bad. We know each other better than if we'd been going steady all that time. I know you're what I need and I may have little enough to offer you in return. But I'm willing to do my best for you. Have pity on a guy. Say yes."

Oh, Mother, she thought, *oh Mother, are you watching? I remember all you said, Mother. Choose carefully, you said. A woman is so much more vulnerable than a man and marriage costs her more dearly than it does him. Marry a good man who you're sure will be faithful. Character counts more than looks. Looks are a snare and a delusion and one day they'll be gone.*

I remember it all, but Mother, this stocky little man with his dark hair and eyes, that soft, pouty sensuous mouth that makes me feel so nice, oh, Mother, Richard is a good man and Tom is awfully naughty, but I could marry him just for his mouth and the curls round his ears, couldn't you, Mother? Say you understand? Mother?

"Yes," Jill said.

The Ashton-Richards had come to an agreement. The previous evening, after Elizabeth had been put to bed and sunk into a sedated sleep, they had had a long talk and they had decided. She must marry Reggie. There was no point in opposing it. They would withdraw their objections to the match and she could marry him as soon as she chose. They communicated this decision to her at the breakfast table and the lack of enthusiasm with which she greeted it, they put down to the lingering effect of the drug.

With a perfectly natural curiosity, Hugh Ashton-Richards had looked at the pictures his daughter had been sent and had been astonished. Not that an unmarried young man like his colleague should have the occasional un-regularised contact, but that he should choose someone like Ann Bone coming from the social class that she did and even more that he should have the crass stupidity to be photographed with her.

Before he got to the Department, the pictures in the hall had been removed and burnt so he did not get the full impact of them. A graphic description from his secretary was all he got. It seemed unduly harsh to blame Tom for what had happened. His instinct was to back his own kind against Ann Bone and her like. So, when Tom came knocking at his door with his letter of resignation in his hand, he was in a mood to be benevolent. He listened and accepted without question, a slanted and slightly fictionalised account of the cause of the morning's events. In the end, the letter went in the bin and the bottle of whisky came out of the private cupboard for congratulations on the engagement. Hugh did not think it was an entirely appropriate match, but Jill was at least a little better than Ann Bone.

And besides, it was such a weight off his mind that at last Elizabeth was settled, or so it seemed.

Chapter 24

Very far from it. Shocks in plenty were still in store for the Ashton-Richards. An encouraging phone call from Erica that evening caused Reggie to try a confident proposal. He was turned down with more than the usual sharpness, for Elizabeth did not care to be taken for granted. They had an extensive and wide-ranging quarrel. She demanded that he took her to the University Summer Ball that Saturday. She had known for weeks, as he reminded her, that he could not because of a tennis tournament. When he refused to change his plans, she announced that she would go to the ball with Sarah and that she never wanted to see him again.

That would mean until about an hour after Sunday lunch, when he would come and lay his newly won trophy at her feet, and mourn that winning it had not been worth the joy of dancing with her.

Tom, meanwhile, in his usual precipitate manner, had dragged the not even slightly reluctant Jill into town at lunchtime to buy her a ring. Later, they were to be seen sitting together on a bench in the park, arms round each other, her left hand in his right, her ring glittering in the sun.

"It's beautiful. I've never seen such a lovely ring."

"Your own is always the nicest in the world. Looking forward to showing it off?"

"Yes, all worked out. In the lab, Sally will probably notice it, but I'll have to wave it under Robert's nose. Then, the office. That'll be the best bit. They'll spot it without fail. When I go to pick up your letter of resignation I gave them to be typed, they won't know whether to congratulate me or commiserate with me. Goodness, look at the time. Shouldn't we be getting back?"

"What for?"

"Well, I should be working."

"I'm the boss, aren't I? As long as you're with me, you're working. We could extend it a bit longer if you want."

"How much longer?"

"Long as you like. Come and see my home, why don't you? It's not far from here."

"Well, I'd better, I suppose, if that's where I'm going to live, but what's the hurry?"

"Can't you guess?"

"No."

"Really?"

"What are you getting at?"

"I'd like to make love to you."

"I hope you don't mean what I think you mean."

"What a crushing remark! Must I put it in words of one syllable? I'd like to go to bed with you."

"You're not serious?"

"Of course I am."

"Well, the answer's no."

"But Jill —"

"There's no 'but Jill' about it. Not till we're married, understand? And I'm not taking any orders about that, so there."

He sighed.

"Why do I have this overwhelming talent for surrounding myself with women who like to have me firmly under their thumbs? Well, there's only one answer to that. We shall have to get married as soon as ever we can."

"Oh, heavens, he's off again!"

"Look, you love me, I love you, what's the point of waiting? Listen, the minute we're married, I shall carry you off to the apartment and we'll run up the stairs two at a time, straight into the bedroom without your feet touching the floor, then we shall spend a whole fortnight in unrestrained debauchery. Since we'll be safely married, even you won't be able to say no."

"Stop, stop, stop!" she cried.

"Did I say something wrong?"

"I hope you're not going to be in quite such a hurry."

"Just try and stop me."

"I intend to do just that."

"Why?"

"Because, unlike you, my dear Tom, I am a virgin. You needn't stare like that, there are still one or two around, despite the efforts of men like you. So, you see, I hope you'll go a bit easy."

He did continue to stare, though, then said,
"I don't know what I've ever done to deserve it, but someone up there's got my number! All right, a change of scenario. I'll install you in my favourite armchair and go through to the kitchen to make coffee."

"Like it so far."

"I'll bring you a cup and you can drink it as slowly as you like — you can even have two if you want — then when you're quite ready and not a minute before, we shall stroll through to the bedroom like two civilised adults. You will enjoy it, I promise you. The rushing about and playing the fool can come later."

"That sounds much better."

"Oh, Jill. I don't know what I've done to deserve you. Do you know, I think I'm going to get lucky now. I can feel it in my bones."

"Me too."

There was another notable virgin in the park that lunchtime too. Despite their squabble of the previous evening, Elizabeth was out walking with Reggie. Still slightly under the influence of last nights' sedative, she simply couldn't be

211

bothered to keep it up. She still looked pale and drawn after yesterday's ordeal, but she was buoyed up by the inner strength granted to those who have been proved totally, indisputably right, in the faces of those around them.

Reggie, who saw only the pale and shaken look, was planning, sometime within the next ten minutes, on proposing to her yet again, fully confident that this time he would be accepted. No one would tell him just what had happened, but it clearly had been something quite catastrophic and with Elizabeth in, as he thought, a weakened state, he felt confident that her resistance would crumble.

They walked by the duck pond and through the rose garden, then up a tree-lined alley towards the river. The romantic atmosphere, the sun shining on the dancing leaves of the trees and glinting on the ripples – that would be the perfect setting. She loved the river, so what better place could there possibly be?

They were passing a gap in the trees when she suddenly stopped. He had walked on a few paces before he realised she was no longer with him. As he looked round, she beckoned urgently and he came back to her.

"That's him!" she whispered.

"Who? Where?" he asked, glancing around, puzzled.

"There! On that bench through the trees! Who's that with him?"

"Oh, the Di Angeli fellow. So it is. Why should you want to know who's with him?"

"I just want to know, that's all. I shouldn't have thought anyone would want to come within miles of him after what happened."

"What did happen, Elizabeth? I wish someone would tell me."

"Oh, I couldn't possibly. It was all too sordid for words. Go and find out who that is, Reggie."

"What, me? How am I supposed to do that? What do you want to know for, anyway?"

"Never mind. Go on, do it, for me."

With his projected proposal in mind, Reggie felt he had better humour her.

"All right, I'll do my best." And he strolled on, as casually as might be, round the corner to where Tom and Jill sat, still holding hands.

As he walked away, Elizabeth looked at his back, wondering if he looked as good as Tom did with no clothes on. How strange it was that Tom should be the only adult male she had ever seen naked, even if only in a photograph. Life did play some unexpected tricks on one!

As soon as she had recovered sufficiently from the shock, she had torn up all those dreadful photographs, with the hateful anonymous letter and burned them in the fireplace of her white drawing room. Her mother felt she ought to keep them and call in the police, but she had adamantly refused. The thought of having to answer endless questions and show the things to a police officer was utterly distasteful to her.

She had burned all the photographs except the one without the unknown girl in it. For some reason she was not really sure of, she had been unable to resist keeping that. She had put it in an envelope and buried it at the bottom of her lingerie drawer where, she hope, no one would ever find it.

Meanwhile, Reggie, unaware of the comparison he was undergoing and trying to look as unconcerned as if he was having his daily constitutional, was approaching Jill and Tom.

"Good afternoon."

"Good afternoon, Reggie. Pleasant day for a stroll," Tom replied in a genial voice.

Reggie's eyes were riveted by the ring, indeed it would be difficult to miss it.

"May I take it that congratulations are in order?"

"You may. This is Miss Jill Adams, who I am delighted to say, is now my fiancée."

"How do you do, Miss Adams. Haven't we met before?"

"About a year ago, at an inter-departmental dance. You danced with me and we talked for a bit."

"Of course. I rarely forget a face. You're a – hmm, let me think – you're a doctor, aren't you?"

"I'm a technician," Jill replied, smiling.

"A technician! Oh, I see!" Reggie glanced at Tom and his face was such a study that Jill was hard pressed not to laugh. "Well, many congratulations to you both. Be seeing you," and off he went.

As soon as he was out of earshot, Jill said,
"Oh, Tom, did you see his face! A technician! He obviously thinks you've sunk to the uttermost depths!"

"He can think what he likes. I'd rather have a technician than an ice maiden like he's got. Well, let's get back so I can start finding out how quickly you can get married in this god-forsaken country. I can't have you hanging about as a sour, frustrated virgin longer than avoidable."

"Do you mind? I'm not in the least sour and frustrated. I've been saving myself for the right man. Aren't you pleased?"

"Of course, I'm pleased. I'm delighted. I'm overjoyed and I think you're the sweetest, loveliest, most un-frustrated, most sensible, marvellous, wonderful virgin I've ever met in my whole life."

"Have you met very many?"

"Well," he said, smiling thoughtfully. "It's not always the first question you ask people, is it?"

Elizabeth was not pleased with Reggie's news. She never liked anything to get away from her, even if she had not really wanted it in the first place. But she was greatly amused to learn who the other party was.

"A technician? Oh, poor Tom, is that the best he could do? Wait a minute, Jill Adams, I think I know who she is. A dark-haired girl, short hair, rather plain, a bit dumpy?"

"Er, well –" said Reggie, who had actually thought her not all that unattractive.

"Yes, of course. She works for him in the lab. She used to glower at me when I went in to see him and if I asked her where he was, she would look as if she wanted to poison me. Oh yes, she'll guard him like a hen with one chick." They walked on for a few minutes and then she said, "I suppose you haven't changed your mind about the Summer Ball?"

Bracing himself for a storm, Reggie replied,
"Darling, I'm playing for the County. It's not as if it's a club match."

"Tom could always take me to things I wanted to go to. He didn't go in for silly things like tennis."

"Well, he can't take you now, can he? "

"Then I shall go to the Ball with Sarah."

Reggie did not feel it was the right time for yet another proposal.

Chapter 25

The University Summer Ball was, as always, a glittering affair. The main hall, in which it was regularly held, was a lofty and handsome structure with an oak beamed roof, and cream painted walls mostly lined with the inevitable oil paintings of retired dignitaries. One long wall consisted almost entirely of windows, with a series of double glass doors opening on to a wide flagged patio. All the doors were open, letting in the evening sunshine and the warm breeze carrying the scent of flowers from the gardens. Within, a good band was playing, there were seemingly unlimited supplies of champagne, strawberries and cream, and the hall was filled to capacity with people dressed in their best, chatting and dancing the warm summer night away.

Paul, tall, fair and very American, elegant in his best suit, was there. Having just returned from holiday, he was not up with the latest developments concerning his friend Tom, so he was surprised he was not present. He had been there for over an hour, but had not so far been able to dance with anyone as he had been buttonholed by a frighteningly intelligent American female Professor of Philosophy, who was bent on putting him right on any and every subject in the world. Her eye was sharp and ruthless behind her gold-rimmed spectacles, and it held him transfixed like a beetle on a pin while her edgy, high-pitched voice went on and on. He supposed he should really have asked her to dance, but it was quite exhausting enough standing listening to her. Besides, she was so plain, with her rather over large nose, thin lips and black hair pulled back in a bun, besides that dreadful dark flouncy peasant style dress which did absolutely nothing for her short dumpy figure. Paul wanted to dance with someone more attractive and listen to someone less clever.

Right now, she was bending his ear on some point from Descartes, about whom, as a scientist, he knew next to nothing and while trying to say yes or no in places that would not make him look too stupid, his eye was roaming round the room, surveying the abundance of pretty, nicely dressed girls from whom he was being so firmly kept. He longed to dance, but was at a loss for how to stem the endless tide of incisive points and arguments in which he was being swamped.

A little flurry of activity at the door caught his eye. A group of men and women entered, followed by Elizabeth and Sarah. They stood at the door briefly, looking for acquaintances, then moved to the side as more people came in behind them.

He quite lost whatever grasp he had had of his philosopher's argument as he surveyed them. What a contrast they were and how mutually delightful they looked. Elizabeth, as always, in white, a very simple dress on slightly Grecian lines, tall, cool, her blonde hair gleaming and smooth, just curled under at the ends. Sarah, on the other hand, wore a black and red dress patterned with roses with a frill round the neckline. Her cheeks glowed pink and her short dark hair was curled all over her head. The lily and the rose, he though, irresistibly. For himself, he really preferred the rose. He had never been able quite to see why other men raved about Elizabeth. True, she was an attractive girl, always well-groomed and beautifully dressed, but to him, she seemed little more than the conventional blonde mantrap. Sarah looked much more vivacious and lively. And, if Elizabeth disliked Americans, well, let her stick to her prejudices and her upper class stuffed shirt of an English boyfriend. Paul had no particular fondness for beating his head against a brick wall.

Paul suddenly realised the Professor of Philosophy was no longer talking to him. A friend of his had appeared at her other side, dared to challenge one of her points and was now suffering for his sins. Seizing his opportunity, Paul melted into the crowd and moved towards the two girls.

Elizabeth saw him coming and smiled confidently. Of course, he was coming to dance with her. Paul intrigued her for, of all the endless stream of Americans who moved through her life, he was the only one who never paid more than the most casual attention to her. He came up now, pushing a lock of his fair hair back with his fingers.

"Good evening, ladies," he said cheerfully. "Isn't it a lovely night? Much too good to spend indoors."

"Delightful," said Elizabeth, while Sarah merely smiled. "Are you enjoying the dance?

Paul?"

"I am now. Would you care to dance, Sarah?"

"Oh, how lovely! Yes, I would!" cried Sarah, only fractionally less surprised than Elizabeth.

Off they went, leaving her more than a little piqued.

Sarah really was such an attractive girl, Paul thought. She chattered gaily about this and that as they danced, laughing delightedly at his jokes. She told him about her holiday. She seemed to fall into the most surprising adventures, and her happy and impetuous spirit let her turn even minor reverses into great fun. She was telling him a tale about how her car had got bogged down halfway up a mountain pass in Switzerland when over her shoulder, her suddenly caught Elizabeth's eye. She was dancing with someone else and she smiled at him charmingly. He smiled back briefly and returned his attention to Sarah. He had better dance with Elizabeth next out of politeness, he thought.

The music came to an end and they walked back to where she had been standing, still conversing. Elizabeth appeared a moment later, as Sarah was finishing her tale and he asked her for the next dance.

Before he had been dancing with her for two minutes, he began to become aware of her overwhelming charm. Everything he said seemed to be of fascinating interest to her. Her eyes never left his face for an instant, her laugh was like the tinkling of a silver bell. Her slender waist moved within his arm to sensuous effect and tantalising whiffs of her seductive perfume lured him nearer and nearer to her. He found her so riveting that when the music came to an end, there was no question but that he should ask her to dance again. She agreed readily and continued to tell him a tale of a horse her friend was thinking of buying. Paul was not the least bit interested in horses, but he would have listened all night to Elizabeth talking even on philosophy.

Halfway through the next dance he said,

"Let's have some champagne, Elizabeth."

"Oh yes, that would be lovely."

She started to move to one of the tables, but he said,

"Let's go to the other side. There's a terribly intelligent woman over there who will buttonhole me again if I get within range of her again and she'll never let me escape again."

"A sad mistake, having all these clever people around," said Elizabeth with a mischievous smile. "Let's find somewhere to evade them."

He smiled back, quite captivated.

They danced together for the rest of the evening. When not dancing, they held hands, smiling into each other's' eyes, sipping champagne, often from the same glass. They drank a great deal of champagne. There seemed so many things to drink to. Sarah watched them with resignation. It happened all the time. Before long, it was plain that, if they had been indifferent to each other before, they were so no longer. She found Paul's easy-going geniality delightful, he, after an hour or two as the target of Elizabeth's practised charm, found himself quite bowled over. The heady cocktail of youth, music and champagne worked its potent magic on them, seeming to fill their world with stars and flowers, romance and beauty, and always, always each other. Nonetheless, it came as something of a surprise to them when they both woke up next morning in Paul's bed.

After the initial shock, they were both quite delighted. Paul even more so when Elizabeth told him she had left her parents with the idea that she might very well spend the night at Sarah's so they would not be panicking and there was no pressing reason at all why she should get up. Paul had one worry, though.

"I don't know how I'm going to explain this to Tom."

"What's it got to do with him?"

"I thought that you and he –"

"Haven't you heard? Tom is engaged and not to me either. To some little tramp or other who works at his Department."

"What! When did all this happen?"

"Oh, a week or so ago. Where on earth have you been? I thought everyone knew about it."

"I've been on holiday."

"Well, goodness, you've managed to miss the most mind-boggling time I've ever known in this University. It's been incredible."

"Just my luck. What's been happening?"

"You'd better ask someone at work. They'll all know. But I don't want to talk about him. You're much more interesting. Better looking, too."

She stroked his chest which was covered with a fascinating fuzz of fine fair hair.

"Well, no one's ever said that to me before. What about your other boyfriend?"

"Reggie? He keeps asking to marry me and I keep on saying no. What's the time?"

"Seven o'clock."

"Seven o'clock on a Sunday! I don't have to get up for at least another hour. How about you?"

"I haven't a single appointment that I can recall to mind."

So the two erstwhile virgins spent the rest of the Sunday morning improving their techniques. At 9.57, he proposed and at 10.01, after a little ritual skirmishing, she accepted. At 11.55, they finally got up, she rang her mother to say she was bringing a guest to lunch but refused to say who or why, they had a delightful and unnecessarily prolonged shower together before he went to select what seemed the most appropriate suit in which go to Sunday lunch with some very proper English parents for the purpose of telling them he had just seduced their daughter. Elizabeth, meanwhile, was picking up last night's clothes from the floor and looking at them distastefully. She must have been very drunk to leave them on the floor like that and now she had no choice but to put them on again.

"Hurry up, Liz baby. Your parents are going to be enough displeased with us without having to wait lunch for us as well."

Elizabeth smiled to herself. Liz baby, indeed!

"If you call me baby, what do I call you?"

"Whatever you like. Sir would do. All right, just joking. What would your parents say if they saw you now?"

Pulling on her creased dress, Elizabeth replied,
"Probably hooray. They've been trying to get rid of me for years. That's why they keep inviting all these awf – oops!"

Elizabeth put her fingers over her mouth.

"All these awful Americans, I guess you were about to say." Elizabeth nodded, eyes sparkling with laughter. "So they've been trying to get you hitched and look, you've managed it all by your clever little self."

"Thank goodness, there is someone who doesn't regard me as the original brainless wonder."

"Yeah, I remember Tom saying that. Boy, was he drunk! Now, let's move and go and ruin your folks' day."

The Ashton-Richards bore the shock with suitable composure, served up Sunday lunch as if their daughter brought home such news often and were relaxing over coffee when Reggie appeared with a huge silver tennis cup.

Poor Reggie!

It was a very civilised interview, with them all being terribly polite to each other, and drinking to each other's future success and happiness – what else could one do, after all? Convention really forbade one from taking the chap outside and beating him into a thousand tiny pieces, so Reggie was compelled to sit there smiling feebly and looking as if he did not mind too much, when all he wanted to do was crawl away into a hole and hide.

Chapter 26

And so, Paul had Elizabeth, greatly to his surprise, and for days he floated about with a faint, foolish smile on his face, feeling happily dazed.

Tom had Jill and he was beginning to wonder what the hell he had got himself into now. He had not had the slightest idea that she was so bossy. Robert could have told him, but he had never asked.

Word of the latest gossip got about quickly in the close knit world of the University and so, on the Monday afternoon, Jill popped into Tom's room to say,

"Have you heard the news?"

"Only tell me if it's good news," he said, wrinkling his brow. He had a headache.

"Don't I always bring you good news? Have you taken those aspirins I gave you?" He muttered incomprehensibly. "No, you haven't. Look, they're still there in your saucer. Oh, Tom, you are hopeless. Why didn't you take them with the cup of coffee I brought you?" He looked at her sideways but said nothing. She picked them up and held them out to him. "Come on now. I'm not having you grumpy all afternoon just because you won't swallow a couple of tablets."

"What's this news anyway?" he asked, ignoring her outstretched hand.

"I'm not telling you till you've swallowed these."

"I'm being managed again. I told you I wasn't going to stand for it."

"Only for your own good, darling. Come on now, don't be silly."

She took his hand and tipped the aspirins into it. He looked distastefully into his coffee cup.

"This is cold."

"And whose fault is that? It was hot when I brought it to you."

Making a face, he swallowed the aspirins with the dregs of the cold coffee.

"Now, what's this news of yours? I doubt if it's worth it."

"Elizabeth's engaged."

He sat up from his slumped position and looked interested.

"Is she now? Reggie's made it at last, has he?"

"That's the best bit. Not to Reggie."

"Who, then?"

"If I gave you a hundred guesses, I bet you'd never get it."

"I'm not in the mood for guessing. Just tell me, please, Jill."

"Still grumpy, eh? All right, your friend Paul."

"Well, I'll be – you don't mean it?"

"I do."

"The old son of a gun! I hope he's up to coping with her. Mind you, he has hidden depths, has Paul."

"It'll make things more comfortable, her being safely engaged, since you're staying. You never told me what the Chief said, by the way."

Rubbing his forehead with his fingers, he said,

"Not all that much really. Mainly, that my private life was my own affair, but he would be grateful if I could try not to visit it quite so dramatically on the Department. I told him I didn't think there should be any more problems of that sort, explained the position to him with as little detail as I could get away with, then he tore up my letter, threw it away and got out the bottle of whisky he keeps stashed in his desk drawer. Quite an honour, I gather."

"Good. Are you feeling better yet?"

"Hmm-mm."

"You'd do anything rather than say you feel better, wouldn't you, just because I twisted your arm into taking those aspirins? Well, I'd better get back to the lab. When you do feel like admitting you're feeling better, come through and I'll tell you what we're doing this afternoon." And she left the room with a determined expression.

"*You'll* tell *me* what we're doing?" he exclaimed, but she was already gone. "She's going to tell *me* what we're doing? What the hell –"

He jumped to his feet and strode off towards the lab with a determined expression that matched hers.

On that very same Monday, Jenny had started a new job. She had found a flat, a pleasant one already occupied by three girls of about her own age and had moved in. While looking in the paper for flats, she had seen an advertisement for a job in a draughtsman's' office, had applied and been accepted. By the time Jason was out of hospital and back to his old ways, she was far from his reach. She had learned from her brothers that an envelope had come to the house with money enclosed and a note to say it was to pay their friend young Tom's fine. Sometime later, she got a card from America sending her good wishes and fond remembrances. She had managed to get Tom to give her his letter and she carried it, with the postcard, in her handbag all the time. She was a little puzzled, though, because the handwriting, though similar, seemed not to be quite the same.

Her new job paid a little better than her old so, on the strength of that, she had her hair done and bought herself a new dress to wear at the office. She was covering her typewriter to leave, a few minutes late, at the end of her first day, when the office door opened and a young man came in carrying some papers.

"Oh, hello. I thought everyone had gone home. You're new, aren't you?"

"Yes, I started today. My name's Jenny."

"I'm Richard. You're late finishing for your first day."

"My boss went to lunch with an American client and they were late back. I thought I'd just finish the work he gave me, so as to make a good impression, I hoped."

"Oh, that's typical of Americans, messing up everyone's lives for them."

"Oh, I wouldn't say that," said Jenny thoughtfully

"Well, I'm a bit anti at the moment. I recently heard that a girl I used to go out with, one I was very fond of, has just got herself engaged to one."

"Oh, that's a shame. I met an American a little while ago. He was a lovely fellow."

"I can't imagine this one is – or at least, I doubt if I'd like him if I was ever to meet him. Is he your boyfriend, this American?"

"Oh, goodness, no. I only met him the once and he's gone back to the States. I haven't got a boyfriend at the moment."

"Oh, haven't you?" said Richard, perching on the edge of her desk and looking at her with greater interest. No doubt about it, she was a nice looking girl and she reminded him, ever so slightly, of his now irretrievably lost Jill. "There's a good group playing at the Town Hall this evening. Are you doing anything tonight?"

Ann never appeared at the University again. Blackgate was her natural habitat, so she went back there, found a new job in one of the factories and set up home with her boyfriend. In the evening, they employed their talents in the production of pornographic photographs for sale and satisfying a small select group of customers with a little titillating flag.

And what of the losers in this game of romantic musical chairs? Monday evening, Reggie could be seen walking home from work, walking instead of using car or bus for the sake of his fitness. His mind was dwelling on that awful moment when he had entered the Ashton-Richards' dining room, seen that tall, fair young American and realised at once what had happened.

Suddenly, there was a cheerful tooting on a car horn behind him and with her usual disregard for life, limb and the traffic laws, Sarah swept up to the kerb in her red sports car.

"Hello, Reggie! What's the matter? You look as if you've lost a fiver and found a bob."

"Worse than that. My life has been ruined and by a damned American."
Sarah's face fell.

"Mine, too and probably by the same one. What's happened?"

"Elizabeth's engaged to him."

"Oh, Reggie, I *am* sorry. Well, I can stop dreaming too, I suppose. I went a bundle on Tom right from when she first introduced us, but he just looks past me all the time."

"Not that guy, another one."

"What!" cried Sarah, brightening up.

"Oh! I mustn't raise your hopes, Sarah. The Di Angeli character is engaged too, but –" Here, Reggie frowned and looked puzzled. "To one of the cleaners or someone like that. I don't know what's going on around here anymore."

"Oh!" said Sarah, looking deflated again.

"Just imagine," said Reggie, waving his arm in an expansive gesture vaguely towards the west, "There's a whole nation of them out there, millions of them, just waiting to come over here and ruin our lives for us."

They both ruminated quietly for a moment. Then Sarah said,

"What you need, what we both need, is a good dinner and a bottle of wine."

"Two bottles of wine."

"Get in. Where shall we go?"

"The Tudor?"

"Great. Get in."

Somewhat reluctantly, Reggie eased himself into the passenger seat and a moment later, his head was jerked backwards as Sarah shot away from the kerb.

"Pass me my handbag, Reggie. It's just behind you," she said as they bulldozed their way out into the traffic stream.

"Er – traffic's pretty heavy, Sarah. You could do with both hands on the wheel."

"Are you suggesting I can't drive? Come on, give me my handbag."

Politely refraining from answering, Reggie reluctantly handed it to her, then watched with concern as she threaded her way through the rush hour traffic, one hand on the wheel and feeling about inside her bag with the other. At last, she came up with her wallet, put in in her lap and pulled out a handful of notes.

"Here you are," she said, handing them to him.

"What on earth do you think you're doing?"

"I'll pay for the dinner."

"You will not! Put that away!"

"Don't be so stuffy, Reggie. I suggested it, so I'll pay for it. Here, take it."

"I'll pay for the dinner."

"I don't want to land you with a big bill when you weren't expecting it. Take it!" And she waved the money at him again.

He took it, but only to preserve the sanity of the driver behind them. Folding it up, he put it in the glove compartment.

"*I* will pay for the dinner. I can afford it, I assure you."

"I know you can, silly, but I suggested it."

They argued about it cheerfully all the way to the restaurant and by the time they got out of the car, they were laughing together as if no blight had ever affected their young lives. They crossed the car park hand in hand. What a happy, easy-going girl she was, Reggie was thinking. Uncomplicated, not the least moody, unlike –

He knew she was a good and keen tennis player, too. He had often seen her running lithely about the courts of the club he belonged to, returning the ball with agile leaps, laughing delightedly at good and bad shots alike. Could it be that they had more in common?

He pushed open the door for her and let her go in front of him.

"Sarah?" he said.

"Yes, darling?" she asked, looking round at him with her bright eyes.

"Do you like Bach?"